Point Horror

COLLECTION 5

A terrifying trio in one!

Have you read these other fabulous Point Horror Collections?

COLLECTION 1
Mother's Helper, The Invitation, Beach Party

COLLECTION 2
My Secret Admirer, The Accident, Funhouse

COLLECTION 3
April Fools, The Waitress, The Snowman

COLLECTION 4
THE R.L. STINE COLLECTION:
The Baby-sitter, The Boyfriend, The Girlfriend

Point Horror

COLLECTION 5

A terrifying trio in one!

The Cemetery
D.E. Athkins

Freeze Tag
Caroline B. Cooney

The Fever
Diane Hoh

■SCHOLASTIC

Scholastic Children's Books,
Commonwealth House,
1–19 New Oxford Street,
London WC1A 1NU, UK
a division of Scholastic Ltd
London ~ New York ~ Toronto ~ Sydney ~ Auckland
Mexico City ~ New Delhi ~ Hong Kong

First published in this edition by Scholastic Publications Ltd, 1994

The Cemetery
First published in the USA by Scholastic Inc, 1992
First published in the UK by Scholastic Publications Ltd, 1993
Copyright © D.E. Athkins, 1992

Freeze Tag
First published in the USA by Scholastic Inc, 1992
First published in the UK by Scholastic Publications Ltd, 1993
Copyright © Caroline B. Cooney, 1992

The Fever
First published in the USA by Scholastic Inc, 1992
First published in the UK by Scholastic Publications Ltd, 1993
Copyright © Diane Hoh, 1992

ISBN 0 590 55877 3

Printed by Cox & Wyman Ltd, Reading, Berks

Contents

THE CEMETERY

For Kim, Kim, Kim

Chapter 1

"If you don't use it, you lose it. Right?" Cyndi Moray laughed. Her blood-red lips drew back to reveal long, perfect, pointed teeth. Darling little fangs.

Lara Stepford didn't notice. Lara never noticed anything unless it was male and breathing on her.

"Right?" repeated Cyndi, turning full face toward Lara. Her smoky black eyes glittered between black tracks of eyeliner, beneath parallel tracks of black-penciled eyebrows. She shook her ice-pale hair over her pale shoulders. Her black dress was cut tight with a long front slit held together by a single glittering button that winked and winked when she moved.

She was a study in black and white.

Lara looked up at last. She'd been lying on her back on Cyndi's snow-white bedspread, contemplating the pink sheen of polish on her nails, the silver sheen of stockings on her legs. "What?" she asked.

"Wake *up*, Lara! Get with the program. I *said*, if you don't use it, you lose it, right?" Cyndi flashed her fangs again.

Lara opened her eyes wide. "Oh, disgusting! How do you get them to stay on like that? Do they come off? Can you kiss with them on?"

"Trust me, I can kiss with these — or without them. And there are other things besides kissing. Don't you ever think of anything else?"

"Yes," said Lara.

"Like what?"

Lara thought for a minute. Then she smiled slyly. "There are *other* things besides kissing," she said.

"Oh, good. Very good, Lara." Cyndi popped open a container and began to dust glittery powder over her hair and shoulders.

Lara kept smiling angelically. With her big brown eyes and pouty lips, and the ridiculous long blonde wig over her own fluffy golden hair, she really did look like an angel.

Maybe that was what made the guys so trusting around Lara, Cyndi speculated. She eyed Lara. "You know, you don't need that wig to look like a princess — whose wig is it, anyway?"

"Rapunzel had long, long hair," explained Lara patiently. "I'm Rapunzel." She giggled. "Only I can't let anyone climb up it, 'cause if anything happens to it, my mom'll kill me."

"Oh, dear. No one can climb up it? Wills will be so disappointed." Then Cyndi pretended to do a

4

double take: "Lara! Your *mother* wears that wig?" She held up her hand as Lara opened her mouth to answer. "No. Don't tell me. . . ."

Cyndi went back to putting the final touches on her vampire look. Dade Walken and William Lawrence Howell would be arriving any minute. They would be escorted to the library to wait. Not that Cyndi's family ran much to books, but they were wonderful for decoration and looked so *right* in the room with leather chairs and a discreet bar. At least that's what the decorator her parents had hired had said. Her parents put a big premium on other people's taste. Living on borrowed class, her father had said, laughing hugely, but not on borrowed money.

Her father, who was inexplicably home tonight, would probably keep the guys trapped in the library, pouring out drinks, and weird fatherly charm. And Wills, who was Lara's current entertainment for, oh, the next ten minutes, would drink his, making that careful, idle, polite, endless conversation that boys with names like William Lawrence Howell were so good at making. Dade, on the other hand, who was all lies and laughter, would say, no, thank you, he was driving. But the truth was, he just liked saying no. He liked being in control. Dade was very big on control.

Cyndi smiled. Dade. What would it take to make him lose control?

Cyndi liked to push people. See what she could make them do.

Her smile widened. Like tonight. She had big plans for tonight. The Halloween dance was only a beginning.

The vampire vixen in the reflection, standing next to the fairy princess, smiled back.

"Come on," said the vampire. "It's Halloween. Let's go down to the library and wait for Prince Charming and Prince Charming."

Rapunzel said, "Prince Charming was in *Cinderella*."

"Give it a rest, Rap," said the vampire. "Let's go. Time to play."

"Wow, it's going to be *sooo* scary," said Rapunzel, turning to follow the vampire out of the room. "I love Halloween."

"But do you love Wills?" quipped the vampire.

Rapunzel frowned. "It's not the same thing," she said.

The vampire shook her head. "Come on," she said. "Let's party."

Across Point Harbor on the other side of town, Georgina Butler was getting ready for the same dance. And the same party.

Not that she'd been invited to the party exactly. But she knew about it. And she was going to be there. What was Cyndi going to do about it? Throw her out?

She hated Cyndi. She hated a lot of people. She liked hating people. It gave her energy. Courage. A kind of high.

She liked being high.

Besides, plenty of people were less than crazy about Cyndi. Cyndi had a fast mouth and a *lot* of money, and she liked to push people around.

But you can't push me, trendy Cyndi, thought Georgina.

She pulled on the black stockings, slipped on the high black heels. Webs of black moved around her, brushing against her, making her shiver pleasurably. For that night only, she had painted silver streaks in her short, spiked black hair. More webs, black gossamer, floated, caught on the spikes. On the front of her short black turtleneck dress was a red design, an hourglass that she'd carefully painted on herself. On the middle finger of her right hand she wore a spider ring.

The room in which she was getting ready was tiny, a big box, really. The walls were lined with blowups of famous people. There were a lot of Liz Taylor when she'd been young and really gorgeous.

Georgie thought she looked a little like the young Liz Taylor. Maybe a little more like her every day.

Georgie's father thought she was crazy. "Liz Taylor, good grief," he said. "What happened to stars your own age? Like . . . Madonna? Yeah, Madonna?"

Her father. What a loser. No wonder her mother had given him the good-bye. Too bad her mother hadn't thought to take her two-year-old with her.

But two-year-olds were brats. Probably even me, thought Georgie.

Georgie the Black Widow Spider Woman

shrugged. "I'm gonna have a good time tonight," said Georgie.

The doorbell rang.

She went to greet her date. Her very *special* date. Cyndi was going to have a fit when she saw them at her exclusive little party.

Yes. Georgie was going to have a very good time.

"Happy Halloweeen," she cried, throwing open the front door.

Foy Villanova was headed up the stairs of the big old house at the end of the long, long driveway, behind the thick, towering hedges that were so important in this part of the world — the rich part. He smiled, passing those hedges, thinking a little of Sleeping Beauty, maybe, and also of the joke his father told: Those hedges don't grow on trees.

They didn't. They took a long, long time to grow. Old hedges meant old money. Very rich people kept very large houses at very discreet distances behind those hedges. And with that kind of money, anything was possible.

Like him and Jane Wales. Except between them, the possibilities had kind of worn out. He and Jane had known each other all their lives. They'd done a little obligatory fumbling. But basically they'd come up just friends.

Just friends.

Why did people say just friends? Friends lasted. The trouble was, he and Jane might not be able to last. Might not be able to be just friends. She might not want to be.

Foy stopped smiling. He was tired of the hedges, tired of the whole bit. But what would happen when he told Jane?

He ducked the thought. Something might happen. Something would happen. He didn't like getting involved in messes. Better to wait and see.

The smooth, golden blond boy nodded familiarly to Hodges, the Wales family's elderly butler — older, possibly, than the hedges — who answered the door.

Hodges betrayed no surprise at the sight of someone dressed in a long robe painted with magic symbols, carrying a necromancer's hat under one arm.

"Miss Jane will be right down," said Hodges. He led Foy at a stately pace past several hangar-sized formal rooms to a small, comfortably shabby living room at the back of the house. Jane's mother, an older version of Jane, in worn, comfortable bathrobe and slippers, was watching TV, flipping the channels with her remote, and trailing the sash of her bathrobe for the cat.

"Mr. Foy," Hodges said, and withdrew.

"Foy," said Jane's mother, beaming. "Now, who are you supposed to be? Let me guess . . . Dracula?"

Above, at the top of the stairs, Jane stopped and watched the top of Foy's head go by. She looked at herself in the mirror. Dorothy in *The Wizard of Oz*.

Was it too juvenile — her brown hair in pigtails, the little stuffed toy cairn terrier in the basket over her arm? But she hadn't been able to resist the ruby slippers — exact copies of the ones in the movie.

She liked the idea. Being able to follow a yellow brick road anywhere it might take you. Making friends with scarecrows and lions and tigers.

Plain rhymed with Jane. Cyndi said anybody with money could look good. But Jane wasn't so sure. She thought, privately of course, that Cyndi just liked the way money looked.

Charity Webster said Cyndi's best color was the color of money.

She'd said it to *Cyndi*.

Jane had been paralyzed. And disgusted with herself for being so taken aback by an only slightly escalated version of the usual dialogue between the two.

But Cyndi, after a slight pause, had lifted an eyebrow and said, "Oh, yes, your parents are artists, aren't they?" and turned languidly away.

And Char had said, "And you're a piece of — art."

Char was outspoken, but not usually in a mean way. Cyndi had a knack for bringing out the worst in people somehow. And, somehow, it made her powerful.

I'd like some power, thought Jane. I'm tired of being in Kansas. What I need is your basic tornado. "Some action, baby," she said aloud, and then rolled her eyes at herself.

I *will* have a good time, she thought determinedly.

She looked down.

I will, I will, I will. She clicked the heels of her ruby slippers together three times. Then she skipped quickly down the stairs.

Rick Carmack was pleased with his costume. It had the maximum shock effect. Even his old man had flinched a little when he first saw it, before deciding on the indulgent smile bit.

"What'sa matter, Father? Never seen any blood before?"

His father kept that automatic smile on his face.

Like a permanent grimace. It probably came with being a mortician. No, not pc. The politically correct title was funeral director.

Right.

Now his father was sort of the McDonald's of the funeral business. A BMIG — Big Man in the Graveyard.

The whole thing made Rick nervous.

Everyone thought he was a big jokester. A party animal. If only they knew the truth. Rick was afraid of being still for even one minute.

When he'd been a kid, he'd even been afraid to go to sleep.

Because being still meant being dead.

And Rick had had his fill of death.

Moving at his usual top speed, Rick bounded toward the front door.

"Happy Halloween, Richard." His father's voice sounded behind him.

"I'll give my regards to the dead," answered Rick as he slammed the door.

Wills was annoyed. Annoyed that he'd agreed to double with Dade and Cyndi. Annoyed that he'd agreed to let Dade drive his big old Chevy. Annoyed with being upstaged.

Trust Dade to upstage everybody, he thought, slamming the car door shut behind him.

As if he'd read Wills's mind, Dade glanced over and surveyed Wills's costume. "Very original, Wills."

"At least people will know I'm Freddie Krueger," Wills said, and then was annoyed that he let Dade know he was annoyed.

"So right for you, Wills. But let me introduce myself — his Lord Highness Death — that's Mr. Death, to you."

Forcing himself to smile, Wills said, "Freddie Krueger and Mr. Death. We're kind of working the same side of the street, wouldn't you say?"

Dade nodded. "And this is Mr. Death's favorite holiday."

"Freddie's too," said Wills. "You know what, we should've borrowed my father's 'Lac."

"Mr. Death and Mr. Krueger cruising in a Cadillac. I like it. But I promised the All-American Metal Machine, since it's been such a good vehicle all year, that it could go out for Halloween."

"Hey, listen," said Wills, "it is no secret you are unnaturally attached to a jacked-up Chevy."

"Mr. Death warns Mr. Krueger to watch his mouth," said Dade.

"Really," said Wills. He wanted to say, who do you think you are? My family can trace its roots back to the Mayflower. Your aunt may be a local personality, but who the hell are you? Maybe you're not even an orphan. . . . Maybe she's not really your aunt. . . .

But he didn't.

Instead, he wished that his costume was real. He'd like to do a Freddie Krueger on Dade. Just to start.

Or a Jack the Ripper. He'd almost come as Jack the Ripper.

He *admired* Jack the Ripper.

A man after his own heart. Stalking the streets of London in the 1800s. Laughing at the cops. Keeping an entire city locked up in a nasty box of fear. Making people pay. . . .

He looked over at Dade broodingly. Dade could be unpredictable. Not safe to confront. Better to get him from behind.

Aloud he said, "Really," again. With an edge.

"Really," said Dade, turning into Cyndi's driveway. "Because Mr. Death, by virtue of who he is, isn't afraid of dying. But Mr. Krueger still has that option."

Jones was ready for the dance early. His costume consisted of putting on a cowboy hat. The rest already matched.

And the hat was real, too. He'd picked it up along the way. More or less honestly.

It would do for Halloween — this Halloween, here and now.

He closed the door of his dark house without saying good-bye to anyone. His car, battered and nondescript and made, lots of it, out of pieces of other cars, cranked to life with a mega-horse roar.

Appearances could be deceiving.

Important to always remember that.

Forgetting could be dangerous.

Believing what you thought you saw could be fatal.

He drove slowly down Main Street, a street lined on either side with small, expensive versions of the larger, expensive shops in the city. Charming town. Quaint. Well-preserved. The foot of the street ran into a dock from which whaling ships had once set sail. At the end of the dock you could look far out into the deep, calm harbor, held between the land on one side, and the long, curving point on the other that gave the town its name.

The tip of the Point was blunt, worn down by the ocean pushing against it, trying to get into the bay. Beyond the Point, a row of rocks, randomly visible, pitched up out of the ocean floor.

Sometimes you could see lights out there, they

said. Long-lost ghost ships that'd once sought the safety of the harbor and been caught by devilish mists and treacherous curling tides and renegade waves — and the rocks.

The Devil's Teeth, they called them. In the old days, people used to scavenge the Point for what washed ashore. And bury their dead there.

Jones glanced out to the Point as he turned and headed for the school. The moon was beginning to rise, laying a path straight across the dangerous waters. Cemetery Point. Once upon a time, and long ago, before the town had become a playground for the rich, that's what the whole town had been called.

The town had a past.

But then, what didn't?

In the school parking lot he pushed the car into a good spot in the shadows at the edge and kicked back to reconnoiter. A few people had already begun to drift into the gym for the Halloween dance, the chaperones and the wannabes, mainly. They'd all be at the dance, of course. But the dance wasn't the thing. Cyndi Moray's party afterwards was what really counted — trendy Cyndi and her too-cool-to-live friends.

He tapped his foot impatiently, scanned the darkening sky. A full moon was going belly up over the roof of the old school. Jones frowned. The old roof, bronzed to green with age (like everything else in this town, he thought) nevertheless gave off a pinkish, coppery glow from the metal beneath, picking up the lights in the parking lot that were beginning to flicker on. And the moon, rising above the Gothic, steeply pitched roof, looked for a moment as if it had caught on a sharp corner, as if the pink color were being drained out of it, to bleed down the roof, down across the building, down across the night. Spooky.

It was unseasonably warm.

"The sulfur fires from the other side," Jones said aloud, and then was annoyed with himself. He didn't like emotion. Feelings caused trouble. They caused you to imagine things: to imagine that you were in love. To imagine that you were loved. To imagine that you were safe. To put another person ahead of yourself.

No.

He would do what he had to do, and then he was out of there. History. Let him be somebody's past.

And somebody else's future.

He shifted in his leather jacket, crossed his cowboy-booted legs on the dash above the glove compartment, punched some heavy bass into the state-of-the-art sound system he'd soldered in under the dash.

He didn't like this night. Didn't like anything about it.

It was always tough being the new kid in town.

Charity Webster was getting ready in the midst of half a dozen siblings of varying degrees of relationship.

"I'll just be a minute, dear," their mother had said vaguely, heading out the door toward the car. The minute had been over an hour. Charity shook her head, smiling. If her mother didn't come back soon from wherever she'd gone, Char would have to think of something — or someone — to step into the baby-sitting breach. Not her stepfather. He was even more vague than her mother. He'd probably wonder where all the kids came from, if he noticed them at all.

He probably wondered how they'd gotten there in the first place.

"Char, Char," squealed her youngest brother.

"What, baby?" she asked, concentrating on making her face pale, pale.

"NOT a baby," he said. He paused. "What are you?"

"A witch," said Char.

"*Oooooh* a witch," screamed five-year-old Kim. The others took up the cry. "Oooh, ooh, a witch, a witch!"

She'd gotten them all ready for trick-or-treating earlier: a collection of ghosts in various colored sheets, with wonderful designs painted on them. That was one of the bonuses of having parents who were artists. And who knew — the sheets might become artworks someday and sell for millions.

In her dreams.

"A *good* witch," Char said, and stepped back to admire the results. Another decent thing about having artistic parents was the scope of their wardrobe. Somewhere it was written: Artists shall wear strange and sexy clothing.

Char was in a very unwitchy black Lurex bodysuit, with a short sequin tunic over it. She'd painted her unearthly red hair liberally with white, put on false fingernails of blood red.

She heard the kitchen door bang shut, and the music go on loud in the room her mother used as a studio. She smiled.

"Time for me to go, kids," she said. She picked up the towering witch's hat and placed it carefully on her head.

"Will you have fun?" asked Kim.

"Yes," said Char firmly.

And who knew? She might. Anything could happen. Who knew what the future would bring.

She *was* going to have a good time. Even if it killed her.

Chapter 2

"Look at the moon," said Jane. It was an unusually warm night for October, but the moon looked round and cool and seductive. Jane tilted her face back and closed her eyes. The moonlight painted the insides of her eyelids silver, making her see stars.

"Moonbathing?" Foy teased her.

She opened her eyes and grinned. That was the nice thing about being with Foy. He was so comfortable. You could say things like, "look at the moon," and he didn't think you were being corny and romantic.

On the other hand, a little romance wouldn't hurt. But Foy was not the one.

Foy took a sip from his flask, offered her some. She shook her head. He shrugged. When he'd had a little more, maybe he'd feel like moonbathing, too.

In the gym the dance was grinding on. Somewhere out there, up and down the pumpkin-lit streets of Point Harbor, the last of the trick or treaters were making their way home, wired out of their little minds on sugar and excitement. Foy sighed. He wished it were that easy to get out of *his* mind.

The back door to the gym opened and a blast of music poured out, bringing Dade Walken with it. Dade didn't wait for Foy to offer. He reached over and served himself from the silver flask Foy was holding. "Bad stuff," muttered Dade, wiping his mouth.

"Where's Cyndi?" asked Jane. Then she wondered why she'd asked. That was Cyndi, thought Jane disgustedly. Even when she wasn't there, people who didn't really want to know still asked where she was.

Dade looked at Jane and smiled slowly. She looked quickly away, feeling her face turn red. Good thing they were outside, in the dark. Or the relative dark. No one could see you blush in the dark, right?

"Moonburn?" said Dade softly, mockingly. Then he looked over at Foy. "Some party hat. Do you need one *that* big for your head? Who're you s'posed to be?"

Foy never let anything ruffle him. He wasn't about to let Dade start now. "Merlin. The magician."

Jane put in, "Mother thought he was supposed to be Dracula."

They all laughed. Then Dade said, unexpectedly, "Sometimes people don't make mistakes when they make mistakes, y'know?"

Shaking his head, Foy took another swig. "Oh, no, it's the Freud dude. Or Dade."

"It makes sense," said Jane. She met Dade's eyes again and forced herself not to look away. She had a moment of seeing him whole, his black shirt and black pants and black boots and long black cape, and the dark mask of pain on his face, a clock with thirteen numbers on it. The hands on the clock were painted so the clock was just about to strike thirteen.

Still holding Dade's eyes, she added, "And who are you supposed to be?"

Dade grinned, an evil, sexy grin. "Death, little Dorothy. As I was saying earlier to everybody's party object, Wills, it's Mr. Death to everyone else." He leaned forward and whispered in her ear. "But you can call me Death."

"This dance is dead!" Rick Carmack came briskly around the edge of the school. He was hyper, as usual. And as usual he was outrageous. Sometimes he was funny. Sometimes . . . not.

Jane checked out his costume and thought, euuww. But it fit him. His costume was classic Rick, just right: a psycho Santa Claus in a blood-spattered suit, holding a plastic ax.

"Where's our host?" Rick addressed Dade. "Cyndi's supposed to be meeting us here, isn't she? I mean, she did promise us a real Halloween party, right?"

On cue the door opened, and a group of people

came out. Cyndi, lethally attractive, had one hand on Wills's arm. Her other hand rested on the new guy's arm. Justin Jones. Only no one called him that.

Lara and Char were behind them, talking.

"You in costume, Jones?" asked Rick.

"Cowboy," said Jones laconically, touching his finger to his Stetson.

"Pretty lame," Richard shot back.

Jones shrugged as Lara drifted over to Wills.

"Is everybody ready?" said Cyndi.

"Trick or treat," said Rick. "Where is this party, anyway?"

"Don't be so pushy," said Cyndi, touching her tongue to the tip of each fang. "The trick will be to keep up with me. If you do, you get the treat."

She turned and headed down the stairs to the parking lot. Obediently, everyone else began to follow.

Beside Char, Jones said, "Do we trust her?"

"No," said Char.

Below, Cyndi turned. "Coming, Jones?"

Typical Cyndi.

Char stole a quick look at Jones. He was definitely worth looking at.

"We'll be right there, Cyndi," she answered.

The vampire teeth showed briefly in what wasn't a smile, then Cyndi whisked ahead to Dade's car. Jane looked back and gave Char a real smile. The rest of them, the Psycho Santa, the Freddie Krueger, the Rapunzel Princess, Merlin, floated fantastically beneath the distorting convergence of parking lot lights and moonlight and began getting into their cars.

And last but not least, a witch and cowboy followed them, all on their way to the real Halloween party.

The red lights ahead lurched crazily, righted, veered sharply left, and disappeared. Char looked over at Jones in the green glow from the dashboard.

"We're headed out to the old Point," she said. "Cemetery Point."

Jones looked back at her, his face unreadable in the dim light. "You scared?"

Char didn't know the answer, didn't want to tell him maybe yes. Instead, she said, "No one goes out there — comes out here — anymore. The road's been sealed off for as long as I can remember. They say it's dangerous, something about erosion and the tides. . . ."

"The road isn't sealed off now," Jones pointed out. Sure enough, just ahead, his lights picked out the huge metal gate, propped open in the barbed-wire fence. He eased the car through, and they caught sight of the taillights of Foy's car just ahead.

As the tires rasped over the metal grating beneath the gate, Char felt a thin shiver across her neck and shoulders, as if someone had laid a single burning finger against the nape of her neck. Almost without knowing it, she reached up quickly — just as Jones pulled his hand back.

"Don't do that," she said, and was surprised at the sharpness of her voice.

"You *are* afraid," said Jones. Then, softly, "That's okay. Being afraid's okay."

What a weird thing to say, she thought.

She frowned. He was new in school. From somewhere in the Midwest, he'd said. Ohio? Nebraska? Had he said exactly where? Maybe he hadn't. Come to think of it, he hadn't said much at all.

"Jones," she began.

"The one and only," he answered. "Listen. How long have you known Cyndi?"

Diverted, Char said dryly, "Too long."

"How long is that?"

"Only a guy could ask that question — let's see. My mother inherited our house here from her great-aunt when I was seven. So ten years."

"Mmm," said Jones. "What about Rick?"

"Ten years," she said impatiently. "He was here when I got here, too. Jones, what about you?"

"What about me?"

"I've known you since school started. Or," she added hastily, "I've known who you are."

"Yeah?" he gave her a sideways leer.

"Well. You know what I mean. But, like, where are you from? What's the story?"

"Well, you know," said Jones conversationally, "I'm adopted. So I couldn't really say."

"Oh." She didn't know what to say to that. She studied Jones covertly. Who was he? She almost forgot, for a moment, the lurching car, the deeply

24

rutted, nearly completely overgrown trail they
were following, the signs that flickered from the
twisted, salt-wind-stunted trunks of trees:

DANGER. NO TRESPASSING. GO BACK.

Go back?

No, that couldn't be.

"Did you see that?" she asked Jones.

He didn't answer.

Instead, he pulled the car to a stop in the thick
darkness. Turned off the motor.

The thick, surging sound of the sea came crashing
through the black velvet thickness of the night.

Her heart jumped. People got killed like this all
the time. Didn't they? All he had to do was reach
out, just like he had before. All he had to do
was . . .

He turned toward her, as smoothly as a cat. She
pressed back against the door, hard.

"J-Jones . . ."

He leaned toward her. Reached out.

"Jones, wait . . ."

And clicked the door handle. The door opened,
almost tumbling her out to the ground, pulling him
with her so he lay on top of her. They stayed still
for a moment, balanced on the edge of the seat.

She felt her breath coming harder now, felt his
breath against her lips. She lifted her face, felt his
lips against hers.

Kiss me, kill me, she thought, half-angry with

herself for letting herself get so scared, half-amused at what a turn-on fear could be.

Was that what Jones had meant?

Was it fear — or pleasure — that was making it so hard to breathe evenly?

To breathe at all.

Whatever it was, it was working.

"Mmm," she murmured deep in her throat.

How long would she have stayed there in the weightless dark, a good witch being bad? And how bad . . .

She'd never know the answer.

Because a sound made her open her eyes. A wrong sound.

For a flash she couldn't focus.

And a flash was all it took.

The flash of moonlight on the blade coming down.

Chapter 3

Trying to scream. To warn Jones.

To twist out of the way.

Trying to close her eyes so she wouldn't see the ax when it came down on her face . . .

Screaming.

Screaming?

She wasn't screaming.

And then Rick was laughing above her.

"It's a trick ax," he chortled. "And you bought it." He laughed harder as Char and Jones pulled themselves out of the car. "Get it? You *bought* it!"

"Funny? *Funny?*" Char said. Her voice was a croak. "*Not*, Rick. No way."

"Every time you thump it against something, it makes that screaming sound," Rick went on, gleefully demonstrating again by whacking the side of Jones's car. "Sometimes I just *kill* myself."

Jones's hand shot out and caught the ax as Rick raised it again.

"Hey! Let go!"

"What're you gonna do, ax murder him?" Wills chortled behind them, silver moonlight flashing on the fake razor-blade fingernails as he made an elaborate show of slapping his hand against his thigh in amusement.

"Shut up, Willie," snarled Rick.

Wills said, "Watch it, Carmack."

"Or what? You'll rip me to death with your fingernails?"

"Lighten up, okay?" drawled Foy.

Char realized that everyone else had gathered around them — the whole sick-looking crew beneath the light of the moon.

Another shudder swept over her, and Jones's hand tightened on her hand. She looked down at his hand holding hers. When had that happened?

She looked over at him. His face was expressionless. He seemed cool, unfazed by the whole thing.

"Pretty decent joke," Rick insisted. "Admit it. You were scared witless."

"You wouldn't have the wit to know when to be scared," Jones answered evenly.

Rick snorted. "Deep. You're drowning us in it, Cowboy Jones."

Then Lara's voice broke through the tension. "Why are we standing around? This is a *party*," she said plaintively.

"You're right," said Dade. "Let's unload the cars. Wills, you and Richard carry the cooler. I'll be in charge of the music. Jones, get that box out of the trunk."

"I'll bring the blankets," said Foy.

"Why do we get stuck with the cooler?" Wills complained. "It weighs a ton."

"What'sa matter, Freddie, afraid you'll break your fingernails?" said Rick.

"Shove it," snapped Wills.

"Just do it, okay?" said Dade. He hoisted the boom box up on one shoulder, slung the CD case over the other.

"I'll come with you," Lara said to Dade.

"And why aren't the girls carrying something?"

"We're carrying the conversation," snapped Char, suddenly sick of the whole scene. Beside her, she sensed Jones's silent amusement.

"Where's Cyndi?" Jane intervened. I'm doomed, she thought. I'm doomed to keep asking the same dumb question. And I don't even want to know the answer.

Lara gave a little gasp. "Look!"

A tall figure in a clinging dress stood silhouetted against a dune just beyond the clearing where they'd parked their cars. Behind her, a faint path gleamed like an old scar in the scrub grass skirting the woods.

The figure beckoned sepulchrally.

"Yo, Cyndi," Rick called.

The figure beckoned again, then turned and glided into the darkness of the trees without answering.

"Creepy," said Lara. She put her hand on Dade's arm.

Wills snapped, "Pick up your end of the cooler, Carmack."

Rick smiled unpleasantly, but bent over and helped Wills hoist the cooler without comment.

"C'mon," said Dade. He nodded in the direction where Cyndi had disappeared. "Let's do like the lady wants."

Jane found herself looking at Charity.

Lady? thought Char as her eyes met Jane's. She raised her eyebrows at Dade's choice of words.

But no one was going to say the obvious.

"Yes," said Charity. "Let's do like the *vampire* wants."

Following the path into the woods, they wound in and out among the misshapen trees. Sometimes the path almost disappeared in the drifts of sand laying siege to the struggling trees. Sometimes the path was erased beneath the trees' gnomic moon-shadows.

"This is nothing but a big sand dune with trees," Wills panted.

No one answered. The wind kept up a steady keen, pushing clouds across the sky, blotting out the moon again and again, making the whole world flicker between darkness and light. And always, beneath the wind, the sound of the ocean could be heard, pounding and sucking against the shore and the ring of the Devil's Teeth beyond.

"Spooky," said Jones to Char in a conversational

tone, as if it were a sort of weather condition.

"Whose idea was this, anyway," complained Wills. "You were in on this, weren't you, Dade? How much longer do we have to walk?"

"Ah, you don't mind a little walk with Death do you, Freddie?" Dade's teeth flashed briefly. "And we got a cooler full of goodies so we'll all be nice and warm when we get there."

"It's really very warm for this time of year," said Jane. "Not cold at all." Then she thought, that's *it*. I get the stupid conversation of the year award. It's Halloween, and I'm talking about the weather.

Dade said, "See, Wills? A little walk with Death doesn't leave Jane cold."

"Just the opposite, sounds like," said Rick.

Wills said, "I wouldn't let Cyndi find out, Jane. She doesn't like to share."

"Low class, Wills," said Char.

"Oh, listen. Charity defends her *best* friend," Wills shot back sarcastically.

Lara said, "I don't think you should talk about Cyndi like that, Wills. *She* never talks about you."

Dade started to laugh.

And at last, the path opened up into another clearing. Only this one wasn't really a clearing.

It was the end of the trail.

They'd reached the tip of Cemetery Point. It was a high, rocky spit of land, pounded by the ocean on one side, gnawed by the currents on the other side where the water of the sound met the ocean. A crumbling stone wall enclosed the cemetery. Inside the wall, a crazy dance of weathered gravestones and monuments waited.

And just outside it stood Cyndi.

She turned and gestured grandly. Beyond her, where the graveyard began, was a huge pile of driftwood.

"Welcome to Cemetery Point," intoned Cyndi.

The moon went behind the clouds, and the rest of her sentence came hollowly out of the dark. "Happy Halloween."

They stood silently for a moment. Then, "Decent," Dade said, and went forward.

Wills and Rick followed to set down on the ground the cooler they'd been lugging.

"Let me do a little magic here," said Foy, dropping the blankets on the ground and kneeling by the driftwood. "Who's got some starter?"

Cyndi dropped to her knees beside Foy. "Yeah. I'd like that. C'mon and light my fire, Merlin."

"Here." Jane fished hastily in her basket and pulled a lighter out from under her stuffed Toto.

"The truth about Dorothy — she smokes," said Cyndi snidely. "Or is it only when you're not in Kansas?"

Jane felt her face flush in the darkness. It was my father's, she wanted to say. But why should she have to explain herself to anyone? Especially Cyndi.

Beside her, Char said, "Jane, I'll help you with the blankets," and bent to pick one up. Jane reached out gratefully to help her unfold it and start spreading it on the ground on one side of the bonfire.

The lighter flickered, and a moment later the fire leapt to life. The silvery darkness, the shadowed woods behind them, were obliterated by the brightness of it.

Dade set up the box on a level spot on the wall and cranked the music. Rick flipped back the lid of the cooler and said, "All *right*."

Finishing with the blankets, Char stepped back from the circle of firelight and turned. The grave-markers made her uneasy. Tilted at their crazy angles behind their low, crumbling stone wall, they seemed to be dancing in the erratic firelight.

"I don't know if this is a good idea," she said aloud before she could stop herself.

"So leave," said Cyndi. She put her hand on Dade's arm. "Dance," she commanded.

"All *right*," said Rick again, popping a top. "Let's party, animals!"

Wills threw his head back in a long, imitation werewolf howl.

"It'd be funny," Jones murmured, "if something howled back." He turned to Char. "Dance?"

A few minutes later, Char thought, I think this kind of dancing is probably illegal, or something. Because in spite of the chop beat of the music, Jones had wrapped his arms around her and was moving slow.

She pulled back. Felt, rather than saw him smile. They had danced to the edge of the circle of light, and she turned impulsively toward a gap in the crumbling wall.

"It's weird, this place," she said to Jones.

Following her into the graveyard, he said, "It's a graveyard."

"Yeah." She bent over, squinting at the words on the weathered stone and read, " 'Believed taken by the sea. May God have mercy on his soul.' "

"Sounds like there was some doubt about the mercy part," murmured Jones. "Maybe the drowning, too. . . ."

"He's buried *in* the graveyard," Char pointed out. "You can't get buried in a graveyard if you aren't, aren't . . . you know, if the church or whatever says it's not okay."

"Like suicides," said Jones.

"Right. That's still true, isn't it? If you commit suicide, then you can't get buried in holy ground, or something."

"For some churches," agreed Jones. "Look at this one: 'Borne on the tides up to heaven.' Kind of nice."

They wandered down the uneven row of stones. "These are all sailors, I guess." Char leaned over the wall to study a lone stone, all worn at the edges. "No, wait — look at this: 'Asleep but not at rest. May death bring her peace.' What does *that* mean?"

"I don't know. What do you think it means?" Jones caught her hand and began to walk back alongside the wall toward the fire.

"Sounds like she got zombie-ized."

Jones looked back, then slid his hand up Char's arm. "Zombi-ized?"

"Mm," she said, forgetting about the tombstone.

Then, for the second time that night, she forgot to think at all.

And just beyond, the music cranked on, and the clouds kept tearing up the moonlight, and everyone kept drinking and dancing and partying. As they came together and danced apart, they made long, strange shadows that leapt and twisted and merged with the shadows beyond the fire.

Jane sat down while Foy wandered over to the cooler where Rick was leaning on the wall, his long legs dug heel-first into the ground. Rick was drinking a lot, but, so far, thought Jane, it hadn't slowed him down.

"Are we having fun yet?" Dade left Cyndi digging through the cooler and walked over to squat down on his heels by Jane. He took a long drag on a cigarette, then snuffed it in the sand.

Jane took a hasty swallow of the warm beer she'd been holding all evening. "Yes."

"Then why aren't you dancing?"

She didn't answer for a moment. They watched the figures in the firelight making bizarre shadowy gyrations.

Wills had come up to Cyndi. He was saying something to her, too low to be heard across the fire above the music. Cyndi was looking up at Wills, a little smile on her face.

Dade followed Jane's gaze. He seemed amused. "Brave man," he commented.

"Does it bother you?" asked Jane impulsively.

"What?"

"About Cyndi and Wills. That he . . . you know, broke up with her, and she was so . . . so . . ."

"Unwrapped? Nah. Besides, there're at least two sides to every story. More, if you're dealing with creative people."

"I'm sorry," said Jane. "I shouldn't have asked."

"No problem. The problem is, why won't you dance with me?"

He caught Jane's hand and stood up, pulling her with him. At almost the same moment, Cyndi threw back her head and laughed. Then she turned and walked away from Wills and over to Rick.

The way she pulled Rick to her made Jones and Char look like the Bobbsey Twins.

Lara, who'd been standing nearby, started laughing.

Furiously, Wills whirled to face her. He raised his hand, and the shadows of his nails made stripes across Lara's face. For one awful moment, Jane thought he was going to lash out at her.

"Shrink's delight," said Dade, watching Wills.

Then Lara laughed again. "Freddie, Freddie, Freddie," she said delightedly.

And Wills slowly turned his hand over and bowed elaborately. "May I have this dance?" he asked.

"Sure," said Lara.

Jane started to dance with Dade, letting him spin her around and around in the firelight. Her dizzy eyes met Foy's once, briefly. He was smiling as if he enjoyed watching them.

But he wasn't enjoying watching half as much as she was enjoying the dance.

Jane had never danced with Dade before. It made her uncomfortable, to stand so close to him. Uncomfortable. Scared. Excited.

Dade was not a too-right guy. Everyone knew that. He was dangerous. There were rumors of drugs and fights and marathon parties where all the other partyers were left low and in trouble, only Dade still standing, able to move out of harm's way.

Some people said he carried a gun.

But no one knew for certain.

She liked that.

A sarcastic voice cut in on her dance. "Well, if it isn't little Dorothy. Close to Death."

The glitter in Cyndi's eyes was unmistakably menacing.

For a moment, Jane was almost afraid. Then, before she could stop herself, she laughed.

"What's so funny?" said Dade, swinging her away from Cyndi and Rick.

Away from harm, and looks that could kill.

"Nothing," said Jane. Her eyes met Char's and Char knew they were thinking the same thing: If Dade didn't carry a gun, having Cyndi around was probably the next best thing.

Char let Jones pull her down to sit beside him on one of the blankets. And Cyndi imperiously grabbed Rick's hand and swept through the gap in the stone wall and into the graveyard.

"Hey!" said Rick.

Cyndi turned. "Lift me up," she said.

Rick bowed. "As you vish, my beautiful vampire." He lifted Cyndi up. Then she got carefully to her feet on top of a low marble crypt. Rick scrambled up beside her. She pulled him to her, her arms locked just below his waist, and began to sway.

"C'mon," she called. "C'mon!"

Stupidly, Jane said, "You shouldn't do that, Cyndi."

"Shouldn't I? Shouldn't I? Who asked you?"

"Cyndi, come down," said Lara.

"You come up," replied Cyndi. "There's plenty of room."

But they all stayed where they were, staring up at Cyndi. The music cranked on. Cyndi and Rick kept dancing, their shoes scraping a protest out of the worn stone.

"What's the matter?" Cyndi taunted. "Afraid of a few dead people? Listen to the *truth*! This is the first party they've had in an eternity. They're happy."

Rick hooted. "Yeah. Grateful. The Grateful Dead, get it!"

"That sucks, Carmack," shouted Wills.

The wind gave a howling gust.

Something crashed in the trees behind them.

Lara was the first to begin to scream.

Chapter 4

"I bet they can hear you all the way back in Point Harbor. What's all the screaming about?" Georgina Butler made her entrance, strolling with studied nonchalance out of the dark fringe of the trees and into the firelight. In spite of the Halloween costumes, it wasn't hard to read the reactions: Jane, looking just like Dorothy, her eyes wide; Char, half-amused; Lara, faintly surprised and a little puzzled. All the guys, Georgie decided, looked appreciative.

But it was Cyndi's face, Georgie concluded, that made it worth the trip. Her eyes had narrowed to furious slits.

And as Georgie's date walked out of the shadows behind her, Georgie watched Cyndi's lip curl into a snarl. *"You,"* she hissed, looking past Georgie. "What are *you* doing here?"

Cyndi Moray's brother, Dorian, walked up beside Georgie and put his arm around Georgie's shoulders.

Georgie looked around innocently. "We're not

late, are we? I mean, it won't be midnight for a while yet."

"Hey, Dade," said Dorian. He nodded offhandedly. "Any brew?" He went over to the cooler and began to study its contents.

"What're you doing here?" repeated Cyndi furiously.

"Dorian invited me," said Georgie, smiling.

"And I invited myself." Dorian reached into the cooler, helped himself, then turned to face his sister. "I figured you'd just forgotten."

The fact that Cyndi was dressed as a vampire and Dorian was dressed as a pirate didn't hide their similarities. They both were striking people, with high-boned cheeks and golden hair and enormous self-assurance. But Cyndi's costume was provocative, outrageous. Dorian was conservative and elegant in an authentic-looking costume, like the well-dressed captain of a pirate ship — with a hook for a hand.

Wills was scowling.

Rick looked over and smiled. "What'sa matter, Wills? Hook envy?"

"Shut up," said Wills, loathing in his voice.

But the loathing was nothing to match the loathing emanating from Cyndi and Dorian toward each other. Pure hatred.

Char, looking at them now, both of them giving off such a shimmer of angry heat that it seemed to dim the fire, thought it might be because they were so much alike. And both of them couldn't be the center of attention at the same time.

Cyndi and Dorian might have stood there in a frozen mutual hatred staring contest for eternity, but the music clicked off.

As Dade headed over to it, Rick said, "Leave it, Walken."

"Yeah?" said Dade.

"Yeah. Let's do something different."

Georgie looked at Cyndi and said sweetly, "I love games. Is that what you had in mind? Pin the tail on the donkey?"

That got Cyndi's attention. She looked away from Dorian, smiled suddenly at Rick, tilting her head slightly in Georgie's direction. "No, I have an idea, Rick. Since we have such a *special* guest. Why don't you just play the game you usually play with her. Hot potato, is it?"

Wills laughed, although no one else did.

Rick said, "How about ghost stories?"

"No way!" cried Lara, looking enthusiastic. "Do you know any good ones, Rick?"

"Naturally. Unless everyone else is" — Rick looked around the circle of faces — "chicken."

"Let's do it," Charity heard herself say, and she found herself sitting abruptly down on the ground, pulling Jones down with her.

He gave her a little smile, and said softly, so only she could hear, "Let's."

Char looked at him out of the corner of her eye,

then turned back to the fire as Cyndi slid down off the crypt. "Okay," Cyndi said. "We'll tell ghost stories. You go first, Rick."

One thing about Cyndi, thought Char, she never admitted defeat. Now she was taking charge of the ghost stories as if they'd been her own idea. And taking charge of Dade and Rick at the same time.

Georgie didn't like it. But she contented herself with snuggling up close to Dorian as they sat down by the fire across from Cyndi.

When everyone else had gotten comfortable, Rick leaned forward and gave the fire a poke. The flames shot up, and smoke rolled in ghostly clouds into the dark. Then Rick lowered his voice:

"Once upon a time, a couple went out parking on a dark, dark dead end road. . . ."

I've heard this one a million times, Char thought. This is so Girl Scout camp.

But she felt a faint thrill of fear in spite of herself. Maybe not the best place to tell ghost stories, thought Char wryly. Next door to a graveyard on Halloween. She glanced again at Jones. He was looking at Rick, his face expressionless.

Char wondered if her own face was as noncommittal. I don't like that graveyard, she thought. Then she thought, you're being stupid, Char. Everyone there has been dead and gone since the turn of the century. They have nothing to do with you. Nothing.

And there's no such thing as a ghost.

Foy had settled down by Jane. He was holding her hand in an absentminded way. Jane's attention didn't seem too fixed, either. She kept looking down, glancing sideways, shifting restlessly.

Is Jane spooked, too? wondered Char. And what is Foy thinking about? What does he see, staring at nothing like that?

Good thing we're not playing Truth or Dare.

Jane and Char hadn't been friends that long. They'd first started talking in art class their freshman year. The art teacher had been praising Char's neat, skillful, lifeless sketches. "Excellent technique," the old wannabe had been saying, and Char had been torn between feeling sorry for him and angry. She knew it wasn't her work he was praising, but her genes — her mother's, anyway.

Then she'd reminded herself, isn't this why you took the course? You knew it'd be an ace.

The teacher had paused again, and frowned. "Really," he had said reprovingly to the student whose sketches were scattered across the table.

When he'd moved on, Char had leaned over. The technique wasn't great, but the imagination was.

"Geez," she'd breathed. "You could really do it." Then she'd realized it was Jane Wales she was talking to. Jane, who didn't need to do anything for her whole life except live long enough to inherit the fortune her father had left in trust for her. Quiet, well-mannered, self-effacing, very rich Jane.

She'd expected Jane to smile politely and thank

her politely and that would be that. But Jane's pleasure had been real. And it had been the start of an unexpected friendship.

Quiet, well-mannered Jane. You wouldn't know she was restless unless you knew her.

Now Char caught another one of Jane's fleeting sideways glances. Dade.

Dade! thought Char. Maybe I *don't* know Jane.

Had Dade noticed?

More important, had Cyndi?

Char looked carefully in Cyndi's direction through the veil of her eyelashes.

Cyndi was tapping one vampire tooth with one long red nail, looking a little bored.

Don't let Cyndi see you, Jane, thought Char. 'Cause if she does, girlfriend, she'll have your blood.

Georgie's applause brought her back to the fireside abruptly.

Dorian said, "A tried-and-true story, Rick. The hook, the car door, the whole bit."

"But it's a great story, anyway," insisted Georgie.

"I like it," agreed Lara. "It's not so scary if you know how it ends."

"Hey, Jones," said Dade. "You got any stories?"

"Nothing you haven't heard," said Jones, his face unreadable.

"I've got one," Dorian cut in.

Without waiting for anyone else to speak, he began. "Once upon a time, there was a vampire. A vampire on wheels, if you know what I mean." His eyes locked with Cyndi's, and Georgie giggled.

"This vampire couldn't keep her teeth off other people's property. Or other people. She liked to take what wasn't hers. So she started getting fat. And then she couldn't catch the people anymore. So she had to go to this graveyard and suck on the dead people."

"Gross," cried Lara. "Isn't that gross?"

Cyndi, her eyes snapping with fury, said softly, "Boring."

"I haven't finished," her brother answered. He smiled, handsome like a golden cat warming itself by the fire.

"Anyway, our fat, greedy vampire, who was nothing but a big fake, because what self-respecting vampire would ever let this happen, made a big mistake. Because all the people in the graveyard weren't quite dead yet. One corner of the graveyard was for the undead. And she dug up one of the undead, and it was a vampire. And it bit her. And you know what happens when a vampire takes a direct hit from another vampire — at least what happens to a bogus vampire?"

"What?" Dade's voice was as soft as Cyndi's. But more frighteningly menacing, somehow.

Dorian seemed unaware of the menace. "Major, permanent bloodletting. Like she'd turned into a hemophiliac. Bleeding and bleeding. So the old vampire was freed, and this new, bloody, bogus vampire got buried in his grave. And she's there to this day, buried alive, too weak to leave. Her blood turning the whole earth around her red. And no one will save her because no one loves her. Or ever will."

"What's love got to do with it?" said Cyndi, her eyes on her brother.

"Disgusting." Lara shook her head. "All that blood."

Jones looked back and forth between them. Then he shook his head. "You guys go too fast for me."

"It's almost midnight," said Georgie. She lowered her voice at midnight. "Ooooooh."

Then she looked around the circle of faces. "I know. Let's all hold hands and see if we can contact the dead. You know, like a séance?"

"Anything to grab onto a guy's bod, Georgie?" Cyndi sneered.

"Afraid?" challenged Georgie.

For an answer, Cyndi grabbed Dade's hand and Jones's.

"Go for it, Georgie," said Dorian, sounding amused.

Jones frowned as the ring of people joined hands in a circle with the fire at the heart of it.

"This," Georgie intoned, closing her eyes dramatically, "is All Hallows' Eve. We call to you, spirits trapped beyond life. We call to you, spirits who wander the earth. We call to youuuu . . ."

Jones's hand twisted in Char's. She tightened her fingers unconsciously.

"Arise!" wailed Georgie, raising up her own hands. Everyone in the circle followed suit.

A blast of wind came out of nowhere, drowning all sound.

A log shifted on the fire, and a tongue of flame shot from the heart of the embers up into the night.

Jones said, "No!" and yanked his hands free, breaking the circle.

"Hey!" cried Georgie. "You ruined it!"

"Let's dance some more," Char said, jumping up. The night was getting too weird. In fact, it had been too weird all along. She thought, it's almost like, put people in disguise and their true nature comes out.

Then Char felt the whole Point tilt fractionally.

No one else seemed to notice. Looking sulky, Georgie was allowing Dorian to coax her into dancing. Lara had started laughing at something Wills had said. Jane and Foy bent over the box, fiddling with the sound. Rick finished chugging his beer, tossed the can over his shoulder, and began to follow the edge of the low wall into the dark, fumbling with his pants. Cyndi and Dade began to dance.

Char lost her balance.

She felt the tremor through her body, a shock and an aftershock.

Dark. Like pain. Pain remembered.

She looked at Jones.

"Jones?" she said.

He was looking at his hands.

"Jones," she said again. "Jones . . ."

"It's time to go," he answered at last, his voice low and urgent.

"You felt it, didn't you?"

"Now," Jones said. And grabbing her wrist in a vise of iron, he began to pull her into the darkness under the trees.

Chapter 5

"Where are you going?" Cyndi's voice cut across the blast of the music.

Everyone turned to look.

"A little Charity work, Jones?"

Char felt the angry heat in her face. She stopped and tried to pull free of Jones's grip.

He didn't let go.

Cyndi put her hands on her hips and smiled. Her vampire fangs glittered. So did her eyes. "Or just going to play a little hide-and-seek? What a *good* idea!"

Behind Cyndi the moon came out.

"I hate this," Jane said softly to Foy. "I wish whatever is going to happen would just *happen*." But she stayed still, waiting.

Everyone seemed to be doing the same thing. They all remained motionless, a game of statues.

Char took a deep breath. She looked past Cyndi, at the graveyard stretching into the shadows beyond where the real statues waited out eternity in memory of the dead.

Jones's hand tightened on her arm.

"What time is it?" asked Georgie, clinging to Dorian's arm.

Her question somehow diffused the moment.

With some difficulty, Dorian turned his wrist over so he could see his watch.

"Three minutes till midnight," he said.

"Excellent," said Cyndi. "When I clap my hands, all the girls can hide. Then I'll count to thirty, and the guys can come look for you."

"What does that make you, Cyndi?" asked Georgie. "One of the guys?"

Before Cyndi could answer, Dade raised his hands. "I'll put my hands together for you, Cyndi. Then you can hide, too."

Dade looked at Cyndi, who stared rebelliously back at him. Then, slowly, reluctantly, Cyndi climbed down off the tombstone.

"Wouldn't it be great to play hide-and-seek and let Cyndi hide forever?" muttered Georgie to Lara. But Lara was busy tucking her short gold hair beneath the long gold Rapunzel wig, and didn't seem to hear.

This time, the tremor was more distinct.

Char looked up at the sky. Although the wind was blowing strongly now, the clouds no longer whipped past the moon. It stood, frozen and alone in its nimbus of fiery light, like an eye in a socket of exposed bone.

This time, Char had felt the tremor through the soles of her feet, up her spine, into her heart.

"Jones?"

"Run," hissed Jones, releasing her arm, his voice as thin as glass.

She looked at his face. It was as bleached as the bone-socketed moon.

"Jones," she said again.

"Ready?" drawled Dade. He pressed his hands palm to palm and raised them high above his head.

"Run," said Jones. "Back to the car. Don't stop. Don't look back."

He gave her a push.

What about you? she wanted to cry. What about Jane? What about everyone else?

But suddenly a cloud came from nowhere, and she felt the earth pitch as if it were about to open and swallow her whole. Just before the moon was blotted out, she had a last glimpse of Dade, high on the crypt in his black-and-silver Death outfit, like a priest in some ancient, evil rite, his hands raised above his head. Like a prayer.

She didn't wait to hear him clap. She was running for the cover of the trees, each breath stolen from the fear that was choking her.

She'd never been so afraid in her life.

But, then, she'd never run for life.

Dade felt a gust of wind almost make him lose his footing. But he caught himself, quick as a panther. He raised his voice and began to count.

Below him, the guys lounged around, their eyes obediently sort of closed, while the girls scattered.

Dade kept counting. He kept his own eyes open. But he didn't watch anyone hide. Instead, he watched Char sprint into the woods. Something about the way she was running . . .

"Twenty-one . . . twenty . . ."

Dade let the pause draw out. This crypt gave you a pretty good view, he thought. He looked down at Foy and Wills and Dorian standing just below, with Jones a little ways beyond.

"Hey, Merlin, use your magic powers and tell me where they're hiding," he said to Foy.

Foy said, "Use your eyes. You haven't got them closed, have you?"

"Who told you?" said Dade, and began to count again.

"It's not fair," said Wills, opening his eyes and leaning over to give the fire a poke with one of his long, plastic-silver razor nails.

Dade said, "Be careful, my man. You'll melt your fingernails. Then we'll have to call you Freddie the unready. . . ."

"Pretty good, Dade." Dorian nodded.

And what are you doing here, college boy? thought Dade. Did you come all the way back to town just to give your sister a little Halloween surprise?

"Where's Rick?" asked Foy.

"I'll check," said Dade. "Twenty-two, twenty-three . . . RICK!"

"Yeah, yeah," a faint voice came back from a dark corner.

"Hey," called Dade, "you're not doing what I think you're doing on those graves, are you, Richard?"

A faint giggle came from another corner of the graveyard.

"What do you think?" Rick's voice was closer now, and in another moment he came into view, wrestling with the zipper on his Santa suit.

"You *are* a psycho Santa . . . twenty-four, twenty-five. Hey, Jones, no fair, getting a head start."

Jones didn't answer. He just stood there.

Dade took a swig from the flask. Oops. Almost lost his footing that time. Had to be careful on these crypts. "Twenty-six, twenty-seven, twenty-eight . . ."

"Just for the record, I plan on taking my time out there in the dark," said Rick, wiggling his eyebrows up and down maniacally.

"Twenty-nine . . . you don't have to spell it out for us, Rick. We'll figure it out . . . thirty." Dade raised his voice.

"Ready or not, here we come!" shouted Wills.

"Death's coming to getcha," Dade called. He leapt off the crypt with a flourish and headed into the darkness in the general direction where Cyndi had disappeared, ignoring the others.

What a creep joint, Dade thought, threading his way across the uneven ground, between the gravestones. And what happened to the moon?

"Cyndi," he said. He heard a faint noise to his left, and smiled. Cyndi was up to something. She always was. If she couldn't make trouble, she'd borrow it. He had pretty low expectations of anything between them. He smiled a different smile, thinking about some of their past dates. Very low expectations.

Cyndi smiled to herself. She'd found a hollow of ground beneath a broken-off monument. She was crouched beneath it. When Dade got closer, she was going to jump out and give him the scare of his hot-blooded, cold-hearted life. She could hear him now . . .

Or maybe it wasn't Dade. That was an interesting possibility, too.

Jane knelt down miserably in the shadows of the cold stones. She should've done what Char had done, and made a run for the woods. But none of them had, except Char. Maybe because Jones had been standing there.

Something about Jones. Something about this whole night.

A shadow passed. Dade?

Then she thought about all the shadows around her. Shadows of tombstones. Shadows of the dead . . .

Stop it, she told herself.

But why did they always end up doing what Cyndi wanted to do?

Foy gave his robe a yank. It kept catching on the underbrush. At least he'd dumped the hat. You could see that hat coming a mile away. He skirted the edge of the graveyard slowly. Up ahead, he thought he saw a figure crouched in the shadow of the crumbling stone of the graveyard wall. Yes.

Georgie peered cautiously over the top of the angel's half-furled wing. What a perfect hiding place. An angel. And speaking of angels, where was Jones? Or Dade? Wouldn't that put Cyndi in a twist? Her gaze swept the fire-lit clearing. But Jones wasn't standing there anymore. Had he headed toward the graveyard, instead of out into the woods after Char?

Stupid Charity. No one would ever find her in those woods. You'd need a bloodhound, or something.

Someone was coming. She slid back down.

Rick didn't care how much noise he made. It didn't matter who he found. Unless it was Cyndi, and she was feeling like making some trouble to pass the time. Which was not a bad idea. If he found Cyndi first, and she was glad to see him, it might be a little while longer before Dade found them.

And Dade wouldn't care. Would he?

* * *

Dorian found a flat, worn-down stone and sat down on it. He lit a cigarette. Waited. He wasn't about to go thrashing through or around a graveyard. He had better things to do.

Wills stumbled over something and cursed. Damn graveyard. Stupid game. He wrinkled his nose. Something stank. Then he saw the deeper shadow on the ground ahead of him. Had someone been digging? He stopped uneasily. Was that what smelled so bad? An open grave?

Then he remembered that the graveyard was long unused. Whatever had been buried wouldn't smell anymore.

Ugh. Maybe something had fallen in, an animal or something, and hadn't been able to get out. . . .

Stupid animal.

Something made William Lawrence Howell turn.

Something was standing behind him. Something big. Not the right costume. Not right. Not . . .

The moon came out.

He had a fraction of a second to see.

It wasn't what he expected.

The world tilted.

He threw up his hand in a futile gesture of defense. The shiny ends of silver-plastic razor nails flew through the air like bits of confetti.

The great glittering blade hooked him under the chin. It caught, fractionally. Wrenched sideways.

The boy dressed like Freddie was in shock long before it was finished.

He never knew he was dead.

Lara was getting bored. The people sneaking around the graveyard were making enough noise to wake the dead. Why hadn't anyone found her yet?

She waited a few seconds longer. An eternity. Then, with a little pout, she jumped to her feet from the edge of the raised gravemarker where she'd been sitting. The graveyard didn't really bother her. In fact, the raised grave had reminded her a little of those raised garden beds made with railroad ties that her older sister was always digging in. The smell of earth wasn't too different from the gardening center her family owned, either.

She sensed rather than saw a movement in the far back corner of the graveyard, where the wall had stopped. Or maybe it had crumbled down. Maybe there had been a wall, and they'd run out of room and had to bury people outside the wall.

It didn't interest her. It didn't really matter.

She raised the hem of her dress and walked lightly across the graves.

The moon came out suddenly. She saw something flash in its light. Wills's Freddie Krueger nails. It had been a pain trying to dance with him while he was wearing those things.

She heard a sound, sort of a muffled ripping sound, the way the wet packed earth sounded when her sister stuck the trowel in.

A wet, protesting sound.

"Wills?" she called softly, rounding the corner of the wall.

The wind had died, but the cloud-blotted darkness remained. Branches slapped her face. She'd lost the path. Dimly, Char thought, if I can just find the edge of the dune. If she could reach it, she could follow the dune's edge back to the clearing where the cars were parked.

"Here we come . . ." Dade's voice.

How long had she been running? Thirty seconds? A minute?

A lifetime.

She shoved the branches aside, peering ahead for the white glint of sand.

The dunes would be treacherous. Walking the edge of them would be like walking in quicksand on the edge of a cliff. To lose her footing would mean a steep fall to the rocky ledge of shore below. Although she'd never been there, she knew that somehow. Didn't have time to think how she knew.

She stopped to catch her breath.

And heard it.

Something was crashing through the woods behind her.

Jones, she thought.

But she didn't say it aloud.

Maybe it *was* someone playing hide-and-seek. One of the guys. Foy or Dade or Rick. Or even Lara or Jane or Cyndi or Georgie, looking for a hiding place.

Maybe.

She didn't move. Tried not to breathe. Crouched down now, hoping the moon would never come out to give her away. At least she was dressed in black. Witch's black.

If she were really a witch, she wouldn't be so afraid in the midnight darkness of Halloween. Why wasn't she a witch? A *bad* witch?

The crashing stopped.

With the cessation of sound, the darkness was complete.

Midnight.

She knew in her bones it was midnight now. High midnight on All Hallows' Eve on Cemetery Point.

Midnight only lasts a minute, she told herself. In one minute, it won't be midnight anymore. In one minute, it will be over.

And then the screams began.

There had never been such a sound. It went on and on. It spread out like a wave, drowning the night. It was raw and terrible. Inhuman.

Instinctively, Char put her hands over her ears. The sound came through, drove through her hands, into her senses. Into her brain.

She ran now, not caring what was behind her, not caring what was ahead. She ran blindly under the blazing light of the moon. She ran with her hands balled in fists, pressing them against her ears, punching her way through the trees.

Until something caught her by the ankle. And the darkness came up to meet her.

She was in the water. The water was warm. The waves had a friendly feel as they pulled at her ankles. As if they wanted her just to come in and play.

But who ever swam in the dark in the ocean? Things could get you. Sharks. Undertow.

Or worse.

She stood in the pull of the waves, the water swelling and pulling at her thighs, the long skirt of her dress twisting like seaweed around her.

Out beyond, the shadowy Devil's Teeth grinned jaggedly. Something was sailing there, just past them. Sailing in the dark and heaving waters, sailing safely among those teeth.

Something was hunting out there.

But she was waiting for it.

And then the water turned to ice around her thighs, and the wind laid cold wet hands against her cheeks and froze her breath, and she couldn't move.

It had come.

" . . . Char . . . Charity?"

"No one calls me Charity," she murmured, coming up out of the nightmare into the dark.

"Don't cry. It's all right."

"I'm not crying." But she was. She could feel the tears on her face, feel how cold they were.

And feel the hand there.

She opened her eyes. The moon was shining. She was lying in soft sand. The branches of trees were silhouetted against the sky above her.

"Can you get up?" A different voice. Familiar. But odd. Not right.

"Yes," she said.

"Let's get out of here," said another voice. Georgie's. Yes. Now Char remembered. She'd been running. Someone had screamed.

They'd been playing a game.

"Is the game over?" she asked.

No one answered. Instead, hands were hauling her to her feet.

"Lean on me," said a voice.

"I'm fine," she said, suddenly indignant.

She began to make her way carefully toward the cars. Someone stepped ahead of her and opened a door. Other figures hurried by her in the silver light. Grotesque figures — Santa Claus and a spider woman and Captain Hook . . . all scurrying, scrabbling.

Halloween. That's right, it was Halloween. That was Jones. And Jones's car.

She put her hand on the car door and looked across the top of the car at Jones. "What happened?" she asked.

"For God's sake, get in the car," someone snarled behind her. She was pushed unceremoniously in. The door slammed behind her. More people piled into the back seat. Jones started it up, slammed it to reverse, turned it around.

Behind them, other cars followed.

Jones drove fast, lurching in the overgrown sand track, scraping against trees. Grabbing the dash to keep her balance, Char turned to look back.

The clearing was empty.

In the seat behind her, outlined in the headlights of the car behind them, sat Lara and Cyndi and Dade.

"Where's Jane?" she asked.

Cyndi answered. "In one of the other cars. Foy's."

"What about . . ."

Cyndi cut her off. "Georgie Porgie is with Dorian, okay? And Rick is probably with them, if he isn't with Foy."

"But what about Wills?" Char looked at Lara. Lara didn't answer.

Char faced Jones. "What's going on? What happened? Is the party over?"

"You could say that," said Jones. He accelerated through the open gate and down the narrow track to the road.

"Where's Wills?" said Char.

"Dead." Cyndi's voice, hoarse and ragged, pulled Char's attention back. The vampire fangs flashed briefly, uselessly, in the dark, as Cyndi licked her lips carefully.

"He's dead," she repeated.

Chapter 6

"Dead." said Char.

Lara turned her head away. Cyndi stared defiantly back at Char.

Dade said, "Yeah."

For the first time, Char noticed the dark stains on Lara's pink princess dress.

It can't be blood, she thought.

They were on the beach road now, twisting and turning back to Point Harbor.

"This is a joke," said Char. "A bad Halloween joke. Cyndi — "

But whatever she'd been about to say, telling Cyndi it wouldn't work, that Cyndi wasn't going to get away with this kind of garbage, was cut off by Jones's voice.

"He was ripped up pretty bad."

"How do you know?" asked Cyndi sharply. Then, "That's right. You stayed. You stayed and *looked* at him."

Dade spoke just as sharply. "Better than running away."

Cyndi jerked away from him and sat rigidly on the seat between Dade and Lara.

"He was on the ground." Jones's voice was flat. "Lara was over him, screaming. I pulled her away and tried to see if he still had a pulse or anything."

Lara's voice, as flat as Jones's: "He was still moving. . . ."

"Sometimes that happens, even after . . . after a person is dead."

"How do you know so much, Jones?" Dade's voice was curious, as if they were discussing a theory, not someone they knew. "Rick knows that kind of stuff, probably, 'cause of his father. Wills was a specialist in it, but then he wasn't wrapped right."

"Stop it! *What happened?*" Char almost screamed.

The lights of Point Harbor came up to meet them. The streets were almost empty now. But jack-o'-lanterns still burned in the windows, silhouettes of construction paper skeletons and cats and pumpkins still decorated the windows. One of the houses had been rolled. Toilet paper fluttered in the branches like shredding flesh on twisted bones. Someone had, as usual, poured soap into the fountain in the center of town.

Jones turned down the street by City Hall. Turned again and slid the car to a stop outside a low, quiet, brightly lit building.

"The police station!" said Cyndi.

Lara's voice, flat expressionless: "Of course it is, Cyndi. What did you expect? We have to report a murder."

"She's expecting me."

Hodges hesitated, then Jane said, behind him, "It's okay, Hodges."

He gave a stiff nod and stepped aside and Jane hurried forward to seize Char's arm. "Oh, Char, I'm so glad you're here. I couldn't sleep."

They'd been at the police station until almost dawn. As they'd left, Char had looked out toward Cemetery Point. Yes. Searchlights. No one had believed them at first. But they'd believe them now.

Only she still wasn't quite sure what had happened.

"Come up to my room. Would you like something to eat? Oh. I guess that's not . . ."

"It's okay, Jane." Char followed Jane up the stairs to her big, immaculately kept corner room. Every light in it was on. All the windows had the curtains pulled back as far as they would go.

"No wonder you couldn't sleep." Char tried to make a feeble joke, motioning toward all the light.

"I didn't want to be in the dark," said Jane simply.

Char sat down in one of the small, down-filled chairs and leaned back wearily. She was exhausted. But she hadn't been able to sleep, either. Jane's phone call had been a welcome relief.

She watched as Jane fidgeted: flopping back across her bed, sitting up, rolling over on her stomach, and pulling a pillow under her chin.

Jane was normally so calm. Normally.

Normal.

We won't be using that word for a while, thought Char. Because what had happened — whatever it was — was definitely not normal.

Jane pulled a tendril loose from her tightly drawn-back brown hair and began to inspect the ends. One foot bobbed up and down over the far edge of the bed.

Not normal. Wills was dead.

"Who?" said Char aloud. "And why?"

Jane got still. She looked at Char, her eyes huge. "It was one of us. Wasn't it?"

"I didn't say that. It could have been some random person out there. Some bum, maybe."

"Yeah," Jane responded lukewarmly, her eyes still fixed on Char's face. "Yeah. Some bum who just happened to walk all that way out to Cemetery Point, and was waiting there for us on Halloween."

"He — or she — could have been living there," Char pointed out. "Or it could have been some pinball crazy person who knew about the party and got there first. . . ."

"Or followed us out." Jane nodded slowly. "Like Georgie and Dorian."

"Yeah," said Char. She hesitated, then said, "Did you notice anything, Jane?"

"Like what? The police asked me that, too."

"I'm not the police."

"I know. It's just that . . . no. No. I don't remember much of anything. I mean it was spooky and all. It was so . . . so Cyndi to have that party . . . I mean, I didn't want to go in the first place. . . ."

"Yeah. I mean, I probably wouldn't have gone if Jones hadn't come along. I think I went with him just to yank Cyndi's chain."

Meeting Jane's level gaze, Char added, "Well maybe not *just* to yank Cyndi's chain." She almost smiled, remembering. Then she remembered the run toward the darkness, the panic like some uncut drug speeding through her veins on its way to stopping her heart, remembered the sound of Dade's voice behind her, counting down the mortal seconds.

Remembered the heaving earth beneath her feet.

"Details," said Char, coming back to the present. "Don't think about the whole thing. Just try to remember the details."

"Well . . ." Jane began slowly, and Char felt a surge of hope. Although what exactly she hoped for, she didn't know.

"I know the way, don't worry," a voice sounded in the hall. A moment later, Jane's door opened.

"I thought *you'd* be here," said Cyndi, by way of acknowledging Char.

The three of them looked at each other in silence. Then Jane said to the flustered-looking maid who had appeared behind Cyndi, "It's okay. Thank you."

Cyndi didn't look good, thought Char. But, then,

who did? She'd washed the witch's paint off her face, removed the red talon press-on nails from her fingers. But vestiges of paint still clung to her skin, and she hadn't had time to wash the white paint from her hair, only to comb it so it at least wasn't spiked straight up.

Cyndi was pale, almost as pale as her vampire makeup had been. Traces of black liner still ringed her eyes, and her mouth looked chapped at the corners where the vampire teeth had rested.

Without waiting to be invited, Cyndi dropped into the other chair and pulled her feet up under her. As usual, she was all in black. It didn't fit in Jane's blue-and-ivory room.

"Cyndi?" asked Jane.

"Jane?" mocked Cyndi.

Char felt her temper rise. It was just like Cyndi to walk in and muddy the waters. That girl was a walking personality disorder.

"We were talking about the murder," Char said sharply. "It kind of ruined your party, didn't it?"

Cyndi said, "Yeah. I guess you could say the murder spoiled all the fun."

"Fun," repeated Char neutrally.

But Cyndi didn't rise to the bait. "I thought you'd be here," she repeated. "Both of you. That's why I came."

"Why?" said Jane.

"Because Wills is dead. And maybe someone might think . . . might think it was my fault."

Jane gasped.

"Is it?" asked Char, watching Cyndi closely.

"Char!" exclaimed Jane.

"It's okay. You're a . . . witch, Char, but you're consistent. I . . . in a funny way, I trust you."

"I'd stick to trusting my friends," muttered Char.

Cyndi hunched one shoulder in a contemptuous shrug. "Friends," she said.

"But Lara," began Jane.

"Home. Doing the grief number. With the help of the doc's prescriptions."

"And you're here," said Char.

Cyndi said to Jane, "You see what I mean about Char?" To Char she said, "And I'm here."

"Why?"

With some difficulty, Cyndi said, "Because the cops think I set the whole thing up: the party, the games . . ."

"The murder," said Char.

"To get even with Wills. To pay him back for us splitting. Someone told them all about it."

"I didn't," said Jane.

Cyndi said, "I know. And I know Char didn't, either."

Jane frowned.

Cyndi said, "You wouldn't. People like you, Jane, don't gossip. To the cops or anybody. You live in a closed circle. You protect what's in it. You don't talk about what's outside it.

"And Char wouldn't because she doesn't like me. It's sort of like a weird code of honor. Am I right?"

"I didn't say anything to the cops," said Char.

Cyndi smiled. "That's the difference between you and me, babes."

"Everyone did know about you and Wills," interceded Jane. "He — they — said you'd had a big fight."

"He said it," said Cyndi. "He told everyone his version. He had a big mouth. Big man. Big stud. He didn't get it, you know? All he wanted was to be somebody famous, even if it was only for fifteen minutes. And even if it was only for going out with me."

Char said, "You were just using him, too."

"So? I'm not on this earth to fall in love, get married, and have babies. . . . And, anyway, it was mutual. I just wish I'd dumped him first. I could've killed him for that."

Her words hung in the air.

Cyndi smiled.

"Jeez," muttered Char.

Cyndi said, "I could have killed him, but I didn't. I've got to prove it.

"And the only way to prove I didn't kill Wills is to find out who did."

Chapter 7

Jones was thinking about murder.

How easy it was. How people got away with it. On TV. In films.

In real life.

Sometimes it was hard to remember what was real. Sometimes it was hard not to believe what wasn't.

Nothing seemed real.

Maybe being dead was what was real. Maybe that was the only reality.

"Heavy," muttered Jones disgustedly.

He was sitting at the overlook by the Back Bay Road. He'd been there all night. Had watched the sun come up over Cemetery Point.

On the previous night, what was left of Halloween night, lights had glimmered and flickered until dawn out on the Point. But last night, it had been dark and still, lit only by the waning moon.

The sunrise had been spectacular, a definite ten for special effects: the sky shot full of colors, a decorator's nightmare, turning the Point gray, then silver, then blood red.

The cops would have the Point roped off. Scene of the crime.

On the Bay Road behind him, the Point Harbor morning traffic had begun — six or eight cars.

Why would anyone live in a place like Point Harbor?

Crazy to live that way.

Unreal crazy.

Almost as crazy as murder.

Another car. This one didn't pass by. It pulled to a stop behind him.

He watched it in the rearview mirror. Watched the driver get out and saunter toward him.

The door on the passenger side of his car opened. Dade slid into the seat next to him. Looked out at the view.

"Say you wanted to off someone," Dade said conversationally. "How would you do it?"

Char was dreaming again. She knew she was dreaming. She knew the dream. She'd been there before, that night on the Point when she'd been running away from Cyndi's party.

This time, she wasn't in the water. This time she was on the dunes above, looking out to sea. Although the moon was waning, the Devil's Teeth glistened with an unholy light: the carnivorous smile of the sea.

The somber, heavy wool dress she was wearing

didn't warm her. She was cold to the heart.

But he was there. Out there. Waiting. Waiting for her to call him to her. They would say she had a demon lover. But it wasn't that.

Because he had taken everything that she had loved, everything that ever mattered. And that had changed her.

She felt the power rising through her veins, more scalding than any passion, more dangerous than any love. Immortal power.

She didn't know where it came from. Or why.

She didn't care anymore.

Whatever it was, whatever he was, she would kill him. And if he would not die, well, then, it would be a fight beyond death.

She would wear out eternity before she rested.

Raising her arms, she began to call him to her.

Char woke. Her arms were raised, as if she wanted to pull the darkness to her and hold it tight.

Like a lover.

No.

No.

She jerked her arms down, scrabbled in the blankets, and pulled them up over her head as if she were a child again.

What was happening to her?

Why?

She had to stop it. She had to fight it.

She was afraid.

The cold cut her to her bones. Mortal fear.

"I'm not afraid of dying," she whispered in the blanket darkness.

I'm not afraid of dying.

I'm afraid of something worse.

Lara slept on. She'd always liked to sleep. Slept liked the dead, her family said.

Sleeping was one of the things Lara did best.

But she'd had trouble sleeping after Wills's death. Even with the 'scrip to calm her down. So the doctor had phoned another 'scrip into the pharmacy, and the pharmacy had delivered it.

And if the dead slept without dreams, without memories, without moving, then Lara was sleeping the sleep of the dead.

"Yo, Father," Rick had said. "A little business for you. Sort of makes us a team, right?"

His father had looked away.

Rick had almost felt bad.

But he'd asked anyway: "Are you gonna be the one who — makes Wills into a beautiful memory picture?"

"The family has contacted us," his father had said.

Rick had felt bad then, a little. Bad and weird.

So he'd said, "Well, you've got your work cut out for you. Get it?"

After leaving the police station, Dorian had sacked it for the day. He got up Sunday evening to find the house empty except for servants. And his sister.

He didn't see her at first. He'd wandered into the library to scrounge in the bar. Something had made him turn.

She was sitting in the window seat, in the shadows.

"Drink?"

She shook her head.

"You look bad," he told her, fixing himself a drink. "Like something the cat dragged in. 'Cept it's Wills that got the cat treatment, isn't it?"

Cyndi still didn't answer.

"Cat got your tongue?" he asked. "Or did Point Harbor's finest wear you out with their relentless questioning?" Pretending to be concentrating on his drink, he watched her from beneath his eyelashes. He thought, but he wasn't sure, that she got even paler.

He smiled unpleasantly. "I'm surprised they let you go," he said. "Do they know how you tried to kill me once? Did you tell them that?"

Georgie woke up Monday morning with a bad headache. Bad dreams. She couldn't remember them, but they were definitely there.

The cops had not been nice to her. They'd treated her differently than they'd treated the others. But she'd made it clear she knew what was what. "I don't have to answer your questions," she'd told them. "Or am I under arrest? I know my rights."

They'd backed off a little at that. Then she'd told them what she knew — about Cyndi. And Wills. And the whole soap opera of the young and the richest. So that even if every one of those babes had lied and stuck together, someone was telling the truth.

Even if it wasn't the whole truth and nothing but.

That made her head stop hurting.

Her father's cat was meowing hungrily.

She hated that cat.

"Hungry?" she asked it.

The cat meowed.

"Thirsty?" she crooned.

The cat meowed.

"Tough, kitty, kitty," she called, and slammed the door behind her, laughing.

Cruising down Back Bay Road, Foy saw Dade slide out of Jones's car.

He almost stopped. But something about the whole setup made him keep going.

And start wondering.

Jones and Dade.

Definitely not situation normal.

What were they up to?

Then he told himself, stop it. You're getting paranoid. They're not up to anything.

They're probably just up. A little preschool meet to get high.

Except that it didn't fit. He'd never seen Dade carrying, much less getting high.

And Jones. Now there was a man who liked to stay in control.

Even that whole scene out at the Point, he'd been the ice of them all. The first one to reach Lara. To pull her away. Kneeling down beside the body and calmly checking for a pulse.

How had he even known where to look in all that — mess?

They said Wills had died instantly.

So everything else that had happened hadn't mattered.

But it mattered to the living. Someone out on the Point had done a Jack the Ripper on William Lawrence Howell.

Ironic.

Wills had always been such a fan of Jack's.

Foy turned into the parking lot.

Did he imagine it, or were the kids hanging nearby turning to stare? To whisper.

"Monday, Monday," muttered Foy, getting out of his car to face the day.

"Hey Foy, how'sit?" said one guy.

Brownie points to you, thought Foy.

Several more heads turned. Watching. Waiting.

Well, they weren't going to get anything from him.

"Hey," Foy said, and began to amble toward the school. He felt the eyes on him. Felt them watching.

He had the odd feeling that if he started to run, they'd all run after him, bring him down.

Then he thought about Halloween night out at the Point. How someone had been watching and waiting, then, too.

And, suddenly, although the day wasn't cold and he was wearing a jacket, he felt a chill down his neck.

It was cold as ice. As cold as death.

He felt fear ripping open his chest.

It took all his willpower not to turn. To make himself believe that nothing, *nothing* could possibly be behind him. That the killer, no way, could be standing out there in the parking lot, watching him.

At last he reached the doors of the school. Pulled them open.

But only when they slammed shut behind him did he feel safe.

Monday was going to be murder.

Chapter 8

"Part of our quaint charm," muttered Char.

She was in the Point Harbor public library, a carefully preserved pile of stones with narrow windows, drafty halls, and dark corners. She'd left school and come straight there to rummage in the stacks of crumbling, yellowing old newspapers that had not yet been converted to film.

Now, pulling a dusty bundle of newspapers off the lower shelf in the back of the stacks, she carried it to the rickety wooden table crammed in one corner of the basement. The corner was lit by an old lamp and the faint afternoon light of day coming through the small rectangular street-level windows at the top of the basement.

She was bored just being in the library. But what else was there to do? Homework? Not likely.

For a moment, she thought of Jones, and a little smile curved her lips. Not homework material. Exactly.

Then, resolutely putting him out of her mind, she blew the dust off the top of the stack and sneezed.

"*Gesundheit*," she said aloud.

She sat down and began to read.

Time passed.

Point Harbor history was hardly newsworthy, even when it had made the local newspaper. She'd started forty years back. That seemed far enough — unless whoever'd killed Wills was some kind of geriatric phenom.

Like Cyndi with a thousand face-lifts, she thought. Nah. I don't like Cyndi. But I don't think she's a killer, either.

Which still didn't explain what she was doing spending her downtime with a bunch of moldy old newspapers.

But maybe there was a pattern. Maybe someone like this had killed before.

"And maybe Jack the Ripper has been reincarnated in Point Harbor," she said sarcastically to herself.

Still, it helped to be busy. To think she might find something. It helped to keep her from thinking about, imagining, Wills's death. She hadn't liked Wills.

But no one deserved to die like that.

The light at the windows turned gray. She sifted through one stack of newspapers after another.

The police blotter reports gave new meaning to petty crime: a dispute over a fish stolen from the back of a truck. A rash of farm equipment thefts.

A local man charged with being a public nuisance for refusing to cut his lawn.

She even read the obituaries. But the deaths were natural. Car accidents, heart attacks, sad stories of illness and loss. Not murder.

Then, in the dead of winter in 1959, the murder-suicide of an old couple on their potato farm.

Expressions of shock on the part of the community.

Someone's car hit by a train.

A brief acknowledgment of the arrival of the Beatles.

And, late in the sixties, arrests for marijuana. One of the arrests had been of a farmer's daughter, growing marijuana in the cornfield.

Char made a disgusted sound and stood up and stretched. I don't spend this much time on homework, she thought. But, then, when was homework ever about murder?

Homework is murder, she thought.

She looked around at the shadowy stacks and thought, if you did your homework down here late enough, I suppose you could get murdered.

Ugh. But she wasn't really scared. The stacks were too depressing to be truly scary. She gathered up the last bundle of newspapers and trundled them to the back of the stacks.

Kneeling to shove the newspapers back in place on the lower shelf, she didn't hear anyone come in.

Instead, suddenly, she felt it — a shifting in the air. A flutter of the dim light.

She wasn't alone.

She straightened up slowly. Tried not to breathe.

The stacks were quiet. From upstairs, faintly, came the sound of the copier.

Nothing else.

Sure, she thought. Someone carrying a twelve-foot butcher knife and an ax and maybe a chain saw just oozed past the librarians on the way down here.

Sure.

Get a grip, Webster.

Besides, even if someone were down here, the librarians are just up the stairs. You wouldn't even have to scream very loud. And as long as you could scream . . .

She thought of Wills. Who hadn't made a sound.

She lifted her chin. Thought of her bare throat. Lowered her chin again. Took a deep breath. "Who's there?"

No one answered.

Her heart began to pound erratically.

"Stop that," she muttered.

And a soft, soft voice whispered in her ear, "Stop what?"

She didn't scream. Instead, grabbing a book from the nearest shelf, she spun around.

Jones said, "Wait."

"You!" Slowly, she lowered the book and pulled it close to her chest. She forced herself to speak. "Jones. What are you doing here?"

He held up a small black book. "I might ask the same thing."

Char recognized the artist's notebook she always carried with her. She'd left it on the table, where she had been taking notes and making sketches from the newspapers. "I might ask what you're doing with my property."

"Interesting stuff," he said, handing it to her casually.

"You had no right to look in that book."

"It was open," he said.

Had it been? She didn't think so. She wasn't sure. Taking the book, she pushed past him and headed back to the table where her leather shoulder satchel hung over the chair. Without looking at Jones, she shoved the book deep inside and hoisted the satchel.

"Hey, wait a minute," said Jones. Then, more softly, "I thought we were friends."

"Friends?" she echoed furiously. She kept remembering all the things she'd written in her notebook — not just notes from today, but personal things. Things she had never told anybody. She hoisted her satchel.

Jones blocked her way.

"I'm leaving now," she said pointedly.

"Char, hey, listen. I'm sorry. It was open. It really was. And I only looked at the open pages."

"You shouldn't have looked at anything."

"No, but I'm glad I did."

Startled, Char turned to face him. "What?"

Choosing his words carefully, Jones said, "We obviously think alike. We obviously pick up on some of the same things."

"We share vibes?" she said with soft sarcasm.

He ignored the sarcasm. "You're doing research on Wills's death, aren't you — looking up other crimes that happened around Point Harbor that might be similar."

"So?" He had her full attention now. Her thoughts took an unexpected spin back to Halloween night, the two of them in the car, right before Rick played his stupid joke.

"So," she repeated.

"The night Wills — died — you knew something was going to happen, too. You felt it."

"I don't know what I felt." She met Jones's eyes and added, "And whatever I felt, it didn't have anything to do with what happened."

They were the same height. Funny, she'd thought Jones was bigger, somehow. Taller.

He moved closer.

Involuntarily, she stepped back.

He stopped. "You don't trust me, do you?"

"Who killed Wills?" she returned. "Tell me that."

"I can't. I can't do that."

"You know," she said softly. "You do know."

They faced each other for a moment longer, both their faces in shadows. Her breath was coming in soft, short gasps. Whether it was rage, or fear, or some other emotion, or some combination of all, she couldn't tell.

Jones was breathing hard, too.

"The name," she said.

He didn't answer.

"Fine. Play the game," she said. "Keep the name. Excuse me. Please."

He stepped back to let her by.

When she reached the foot of the stairs, he said, "Char."

She stopped. She didn't turn around.

"It's not a game, Char."

"Then you won't mind if I don't play by the rules," she answered and went up the stairs.

Chapter 9

Georgina was bored.

Bored, bored, bored.

Bored to death.

The Halloween party had been ruined. Rotten party. And the weekend was still days away.

And Dorian hadn't called her, either. He'd said he would. Hadn't he? She was pretty sure he had. She'd had a little too much to drink, of course. She wasn't drunk. Never drunk. She could handle it. Quit any time.

But she didn't remember the whole evening all that clearly.

She hunched her shoulders and poured herself a little bit of vodka that she'd siphoned off the top of her father's supply. Fancy stuff he saved for special occasions. Made from potatoes.

It didn't matter. It all tasted the same. She took a sip and tried to think clearly now, her pale blue eyes squinting with the effort.

The cops had asked all kinds of questions. Had they believed her? What had Dorian told them? What had the others said about her?

She could just imagine. They always talked about her. Thought they were better than she was. Scared little girl Jane. That rich witch Cyndi. And Char. Charity. Ha. Ha to Lara, too. Looks weren't everything. You had to have brains, too.

What had happened to Wills was the least of what any one of them deserved. And weren't they scared now! Scared it was one of them. Trying to figure out who to blame.

Well they weren't going to blame her.

It served them all right.

Sorry. They'd all be sorry someday about how they'd treated her. When she was famous. Sorry.

But it was such a long time to wait. She wanted them to start being sorry sooner. Much sooner. Like now.

She finished her drink and picked up the phone.

"I don't think this is such a good idea." Dorian kept the BMW idling at the curb. A break-my-window, he called it. You can't park these in the city, he'd said. They break your window and take it all.

My next car is going to be a Jag, he'd said. This one will be the down payment.

She drove a two-door Toyota. When her father wasn't using it.

"Drive," she said now. "Or my old man'll come cracker-jackin' out the door, telling me it's a school night."

"Well, isn't it?" asked Dorian.

"Dorian."

"I'll drive. But Georgie-girl, my favorite brunette, what's the point?"

Why did he call her that junk name? Probably from one of those stupid old movies he was always watching. At first she'd thought they'd had something in common. But she couldn't stand the movies he liked. He was practically a freak.

But a rich freak.

"You have anything to drink?"

"Thanks, but I'm driving."

"Don't be stupid, Dorian."

"It's a school night for me, too."

"Yeah," she sneered. "You're on what? Halloween break from college? Why did you come home, Dorian?"

"You called and made me an offer I couldn't refuse," he said lightly, but she could see it annoyed him. Good. She liked him a little annoyed. A little upset.

She said, "I'm flattered you decided to stay on. Or maybe the cops asked you to."

"Or maybe they didn't." Dorian turned the car into a convenience store parking lot and got out. A few minutes later he returned with a six-pack in a brown bag.

"For me? How sweet."

He didn't answer as he started up the car. Then he said shortly, "Keep it down, okay. I don't want my license pulled for having an open beer in the car with a minor attached to it."

"You don't mind having a minor in your car doing other things," she said.

"Dif, Georgie. Big time."

"Bogus, Dorian. It's just as illegal. Isn't it?"

They were out of town now, negotiating the narrow turns along the Back Bay Road. The houses along Back Bay weren't as impressive as the ones on the beach. But those houses, sitting deep in their nest of woods with their walks to private bay beaches and their waterviews, they cost enough, thought Georgie.

"Why are we doing this?" asked Dorian.

Because I'm bored, thought Georgie. Because I like a little thrill, and you aren't cutting it.

Aloud she said, "You remember Nancy Drew, girl detective? Or how 'bout Sherlock? Well, I thought it might be fun to look for some clues. You know?"

"I don't know," answered Dorian impatiently. "It's a mega-ditz idea, Georgie. The whole Point is sealed off, for one thing. And it's almost dark, for another."

"It won't be dark for at least another hour," she said scornfully. "What'sa matter. Scared?"

His lips tightened. "No."

"They think Cyndi did it," she said, just to see his lips tighten a little more.

89

He didn't answer, so Georgina went on. "She's capable of it, don't you think? I mean, she's got such a bad temper. And she's strong. A big strong . . ."

"What about it?"

"Why do you always get so bent over Cyndi?" asked Georgie. "What's with you and her?"

"We're going back to the scene of the crime, Georgie. We're going to look for clues, as you so professionally described it. You're going to get to be Nancy Drew for an hour. So just be quiet."

Georgie leaned back, satisfied. For the moment. "Nice sunset," she said.

Dorian didn't answer.

The gate to Cemetery Point was padlocked shut. The "No Trespassing — Danger" sign was back up. Neon police tape sealed the scene of the crime.

"What now?" said Dorian.

"Can you walk?" asked Georgie.

Without waiting for an answer, she slid out of the car and headed toward the gate. "C'mon," she said. "Help me."

She slithered through as Dorian reluctantly held the strands of barbed wire apart. He followed, being careful not to snag his lambskin jacket.

"Start looking for clues," she said, taking a long swallow of beer.

"For clues. Yeah, sure. If I see any suspicious trees, I'll run right over and make a citizen's arrest."

They walked in silence down the sandy, rutted path.

"Oh, wow," said Dorian sarcastically. "Something big's been here. Look at those tracks. And the broken branches. Maybe a car?"

"Oh, Sherlock, you really turn me on," Georgie snapped back.

The silence descended again. So very quiet. Dorian couldn't quite put his finger on it. . . . "Doesn't this give you the creeps?" he asked.

"No," said Georgie. "It's exciting."

In the clearing by the graveyard, they stopped by the charred remains of the fire. "The cooler's gone," he noted. "Guess the cops took it."

He started to kick ashes and rubble, then thought about all the television shows he'd seen about preserving the evidence, and stopped.

"Wills brought it back this way." Georgie caught his hand.

Her hand was very warm. Hot. She squeezed his fingers and smiled brilliantly back at him.

Tough cookie, Georgie. With *a lot* of weird energy. But exciting. Something about her excitement now, the way she was obviously getting off on this whole sick scene, was turning him on, too, now.

Sick.

"It's getting dark," he said.

"You are *such* a chicken." She turned to face him, her eyes shining. "Come *on.*"

Dorian tugged her toward him. "What's in it for me?"

"What d'ya want to be in it?" She pulled back, keeping just out of reach of his other arm, her smile bright. "Come with me, and I'll show you."

"What a bad little girl you are," he said, following. "You're really getting off on this, aren't you?"

"Aren't you?" she asked. "Nothing ever happens. Now something has. Doesn't that do anything for you?"

"Murder doesn't."

"Danger, then."

He started to point out that there wasn't any danger. Whoever'd done Wills was long gone. The only danger was someone finding out.

Instead, he allowed himself to be led along, trying to step in the footprints Georgie made. If anyone found out about this, he didn't want his footprints all over the place. Although, come to think of it, he could have made those footprints on Halloween.

Suddenly Georgie stopped with a little gasp. Her fingers tightened on his.

The chalk outline where Wills's body had been glowed eerily in the early dusk. More darkly, great stains grouted the cracked earth and seared grass inside and around the outline.

Blood.

All of the blood in Wills's body, from the look of it.

"Wow," breathed Georgie. She strained forward, gazing avidly.

"Careful," he said. She seemed not to have heard him as she dropped his hand and walked closer.

"Look, Dorian. This is where Wills fell. Backwards. And Lara must have knelt down here. That means whoever stabbed him, stabbed him from the front."

"That doesn't necessarily mean you fall backwards," said Dorian.

"Then maybe he was tripped. Or dragged."

In spite of himself, the whole grisly scene was getting to him. He said, softly, "Do you see any drag marks, Georgie? Look, we don't know enough to find any clues. And whatever clues there were, the police found them."

Georgie remained a moment longer, kneeling where Lara had knelt. She was imagining herself as a great actor. The cameras were all on her. She'd handle it better than Lara. . . .

"Georgie."

"Oh, all right!" She got up crossly and brushed the dirt off her jeans. "We're going, we're going." She looked up at him. "Kiss?"

When he looked up again, it was almost dark.

"We gotta go."

Georgie pressed against him. "Now?"

For an answer, he pulled her against him and started toward the graveyard entrance.

"Wait," said Georgie. She reached down, picked up her beer, and finished it. Then she threw the bottle as far as she could.

"Why don't you just leave a note saying you were here," said Dorian.

"I dropped it that night. When we were playing hide-and-seek. You're the only one who knows different." She smiled suddenly. "Let's go, Dorian. Let's go have some *fun*."

He didn't want to admit how relieved he was. Instead, he said, "Tell me about it." If they walked quickly, they'd be out of there before it got too dark.

He was wrong. The darkness in the woods was already complete. He picked up his pace.

"Hey," Georgie complained. "I've got on boots with heels, okay?"

"Come *on*." He hurried ahead. An uneasy feeling was growing on him. The branches of the trees felt disquietingly like hands, holding on to him. And the silence.

That silence. No birds. No animals rustling in the undergrowth. No squirrels or gulls. *Nada.*

Nothing. Complete silence.

Like the grave.

"You're scared, aren't you?" Georgie's voice took on a mocking note. "You're really scared."

"Will you come on?" They were in the clearing. He was almost running now.

"What a cowardly little boy." He reached the head of the rutted sand track leading back to the gate. Looked back.

Georgie had stopped dead and was standing there, her arms folded, one hip thrust out provocatively, her black hair like a dark halo around her head. While he watched, she ran her tongue over her lips, then caught the lower one in her teeth. Her eyes were bright, supernaturally bright.

"Don't you want to stay for a while, little boy?"

She unfolded her arms, and ran one hand down her hip.

For a moment, he almost turned around.

Then he heard it. The faintest of sounds in the undergrowth.

"Hurry," he said.

He crashed forward, pushed his way toward the gate. The last sliver of sun snuffed out below the horizon.

"Dorian!" Georgie's voice, suddenly sharp. Looking over his shoulder, he saw her behind him.

"Run," he ordered. He didn't stop.

The barbed wire tore at his hands. At his jacket. He didn't care.

He didn't care about the torn leather, the torn flesh on his palms and fingers.

For a moment it felt as if the wire were holding on to him. He gave a strangled cry and tore free.

Crouching, sobbing, he reached the car. The blood on his hands made the door handle slippery.

"C'mon, come on," he sobbed.

Then he was inside. He slammed the door shut behind him.

Georgie's window was down. Frantically he fumbled for the button to roll it up.

It wouldn't work.

Power windows.

Break my window.

He jammed the key into "on." The engine screamed.

The window began to grind shut.

"Dorian!" He saw her just beyond the gate in the trees.

"Dorian!" she screamed. It was a voice he'd never heard before.

"Come on, dammit!" At the same time, almost involuntarily, his fingers found the automatic lock.

All four doors locked with a clunk.

"Runnnn!" he screamed.

But Georgie wasn't running. She wasn't hurrying at all. It was almost as if she were moving in slow motion. In slow motion, she turned her head. In slow motion, she stumbled.

"Dor . . ."

Something dark leapt out of the woods.

He shifted into gear.

There was a glint of burning metal light.

Georgie turned back to face it. Whirled in a grotesque dance. And then jumped, as if she were rising up to meet the glittering blade.

The car bucked wildly in the soft earth. For one awful moment, he thought it was going to stall.

He didn't see Georgie fall.

He tore down the track, heedless of the branches scoring the side of the car.

Heedless of what had fastened to the door handle.

Chapter 10

Cyndi was driving. She'd started out driving aimlessly. Then she had started tailing people, trying to guess where they were going by their cars, then following them to see how close she came.

The Mercedes had stopped at the grocery store. Not even close.

The farm truck had pulled around behind Finisterre, the pricey hotel overlooking the bay.

She'd missed that one, too. Some detective.

A police car cruised by. Was she being followed?

So far, there had been no more questions from the cops. It was one of the advantages of having rich parents and a nasty lawyer in a nice suit.

But that didn't mean she wasn't being followed.

She edged out of town. Maybe if she laid down some fast miles, she'd feel better.

And if someone *was* following her, let them try and keep up.

After all, a suspected murderer wouldn't mind playing a little chicken.

"I'm home," called Char.

At almost the same instant, a herd of snorting, stamping, mooing children shot by, pursued by her stepfather and one of her sisters riding on her stepfather's shoulders.

"Giddyap, bang, bang, bang!" screamed her sister.

"I don't think you're supposed to shoot the cows," said Char wryly.

Her stepfather rolled his eyes.

"Bang, bang, bang!" shrieked her sister, pointing at Char. "You're dead, too."

"Not quite," said Char. She went back to her room and shut the door.

Slinging the satchel on the desk, she reached inside for her notebook. She found it . . . and another book.

A pale rusty-colored book, the rust of black cloth faded with age. Nothing was written on the outside. Inside, the printing was close and faded to an even paler rust. Almost indecipherable.

Almost.

"Where did this come from?" she muttered. She fluttered the pages. The book smelled old, as if the pages had not been turned in a long, long time.

Had it fallen into her pack at the library? She tried to remember if she'd seen any other old books like this.

And then Char felt the hair rise on her neck. In her own house, in her own room, and she was spooked. Worse than the time she'd read that book, what was it — *Interview with the Vampire*.

Only this wasn't an interview, and this wasn't fiction. It was an old whaler's journal. Something printed before the turn of the century.

And across the title page, in the same faded rusty script, was the title: *Of Darkness and Its Minions*.

"No," she said aloud. And in spite of herself, began to read.

What am I doing here? thought Cyndi. Who do I think I am, Florence Nightingale?

More like Dr. Strangelove. Or something.

She rang the front doorbell.

A few minutes later she was standing just inside the door of Lara's bedroom.

"Lara?"

Lara was sitting in a chair by the window. The curtains were almost drawn shut, and the room was in near darkness.

"Lara?"

Without turning her head, Lara said in a flat, lifeless voice, "What."

"It's me. Cyndi. Remember me?"

"I'm fine," said Lara. "Thanks for stopping by."

"And I can go now? C'mon, Lara."

Slowly, at last, Lara turned to look at Cyndi. It was hard to see her expression in the dim room. The silence between them lengthened.

"Knock it off, Lara," Cyndi said abruptly, and sat down on the bed and folded her legs beneath her. "What's going on here?"

That made Lara sit up. "Wills is dead. I was *there*."

"So was I. And I wasn't any more in love with him than you are — were."

"There's blood all over my dress. Blood all over me. . . ."

"Get a new dress. Take a bath."

"Oh! You are hateful. A real piece of . . ."

"I am, but what's that got to do with it? C'mon, Lara. This is the kind of thing Georgie would do — Melodrama 101."

The hiss of Lara's breath told Cyndi she'd scored. She waited.

Then Lara said, "Why are you here?"

"Why are you? Gonna hide out until it's all over?"

Then Lara said, in a smaller, different voice, "Yes."

Cyndi leaned forward. "Why?"

"Because," said Lara.

"Lara."

"Because," repeated Lara. "Because . . . I saw who killed Wills. And I don't want him to kill me."

Ghost ships. Monster sharks.

Superstition and blood. And death.

A history of it. One that came at last around to Point Harbor.

Only it wasn't Point Harbor then. It was Cemetery Point.

"... Because there be besides a graveyard
on that tongue or spitt of land that enfoldeth
the harbor, just beyond as grave a stretch of
treachery water, marked by ungodly tyde and
hidden rock, as ever known to man, and beying
called the Devil's Teeth."

Not big news. All other things being equal, she
was surprised they hadn't made old Cemetery Point
into a sort of amusement park, with quarter-
operated telescopes for a closer look at the Devil's
Teeth.

But there was more. The sudden closing of Cemetery Point, alluded to only as a done deal in the
local newspaper she'd read earlier in the library,
was foreshadowed here in the unidentified author's
words.

No one went to Cemetery Point now, the author
noted, to bury their dead. They chose the newer
graveyard inland. For though it was true that those
sailors who were not "gatheryed into the bosom of
the waves" might prefer a burial within sight of the
sea, it was also true that "upon that once hallowed
land there now be hauntings.

"For it is the port of call of one fiend ship,
that doth sail easily among the rocks and

across the tydes, doth land where no ship can land, doth lure other mortal ships to immortal death, that it might gathyr souls from proper burial. That evidence be those who search the shore after a ship goeth down, they find no bodyes whole, but such rendered parts as was done by no earthly element.

"Some do saye that the master of the fiend ship be a foul dark creature, huge and graven, escap'd from Englund by reason of unspeakable renderings of human flesh therein that country, and thus driven forth to come hence here to our sorrow, having devoured his crew in feasts of blood."

"Sharks," she whispered. "It was sharks." She read on:

"Some do say that Thing which waityth upon the Cemetery Point and beyond, cannot be destroyed. That it hath Powers: to fly, to mimick form and life and shadow, to come and go, to suck upon the heart all that is hiddyn there. That it can only be stopped before it grow yet stronger still. But none have come upon the means to stop it, not one yet having seeing its face and lived."

Char swallowed, her mouth dry. "Impossible," she whispered.

Then, much later, a final entry, the handwriting

suddenly shrunken, as if written by a shaken, aging hand:

"I have seen Her there. She hath died outside Godliness for she movves yet upon the land and water. Howsomever, I do not belieyve she did mayke tryst and pact with the Dark. What was buried was not buried arright. The Peace is made of wronged blood.

"She was beautiful once."

The journal ended abruptly. There was no more.

It's not possible, Char repeated to herself. What had happened is someone had found this account, or one like it, and had used it to stage Wills's murder.

But if someone had it, and had used it as a handbook for murder, what was it doing in her pack? How had it gotten there?

Then she remembered Jones, standing there in the shadows in the basement in the library.

And it suddenly made vampires seem easy.

Chapter 11

I handled that all wrong, thought Cyndi.

I've got to be careful. Or people really will think I did it.

Because Lara had suddenly gone still. And silent. "Go away," was all she would say. "Go away."

And I made a fool of myself, thought Cyndi. I actually begged Lara to help me.

Cyndi flushed, remembering her words. "For me, Lara," she'd said. "We're friends."

"Friends?" Lara had answered slowly, in a considering voice.

And nothing more.

Maybe she won't remember that I begged, Cyndi thought. Maybe she's too scared.

But who had Lara seen?

What had she seen?

Maybe they'll believe Lara did it, Cyndi thought. After all, she had all that blood on her dress. What if she didn't get it kneeling down beside the body?

Maybe that's *why* she threw herself down by

Wills. To explain why she already had blood on her dress.

What normal person would throw themselves down by a hacked-up corpse?

Then she thought, Lara? A hatchet woman? Cyndi, get real.

The car purred along. No one knew where she was. Not that anyone cared. The parental units were out partying for charity at some big-bucks-a plate dinner. Her brother was holed up in his room.

Her brother. As always, the thought of Dorian made her feel crazy. What a sick puppy he was. She hadn't liked him from the moment she was born.

But, then, he hadn't liked her, either.

Still, after what had happened, you wouldn't think he'd have the nerve to go on scorching her.

Scorching. Funny she should choose that word.

Where was Dorian? Strange big bro Dorian. Now *he* was someone who was capable of murder.

A little smile curved her lips. Yes. Dorian. Maybe Dorian did it.

When she got home, it was late. But she wasn't tired. In fact, she was high. Manically high. The energy poured through her, bright, unstoppable.

Her parents' Continental was still out. So was Dorian's BMW. She slotted her car into its space, powered the garage door closed behind her. She'd just gotten out of her car when she heard the sound.

Dorian's car.

She stepped back in the shadows and waited as the garage door went back up.

He was driving like a bat out of hell.

He slammed the car into the last space at the far end of the garage, fendering the wall at the end and bouncing back. He slammed the door open so hard, it rebounded against the wall.

That, thought Cyndi, is going to make a nice dent.

He staggered around the front of the car, his breath coming in rasps.

Cyndi smiled a little.

She stepped forward from the shadows.

"Hot date?" she asked nastily.

And her big, brave brother screamed.

The lights of the patrol car swept the gate. The cop behind the wheel frowned. Something wasn't right.

She swore softly and began to report back on the radio. The other cop got out, one hand on his gun, and played this flashlight over the scene.

"Ten-four," she said. She slid out of the car and flicked on her own flashlight. The shadows jumped in the crisscrossing beams of light. The gate made long bars of darkness on the other side.

"Can you see anything?" she asked.

"I'm not sure."

Leaving the car lights on and the motor running, they cautiously approached the gate.

"Look," she said.

Something torn fluttered on the barbed wire. They bent down to examine it.

"Leather," she said at last. "A strip of leather. A shoe?"

"A jacket," suggested her partner.

"Yeah . . . it wasn't here before. . . ."

She shone her bright light through the wire, back into the shadows, quartering the darkness.

The silent eerie darkness.

"You watching my back?" she asked.

Any other time, he might have made some pig joke. And she would have called him a pig. Laughed. Or given him grief, depending.

But, tonight, he just said, "Yeah."

"There are two of us, anyway," she went on.

"There were ten of them," he answered. "To begin with."

"Who would be stupid enough to come out here after something like that?"

"Thrill-seekers. Ghouls."

It was her turn to answer, "Yeah."

She turned her flashlight to a new section of darkness. Swept it again. Froze.

Something lay motionless in the white beam.

Something horrible.

Something that had once been human.

For one moment, she wanted to say, "Call the cops."

Then she remembered: *I am one.*

Whatever — whoever — it had been, it was still oozing.

Maybe whoever it was, was still alive.

Sort of.

"Oh, my god," said her partner behind her.

Cyndi walked across the garage. She'd never seen Dorian so scared.

Or almost never, anyway.

He'd bolted out of the garage like the devil himself was following.

She was smiling, a little. Funny how, if you did something and someone blamed you for it, it made you hate them worse than ever.

The way she hated her dear, sweet brother.

Then she stopped, the smile leaving her lips.

Her heart began to pound heavily.

"Dorian?" she whispered. She walked forward again, stopping by the driver's side of the door.

Dorian had a lot more to worry about than a little dent in his car door.

The words of Rick's stupid, tired old Halloween tale came back to her.

Only it didn't seem like such a stupid story anymore, did it?

Because a deep gouge ran down one side of the car. And hanging on the handle on the driver's side was a bloody hook.

"Dorian."

No answer.

"Dorian. I know you're in there."

A long pause. Then he said, "Why don't you just

go away, Cyndi. Don't you think you've done enough?"

She tried the handle of the door. It was locked. She jiggled it impatiently.

"I think we need to have a little talk."

He didn't answer.

"I think we need to talk about what happened . . . tonight."

No answer. But a minute later, the doorknob turned in her hand.

He didn't open it for her. "It's unlocked," he said and had already started retreating to the other side of the room when she pushed her way in.

He turned to face her from the corner. Like an animal, his back against the wall.

"What do you want, Cyndi?"

"What happened tonight?"

His face, if possible, got paler. "Nothing."

"Nothing?" She raised her brows. "Nothing?"

He remained silent. Watching. Waiting.

"Where did you go, Dorian?"

"Out."

"Who'd you go with?"

"Nobody."

"And you didn't do nothing," she mocked him.

"I drove around," he said.

"Well, you must have hit something." She paused, watching him watch her.

He made a sound. A strangled sound.

She was enjoying this. She was. She said, softly,

persuasively, "Remember, Dorian? Remember when I was five, and you were seven?"

That sound again. But now color was coming back into his face. Color and rage.

"Remember how you used to play hide-and-seek with me, Dorian? And how you locked me in the trunk in the attic? And how you were going to leave me there?"

"You're lying."

"Nooo. No. It's the truth. Only you wimped. *After* I'd been there for hours. Alone. Buried alive. In the dark."

The strangled sound again.

Her voice grew soft. "You'd think I'd be afraid of the dark, after that, wouldn't you, Dorian? A scared little kid. A coward. But it didn't work out that way."

"I came back for you," he whispered. "It was a joke."

"No, it didn't work out the way you planned. Because what doesn't kill you makes you stronger."

"It was a joke." He licked his lips. "A joke."

She smiled. "I'm laughing. See?"

He rasped out, "What you tried was murder."

"But you *made* me keep playing hide-and-seek. That stupid game. Why did you? So you could try to scare me to death again? Or so you could really kill me?"

"You're crazy!"

"I don't think so. Then I was. A crazy little kid,

to keep playing a crazy little game with her crazy big brother."

She paused. Smiled. "But not now."

"It wasn't me. Not . . . it wasn't me who tried to do the killing," he said raggedly.

"Oh, Dorian. What *are* you saying? I locked you in that closet because I was afraid of you. Then. Did you think I would do to you what you did to me? That I wouldn't let you out?"

"The fire," he said.

"An accident, Dorian."

"It was the fire department that let me out!"

She said softly, "I told them you were there. I told them. I told them. I saved your life. You should thank me."

"Get out," he said.

"And I've been the one they've blamed ever since. Not you. Me."

"Get out!"

"I'm going," she said. "But if I were you, I wouldn't let anybody else drive my car."

Chapter 12

"I don't like you, Dade," said Jane.

Dade leaned out of the car window, one hand draped over the steering wheel, the other resting on the car door.

"If you don't like me, why are you talking to me?"

Jane shook her head and kept walking.

"You shouldn't be out so late alone," offered Dade.

"And you should?" she shot back.

"I'm with you."

She spun to face him. "You are not! Can't you just leave me alone!"

He twisted the car up onto the grassy verge just in front of her and stopped. With one quick, easy motion he jumped out and stood facing her.

She stepped back. It was hard to read his expression in the dark.

"What do you want?" she asked, keeping her voice cold.

"I'll walk with you," he said. "Unless you want me to give you a ride."

She hesitated. Which was worse — walking alongside Dade? Or riding in the car with him — alone?

She was so tired. So afraid. So alone. The cops had been back. Everyone at school kept watching. Waiting. Foy was acting weird. Like he wasn't all there. And Char wasn't even home. Where was she?

What was going on?

Murder, she thought. Murder is what's going on. No one was acting normal.

She didn't have anyone to talk to. So she'd come for a walk. Just a short walk in her very well-tended, carefully guarded neighborhood.

The hedges were way too thick for anyone to hide in. The private security force had already swung by once. She'd waved, and they'd recognized her.

Safe. Probably safer to walk than to get in the car with Dade.

So why, then, did she suddenly want to live dangerously?

"Does Cyndi know where you are?" she asked.

His teeth flashed white in the dark. "And I don't know where she is, either."

"Let's go for a ride," she said recklessly.

He held open the driver's door with a little bow, and she got in and slid across to the passenger seat.

She'd never been in Dade's car alone before. It

felt bigger. The motor sounded like one of those cars her father used to drive.

Her father. She missed him. But missing wouldn't bring back the dead.

They pulled away from the curb. Drove down the manicured lanes between the hedges.

"Where do you want to go?" asked Dade.

"Far, far away," she answered without thinking.

"Oz?" he said.

"Not exactly," she answered slowly. "But somewhere that isn't here."

"No place that isn't," he said. "Every place turns into here sooner or later."

She thought about that. Shook her head. "Wherever I go, it's going to be different. I'm going to be different."

"Changing the props don't change the performer," said Dade.

"Maybe I just don't want to perform anymore," she snapped.

He turned to look at her quickly. Grinned. "Good," he said.

"You're strange, Dade," she said. She couldn't believe she was sitting here, talking to him like that.

"Wait'll you get to know me," he said.

She slid a little closer. This isn't me, she thought. Does Cyndi act like this all the time? Is this what it feels like for Georgie when she's after someone? Or Lara?

"I don't want to wait," she said. *Oh, my god, I can't believe I said that. It's like I'm possessed.*

But Dade didn't seem to mind. He pulled the car to a stop.

Jane looked out. They were on the beach, above the dunes, opposite Cemetery Point.

She had a brief moment to think about Halloween and Cemetery Point and Wills.

A briefer moment to think about Cyndi.

Then she stopped thinking altogether.

Dorian's face was ugly. His hands were shaking.

In the harsh overhead light of the garage, he was staring at the door of his car. At the bloody gouge scored down one side.

At the bloody hook hanging on the door.

Someone is trying to scare me, he thought. It was an oddly comforting thought.

Because if someone wasn't, if this wasn't some sick, elaborate joke . . .

But it had to be. Georgie probably wasn't even dead. This whole Captain Hook routine was . . . was . . . yes, probably Cyndi's idea.

Or it was a frame-up?

No.

No one would believe it.

He wasn't thinking clearly. He had to stop panicking.

He took a deep breath. Time to ease on down the road, he thought.

Like now.

But where?

He couldn't go back to school. Being suspended

for cheating had put that away for him.

Money, I've got plenty of money, he thought. I'll think of something.

The important thing was to get away.

He turned.

He almost screamed.

Someone was standing in the corner of the garage. She walked toward him. He raised shaking hands, as if to ward her off.

Then he realized he was right. It had all been some awful joke. His worst fears weren't coming true.

Georgie wasn't really dead.

"Sick," he said. "You're sick, Georgie. Did that turn you on, doing that to me? You got so hot off it, you had to come and find me? That it?"

Georgie stopped.

She tilted her head. "Is that what you think?" she asked.

Dorian started toward her, his hands clenched.

Georgie waited. Smiling.

"Jane," Dade said softly.

Jane laughed. Phooey on Foy, she thought. Why didn't someone tell me the truth?

She sensed, rather than saw Dade smile.

"Having fun?" she whispered.

"Umm."

"I am. So far."

He shifted a little, holding her. She felt his breath in her hair.

They stayed that way for a while. Still. Which wasn't bad, either.

Then she turned toward him. Pulled him against her hard.

His arms tightened for just a moment.

Then he said sharply, "I don't believe this."

That made her remember who she was. And what she was doing.

She tried to twist free, but his arms tightened even more.

"Dade," she gasped.

"I don't believe this," he repeated.

And then she saw it. Saw the flashing lights out on Cemetery Point. Saw them careening away toward town along the coast road.

Dade let her go abruptly. As Jane caught her breath, he kicked the car into gear.

A moment later they were speeding back toward Point Harbor.

"It's happening again, isn't it?" she said, almost to herself, as they roared through the night.

And then she thought, I wonder which one of us it is this time.

The nice thing about the BurgerBurger was that they didn't care how long you stayed, as long as it wasn't crowded, thought Char. She'd been there for a couple of hours. It was comforting, the jelly bean colors, the relentless piped-in music. It had driven her crazy when she'd worked there, but now she liked it.

She watched the sophomore behind the counter, an intense kid with sandy hair and a collection of earrings in one ear. She was flirting, carefully, with a couple of guys who were sitting at the table closest to the counter.

Char would have told her from long experience that no matter how carefully she flirted, the manager knew. It was like she had eyes in the back of her head.

But she'd let it ride as long as the counter help didn't take it too far. Or give away too many free fries.

I should go over to Jane's, thought Char. But she didn't want to. She just wanted to sit there. Peacefully. Safely.

She wanted to sit here and not think about Jones. Or love. Or death. Funny how those three things seemed to go together.

About as funny as her dreams.

She slid her hand into her pack and touched the spine of the journal. Next to it was a fat paperback full of explanations of dreams and their symbols that she'd found on her mother's shelf. Her mother said books like that helped her understand what the art critics were talking about.

It hadn't helped Char.

Because it wasn't a dream, thought Char. *It was real.*

Suddenly the BurgerBurger felt confining. She needed to move. She needed to think.

118

No! She needed to stop thinking.

She gave herself a mental shake and looked at her watch. It *was* getting sort of late. Time to cruise.

Char walked slowly across the parking lot of the BurgerBurger. I smell like McGrease, she thought wryly. But she'd needed the comfort food. Funny, when she'd worked there, she'd sworn she'd never eat another burger. But, now, sometimes, it was just what she wanted.

Her pack bumped against her. She felt the edge of the book.

She took a long, comforting slurp of mocha shake.

Then she heard it. No, sensed it.

Someone was behind her.

But that was crazy. Of course someone was behind her. This was the Point Harbor town parking lot. The BurgerBurger was doing a brisk business. And some of the other stores, the ones that were still open, had just started to close for the night. People were coming out of them now, headed toward their cars.

Car doors slammed. Motors idled. People talked and waved.

She looked behind her, anyway.

No one.

She hurried more quickly to her car and fumbled with the key. Why wouldn't the door open?

There. Now. A quick check of the back seat, and then . . .

The blinding glare of headlights pinned her against the darkness.

Even though she'd never seen Georgie's father, she knew that was who was standing at the Emergency Room door. For one thing, they looked alike.

For another, Jane recognized the battered two-door Toyota next to him, the driver's door still open. A police officer was saying something to him, her face a frozen mask of professional sympathy. But he didn't seem to be listening.

Dade pulled into the parking lot and led the way toward the ER entrance.

It was a small hospital. A small hospital in a quiet town. It wasn't accustomed to handling anything like this. But, still, the professionals had stepped into their roles, bustling, rapping out orders as a stretcher was lowered gingerly from the ambulance and hustled through the ER doors. Beyond, the scene was one of frantic motion and scalding white light. But the bundle lay motionless and silent.

It was done with all the noise.

Jane swallowed hard and looked quickly down at her fists.

"What happened?" Dade asked the driver of the ambulance.

The driver shook his head. "Nobody knows. But it looks like she really bought it. Like that other guy out there. Looks like she got a dose of Jack the Ripper."

"Georgina," said Jane softly. "It was Georgina."

"They dunno yet," said the driver. "Hey, you shouldn't be here."

He got back in the ambulance and began to back it away from the ER door.

Georgina's father had gone inside. They could see him, two more cops with him now.

Just then a tall man with streaks of silver in his short, tightly curled black hair came toward them. He was in a white coat and had a stethoscope around his neck. He took off his glasses. Rubbed his nose.

For a moment, it seemed as if all the movement had stopped.

Just like a play, thought Jane wonderingly.

Then the doctor slowly shook his head.

And Jane knew Georgina was dead, too.

"Rick! Foy! You guys scared me! Don't you know how to honk or something?" Char was really annoyed, more at herself than anything.

"Yo, Charity," said Rick.

"What d'you want, Rick?" she asked.

"Nothing. We were just hanging and saw you and . . ." he shrugged.

"Well, nice seeing you and all, but I've got to get home."

Foy said, "We were kind of looking for Jane."

Char frowned.

"I called. She wasn't home. She was out for a walk," Foy explained.

"Well, she didn't walk this far." Char was still frowning. She knew Jane liked to take walks sometimes. But this wasn't exactly the safest time to do it.

Rick said, "So she's probably back home by now, my man."

But Foy looked as unconvinced as Char felt. Fishing in her pockets, Char brought up some change. She nodded toward the phone booth at the corner of the parking lot. "I'm going to go give her a quick call, okay?"

"Good idea," said Foy. "We'll wait."

But when Char reached Jane's house, Jane wasn't back yet.

"I'll tell Miss Jane you called," Hodges said firmly when Char tried to ask more questions.

And Char suddenly began to feel very, very afraid.

"Georgie? Georgina?"

She took a step toward him this time.

He took a step back.

"You're not really dead," he insisted. His voice was a croak. He could feel the sweat on the palms of his hands. Feel it starting up on his forehead. Funny you could be so sweaty and so cold at the same time.

"Oh, I'm not dead," Georgie agreed sweetly. "I'm very, very hard to kill." She took another step toward him.

He took another step back. Felt the cool metal of his car beneath his hands.

Smelled the rank smell of sweat. And another

smell. A cloying stench. A dead smell.

"Georgie," he whispered.

And now another, sharper smell. Gasoline.

"Get away," he said hoarsely. "Don't come any closer."

The sweat ran into his eyes. He blinked, brought his arm up and dragged it across them.

The figure blurred.

"Who are you?" he asked. He could barely breathe. Darkness swam at the edge of his senses.

The figure smiled. "Who do you want me to be?" it asked coquettishly. It reached down, came up with a pack of cigarettes and a match. It took a cigarette out of the pack.

"You killed Wills, didn't you?" gasped Dorian. "And . . . and Georgie."

It smiled, the unlit cigarette clenched between its teeth.

"Who shall I be?" it asked. "The first time, I was a sorry sight. I could barely get it together to give Wills, what he . . . wanted. But, then, with sweet Georgina, I could be a little more creative."

"Jack the Ripper?" Dorian could feel the cold to his bones. Could feel how the horrible cold was making his bones crumble inside him.

He was shaking.

"Cold, Dorian?" The figure flipped open a book of matches. "Jack the Ripper. Hmm. Or Clarence. Or in the nautical line, Captain. Or Charon. But I like Jack. A very high profile image. Yes. Jack will do for now."

The figure struck the match. Made an elaborate show of lighting the cigarette. "Care for a light?" it asked.

Dorian felt himself losing consciousness.

"Get away . . . get away," Dorian gasped. He felt himself sliding into unconsciousness.

The lit match flew through the air.

And the world exploded into flame and darkness.

"Yes," it said. "Yes. Tell them — Jack's back."

Chapter 13

Char was halfway back across the parking lot when she heard the explosion. For a moment, she didn't believe it was real. For a moment, she thought it was her senses, playing that trick on her. Making bogus earthquakes.

Then she heard the fire station's siren down the street go into action, calling all the volunteers.

"Hot, hot, hot," cracked Rick as she reached her car.

"Jane's still not home," Char told Foy. "I — "

"Let's go see the fire," interrupted Rick.

"You are so cold!" She felt her temper flare up. "Don't you care that something might have happened to Jane?"

"Maybe it's her house that's on fire," said Rick. "It's in the right direction."

Controlling her disgust — barely — Char swung around. It *was* the right direction.

"It's not Jane's house," Foy said, but he was getting back into his car.

"Yeah, maybe it's your house," said Rick.

"Give me a break," Foy said.

"Grow up," muttered Char. She wheeled and raced back toward her Mom's old Volvo. Miraculously, it started on the first try.

She could hear the sirens of the fire truck as it pulled away from the station. Ahead of her, Foy and Rick were turning out of the parking lot. Too slow. Too slow.

She put her hand on the horn. "Go, go for God's sake, move it!" she screamed.

The hospital had disappeared into the night behind them.

They were tracing their way through the dark, following the flickering light.

The light of a fire.

Whatever it is, thought Jane, it can't be any worse. "Turn here," she said aloud.

And then she realized who lived at the end of that street, and she knew Dade realized it, too.

And realized that, yes, it could be worse. Much, much worse.

A fire in Point Harbor was a big event. But a fire in the rich section of town was ranked public entertainment. The public was already there, pulling up in its cars, leaning out of windows, standing on roofs to see the show.

Ahead of her, Dade pushed his way unceremoniously through the gathering crowd. A few muttered complaints. But no one tried to interfere with him.

A fire fighter stopped them at the edge of the tangle of hoses.

"It's the garage, Dade," Jane said. "Just the garage."

But just the garage was enough, burning like the fires from some Bible-thumper's sermon, lighting up the sky. The fire fighters worked frantically, trying to contain it, trying to keep it from spreading.

"What happened?" Jane asked the beefy guy next to her.

"Like, an explosion," said the beefy guy. He burped. He was holding a beer, and his pot belly threatened to pop the zipper on his jacket.

A murmur went up from the crowd as the front door of the house opened and a figure in a uniform tottered out escorted by a fire fighter. She joined two other figures at the edge of the lawn.

"Is that everybody?" shouted the chief.

Jane knew the answer before the fire fighter could start shaking his head.

"No!" he shouted back. "That's all the servants. The parents are out for the evening. But the son and daughter aren't accounted for!"

Suddenly Dade had pushed his way past the barriers.

"Hey, you!" shouted the chief. Two other fire fighters made a grab for him.

With an inhuman cry, Dade shook them off. He

leapt away. Then he was at the front door and was gone.

"Get him!" roared the chief. "That's all we need . . ."

A gust of flame shot up into the night as a section of the garage roof fell in. The molten outline of a car could be seen beneath it.

Someone in the crowd began to cheer.

"Pigs," shouted Jane. "Pigs!"

"Cook the rich," someone else shouted, and she heard whistles and catcalls.

Tears filled her eyes. How could people be so evil?

Then through the tears, she saw the front door open.

Around her, the jeers turned to cheers.

It was Dade. He had his arms around Cyndi. She was struggling with him, trying to pull free, trying to go back into the house.

"Let me go!" she cried. "Let me go!"

Another section of roof fell in.

Jane could feel the heat of the fire from all the way back where she stood.

Cyndi twisted as if she could feel the flames. "Dorian," she screamed. "Dorian!"

"Jane." In all the noise, she heard the soft voice.

"Char," she said gratefully, moving to let Char in beside her. "What are you doing here?"

Char put her hand on Jane's arm. "I was on my way home from the BurgerBurger. It's Dorian? He's in there?"

Jane nodded numbly. She saw Foy and Rick over Char's shoulder. Jane took a deep breath and said, "Georgina, too."

Rick said. "You're kidding. Georgina was in there, too?"

Shaking her head, Jane tried to explain. "No. But she's dead. They found her out on the Point tonight."

Char's face looked frozen, her eyes enormous. "Georgie? Like . . . like Wills?"

"Yes. At least, that's what it looked like. . . ."

Suddenly, the noise seemed to recede. It was just the four of them, staring at one another — Rick's face twitching, every emotion showing; Foy's unnaturally blank; Char's pale, paler; Jane's struggling for composure.

Then a fire fighter was escorting Dade and Cyndi toward them. Cyndi was crying.

No one had ever seen Cyndi cry before.

The fire fighter looked grim. "Stay here," he said. "I'll send a paramedic over."

"Dorian," wept Cyndi brokenly.

"Cyndi?" said Char.

"I killed him. I killed my own brother. The first time, I meant to, but I didn't. This time, I didn't mean it. *I didn't mean it.*"

In the cozy den in Jane's house, the fire burned softly, tamely in the grate. Cyndi held a mug of hot milk in her hands. The paramedic had given her something to calm her. She'd stopped crying.

Stopped talking. Now she just stared down at nothing.

They were waiting for her parents to be located and told the news.

"It's not your fault," said Jane again.

A long silence fell. Then Cyndi, not looking up, said tonelessly, "You don't know the whole story." Her fingers whitened on the mug. She raised it to her lips like a blind woman, held it there, her head bent.

Then she started to talk.

"Dorian and I hated each other," she said. "We used to do awful things to each other. It got so our parents had to hire different nannies, just to keep us separated.

"But we'd find ways to get together. And then we'd start on each other. Only we'd never admit what we were up to. It was always a game.

"Until one day, when Dorian and I were playing hide-and-seek. I was five. I hid in a cedar chest in the attic. Dorian found me. Only instead of letting me out, he locked the trunk.

"I don't know how long I was there. Hours. It was daylight when we started playing. It was dark when they found me.

"I thought I was going to die there.

"After that, I knew nothing would ever scare me again. And nothing was going to stop me from getting even with my brother."

"Cyndi," said Jane softly.

"Let me finish," said Cyndi harshly. "I waited.

Told Dorian I wanted to play hide-and-seek again. Pretended I really believed that the trunk had locked by accident.

"He hid in a closet. I think he thought he would jump out and really scare me.

"Only he didn't hear me. Not until I locked the door on him. Then I found some matches. I set fire to a wastebasket in the room.

"He smelled the smoke. He was terrified. He begged me to let him out. Just like I'd begged him. I wonder if he stayed and listened to me beg the way I stayed and listened to him. . . .

"We have a very good security system in our house. Always have. The fire department's connected directly to it. So they got there in time. I told them where he was. I was crying.

"I got into a lot of trouble for playing with matches.

"No one ever asked why Dorian was locked in the closet. But after that, we lived in separate wings of the house. Until we were older. Until we had 'outgrown' it.

"I was always bad after that," she said. "A bad girl."

A thin, ghastly smile crossed her face. "And Dorian was always very, very good."

"It's okay, Cyndi," said Dade.

Cyndi looked at him. "No. Because Dorian was in the garage tonight."

"Dorian?" repeated Jane.

"How do you know?" asked Dade.

"It's where he went when he left me. He was there with his car . . . his car . . ."

She took a deep shuddering breath.

"I think he'd been with Georgie. I think now, whatever was after Georgie, was after him.

"I think something is out there. And it's going to get us all."

Chapter 14

"That's crazy," said Rick.

Foy was shaking his head slowly.

Jane, meeting Charity's eyes, felt a tremor of fear go through her.

Char didn't think it was crazy.

Char believed Cyndi.

Dade looked past them all with a curious smile on his face.

Then a voice said, "She's right, more or less."

Jones walked into the room. For a moment, they were all silent. He didn't look any different. But something had changed. Something about him . . .

"How did you get in?" said Jane.

"The old-fashioned way," said Jones. He jerked his head toward the door. "Your guy let me in."

In spite of himself, Foy smiled, suddenly imagining how Hodges would react to being called "your guy."

Cyndi was regarding Jones with angry suspicion.

"You know what?" she said. "*Nothing* had ever happened until you got here. What have you got to say about that?"

Jones shrugged.

"No one was dead before you came along," Cyndi persisted, her voice low and threatening.

Jones shrugged again. "So? If I confess, will it make you feel better?"

Cyndi's head snapped up. "You're despicable."

Jones ignored her. His eyes met Char's. Looking at her, he said, "Something is out there. I'm not even sure what it is. But it is after us. Collectively. And individually."

Char took a shallow, sharp breath. Why was Jones looking at her?

"Great," said Rick. "It's big. It's bad. It's mad. And it's out there, looking for . . . us."

Char made an impatient gesture with her hand to silence Rick. "How do you know? Are you some kind of, some kind of supernatural bounty hunter?"

"How do we know it isn't some kind of trick," Foy drawled. "Maybe he's just some kind of a bounty hunter. Period."

"Three of us are dead," Jane pointed out.

"Us?" croaked Rick.

"This is stupid," said Cyndi. She was clenching and unclenching her hands. Whatever the doctor had given her wasn't working. "You're all stupid. Go away."

Jane put her hand on Cyndi's arm. Cyndi shuddered at the contact, and huddled down again.

"Someone killed Wills on Halloween night. Three days later, in the same place, Georgie is dead. And Dorian — "

"Is burned alive." Dade finished Jones's sentence.

"What happened to Dorian could have been an accident. It's not the same as what happened to Wills and to Georgie," said Foy.

Cyndi started to rock slowly in her chair. Her voice, when she spoke, was almost a singsong. "It wasn't an accident. I saw it."

"You saw it *happen?*" Jones's voice sharpened.

"I saw it on the door. Dorian's car. He came back tonight, and I was waiting when he pulled into the garage. Scared. Scared. Scared."

"Cyndi," said Jane softly.

"So scared. I thought it was a joke. I thought Rick did it."

"Hey!" said Rick. "I haven't done anything!"

Jane gave Cyndi a quick shake. "Cyndi! What are you talking about?"

For a moment, Cyndi didn't move. Then she seemed suddenly transformed. Her lips curled back in a sneer. "What am I talking about? Tonight, when Dorian got home, I saw his car in the garage. Something had made gouges all down the side of the car. And on the handle of the driver's door, there was a hook."

Everyone stared at Cyndi, at the gleeful, awful smile on her face. "A hook," she said. "A hook. Just like that stupid story of Rick's."

And, then, just as suddenly, Cyndi retreated back into herself, seemed to shrink and grow smaller, pulling her legs up and wrapping her arms around them, pressing her forehead to her knees. "Go away," she moaned.

"*I* didn't do it," said Rick.

"That book," said Char. "The one *you* gave me, Jones." She didn't wait for him to confirm or deny her statement. "It talks about something that happened in Point Harbor when it was a whaling port. Something that caused ships to sink, that haunted — is that the right word, Jones — that haunted Cemetery Point. Not just out there, but the whole town."

Rick said, "What book?"

"Shh," ordered Dade.

Jones nodded.

"And it got stopped. Somehow."

She waited. Jones said, slowly, almost as if he were in pain, "I don't know how."

This time, he didn't quite meet Char's eyes. She said, softly, "Don't you?"

Foy said slowly, "Something inhuman. That got . . . dead and buried, would you say? Out there, in the graveyard? For a long, long time?"

"Dead and buried," agreed Jones.

"Until something woke it up," said Foy.

Although she was sitting with her back close to the fire, Char felt the chill on her neck.

"We woke it up, didn't we, Jones? That night.

Halloween night," said Char. "We went to a party in a graveyard and we woke the dead."

The fire had started to die out. Cyndi's parents had come and gone. Cyndi was staying with Jane that night.

Horror makes strange bedfellows, thought Char wryly.

The cops had been there, too. Dorian had been in the garage. They'd found his body. They were looking at a possible link between Georgie's death and Dorian's, the cops said. Murder–suicide, they said.

No one bothered to disagree.

They sat still by the dying fire, listening as Char finished reading aloud from the book.

"So it *has* been around for a long, long time," said Jane. "They *must* have buried whatever it was — is — out there on Cemetery Point, maybe did something to make it stay put, like how they bury vampires with a stake through the heart. . . ."

"And closed up the joint," said Dade.

"Until we came along," said Jane.

Cyndi, who had resumed her motionless pose in her chair, with her forehead resting on her drawn-up knees, sing-songed, "It's my party and I'll cry if I want to, die if I want to . . ."

"We can't trust *anyone*," said Jones. "Not the cops. Not our parents. Not our friends."

"Look around," said Dade genially. "We're all friends here."

Rick broke in. "We should tell the cops."

"Right," said Foy. "Like we're going to tell the cops: 'Oh, Officer, there's a serial killer out there. It likes knives and fire. And it isn't human and has superhuman powers.' "

"Supernatural powers," whispered Jane.

"We can't trust anyone," insisted Jones. "Think about what we just heard. Think! Whatever it is, it has supernatural powers."

"It can change shapes," said Char abruptly. "That's what that meant: 'Power to mimic form and life and shadow.' "

"No way," said Rick. "Get real."

Foy interceded. "We have to do a little reality check here. Something — or someone — is stalking us. Maybe it's some flipped-wig weirdo we unwrapped when we did the graveyard party. *Maybe.* But an old book and a bunch of words are *not* what's real in all this."

"I hope it turns into a babe, a built blonde babe, before it goes after me," said Rick.

"God, Rick, you're disgusting." Cyndi roused herself to give Rick a withering look.

"Why don't you believe me?" asked Char.

"I don't know what to believe," whispered Jane.

"So what're we supposed to do while this alleged supernatural serial chopper is in town?" snarled Cyndi. "Only travel in threes for the rest of our lives?"

"I don't even think threes would do it," answered Jones.

No one had a comeback for that.

The silence fell again. Char listened to the sound of the wind outside. Cold, cold wind. Cold as death.

Cold as the thing that stalked them. Char believed in it now. Whatever it was, it had no human feelings. If it had ever been alive, it was no more. It would not understand mercy, or pity. Or love.

It wouldn't matter to it that Wills, crazy, mean Wills, might have been something different someday. Something better. Something good.

It wouldn't care about Georgie's energy and dreams, and why she'd had them, and what had made them so much too big for her. Dreams that Georgie would never make real-life sized, now.

It wouldn't care that Dorian was dead, horribly, in the way he feared the most. Gone forever.

It wasn't human. Or even alive.

But it was real. A hunger. An evil inhuman force. So much bigger and stronger than any of them could ever be.

It didn't even matter if they hated it, feared it. It didn't do any good. It didn't matter at all.

Rick, for once not joking, said, "We're all going to die. Is that what you're saying Jones?"

"God," said Foy softly.

"No!" shrieked Cyndi. "I'm not. You can't make me. I'm going to fight! I'll stop it. I'll . . ."

She jumped up. Dade grabbed her shoulders. "Cyndi!"

"No!" she screamed and, with almost superhuman strength, tore loose from Dade and ran out of the room.

"Stop her," commanded Jones. "We have to stop her!"

Chapter 15

Cyndi ran wildly down the long driveway toward the shadow of the hedges. The front door swung wide behind her.

It was almost uncanny, how fast she could run.

They ran after her, into the night.

But Cyndi was faster. Char heard a car door open. Then a car shrieked out of the shadows, bearing down on them, accelerating.

Char had one glimpse of Cyndi's white, mad face, and then she threw herself out of the way.

The car swept by without even stopping.

Rolling to her feet, she caught Jones's arm. "Your car!" she cried. "Cyndi took your car."

"Let's go," said Dade, wheeling without breaking stride. "In mine."

It was like the Keystone Cops, thought Char dazedly. The way they piled into Dade's car. How many potential murder victims can you get in a heavy metal Chevy?

The needle on the car shot upward from zero to

seventy in no time. Dade cornered on two wheels, sat the car back down, and hammered it into the dark.

"We'll catch her," he said. "This car can do it."

Then he glanced sideways quickly at Jones. "But, then, maybe yours can, too."

Jones didn't say anything. He just jerked his head forward in a nod, once.

The taillights of the disappearing car were a bloody smear in the darkness.

Why didn't the cops appear out of nowhere, like they usually did? wondered Char. Why weren't they lurking, waiting to yank some kid's chain?

As if he could read her thoughts, Dade said, "I hate the cops."

"They're probably all out at the Point," said Foy.

"It's been hours," Char said. "Maybe they've sealed it off and all gone home."

"Well, they're not around here," said Rick.

It was true. No cops. Nobody at all. No one was on the road except them. And Cyndi.

"It's like the lights are on, but no one is home — anywhere," muttered Char. Beside her, she felt Jane's hand on her arm.

The distance between the cars stopped widening. But it didn't grow any narrower.

They were traveling at the speed of light.

No. At the speed of darkness.

Then Jane gave a little gasp. "The Back Bay. She's going down the Back Bay Road."

Char said, "To the Point."

"Let's hope the cops *are* still there," said Dade grimly.

Jones said, so softly that only Char heard, "They won't be."

"We're not going back out there?" croaked Rick incredulously.

"We don't have a choice," Foy shot back.

"*I* have a choice," snapped Rick. "I'm not going out there."

Without slowing down, Dade said, "You wanna get out, be my guest. The door's right there."

For a moment, Char thought Rick might actually do it. Then he said sullenly, "Dade, you're jack crazy, you know that? Like I'm gonna hit the black-top doing ninety."

"Then you're in for the haul," said Dade.

He pushed the accelerator.

The wheels didn't even touch the ground on that curve, thought Char dispassionately. Beside her, Jane's hand tightened on her arm, then relaxed.

Jane the calm, thought Char. Or maybe she's just gone fatal. Then she caught a glimpse of Jane's pale, set face. And saw the direction of her gaze.

Jane wasn't staring out at the night, screaming by the window. She wasn't staring at the red lights ahead that had just turned down the road to Cemetery Point.

She was staring at Dade.

True love, thought Char. Spare me.

"She's got to stop for the gate, man," said Rick.

"Don't count on it," said Dade.

"Look out!" screamed Rick.

Dade didn't even slow down.

"Did you hit it?" asked Rick.

"I don't know," said Dade tersely.

Jane said firmly, "He didn't hit it, whatever it was."

Rick gave a half-hysterical laugh. "Yeah. Good. That's what's important here."

"Maybe it wasn't anything at all," said Jones softly.

And Char felt the hair on her neck rise again. *Shape-changer*, she thought.

Able to skitter out on a road and make a car go over a cliff?

"Jones," she said softly.

"Yes," he said. And she knew he was answering her unspoken question.

Even if she didn't know how he knew.

They'd slowed down a little now. The road was just as bumpy as it had been on Halloween night. The trees leaned in just as closely. Only the moon wasn't full.

Char was afraid. But this time, it wasn't a pleasurable fear. It wasn't the comfortable creepy-crawlies of Halloween, the little thrill at the idea that a witch or a ghost might be lurking just out of sight, just out of belief, dressed up in childhood story-clothes, something familiar and simple. Your basic Halloween apparition.

This was real.

This was death.

"Look out!" Foy, this time, leaning forward to peer over Dade's shoulder.

Dade slowed fractionally.

The metal gate was burst apart, twisted all out of recognition.

"Your car's dead, fella," said Dade to Jones.

But it wasn't. Somewhere just ahead, the red of the taillights kept flickering in and out as Jones's car disappeared down the trail.

"It should be dead," said Char. "What's that car made of, Jones?"

"Kryptonite," said Jones.

"I wish," said Dade. He fought the wheel, scraping trees, bucking the car over ruts and through the sand.

And then they were in the clearing.

Dade slammed on the brakes. The Chevy slewed sideways. Kicked back as he wrestled with the wheel.

Then it shuddered to a stop.

Inches away from Jones's car.

The front of Jones's car was twisted all out of recognition, the glass broken, one light on, the other shattered and dead. The driver's door was open.

Cyndi was nowhere in sight.

"We're heeere," Rick said feebly.

No one even bothered to tell him what to do with it.

Char took a long, shaky breath. "What are we going to do?"

"Let's go," said Foy.

Jane glanced at Foy in surprise. Foy wasn't usually a leader. Not a follower. But not a leader, either.

Char said, "No, wait." Staring out at the dark, she asked, "Have you thought of this? Maybe that's not Cyndi up there, leading us all out here. Maybe it's not Cyndi at all."

Chapter 16

"Not," said Rick.

"We were with her all night," said Jane.

"We weren't with her when her brother died," said Char softly.

A shaken, disbelieving silence answered her.

Then Jones said calmly, "Whatever. We need to stay together. That's critical."

Jane said, "We could hold hands. Form a chain."

"Or, how 'bout the buddy system." Rick tried for sarcasm.

"Holding hands is not a bad idea," said Jones. He got out of the car and held out his hand to Char.

"Let's do it." Taking a flashlight out from under the seat, Dade jumped out, pulling Jane with him with his free hand.

Foy took Jane's hand.

"I want you to know, Foy, that this doesn't mean we're going steady," said Rick. Unexpectedly, Dade gave a crack of laughter.

This is how it started, Char thought. We were

all holding hands in a circle around the fire. Taking Rick's other hand, she suddenly remembered something. "Lara," she said. "What about Lara?"

"She's still at home," said Jane.

"At least *she's* safe," put in Rick.

With Dade leading and Jones bringing up the rear, they walked across the clearing. One by one they stepped out of the light and into the darkness, clumsy, stumbling, following the pale beam of the flashlight into the woods.

"Anybody know the words to 'Chain of Fools,' " quipped Rick.

Foy groaned, and Jane gave a nervous giggle.

Rick began to sing. Foy groaned again and said, "Don't sing."

"Think of it as a secret weapon," said Rick. He kept on singing.

"It's ruining the element of surprise," suggested Foy.

"I dunno," said Dade. "I'm surprised. At how bad he sings."

"What are you thinking about?" Jones asked softly. He was walking just at Char's shoulder. She felt his breath on her ear.

Turning her head slightly toward him, she whispered back, "Sunrise. I was thinking how in the vampire movies, the sun always comes up."

"Usually following a period of extreme darkness," said Jones.

"In the movies, it's when the vampire dies."

Rick began the chorus of "I Heard It Through the Grapevine."

Typical Rick, Char thought. But the sound did push back the dark. A little. She could still feel the silence, the waiting stillness just beyond.

"What are you thinking?" she asked Jones quickly, willing the silence away.

"You can't see anything if you look at it head-on in the dark. It works better if you look a little to one side."

"We have a tree in our backyard," said Char randomly. "I used to like to sit in it at night and look into our house. You could see everyone, like in a play. I never used to believe they couldn't see me. I thought they were just pretending."

"The light makes the dark pretty intense," said Jones. "It's all in how you look at it, I guess."

"Blinded by the light," said Char. "Not very useful."

"Unless it helps to see what you're afraid of."

"Unless it scares you to death. . . ."

"If you let something scare you to death, then the worst has happened," said Jones.

"This is comforting," said Char. "Should my life be in danger, remind me."

"I will." Jones squeezed her hand.

The silence fell again.

Ahead, Dade said, "We're here." The beam of the flashlight bored through the trees.

They'd reached the graveyard.

Rick stopped singing abruptly. Char felt how cold Rick's hand was in hers. And how warm Jones's was.

Dade took his breath in sharply.

"Uh-oh," said Rick. For once, he didn't sound like he was trying to be funny.

Something was waiting for them up ahead.

Dade kept walking. Behind him, the human chain stretched out to breaking point.

Dade raised the flashlight.

"I love parties," said Cyndi. "It's time for a party. Don't you love parties?"

"It's time for this one to be over," said Dade.

Cyndi smiled. "I love parties," she repeated.

Keeping his flashlight on Cyndi, Dade stopped. "Hey, Cyndi? This has been done. It's old. Let's go somewhere else."

"Okay," said Cyndi, still smiling. "Let's." She leaned forward — then snatched the flashlight and threw it up in the air. As it fell, she turned and darted into the dark.

Dade dropped Jane's hand. "Cyndi," he shouted and plunged after her.

Jane hesitated only a moment. Then she wrenched her hand out of Foy's and started after Dade.

Behind Char, Jones raised his voice desperately. "Stay together! We have to stay together!"

But it was too late.

"This is bad," said Rick harshly. "This is crazy. We've got to get out of here. We can't . . ."

"Settle down, Rick," said Foy.

In answer, Rick pulled his hand free of Char's and yanked so hard on Foy's hand that Foy almost fell. But he regained his balance and the two of them began to circle in a grotesque dance, pulling on each other.

"Calm down," Foy said.

"Let go, man, let go!"

"C'mon," pleaded Foy. "If we're not going steady, I don't want to dance. . . ."

"Let go!" shrieked Rick.

Without warning, Foy raised his arm. He punched Rick in the jaw. Rick's head snapped back. He staggered. Then he fell like a stone.

Letting go of Rick's hand, Foy bent over him. "Out cold," he announced.

"I don't believe you did that," said Char.

"Now he can't run away," said Foy, rubbing his knuckles.

"And he can't stay with us, now, either," said Jones. "Unless we carry him."

"Why?" asked Foy impatiently.

"We can't leave him here. Not by himself."

"Listen," said Foy. "What did you want me to do? Let him tear out of here like everyone else?"

Char stopped listening. She was frowning. It wasn't the silence that was bothering her. What was it?

And then she realized what it was. The darkness. It was gone. The moon was out, flickering in and out among the clouds that blew above.

But there was no wind.

In the unnatural moon-strobe, she watched Foy and Jones. Jones had let go of her hand. He and Foy were propping Rick up against the wall, trying to get him to wake up.

Just like on television, she thought dreamily. Just like when I used to sit in that tree . . .

A vast lethargy washed over her. She wanted to sit down next to Rick. To go to sleep.

She yawned hugely.

"I'm getting the flashlight," she said.

She giggled. How mortifying, she thought. I never giggle.

Rick groaned.

Something moved in the corner of her eye.

No. No, it was the flashlight.

"Char," said Jones.

"I'll be right there," she said. "I'm just going to get that flashlight. . . ."

"Wait."

"No no no . . . now don't worry. I'll be right over. . . ." Like a sleepwalker, she turned in the direction of the flashlight.

Rick let out a yell and came to, swinging and punching.

Leaving them to scuffle, she strolled into the dark.

There. There it was.

She bent to pick it up. And saw the writing on the tombstone.

Chapter 17

"No," she whispered.

"Char!" Jones's voice.

She ignored him. Picking up the flashlight, she turned it on the gravemarker.

CHARITY WEBSTER
1888–

At least I'm not dead yet, she thought, and felt the bubble of hysterical laughter rise in her throat.

"Char." Jones was closer now.

Jones.

Jones knew . . .

Knew what?

Then he was beside her. She'd begun to shake. The light shimmied in her hand. But she held on to it, even when Jones tried to pry her fingers loose.

"No," she said.

Then she turned the light on him.

The light made his face look bleached and old.

He held up his hand to shield his eyes, wincing. "You're blinding me," he said.

"Not me," she said. "The light."

"Char," he said.

"No. No, you tell me. Tell me *now*. What is going on here?"

"If I knew . . ."

"You knew about that book. *You're* the one who gave it to me. Where did you get it?"

"I can't explain now."

"When I'm dead is *too* late. Way too late."

"You're hysterical."

"Why do guys always say that?" She laughed. Good. That stupid giggle was gone.

She was trembling. She was afraid. No. No, she felt powerful. Strong.

Immortal.

She felt the power rising up through her body. More scalding than any passion. More dangerous than love . . .

A terrible shudder rocked the earth.

She stumbled. Watched indifferently as the flashlight fell from her hand and went out.

Again the earth moved. There was a roaring sound this time. A rending sound.

Was it a loud sound? She couldn't tell. Sensations poured over her, a thousand impressions, each distinct and clear. Her human senses were gone. This was something more. Something much, much more.

In the darkness, she saw Jones's mouth move.

But she couldn't hear him.

She smelled it first. A familiar smell, somehow. Rank and ashy.

She heard it next. The light tread of something heavy. Something heavy and extremely quick. Something hunting.

Then she felt it.

It was standing behind her.

She closed her eyes, and the terrible power coursing through her brought with it a vision.

A woman was standing at the edge of the sea. The water boiled around her. The smoke of torches lingered in the air. But the others were gone. They'd run away.

They'd left her there.

Not me, thought Char. The woman is *not* me.

She opened her eyes. She was still in the cemetery. And it was still behind her.

But a grave's length away, another figure waited, pale and shimmering by the graveyard wall.

It was the woman. The woman from her vision. The woman from her dreams.

"Who are you?" Char whispered. "What do you want?"

The woman raised her arms.

Char took a step forward.

It was as if she'd been punched in the chest. Gasping, she stopped. Roaring filled her ears. But beneath the roar, a fierce and ancient voice whispered, "Turn. Turn. Turn."

Char turned.

A river of fire poured toward her.

Run, something inside her screamed.

She crouched for flight. "Stay," commanded the woman's voice. And with the voice came that sense of scalding, dangerous power.

Char obeyed the voice.

The woman owned her now. Char had been chosen. And she had made her choice.

The molten river parted and sank into the earth around her with a hiss.

Trembling with mortal fear and immortal rage, Char faced the thing that now waited in the shadows before her.

A black cloud covered the moon. The darkness was complete.

The shadows began to move, writhing, with an eerie shrill sound and the sucking of the air. Unmoving, she watched.

Without breathing. Without thinking.

A figure walked out of the contorted dark.

"What do you want?" it mocked. If the woman's voice was a fierce and ancient whisper, this voice was shudderingly smooth, warmly seductive.

"Lara?" Char asked.

"That's right," Lara said. "It's me."

"No," said Char. "You're not Lara. Lara's safe."

"No one's safe from *me*." The figure pirouetted, then dipped in a curtsy. "I took Wills. And then I took Lara. Do you believe me?"

Jones said, "No, you didn't . . ."

"Silence!" Lara lashed the air with her arm, and Char heard Jones gasp and stumble and then thud against the gravestone. Her gravestone.

"Jones?" she said. For a fraction of a second, she became herself. She turned her head.

"No!" said the woman's voice, and Char looked back at the thing that had taken Lara's shape.

"Ah!" Lara stopped. But she was much closer now. The bloody princess dress she wore moved of its own accord, tugged by invisible eddies, unspeakable tides.

"Is this a game?" asked Char. "Like blindman's bluff?"

"No game," purred Lara.

Char stepped back.

"Ah," said the woman's voice, much closer now.

Lara smiled. She took two steps forward. "I've been waiting for you," she said.

"You're not Lara!"

"But I could be. . . ." It tilted its head coquettishly. "If you were Lara and you met me, would that scare you?"

"NO!"

"Oh, dear," said Lara mockingly. She smiled, and the smile began to split her face.

Char took another step back and another.

And felt something brush her shoulder.

"It's me," said the woman's voice. Char waited for her to continue, to say, "Don't be afraid."

But the woman didn't.

Instead, her hand closed on Char's shoulder. Where it touched her was cold. But the power in her surged up to meet it, making her back arch as if she were caught in an electric current. "Now," said the woman. But the voice was no longer a whisper in Char's ear. It was in her, in her mouth. How can I feel so helpless? thought Char. How . . .

Char felt her lips move. She heard her voice say, "It's me."

Her voice. The woman's words.

The thing wearing Lara's face smiled. And now another face began to pulse into shape beneath the rims of flesh.

"Yess . . ." said the lips, and the thing took two steps forward.

The rotting, scorching smell filled Char's lungs.

She couldn't breathe.

She was going to die.

"No," she gasped.

She rocked back. She would run. Save herself.

But she couldn't

I won't give up, thought Char. I won't, I . . .

She lunged forward and seized the Ripper in her arms.

And it was Wills she held, Wills dead, Wills dying.

"Help me," he pleaded. "Help meee. . . ."

"I can't," she said. He was so strong. But she held on. She didn't look away.

The figure threw back its demon head and howled. There was a sound of skin splitting like ripe fruit. Beneath the shining blood now, the face of Georgina looked back at Char.

"You hated me," she hissed. "You killed me."

"I was wrong," Char gasped. "But I didn't kill you."

It twisted wildly in her arms. The shedding layer of skin felt like an old blouse over her arms. The thing raised its head and locked eyes with her.

"You could save us now," said Dorian's voice. "Let me go."

"No," she said.

"Let me GO!"

"NO!" she said between gritted teeth.

Dorian's face tore open before her eyes.

And she saw herself.

"Mirror, mirror, on the wall," it said. Her face. Her voice.

Her smile.

"What you see is what you get," it said. And Char felt her own body. Felt it turn to slime and gore beneath her hands. Saw her own lips draw back and spit: blood and gobbets of flesh.

She held on.

The pain began. The awful grief. For the killing. For the rage. For the eternity of loneliness.

Her own pain. Her own grief.

And the woman's

She tightened her hold.

Something sharp as death pierced her above the heart.

Her heart contracted with sorrow and pain.

And awful joy.

Then the thing gave one last shape-rending twist in her mortal arms and the earth tore open beneath her feet and she was falling and as she fell she knew she was falling into her own grave where it had waited for so long.

No. Not her grave.

I am not you, Char told the woman who possessed her. And at that moment, with a pain more awful than any imagining, Char felt the power that had taken her begin to subside. The phantom woman, her other self, had been received into the earth. Char was alone inside herself now. She was free.

Behind her, as Char fell into the grave, the sun began to rise. And the thing in her arms began to howl.

Rest in peace, thought Char, and the howl began to dwindle and die as the earth closed over them all.

And she held on.

Chapter 18

She was in a grave. Buried alive. It had her by the ankle. Pulling her deeper as the earth shuddered and sealed itself together over her face.

She kicked. Tried to breathe and tasted dirt and whatever graves were made of. Gagged.

And then she was blinded by the light.

It was morning.

She sat up. She was safe. It was over. She was in her own bedroom. In a little while, it would be time to get up. She had the whole day ahead of her.

She had the rest of her life.

Jones pulled his car into the overlook. Char got out and walked to the rail and looked out at the Point. It was just a curve of land in the water now. Not so big a curve as it used to be. The morning after she'd met the Ripper, a chunk of the Point had torn away and fallen into the ocean. The grave-yard was gone.

But that had been a while ago. Autumn was turning into winter now. The nightmares were going away. The killings had ended.

"Hey," said Jones.

Char turned to him and smiled. "Hey."

"You did good," said Jones.

"I didn't have a choice, did I?"

"I'm sorry," he said.

"It's okay." She shrugged. "You made up for it when you grabbed my ankle and hauled me up out of that grave."

"You saved us all. It was the least I could do."

She suddenly grinned. "Just admit it, Jones. You couldn't keep your hands off me."

High above, an arrowhead of geese started their descent for a landing. Their honking sounded clear and strong on the cold air.

Char said thoughtfully, "It was her. She needed me to help her be buried *inside* the graveyard. That was her grave on the outside. She'd stopped it somehow, and they thought she'd made an unholy pact with it. That's why they kept her out.

"And whoever kept that journal had a grave made for her inside, just in case.

"She had my name. . . ."

"Whoever she was," said Jones, "she took the Ripper with her."

"We raised that thing, didn't we, that night at Cyndi's party?" She didn't wait for Jones to answer, but went on. "If we hadn't done that, Wills, Georgie, Dorian — they might all still be alive."

"But if we hadn't done it, something else might

have wakened it up. And because you did, that first Charity had a chance to rest in peace at last."

"I hope she is," said Charity. She paused. "But is the Ripper dead?"

"The graveyard is gone," said Jones. "I don't know. Maybe it just changed shape again."

"I thought it had gotten Lara, too," Char said. "That's what the Ripper told me. You tried to warn me that it was a trick."

"Just another gruesome trick . . . to confuse you. To distract you," said Jones. "I don't think Lara saw the Ripper. I think she just saw enough to scare her out of her wits." He paused.

"But it would have gotten Lara, too. It would have gotten all of us. Each killing made it stronger."

Char asked, for about the hundredth time, "How did you know what would happen?"

And for about the hundredth time, Jones answered, "I didn't."

"What about the book?"

"I found it in my travels," Jones said. "I believe everything I read."

"But why me? Why my name? When I saw it on that tombstone . . ."

Jones said, "You can't believe everything you read." He pulled her closer to him.

She didn't have time to ask him the other question: Who are you?

The last time she'd asked, he hadn't answered, as usual. Instead, he'd said, "Have you ever thought about who you are? I mean, if you were named another name, would you still be you? Take away your name, and what you do, and where you live, and who your parents are. Then tell me who you really are."

Once, the idea would have bothered her. Now, it made a sort of sense. So she left the question for the others.

Like the questions about where he came from, and where he was going. Those were answers nobody had. Not for their own life. Not for anyone else's.

"Hey! Hey!" Dade's voice. He'd pulled up to the edge of the overlook and was leaning out the window. Jane was with him. She leaned across Dade and said, "Char. Come on. We're going over to Lara's."

"Who's we?" asked Jones.

"You know — Foy, Rick, Cyndi." Jane made an airy motion with her hand. "Like that."

"The usual party animals," said Dade, grinning.

"Later," said Char.

"Serious," said Dade. He kicked his car into gear and took off.

"Sorry," said Char. "I should've asked. Did you want to go?"

"Later," said Jones. He leaned closer. "But for now, I like this party here just fine."

FREEZE TAG

Prologue

"Suppose," said Lannie dreamily, "that you really could freeze somebody."

The setting sun seemed to shine right through Lannie, as if she were made of colored glass and hung in a window.

Lannie's eyes, as pale as though they had been bleached in the wash, focused on Meghan.

Meghan gulped and looked away, queerly out of breath. If she kept looking into Lannie's eyes, she would come out the other side.

Into what?

What was the other side of Lannie made of?

Meghan shivered, although the evening was still warm. She felt ancient. Not old herself, but as if something in the night had quivered free from an ancient world. Free from ancient rules.

Tonight something would happen.

Meghan stared at her bare arms. A thousand tiny hairs prickled in fear. Even her skin knew.

The sun was going down like a circle of construction paper falling off the bulletin board. No longer the yellow bulb of daytime, it was a sinking orange half circle. Meghan yearned to run toward the sun and catch it before it vanished.

Meghan tried to ignore Lannie. This was not easy. Lannie always stood as close as a sweater, trying to take your share of oxygen.

Lannie stood alone, but Meghan sat on the second step with her best friend, Tuesday, and admired the silhouette of West Trevor as he mowed the lawn.

Meghan adored the Trevor family. They were what families should be. First, the Trevors had had the wisdom to have three children, not just one like her own parents. The Trevors were always a crowd, and Meghan loved a crowd.

Second, the children had wonderful names. Mr. and Mrs. Trevor had not wanted their children to be named Elizabeth or Michael and thus get mixed up with dozens of classmates. Mixing up the Trevor offspring would never happen. There was, thought Meghan, probably no other family on earth with children named West, Tuesday, and Brown.

West Trevor. It sounded like a street, or perhaps a town in Ireland. But West Trevor was the boy on whom, in a few years, all the girls would have crushes. Meghan was slightly ahead of them. She had adored West all her life.

He was mowing around the beginner-bushes. (That's what Mrs. Trevor called them, because they were so young and newly planted they hardly even formed knobs in the grass.) Meghan admired how

West so carefully overlapped each pass, making sure no blade of grass would escape untrimmed.

"Suppose," said Lannie dreamily, "that *I* could freeze somebody."

Meghan could just see Lannie opening a refrigerator, stuffing a classmate in to freeze, and walking off. Just thinking about it chilled Meghan. Even as Lannie talked, Meghan's joints seemed to harden like a pond surface turning to ice.

Meghan hated it when Lannie joined the neighborhood games.

The houses on Dark Fern Lane were new, but the families were old-fashioned. The lawns ran into each other, the kitchen doors were always open, and the children used each other's refrigerators and bathrooms.

Since the houses were so small, and everybody had a little brother or sister who was cranky, or needed a diaper change, or wanted to be carried piggyback, the older children on Dark Fern Lane stayed outside whenever they could.

Even though the Trevors' front steps were exactly like everybody else's front steps, this was where the children gathered. Mrs. Trevor was generous with after-supper Popsicles, and the Trevors had a basketball hoop on the garage where everybody learned to dunk and dribble.

West's little brother Brown hurtled out of the house, taking the four cement steps in a single bound. Brown leapt onto the back of the ride-upon mower, shouting horse commands at his big brother. He had a long leather bootlace in his hand that he swung like a lasso, telling West to jump the fence and head for the prairie.

West simply mowed on, ignoring the presence of a screaming five-year-old attached to his back.

Brown began yodeling instead. He had heard this sound on public television and now planned to be a yodeler when he grew up, instead of a policeman. Tuesday yodeled along in harmony. The Trevor family sounded like a deranged wolf pack.

For Meghan, this was yet another Trevor attraction: how close and affectionate they were. Friends, mowing partners, and fellow yodelers.

Meghan knew exactly what would happen next. Tuesday would realize that she was thirsty from all that yodeling. She would get up off the step and go into the house. Several minutes later, she would bring out a tray of pink lemonade and jelly-jar glasses. Her brothers would spot her, and come running. They'd all slurp pink lemonade and listen to the summery sound of ice cubes knocking against glass.

Tuesday would not carry the tray back. That was West's job, along with carrying back all other dishes the Trevor family dirtied. And West would never complain. He accepted dishes as easily as Meghan accepted new shoes.

Whereas in Meghan's family, everybody hated dishes. It was hard to say who hated them most — her father, her mother, or Meghan. Sometimes Meghan thought the only thing the Moores ever said to each other was, "No, it's *your* turn to do dishes."

West and Brown were framed like an old photograph: sunset and small tree, older brother and younger. They were beautiful.

"You want to spend the night, Meghan?" said Tuesday, measuring her sneaker against Meghan's. Tuesday's was larger. The Trevors were a very sturdy family.

Of course Meghan wanted to spend the night. Everybody always wanted to stay at the Trevors'. Mrs. Trevor would throw the sleeping bags down on the playroom floor and let everybody watch Disney videos all night long. She would put brownies in the oven and, just when you were ready to fall asleep, Mrs. Trevor would waltz in with hot rich chocolate treats scooped over with cold melting vanilla ice cream. Meghan sighed with pleasure.

Through the screen door, Tuesday shouted, "Meghan is staying over!" and her mother said, "That's nice, dear."

Meghan's mother would have said, "Not tonight, dear, I have to get up in the morning." Meghan could never understand what getting up in the morning had to do with going to bed at night.

Meghan smiled, in love with every member of the Trevor family.

"I'm spending the night, too, Tuesday," said Lannie. She always kept you informed of her plans.

"No," said Tuesday quickly. "Mother said I could have only one person over."

Lannie knew this for the lie that it was. Her heavy eyelids lifted like cobra hoods. For a long time she said nothing. It was cold and frightening, the way she could stay silent. No other child knew how to stay silent. They were too young.

But Lannie had never seemed young; and as the rest grew up, Lannie never seemed old either.

The fireflies came out. They sparkled in the air.

We're being mean, thought Meghan. We're treating the second step as if it were a private clubhouse.

Meghan wanted to do the right thing, the kind thing, and have Lannie sleep over, too, but Lannie was too scary. Meghan never wanted to be alone in the dark with Lannie Anveill. Lannie never made any noise when she moved. When you thought you were alone, the hair on the back of your neck would move in a tiny hot wind, and it would be Lannie, who had sneaked up close enough to breathe on your spine.

Lannie could creep behind things that hadn't even grown yet. Dark Fern Lane was a made-up name for a new little development. There was hardly even shade, let alone tall deep ferns gathering in damp thickets, behind which a child could hide. Yet Lannie crossed the street and passed through the yards as if behind screens of heavy undergrowth, unseen and unheard.

"I hate you, Meghan Moore," said Lannie.

She meant it.

Meghan had to look away from those terrible eyes, bleached like bones in a desert.

Once Tuesday and Brown announced that they were going to give Lannie sunglasses for a birthday present. They chickened out. But Lannie didn't have a birthday party after all, so it didn't matter.

Dark Fern Lane was where grown-ups bought their "first house." They said that when they entertained. "Of course, this is just our first house." Meghan kept expecting her parents to build a second house in the backyard, but they didn't mean that; they meant they lived on Dark Fern Lane until they could afford something better.

Lannie's parents had a raised ranch house the same size and shape as the rest, but there the similarities ended. Her parents were rarely home. Mr. and Mrs. Anveill did not set up the barbecue in the driveway on summer evenings. They did not have a beer and watch television football on autumn weekends. They did not make snow angels with Lannie in January. And come spring, they did not plant zinnias and zucchini.

They weren't saving up for a second house either.

They spent their money on cars.

Each of them drove a Jaguar. Mrs. Anveill's was black while Mr. Anveill's was crimson. They drove very very fast. Nobody else on Dark Fern Lane had a Jaguar. It was not a Jaguar kind of road. The rest of the families had used station wagons that drank gas the way their children drank Kool Aid.

Mrs. Anveill talked to her car, which she addressed as "Jaguar," as if it really were a black panther. She talked much more often to Jaguar than to Lannie.

Lannie was a wispy little girl. Even her hair was wispy. She was skinny as a Popsicle stick and pale as a Kleenex. Meghan felt sorry for Mr. and Mrs. Anveill, having Lannie for a daughter, but she also felt sorry for Lannie, having Mr. and Mrs. Anveill for parents.

The sun fell like a wet plate out of a dishwasher's hand. Meghan half expected to hear the crash, and see the pieces.

But instead, the light vanished.

It was dark, but parents didn't call them in yet. Shadows filled the open spaces and the yards became spooky and deep, and faces you knew like your own were blurry and uncertain.

Lannie's searchlight eyes pierced Meghan. "I hate you," she repeated. The hate grew toward Meghan like purple shadows. It had a temperature. Hate was cold. It touched Meghan on her bare arms and prickled up and down the skin.

Why me? thought Meghan. Tuesday's the one not letting her sleep over.

Again the warm glow of being wanted by a Trevor filled Meghan Moore, and then she understood Lannie's pain. Lannie loved the Trevor family as much as Meghan did. Lannie yearned to be part of that enveloping warmth and silly love and punchy fun. Lannie would never hate Tuesday. She wanted Tuesday. Lannie would hate Meghan because Meghan was the one chosen.

Lannie left the steps, silently crossing the soft grass, walking toward the lawnmower on which West and Brown still rode.

Meghan and Tuesday leaned back against each other, little girls again, and rolled their eyes, and breathed, "Whew!" and "Close one!"

Lannie heard. She looked back, her little white

skirt like a flag in the dusk. Meghan hunched down, as if Lannie might throw things. Tuesday's warmth was at Meghan's back, but Lannie's hate was on her horizon.

"Hello, West," said Lannie. This was unusual. Lannie never bothered with conventions of speech like hello or goodbye.

"Hello, Lannie," said West politely.

"Are you mowing the lawn?" said Lannie.

"No," muttered Meghan, sarcastic because she was afraid. "He's painting the Statue of Liberty."

It was impossible for Lannie to have heard all the way across the yard, but she had.

"You'll be sorry, Meghan Moore," said Lannie Anveill.

Meghan was only nine, but she was old enough to know that she had made a terrible mistake.

You'll be sorry, Meghan Moore.

I am sorry, she telegraphed to Lannie Anveill. I'm sorry, okay?

But she didn't say it out loud.

"Get off of there, Brown," said Lannie sharply to the five year old. "It's my turn."

"Actually, I'm not giving turns," said West mildly. "Sorry, Lannie. But this really isn't safe and — "

"Get off, Brown," said Lannie. Her voice was flat like a table.

Brown got off.

"Stop the mower, West," said Lannie, spreading her voice.

Meghan tucked herself behind the morning glory

vines that had climbed to the top of the trellis and were stretching into the sky, looking for more trellis. Their little green tentacles were more alive than a plant should be, as if they were really eye stalks, like some creepy underwater jellyfish.

"Lannie," said West, "it's getting dark and — "

"Take me for a ride," said Lannie in her voice as cold as sleet, "or I will freeze Meghan."

There was a strange silence in the yard: a silence you could hear and feel in spite of the running engine.

They expected West to sigh and shrug and tell Lannie to go on home, but he did not. West obeyed Lannie, and she got on behind him as Brown had.

How could West stand to have Lannie touching him? Her long thin fingers gripping his shoulders like insect legs?

It seemed to Meghan that West and Lannie circled the lawn forever, while hours and seasons passed, and the grass remained uncut and the darkness remained incomplete.

"Stop the mower, West," said Lannie in her flat voice. "I've decided we're going to play Freeze Tag."

Brown fled. He hated Freeze Tag. Too scary. Brown usually decided to watch television instead.

"There aren't enough of us," objected West.

"Stop the mower, West," repeated Lannie. She did not change her voice at all. "I've decided we're going to play Freeze Tag."

West stopped the mower.

"I," said Lannie, "will be It."

"Surprise, surprise," muttered Tuesday, getting up and dusting her shorts.

Meghan loved Freeze Tag.

Whoever was It had to tag everybody. Once you were tagged, you froze into an ice statue, and didn't move a muscle for the remainder of the game. Eventually the whole neighborhood would be frozen in place.

You tried to impress people by freezing in the strangest position. It was best to freeze as if you were still running, with one leg in the air. It was difficult to balance while the rest screamed and ran and tried not to get tagged. But that was the challenge. Another good freeze was half-fallen on the ground, back arched, one arm frozen in a desperate wave. Good freezers didn't even blink.

At some point in the game, Meghan would get to touch West.

Or he would touch her. Meghan yearned to hold West's hand and run with him, but tag was a solo effort.

You ran alone.

You caught alone.

You froze alone.

Meghan tried to cry out, and run away, but no sound came from her throat and no movement entered her legs.

"Brown!" called Lannie.

He came instantly. Lannie's orders pulled like magnets.

"I could call my brother all my life and not get him to come," said Tuesday.

Lannie smiled at the three Trevors and the one Moore.

She still had her baby teeth, but her smile was ancient and knowing. Her eyes stretched out ahead of her fingers, which were pre-frozen, like a grocery item.

"Run!" she whispered gleefully.

They stumbled away.

The sky was purple and black, like a great bruise.

"Run!" Lannie shouted.

Meghan could not seem to run. She could only stagger.

Lannie laughed. "Try to get away from me," she said to Meghan. "You never will," she added.

This is not a game, thought Meghan Moore.

Her feet found themselves and ran, while her mind and heart went along for the ride. She kept looking down at those strange bare white sticks pumping frantically over the blackened grass. Those are my legs, she thought.

A queer terror settled over the flat ordinary yard. The children ran as if their lives depended on it.

Nobody screamed. Silence as complete as death invaded Dark Fern Lane.

They ran behind the house. They doubled back over the paved driveway. They tried to keep the parked lawnmower between them and Lannie.

One by one, Lannie froze them all.

She froze Brown first, and easily, because he was so little.

She froze West second, and just as easily as if West had surrendered. As if West, although oldest and strongest, was also weakest.

Tuesday uttered the only scream of the night, as terror-struck as if her throat were being slit.

Lannie touched her, and the scream ended, and Tuesday froze with her mouth open and her face contorted.

Lannie closed in on Meghan, fingers pointed like rows of little daggers.

And yet Meghan slowed down. In some primitive way, like a mouse in the field beneath the shadow of a hawk's talons, she wanted it to be over.

Want what to be over? Meghan thought. My life?

"I won't be rude again!" cried Meghan. "I'm sorry! You can spend the night at the Trevors' instead of me."

Lannie smiled her smile of ice and snow.

Meghan's knees buckled and she went down in front of Lannie like a sacrifice. How real, how cool, how green the grass was. She wanted to embrace it, and lie safely in the arms of the earth, and never look into Lannie's endless eyes again.

Lannie stood for a moment, savoring Meghan's collapse, and then her fingers stabbed Meghan's arm.

Meghan froze.

The air was fat with waiting.
Lannie surveyed her four statues.

None of them moved.

None of them blinked.

None of them tipped.

Lannie chuckled.

She rocked back and forth in her little pink sneakers, admiring her frozen children.

Then she went home.

The soft warmth of evening enveloped Dark Fern Lane. No child shrieked, no engine whined, no dog barked. The air was sweet with the smell of new-mown grass. All was peaceful.

Mrs. Trevor came to the front door and called through the screen. "Game's up! Come on, everybody. One cookie each and then it's home for bed." Mrs. Trevor was accustomed to obedience and did not stay to be sure the children did as they were told; of course they would do as they were told.

But only the fireflies moved in the yard.

Meghan's eyes were frosty.

Her thoughts moved as slowly as glaciers.

As if through window panes tipping forward, Meghan saw Lannie leaving the yard. Lannie was happy. Meghan knew that she had never before seen Lannie Anveill in a state of happiness. Her smile shone on Meghan, as she lay crooked and stiff on the grass.

Time to go in, thought Meghan. Her expression did not change, her muscles did not sag. Her mouth was still twisted in fear, her eyes still wide with desperation.

Time to go in! thought Meghan.

But she was frozen. Time was something she no longer possessed and going in was something she would no longer do.

Lannie stepped down off the curb, contentedly glancing back at the statues of Brown and Tuesday. She headed for her house.

Mrs. Trevor came back to the screened door. "I am getting annoyed," she said, and she sounded it. "Everybody up and get going, please. I'm tired of all these grass-stained shirts. Now move it."

She returned to the interior of the house. The lights and music of the Trevors' living room seemed as distant from the dark yard as Antarctica.

Lannie stood invisibly in her own front yard.

The dark swirled around her and Lannie, too, went dark, her usual ghostly paleness pierced by night as it had been pierced by sun.

After a few minutes, she walked back across the street. Gently as a falling leaf, Lannie brushed the rigid shoulder of West Trevor.

West went limp, hitting the ground mushily, like a dumped bag of birdseed. Then he scrabbled to his feet. He shook himself, doglike, as if his hair were wet.

Meghan wanted to call out to him, but nothing in her moved. When he walked forward, she tried to see where he was going but her eyes would not follow him. Her neck would not turn.

"Come on, Brown," said West to his brother. "Come on, Tues." His voice was trembling.

Brown and Tuesday stayed statues.

"You guys are freezing so well I can't even see you breathe," their brother said. A laugh stuck in his throat.

"They're *not* breathing," explained Lannie.

West sucked in his breath. He stood so still he seemed to have been tagged again. In a way, he was. Lannie had placed him in that tiny space after understanding, and just before panic.

Through the frost over her eyes, Meghan saw Lannie's smile, how slowly she reached forward, savoring her power, being sure that West understood. Then, making a gift to West, Lannie touched first Tuesday and next Brown.

Tuesday whimpered.

Brown moaned, *"Mommy."*

"I froze them," said Lannie softly, as if she were writing West a love letter.

Meghan could see her own hair, sticking away from her head without regard to gravity, carved from ice.

"I can do it whenever I want," said Lannie. She seemed to be waiting for West to give her a prize.

West, Brown, and Tuesday drew together, staring at Lannie. In a queer tight voice, as if he had borrowed it from somebody, West said, "Undo Meghan."

Lannie smiled and shook her head. "I hate Meghan."

Tuesday began to cry.

West knelt beside Meghan, putting his hand on her shoulder, Meghan did not feel it, but there must have been pressure, because she tipped over stiffly. Now her eyes stared at the stems and mulch circle of one of the beginner-bushes.

I will be looking at this the rest of my life, thought Meghan Moore. This is what it's like in a coffin. You stare for all eternity at the wrinkles in the satin lining.

"Meghan?" whispered West.

But Meghan did not speak.

"Lannie," whispered West, "is she dead?"

"No. I froze her. I hate Meghan. She gets everything." Lannie chuckled. "Look at her now. No blinking. No tears. Just eyeballs."

West tried to pick Meghan up. Her elbows did not bend and her ankles did not straighten. "Lannie! Undo Meghan."

"No. It's Freeze Tag," said Lannie. "So I froze her." She turned a strangely anxious smile upon West. "Did you see me do it, West?"

They were too little to understand boy-girl things, and yet they knew Lannie was showing off for West. He was a boy she wanted, and she was a girl flirting with him, the only way she knew how.

And West, though he was only eleven, knew enough to agree. "Yes, I saw you. I was impressed, Lannie," he said carefully.

Lannie was pleased.

West wet his lips. He said even more carefully, "It would really impress me if you undid her."

"I don't feel like it," said Lannie.

Meghan stayed as inflexible as a chair, as cold as marble.

West took a deep breath. "Please, Lannie?" he said.

West, the strongest and oldest on the street, the big brother who could mow lawns, and baby-sit on Saturday nights, had to beg. Brown and Tuesday were both crying now.

"Well . . ." said Lannie.

"Promise her anything," said Tuesday urgently.

The only one who knew that West must not promise Lannie anything was the one who could not speak.

Meghan, alone and cold and still, thought: No, no, no! Don't promise, West. Better to be frozen than to be Lannie's!

The Trevors stood in a row, the three of them as close as blankets on a bed.

"You must always like me best," said Lannie.

"I will always like you best," repeated West.

Lannie smiled her smile of ice and snow.

She touched Meghan's cheek, and Meghan crumpled onto the grass. A normal child, with normal skin, and normal breathing.

"Don't forget your promise, West," said Lannie.

They had been whispering. When the screen door opened so sharply it smacked against the porch railings, the children were badly startled and flew apart like birds at the sound of gunshot.

"I am very angry," said Mrs. Trevor. "You will come in now. West, why is the lawnmower not in the shed? Do you think Freeze Tag comes before responsibility?"

Lannie melted away.

Meghan got up slowly, sweeping the grass cuttings off her shorts and hair.

"Don't tell," whispered Tuesday.

Nobody did tell.

Nobody would have known what to say.

Nobody quite believed it had happened.

They never did talk about it.

Not once.

Yard games went into history, like afterschool television reruns.

When Meghan grew up, and remembered the yard games, her memory seemed to be in black and white, flecked with age. Did we really play outside every night after supper? she asked herself.

Meghan could remember how it felt, as the hot summer night turned cool in the early dark.

She could remember how it looked, when fireflies sparkled in the dusk, begging to be caught in jars.

She could remember how it sounded, the giggles turning to screams and the screams turning to silence.

But they never talked.

Were their memories frozen? Or were their fears hot and still able to burn? Did they believe it had happened? Or did they think it was some neighborhood hysteria, some fabricated baby dream?

Meghan never knew if Tuesday remembered that brief death.

She never knew if West woke in the night, cold with the memory of Lannie's icy fingers.

She never knew if Brown was slow giving up his

thumb-sucking because he remembered.

The only thing she knew for sure was that the neighborhood never played Freeze Tag again.

But Lannie . . .

Lannie played.

Chapter 1

For his seventeenth birthday, West Trevor was given an old Chevy truck. It was badly rusted, but this made West happy. He was taking courses at the auto body shop and would rebuild the exterior himself. The engine ran rough, but West was happy about that, too; he had had two years of small engine repair and, although this was no small engine, he ached to use what knowledge he had, and bring that Chevy truck back to strength.

Over the years, Dark Fern Lane had achieved its name. In the deep backyards near the shallow, slow-moving creek, bracken, ferns, and bittersweet had grown up in impenetrable tangles. Mrs. Trevor would not let West leave the truck in the driveway because it was so repulsive, and there was not room for it in the garage, so he drove it down the grassy hill and parked it at the bottom among the weeds and vines. From his bedroom window he could admire its blue hulk and dream of weekends when he would drive it to the vocational school shop and work on it for lovely grimy greasy hours on end.

Sometimes West just stood on the back steps of the house and stared down into the yard. "You can't even see your truck from here," Brown would point out. But West didn't care about that. He knew it was there.

West liked almost everybody. He was not discriminating. He thought most people were pretty nice. He preferred the company of boys, and next to rebuilding his Chevy, the best part of his life was managing the football team. He wasn't big enough to play, but he was crazy about the sport. Fall of his senior year in high school, therefore, was spent on playing fields or in locker rooms instead of working on his truck.

Football season would be over after Thanksgiving weekend.

West spent a lot of time thinking about what he would do next on his truck. He read and re-read his extensive collection of *Popular Mechanics*, *Popular Science*, and *Car and Driver*. He thought he was the happiest guy in town. He thought his life was perfect and it never occurred to West to change a molecule of his existence.

But something happened.

West Trevor fell in love.

He fell so deeply, completely, and intensely in love that even the truck hardly mattered, and football seemed remote and pointless.

What amazed West most of all was that he fell in love with a girl he had known — and hardly noticed — all his life.

Meghan Moore.

* * *

Meghan Moore, of course, had been planning this moment for years.

Girls always think ahead, and Meghan thought ahead more than most. Meghan had worshipped West since she was eight. I'm fifteen now, thought Meghan. That means I've spent half my life adoring the boy next door.

It seemed perfectly reasonable.

West had grown broad, rather than tall. Meghan was crazy about his shoulders and had spent all last year imagining herself snuggling up against that broad chest.

This year she was doing it.

Sometimes, cuddled up against West, her long thick hair arrayed across him like a veil, Meghan would feel the joy rise up in her chest and throat, and envelop her heart and mind. She would actually weep for love of West Trevor.

Furthermore, West was dizzy with love for her. West could not go down the school hall without detouring to her corner, and waving. (Making, said his brother Brown gloomily, a complete idiot of himself.) West could not have a meal unless he was sitting beside her. West could not be near a telephone without calling her. West could not sleep at night without slipping through the privet hedge that had grown tall and thick between the houses, running in the Moores' back door, and kissing her good night.

The only thing better than having a terrific boy in love with you was having the entire world witness it, and be envious, and soften at the sight.

Meghan was the happiest girl on earth.

Mr. and Mrs. Moore were not sure they liked this situation.

Meghan's interests had previously been confined to music. She was in the marching band, concert band, and jazz ensemble. She played flute and piccolo. Since she planned to be a band teacher when she grew up, she was now studying other instruments as well: trumpet, and the whole noisy range of percussion.

The entire neighborhood had been forced to follow Meghan's musical progress. There were those who hoped Meghan would attend a very distant college. Mr. and Mrs. Moore were tremendously proud of Meghan and were sure she had abilities far beyond teaching high school band. They expected her to be first flutist with the Boston Symphony Orchestra, and cut records, and be on television.

They were not thrilled that West Trevor was cutting into Meghan's practice time. With much difficulty (they had to look out the window or down at the table instead of at their daughter) they gave stern talks on sex, babies, AIDS, and life in general.

Meghan nodded reassuringly, said the things she knew they wanted to hear, and went ahead with her own plans.

Two houses away, the Trevors had other things to worry about than West's love life. Tuesday and Brown, so delightful and compatible as small children, had become extremely difficult teenagers. Mr. and Mrs. Trevor were worrying pretty much full-time about Tuesday and Brown. They could not imagine where they had gone wrong. Tuesday and Brown's being horrible was very gratifying to the rest of Dark Fern Lane, after having had the perfect Trevor family held up in front of them all those elementary school years.

West, at seventeen, with his driver's license and his good grades and his busy life, was their success story.

Still, his mother was not sure she liked the intensity of this relationship with little Meghan Moore. "He's only seventeen," West's mother would say nervously, as if she thought West and Meghan were going to get married when she wasn't looking.

It wasn't marriage that worried West's father. He chose not to say what he had been doing with girls when he was seventeen. He thought it was just as well that the Chevy truck was not in good enough condition to drive farther than the vocational school repair bays. He tried not to laugh when he looked at his son. He had never seen a boy so thoroughly smitten.

Young love, thought West's father, smiling. There's nothing like it.

Meghan herself had everything: two parents who lived together and loved her, neighbors who included her, a boy who worshipped her, and a school in which she was popular and successful.

Meghan did not analyze these things. She did not ask why she was so lucky, nor worry about the people who were not. She was fifteen, which is not a particularly kind age. It's much better than thirteen, of course, and greatly superior to fourteen, but age sixteen is where compassion begins and the heart is moved by the plight of strangers.

Meghan was fifteen and her world was West and West was world enough.

Nobody knew what Lannie Anveill thought.

And nobody cared.

Meghan danced down the hall to West's locker. In the shelter of the ten-inch wide metal door, they kissed. Then they laughed, the self-conscious but wildly happy laugh they shared. Then they held hands and admired each other's beauty.

"I've got Mom's car for the day," said West.

They were airborne with the thought of a front seat together.

Meghan slid the strap of her bookbag over her shoulder. West slid his over his opposite shoulder. They wrapped their arms around each other's waists, and slowly made their way out of the school.

Every girl daydreams of a boy so in love he can't bear spending time away from her. There were a thousand boys in that high school and maybe ten had ever behaved like this. The girls watched West watching Meghan. They ached to be Meghan, to have West, to be adored like that. They saw how his hands and his eyes were all over her. How he was thick in the clouds of his love.

West did not see a single girl except Meghan.

Meghan, of course, saw all the girls, and knew exactly how envious they were, and got an extra jolt of pleasure from it.

Lannie Anveill fell in step with them.

Meghan could not believe it. There were certain rules of etiquette, and one was that you did not join a couple who were linked body and soul. Meghan glared at Lannie to make her go away, and Lannie glared right back. Meghan flinched. She had forgotten the power of Lannie's eyes. They went too deep.

West remembered his manners — he had fine manners; sometimes he stood behind his manners like a safety rail — and said cheerfully, "Hi, Lannie. What's up?"

Lannie stood still. She was still thin and wispy, looking little older than she had when they had played yard games. It was a little spooky, really, the way Lannie did not age. As if she would bypass all that tiresome human stuff of stages and ages. Her bleached-out eyes passed straight through Meghan and came out the other side.

Meghan, lovely in casual plaid wool pants and clinging dark sweater, felt stripped. As if Lannie did not see clothes. Only interior weaknesses.

Lannie discarded Meghan from her sight. She focused on West. Sternness left her. Hostility left her. With unusual softness, Lannie said to him, "It's time."

Meghan felt a strange tremor.

West smiled politely. "Time for what, babe?" He called girls who did not interest him "babe." He did not know how much this annoyed them.

"You remember," said Lannie.

West considered this. One of his nicest traits was

being serious when being serious counted. Not every seventeen-year-old boy had figured out how to do this. "Remember what?" he asked her at last.

"Your promise," said Lannie.

Something cold shivered in Meghan's memory.

West was blank. He said, "Am I taking everybody to a movie or something? Sorry, Lannie, I'm a little off-center today." He pulled Meghan close, to demonstrate what put him off-center. "Remind me, babe."

Lannie tightened like a bow and arrow. "You must remember!" she whispered so hotly she could have lit a match with her breath.

West frowned. "Ummm. Lannie, I'm sorry, I'm not sure what we're talking about."

"Give us a hint," said Meghan. From the lofty position of Us — she had a partner, she had a boyfriend, she was a pair — she could look down on Lannie, who was alone and unloved and unpaired. It was more comfortable to be scornful than to be scared. So Meghan looked down on Lannie, and it showed.

Somewhere from the distant past she heard Lannie say, *You'll be sorry, Meghan Moore.* Something in Meghan Moore quivered like a rabbit as the fox's jaws close on its leg.

"You want a reminder, Meghan Moore?" said Lannie Anveill. "Fine. Tomorrow. You will be reminded."

Meghan's knees were weak. She could remember that, too. That moment when her body failed her.

Lannie turned and walked away, vanishing in the

high school crowds with the same ease she used to vanish on Dark Fern Lane.

Meghan forced a giggle. When she took West's hand, hers was sweaty. *I always hated it when Lannie joined the neighborhood,* thought Meghan. *The last thing I want her to join is* us. *She has no right.*

West said, "Didn't she sound like the voice of doom?"

Meghan dropped her voice an octave. *"You will be reminded."*

They actually laughed.

Chapter 2

It was a good morning. One of the best.

In geometry Meghan learned the new formula right away and her mind glittered with pleasure. There was nothing like mastering math to make you feel like a genius.

In history, usually so dusty and remote, the teacher read an exciting passage from an old, old journal. Meghan's skin prickled, imagining how it had been back then.

"Why is history important?" said the teacher. His voice was soft, uttering a sentence he wanted the students to carry through life. "Because . . . if you forget history, you are doomed to repeat it."

Where did I just hear that word? thought Meghan. You don't hear it very often. How dark it is. A word for death and eternal sorrow.

"*Doomed*," repeated the teacher softly.

But I have no history, Meghan thought. So I am not doomed to repeat anything.

In Spanish, Meghan was required to read a passage aloud. For the first time ever in foreign language class, her tongue knew how to sound. She felt a wild surge of triumph, and yearned to speak with somebody Spanish.

She could hardly wait for lunch, to tell West.

Sometimes school frightened Meghan. Sometimes she failed, or it failed her. Sometimes it puzzled her or left her behind.

But this was not one of those days.

She burned with excitement. She savored the feel, even the taste of the new Spanish syllables. She planned the phrases she would use to describe the new knowledge.

She danced down the hallway to where they always met, at the drinking fountain.

He was there already, smiling.

Oh, how she loved him! He was West, wide and handsome and fascinating and wonderful, and most of all, *hers*.

For years she had averted her eyes from any boy she liked. All through middle school, the more she liked a boy, the less able she was to look at him.

But she could look at West. Soak him up. Like a flower facing the sun.

He started talking first. "Guess what."

"What?" They saved things for each other; tiny tales of success to hand each other at lunch, and after school, and on the phone.

"We had a quiz in physics. Guess what I got." West was shining.

He wanted to be an engineer and design cars. He loved anything to do with motors or movement. "A hundred," guessed Meghan.

"Yes!" West hugged her with his pride. "I raised the curve," he bragged.

"Yeah, you toad," said another kid from physics. He punched West cheerfully. "I was the next highest," he confided to Meghan. "I got eighty-nine."

"Congratulations," said Meghan. West's hand on her waist was opening and closing, going nowhere and yet exploring. She loved being possessed like that — the proof of his clasp like a bracelet: this is mine, it stays here.

"You want to get in the sandwich line or the hot line?" asked West.

They checked out other people's trays. The hot plate was unrecognizable. It was brown and it had gravy, and that was all you could be sure of.

"Sandwiches," said Meghan.

"Sandwiches," agreed West.

They laughed and wanted to kiss in front of everybody, but didn't. Still, it was in their eyes and in the way they walked.

"Guess what," said Meghan.

"You got a hundred in Spanish."

"We didn't have a quiz. But listen to me talk. I'm going to knock your socks off with my accent."

"I'm ready," said West. He tugged his pant legs up so they could watch when his socks came off. Meghan giggled.

Somebody screamed.

Of course, the cafeteria was always noisy. People yelled, laughed, talked, gossiped, burped, scraped chairs, and dropped dishes. A scream was not extraordinary.

But this was a scream of terror.

It was the kind of scream that grabbed at the roots of your heart, and wrenched the air out of your lungs, and made you want your back against a wall.

Five hundred students went silent, breath caught, looking for the source of the terrible scream. Eyes sped around the room like paired animals, seeking the terror.

Meghan had a queer slicing memory, like a knife, a knife dripping with blood, and somehow it was mixed with Tuesday, and grass, and darkness, and childhood.

The last time I heard a scream like that . . . thought Meghan.

But she could not quite remember the last time she had heard a scream like that.

West sucked in his breath. Her hand was on his back and she felt his ribs and chest expand, and felt them stay expanded, as if holding onto his lungs would keep him alive. As if there were danger of not being alive.

Toppled on the floor, like a statue knocked over by a vandal, was a girl. One leg remained raised and off it, a long skirt hung like drapery.

"She fainted," said somebody.

"Give her air."

"Call an ambulance."

Teachers and cafeteria workers rushed over to help.

The girl was stiff.

"She's . . . sort of . . . frozen," said the cafeteria

monitor, backing away, as if it were a virus, and would leap free of the fallen girl and attack the rest.

People touched the frozen girl with a single extended finger, and then pulled back, afraid, even wiping their hands off on their trousers.

The air swirled around Meghan Moore and West Trevor.

Old air. The air of their childhoods.

Memory.

The quiet of the night came back, and the softness of the summer, and the deepness of the horror.

Meghan remembered the morning glory by the steps, whose bright blue flowers had slid into their green envelopes, saving its glory for dawn. Meghan had always wondered what morning glories knew that people did not.

She remembered the lawnmower and the scent of the cut grass, the setting sun and the thickness of dusk.

She remembered the calm explanatory voice. *It's Freeze Tag. So I froze her*.

"Who is it, does anybody know?" said the teachers.

"Jessica," said somebody else.

The school had at least fifty girls named Jessica. Meghan did not know if this was a Jessica she knew, or a stranger Jessica.

Meghan moved slowly, dizzily, forward. The fallen girl was still and solid. Her skin did not seem tan with summer, but icy blue with winter. Her hair stuck out from her head without regard to gravity, as if carved from ice. Her shoulders did not rise and fall with the filling of lungs.

"She *is* frozen," whispered a horrified adult.

I didn't run fast enough, thought Meghan. *Lannie hated me.*

She remembered Lannie's fingers, burring into her soul. She remembered being frozen. It didn't hurt. And I wasn't afraid, either, thought Meghan. I was just suspended. Perhaps hibernation is like that. Bears survive the winter, don't they? They just turn down the heat until spring.

But a human would not live till spring.

"It must be a seizure," said a teacher, voice trembling. He tried to move her into a sitting position, but the body did not bend. It was sickeningly stiff, as if she had died yesterday and gone into rigor mortis. "Call an ambulance!"

The girl's leg stayed high in the air, like a gymnast's photograph.

West had had to say *please.* West had had to beg.

Lannie had said, *You must always like me best.*

And West repeated like a little boy learning a little lesson, *I will always like you best.*

He never thought of Lannie again, let alone liked her best, Meghan realized. He liked cars best, and football best, and then finally he liked *me* best.

West set the lunch tray down, his face pale, upper lip fringed with sweat. "I remember," he said. His voice was vacant.

Meghan was afraid to look around. What if she met Lannie's eyes? Those terrible bleached eyes could illuminate a dark yard, like headlights of a car. Perhaps Lannie could freeze you with her eyes.

West murmured, "She's over by the windows."

Meghan forced herself to look over by the windows.

Lannie stood alone, her little wispy frame very still. As Meghan had soaked up the sunshine of West's greeting, Lannie soaked up the darkness of Jessica's freezing. Her smile was tender. Her head was tilted to the side, an artist admiring her exhibit.

West mumbled something unintelligible. He shoved both hands deep into his jeans' pockets.

He was separating himself from Meghan, and from the disaster, and even from the future.

Meghan stared at those wrists, at those pockets, and saw a different West: a West who did not want to face this. A West who was going to stand very still and hope it all went away.

She was aware of a deep disappointment in West. His broad shoulders and his fine mind did not match his strength of soul.

It was a thought too terrible to allow. Meghan knocked it away.

Lannie slid between them, materializing as completely and silently as a chemistry experiment. Meghan's body jerked with fear. Lannie was so close, Meghan flinched. Don't touch me!

She gave Lannie another inch and Lannie smiled into the air, but did not bother to look at Meghan. She did not bother with greetings or small talk either. She never had. "We are going out now, West," she said firmly. As if West were a lottery ticket, and Lannie wanted to buy in.

West jammed his hands deeper into the pockets.

"This is your fault, anyway," Lannie said. "You should have discussed this last night, after I talked to you. I warned you this would happen."

Meghan was afraid, and fear made her stupid, and stupidity made her rude. "Lannie," she said sharply, "we had better things to talk about than you."

In the short space of time before Lannie retaliated, Meghan saw that Lannie actually experienced emotion. It had hurt Lannie's feelings that West and Meghan had not talked about her last night. Lannie looked up at West with a kind of grief and sorrow.

Lannie knew nothing of love. Yet she ached for it; all the world ached for love. Somehow Lannie could not understand why she couldn't just take West and walk off with him. Sort of like shoplifting a lipstick.

In the distance came the peculiar rise and fall of an ambulance siren, as harsh and upsetting as chalk on a blackboard.

"Lannie," said Meghan, "undo her. Jessica didn't do anything to you."

The revolving lights on top of the ambulance cast on-and-off rainbows through the slanted cafeteria windows. When a backboard was slid under Jessica, the body remained stiff and splayed.

"Get out of here, Meghan," said Lannie calmly. "West is mine now."

She's in love with him, thought Meghan. She always has been. How could I have forgotten that? We marched our love up and down Dark Fern Lane, showing off for the world. We forgot that Lannie is part of our world. "You can't do that to Jessica," said Meghan softly. "Undo her."

"It isn't a true demonstration if I undo her," said Lannie. "You would relax. You must never relax around me, Meghan. Now go away. West is mine."

"Lannie," hissed West, "what did Jessica do to deserve that?"

"She didn't do anything."

"You can't go around freezing people!" said West.

"Of course I can," said Lannie, with the annoyed air of one having to point out the obvious. "Now if this was not enough for you, I'll do another."

"No!"

"Actually," said Lannie, "I could freeze lots of people. They would close the school down. They would think they had a weird epidemic."

"I would tell them what you were doing," said West.

Lannie put her thin little arm around his big waist. She hugged him affectionately. "Would they believe it?" she said, smiling.

Across the silent frightened room a teacher said, "It must be some kind of virus. One of those new diseases. Like Legionnaire's Disease."

"Unfreeze her, Lannie!" hissed Meghan.

"No. Come on, West. We're eating together."

West actually took a step with her. Actually picked up the lunch tray on which his and Meghan's sandwiches lay.

"Let's talk about this," said Meghan quickly.

"There's nothing to talk about. West promised to like me forever, and forever is here."

Forever is here.

The words strapped Meghan down. Lannie would have West for eternity, while Meghan would go to school alone and grow up and move away.

"Actually I think I promised to like you best," said West.

"That, too," said Lannie happily.

"Undo Jessica!" shouted Meghan.

The cafeteria turned to stare in their direction.

Lannie shook her head gently, disassociating herself and West from Meghan's crazy behavior.

"You're a virus, Lannie," said Meghan.

Lannie had had enough of her. "And you're frozen, Meghan," said Lannie, reaching out.

Chapter 3

West jerked Lannie backward. Her finger missed Meghan by a molecule's width. Lannie's hand trembled, stuck out into the air, touching nothing. The finger pointed evilly on, as if it could freeze by invisible waves. But it could not. Meghan could move and breathe.

Not easily. Fear tightened her up. Her stomach was cinched in, her ribs were rigid, her ankles were stiff. Meghan managed a single half step away. It was not enough. A river between them would not have been enough.

She was going to freeze me! thought Meghan. She was tired of me and that was the answer.

After a long time, she wrenched her eyes off that shivering fingertip — was it shivering because it delivered a freeze? shivering because it was still straining forward? — and looked at West.

How large West was, how slight Lannie looked against him. She was as insubstantial as a tissue, and yet he had to struggle to hold her. West seemed both stunned and certain. Of what was he certain?

Meghan did not know. She was certain of nothing now. She did not see if she could ever be certain again.

What weapon was this — this threat Lannie could carry out?

How would any of them behave normally ever again, when that finger could . . .

"I like you best, Lannie," said West. His voice was calm. It was even friendly. It did not sound like a lie. Anybody listening would have thought that West Trevor did, indeed, like Lannie best.

Meghan was no longer stiff with fear but limp with shock. Was West acting? If so, he was a brilliant actor. Or was he impressed? Memory returned to Meghan Moore. *I'm impressed, Lannie*, he had said that evening on the grass.

Power is impressive, she thought. But he has to like me best!

"We'll have lunch over by the windows, Lannie," said West in his firm adult voice. "And on our way over, Lannie," he said, giving an order, sounding like a parent, "you'll brush against Jessica. It'll count. It'll undo it. The ambulance won't have to take her. Right?"

Lannie pulled her lips together in a little girl's pout.

How strange she looked. A moment ago Lannie had been as ancient as evil, as timeless as cruelty. Now she was a little girl, lip stuck out because she had to do something she didn't feel like doing.

"I mean it, Lannie," said West. "I can't hang out with you if you're going to freeze people."

Meghan suppressed an hysterical desire to laugh.

"Okay, fine," said Lannie irritably. She snuggled herself up against West and walked so close to him she might have been standing on his shoes to walk, the way Brown used to love to do with his big brother when he was about three.

It was good that everybody in the cafeteria was so absorbed by Jessica's condition. Nobody saw the amazing combination of Lannie and West.

Actually, thought Meghan, a combination of Lannie and anyone at all would be amazing. She's always alone. Everybody's afraid of her.

Meghan's hair prickled.

Why? Why were they afraid? What experiences had other people in here had with Lannie Anveill? What had happened off Dark Fern Lane?

Meghan closed her eyes, blotting out her imagination, and in those few brief moments, West and Lannie brushed by the stretcher just as it was sliding out the cafeteria door and toward the waiting, open ambulance.

Jessica tried to sit up on the swaying stretcher, miraculously regaining consciousness and muscle.

"Oh, thank God!" cried the teachers.

Lannie smiled, accepting this description of herself.

Lannie and West really did sit together for lunch. They even talked, and faced each other, and handed each other napkins. West actually seemed to listen to Lannie, and when it was his turn, he seemed to be telling her important things, things worth focusing on.

Meghan could not seem to function. She could not figure out whether to sit alone, or find an old friend, or hide in the girls' room, or go back to class early.

My perfect day, thought Meghan Moore. My wonderful classes, my fluent Spanish, my lovely, lovely West.

Meghan hurt somewhere inside. How could West be so easy about this? How could he saunter across the cafeteria, relax with that terrible hand so close to him — touching him, even?

Was he acting?

Perhaps she froze part of me after all, thought Meghan. I'm not completely here. Part of my mind is ice. Part of my heart is snow.

Eventually lunch period ended.

Eventually Meghan found herself in gym.

She was taking tennis. The school had an indoor court. Never had it been so satisfying to whack a ball. Meghan hurled all her strength into the drills. The coach was thrilled. "Meghan, you're vicious!" said the coach happily. "I love when you play like this! This is winning!"

I will hit Lannie Anveill like this, thought Meghan Moore. I am not giving up West Trevor. And *he* is not giving *me* up, either. She's not allowed to go running around freezing people or scaring me that she might. I won't put up with it.

Meghan smashed a ball down into the opposite court. Whatever had been frozen in her melted. She was all heat. All rage.

All hatred.

Once she had thought hatred was cold. Wrong. Hate boiled in her mind and her heart. The steam of hate rose in her throat. Bubbles of hate raced through her blood.

She could actually *feel* the hate.

She could feel hate take over her body the way Lannie Anveill's evil touch had taken over Jessica's.

Meghan Moore set down her tennis racket. Meghan Moore backed away from the court, away from the shouting coach, away from the beaten opponents.

No.

I refuse.

I will not be filled with hate. I don't like people who are hateful. I like nice people. I am a nice person. I will not hate.

Meghan walked into the girls' locker room early and stood alone among the slick tiles and the stuck lockers.

She let the hate seep out of her. It did not leave quickly or easily. Hate was a lingering thing. It liked ruling the body.

She shook her hands as if shaking water off her fingers. She lifted each foot and shook it. The last little droplets of hate seemed to leave.

I won't beat Lannie with hate, thought Meghan. But I have to beat her with something. So what will it be?

". . . because knowing your opponent will give you an edge," the coach was saying out in the gym. "You must study your opponent's technique. Then you can see the weaknesses and the flaws, and move in on them."

Know your opponent, thought Meghan Moore.

Did Lannie have weaknesses? Did she have flaws?

Meghan would have to get to know Lannie.

There was no other way.

Meghan had a study hall last period. She usually made excellent use of it. Today, as usual, the forty-four minutes were not wasted. She did not doodle or daydream. But she did not study math or literature, either.

She reviewed her knowledge of Lannie Anveill.

Lannie never seemed to get older, or taller, or curvier. She had stayed wispy. Her hair was dry and brittle. It reminded Meghan of herbs that people who had country kitchens were always hanging from their ceilings. There was a dustiness to Lannie, as if she were very old, and had been stored somewhere. Unused.

Or unloved, thought Meghan. Nobody ever had less love.

Meghan's mother used to say that, when she insisted Meghan had to be kind to Lannie. It was blackmail kindness. You could not really feel sorry for Lannie. You were more apt to feel sorry for her parents. There was something in Lannie that precluded sympathy.

Except for the growing of trees and children, Dark Fern Lane had seen few changes when

Meghan was in elementary school. Most of the families who had bought first homes there still owned those first homes.

Lannie's father was the only one on Dark Fern Lane who actually did get a second house. Lannie had been about ten.

Getting a second house, it turned out, was not necessarily good news. For Lannie's father was not going to bring his wife and daughter along to this second house. He was going to live there with his girlfriend, Nance.

Mr. Anveill promised that he would take Lannie one weekend a month. It did not sound like a lot of time to spend with your father, but it sure sounded like a lot of time to spend with Lannie. Meghan had shivered for Nance, who surely did not know what that weekend and that stepdaughter were going to be like.

And when Lannie's mother remarried, too, Meghan shivered for Jason. Jason moved into the house on Dark Fern Lane, and had to live with Lannie all the time.

One Friday, Nance and Mr. Anveill were picking Lannie up for The Weekend, and Nance happened to have a conversation with Meghan's mother, who was raking leaves across the yard and into the street. "I've been reading up on stepparenting," said Nance.

"Oh?" said Mrs. Moore.

"Experts say not to expect to get along for at least two years, let alone feel any love for the stepchild. So I don't expect a thing, and I certainly don't love Lannie, but I wish she would brush her teeth more often."

Lannie was standing there at the time. She had chosen a few pretty orange and yellow maple leaves to admire. But she did not take them inside with her. She crushed them in her hand.

And then there was the day when Jason, waxing his car (he drove a classic Corvette; the former Mrs. Anveill was not interested in men who drove dull cars) talked to Meghan's father. "I don't know how to be a parent," he confided. He seemed to feel this freed him from having to try.

That year, Lannie skipped a grade, catching up to Meghan. Lannie had never seemed especially smart, and many people were surprised that Lannie was skipped up. Meghan understood perfectly. Lannie's scheduled teacher was afraid of her. What better way to breathe easily than to bump up the source of your fear?

Beside her in study hall somebody coughed. Somebody moved his chair. Somebody dropped a book on the floor.

Meghan heard none of it. For she had remembered the dog. She had not thought of that dog in years!

Why didn't I remember? she wondered. Why didn't I add things up? What took me so long?

Jason had brought home an Irish setter. Such a beautiful dog!

Dark red, lean, and graceful.

It bounded across the narrow yard on Dark Fern Lane, whipped around the Jaguar and the Corvette parked in the drive, and rushed back to Jason to lick his hands. Jason, impossibly handsome in his sporty jacket and jaunty cap, knelt to fondle the dog.

How attractive everybody was! The fine strong stepfather! The magnificent cars! The lovely fluid Irish setter! Meghan had been awestruck. Her own family was dowdy and dull.

Jason, laughing happily, had hugged the dog.

"He's never hugged me," said Lannie.

The dog did not yet have a name. Lannie's mother came out and she too admired the beautiful dog. "We need a name for it," said Lannie's mother with great concentration. "It must be a perfect name."

"For a perfect dog," agreed Jason.

They hugged each other, and leaned against each other, as if they and the dog were the family.

As if Lannie did not exist.

The Irish setter, loping over the green grass, passed near the two young girls. Meghan, who was not fond of dogs, shrank back.

But Lannie had put her hand out.

Meghan, in the study hall, clung to the table, sick with dizziness, as if she were about to faint. *I knew*, thought Meghan, *I knew even then*. I knew what was going to happen.

How vividly Meghan remembered Lannie's fingers. Too long for a little girl's hand. Her wrist too narrow, skin too white.

The dog tipped over, as if made of cast iron. It

lay on the ground with its legs sticking out like chair legs.

"Oh, no!" cried Jason. "What's the matter? My beautiful dog!"

Lannie's mother said, "Quick! We'll take the dog to the vet."

They crooned and wept.

They rushed for help.

They showed the paralyzed dog more affection and worry than they had ever shown Lannie.

Lannie's skin was as cold and white as snow, but her eyes, her pale dead eyes, were hot and feverish with pleasure.

Meghan remembered backing away, trying to slip unseen into her house. She had accomplished it easily. Lannie had forgotten Meghan. Lannie's satisfied eyes remained for hours on the place in the grass where the dog's frozen outline was impressed.

The following spring there was another ending in Lannie's life.

People who drive Jaguars as fast as Lannie's mother either lose their driver's license or get killed. With Lannie's mother, it was first one and then the other.

Everybody on Dark Fern Lane felt obligated to go to the funeral.

Only Meghan had refused to attend.

"Darling," said Mrs. Moore, "I know funerals are upsetting, but Lannie is in school with you, and she's your across-the-street neighbor, and you owe it to Lannie to show support."

Why didn't I want to go? thought Meghan, tapping her pencil against the cover of her unopened literature book. The boy next to her stared pointedly until she flushed and stopped tapping.

Meghan tried to remember the funeral.

I didn't go, thought Meghan. I stayed home. Why?

The answer did not come, and yet she felt it there: a piece of knowledge she had chosen to bury when she was young. When she was thirteen. A terrible age. Meghan was very grateful not to be thirteen any longer.

In any event, Lannie, at twelve, had no mother, and so of course went to live with her father and Nance. Nobody on Dark Fern Lane missed Lannie. Meghan breathed deeper and laughed longer with Lannie off the street.

Not a month later, Nance drove into Lannie's old driveway. Lannie was in the front seat with her stepmother.

The weather had turned unseasonably hot, and everybody was outdoors — because nobody on Dark Fern Lane had air conditioning — and therefore everybody saw and everybody heard what happened next.

"Lannie's father," said Nance to Jason, "has deserted us."

Jason said he was sorry to hear that, but he did not know how it involved him.

"Lannie is yours," said Nance, and she drove off faster than Jason could think of an argument.

There was Jason, in his driveway, with Lannie

Anveill. "Well," said Jason. "Well, well, well."

Lannie stayed. Jason continued to lead his own life. Lannie always seemed to have clean clothes and a recent shampoo. But that was all she had.

Absolutely all.

The children on Dark Fern Lane graduated from elementary school, left middle school, and entered high school.

They no longer had neighborhood birthday parties to which Lannie must be invited. They no longer went to the same ballet classes and had to give Lannie rides. They no longer gathered for afternoon snacks at the Trevors', and had to give Lannie a plate of nachos as well.

High school was big and airy and full of strangers. Even when they had attended it for years, it was still full of strangers. Sometimes they went days without running into Lannie.

Even when they saw Lannie, they didn't think of her. They were completely absorbed by their own lives. The whole world, from the President of the United States to their mothers, was remote and bothersome.

Had any of them noticed Lannie?

Even once?

The final bell rang.

Meghan stood up, dazed.

Here's what I know about Lannie Anveill, thought Meghan Moore. Nobody loves her. Nobody ever has.

Chapter 4

And yet, for all that, when Meghan went down the usual hall at the usual time, there was West, in his usual place. And as usual, her heart leaped, her legs danced, and her lips smiled.

"West!" she said.

His smile filled his face. "Meghan."

They hugged at the locker and went arm and arm to the car.

Lannie had fallen away from their thoughts and their lives like a piece of paper dropped to the floor. How remote those hate-filled tennis-ball-smacking minutes became. How meaningless the knowledge of Lannie's loveless life. Meghan forgot again. Only teenagers can forget so completely, so often.

Meghan knew nothing except the joy and the warmth of the boy she adored. Her world was very small, and very full.

"This afternoon I'm going to work on my truck," said West happily. "It's cold out, but the sun will be shining for probably another hour and a half. I'm trying to fix the door handles."

"That's a good project," said Meghan, who thought it was the most boring thing she had ever heard of.

West beamed, and shared his door-handle restoration plans with her. It seemed that both handles had broken off on the inside. "You have to keep a window rolled down in order to get out," he explained. "And I can't be letting it rain and snow inside my truck!"

Considering that it had been raining and snowing inside that rusty old hulk for a decade now, Meghan didn't see why he felt so deeply about it. But she loved him so she said, "I could help."

She knew West didn't really like help when he worked on his truck. In fact, West didn't like company. He liked to be alone with his toolbox and his chore. But she loved him a whole extra lot today, and she wanted to sit on that dumb old front seat and watch him sweat.

"Okay," he said reluctantly.

They threaded through the escaping cars — hundreds of kids leaving school as fast as they could — and found West's mother's car. West measured his happiness by the number of days he was allowed to take the car to school. It wasn't all the time, by any means. It wasn't even half the time.

"How long before the truck is up and going?" said Meghan, meaning, How long before you and I can ride together every day?

"Long time," said West, half gloomy because there was so much to do, and half delighted because there was so much to do.

West got in his side and Meghan opened the door to hers.

Lannie was sitting in the middle of the front seat.

West froze in the act of getting behind the wheel, looking exactly like a statue in Freeze Tag — one leg in, one leg out, half his body on the seat, half still outside the car.

Meghan froze all over again. Her hand froze on the door handle and her face froze in shock, seeing Lannie ensconced in West's mother's car. Meghan's mind and heart and body raced through every emotion of the day: fear, panic, rage, and finally knowledge.

I know she isn't loved, thought Meghan, striving for understanding and decency. But I don't want her to start with West!

And Meghan especially didn't want to see Lannie so pleased with herself.

West evidently decided that good manners would carry the day. West hated not getting along with everybody. It was a character flaw, in Meghan's opinion. You couldn't always be friends with everybody. But West, like the rest of the Trevors, was endlessly polite. It gave them protection; they could stand neatly behind their courtesy.

"Hey, Lannie," said West easily. As if it were quite ordinary to bump into her in his car. As if it meant nothing now, and was not going to mean anything later. "Want a ride home? We'll drop you off."

But it did mean something, Lannie being there in Meghan's place. Meghan could not quite get in the front seat and sit next to Lannie. Not after she had remembered the dog.

West did not look at Meghan. She could not exchange thoughts by eye. What shall I do? thought Meghan, as if her life depended on it. After a moment she got in the backseat by herself.

Lannie smiled victoriously and rested a hand on West's thigh.

Meghan was outraged. That's my place! she thought. Don't you touch him! He's mine!

But she did not say anything.

None of them said anything. Meghan did not think she had ever driven down these roads and kept silent. She did not think she had ever come out of school without a thousand stories and complaints and jokes to tell.

West seemed to sit very casually in the driver's seat, rather like a van driver who'd been giving rides for a hundred years and drove with a single fingertip, a slouch, and a shrug.

They reached Dark Fern Lane without having uttered a word. And it was Lannie, taking control, who spoke first. "Drop Meghan off," said Lannie. Her voice was as cold as January.

Meghan pressed back against the upholstery. Lannie seemed to have lowered the temperature in the whole car, just by speaking. As if her breath carried frost with it.

"Aw, come on, Lannie," said West. "I had lunch with you." As if that were enough. As if Lannie Anveill would settle for that. "Meghan and I have plans." As if Lannie cared. As if Lannie were going to allow those plans to be executed.

Outside was very January. Cold and waiting, the weather hiding behind a gray sky, waiting to blast them out of their safe houses. The ground hard as iron, expecting snow, needing snow.

In the backseat, Meghan felt queerly numb. She lifted her hands, to be sure she still had them. Drop me off, she thought. Off what? A cliff?

And suddenly she knew.

A glaze frosted her eyes, like the day she had been frozen in the yard.

A glaze of knowledge.

Lannie turned around to glare at Meghan for taking so long. Her hooded eyelids lifted and the dark irises glowed like the Northern Lights. "Get out of the car, Meghan," said Lannie, in a voice as flat as a table.

"Lannie," breathed Meghan. She was trembling so hard she did not see how she could pick up her bookbag, or find the door handle.

Lannie smiled her smile of ice and snow.

"Did you freeze your own mother?" said Meghan. "Is that why the car crashed? Because she was frozen?"

Because that's why I didn't go to the funeral, thought Meghan. I remember it now. I was sure Lannie made her mother pay for loving the dog more.

The bleached eyes swung from Meghan to West.

West's big hands tightened on the steering wheel.

"Look at me, West," whispered Lannie.

"Don't look at her," said Meghan. But Meghan couldn't look away. Nor could she move. She was afraid to lean forward and so much as rest her hand on West's shoulder. She was afraid to touch the door handle, for fear that Lannie had infected it, and it would be a carrier, as wires carry electricity.

"Is that why the car crashed?" said West. His voice, too, was flat. But his throat gave him away. It gagged.

Lannie's smile was as sharp as a splinter. "Maybe," she said. And then she laughed, and the laugh pierced Meghan's skin and hurt.

A few houses down Dark Fern Lane, the school bus stopped.

Children poured out.

Tuesday, who had a generous and romantic nature, and therefore usually let West and Meghan ride home by themselves, got off last. She separated from the little ones. Her dark blonde hair bounced against her neon pink windbreaker. She swung her yellow bookbag in a circle and jumped successfully over an ice-crusted puddle in a driveway. She was laughing. She must have had a great day, or a funny ride home, because even though she was on her own now, the laugh was still carrying her.

"Why, it's Tuesday," said Lannie sweetly. "Dear Tuesday. I've never liked her either, really. Wouldn't it be unfortunate if . . ." Lannie smiled. Then she said once more, "Get out of the car, Meghan."

Tuesday hurled her bookbag toward her own

front steps — missing by a hundred yards — and headed toward her brother and her best friend. "Hi, Meggie-Megs!" shouted Tuesday.

It was a very old nickname.

Meghan hardly knew which person it meant: she felt at least a century older than the little girl who had once been called Meggie-Megs by the neighborhood.

The only sound inside the car was the sound of West trying to swallow and not managing.

For a moment Meghan was furious with West. What was the matter with him? What did he think those big wide shoulders were for? They were for taking control and throwing people like Lannie Anveill out into the street.

But muscles meant nothing.

Not against a touch like Lannie Anveill's.

West's and Meghan's eyes met. This time the message they exchanged was very clear. They were trapped. "You better get out of the car," said West, his eyes going helplessly to his little sister.

Meghan got out slowly, holding the door open, as if nothing more could happen until the door was closed: The car could not leave, Lannie could not have him, nobody could be frozen, all was well, as long as she held the door open.

"Get out," said Lannie, "or I'll freeze Tuesday."

Meghan slammed the door. She ran forward to deflect Tuesday from her path toward the car.

Lannie shifted her insubstantial weight closer to the driver. She said something. Her tongue flickered when she spoke. Snakelike.

West drove away.

"West is going somewhere with Lannie?" Tuesday said. "What is he — a mental case? Nobody goes anywhere with Lannie."

"Lannie needs to talk," said Meghan. This was an accepted teenage reason for doing anything: if people needed to talk, you needed to listen.

"Lannie?" said Tuesday skeptically. "Talk? Right. Lannie doesn't *do* talk, Meggie-Megs, you know that."

Meghan changed the subject. "You're pretty bouncy, Tues. What happened today?"

"Well!" said Tuesday, beaming. "You'll never guess!"

"Tell me," said Meghan, linking arms with her.

What would West and Lannie do on this afternoon? Where would West drive? What would Lannie want from him? Meghan tried to imagine what it would be like for West, sitting in that front seat, Lannie inches away, with her contented chuckle and her pencil-thin arms and her terrible touch.

But from the way Lannie had moved, she was no longer inches away. She was there.

The emotions ripped through her all over again: the fear, the panic, the rage . . . and even a very little bit of the understanding.

Meghan followed Tuesday into the Trevors' house. There was always a lot of food at the Trevors'. Nobody ever dieted there. There was chocolate cake and rocky road ice cream and mint candy and cheese popcorn and onion bagels and sliced strawberries. Meghan's family had things like diet Coke and celery sticks.

The kitchen was entirely white: Mrs. Trevor had redone it a few years ago and it reminded Meghan of a hospital room. It looked like the kind of room you'd hose down after the autopsy.

But the family left debris everywhere: on the counter were a bright plaid bowling ball bag, a pile of trumpet music, a stack of old homework papers, a folder of phone numbers, two pairs of sneakers, folded laundry, and breakfast dishes piled with toast crusts.

It was so real.

So ordinary.

So comforting.

Meghan knew right away that her worries were false and exaggerated.

Nobody freezes anybody, thought Meghan. I can't believe that West and I let ourselves fall for Lannie's silliness. No wonder she was laughing at us. We fell for her dumb story. Poor old Lannie needs to be the center of attention and did she accomplish it this time! I'm such a jerk.

Meghan helped herself to a handful of cheese popcorn and then a dozen chocolate chips from the bag — nobody ever got around to making cookies in this family; they just ate the chips straight — and then a glass of raspberry ginger ale and finally some of the strawberries. Tuesday meanwhile had strawberries on Cheerios with lots of milk, tossing in a few chocolate chips for variety. For quite a while there was no sound but the contented intake of really good snacks.

"They chose me to hostess the JV cheerleaders' slumber party!" said Tuesday, sighing with the joy and the honor. "It's going to be here, Meggie-Megs! Isn't that wonderful? They want to have it at my house."

It did not necessarily indicate that Tuesday had become the most popular girl on earth. Mrs. Trevor was probably just the only parent willing to have a dozen screaming ninth- and tenth-grade girls overnight. Plus Mrs. Trevor would certainly have the most food and be the most liberal about what movies they could rent.

But Tuesday didn't see it that way. Nobody ever sees popularity that way. And Lannie probably didn't see that she had blackmailed West into driving away with her; Lannie probably thought she was just getting her fair share of popularity at last.

At that moment, Mrs. Trevor came home. She was a very attractive woman. Heavy, but the kind of heavy where you would never want her to lose weight: she was perfect the way she was. All the neighborhood children called her Mom even though everybody but Lannie had a mom of their own. "Hi, Mom," said Tuesday happily.

"Hi, Mom," said Meghan.

Mrs. Trevor hugged and kissed and made sure everybody had had enough to eat. Then she made sure she had enough to eat, too. "Tell me that I did not see my son driving around with Lannie Anveill."

"You did not," said Tuesday agreeably.

"Yes, I did," said her mother. "What's going on?"

"Lannie has a crush on West," said Tuesday, "didn't you know that?"

"Of course I knew that. But West is dating Meghan."

"They're just going to talk," said Meghan.

Mrs. Trevor got out her huge coffeemaker, the one that dripped and kept for hours. Meghan was happy. She loved the smell (but hated the taste) of coffee. For a really good kitchen smell, you needed bacon, too. If Meghan told Mrs. Trevor that, Mrs. Trevor would have bacon in that skillet in a second. She would think it was a perfectly good reason to cook some: because Meghan wanted to smell it.

"I feel funny," said Tuesday suddenly.

"You do?" said her mother, all concern. "In what way, darling?"

"Frozen!" said Tuesday. She rubbed at her own skin, trying to warm herself with friction.

There is such a thing, thought Meghan, as being too understanding. Or perhaps that's not it at all. Perhaps I'm just too afraid to think about what's really happening. I'm too eager to put it on the shelf and pretend it's not there. But Lannie's come off the shelf. She's here. She's not going away.

She has West.

She could have Tuesday.

What am I going to do?

Meghan thought of saying: Mom Trevor, Lannie

has evil powers, she can freeze people, she froze me once, she froze the Irish setter, and probably froze her own mother. Now she's threatening to freeze Tuesday. So since we now both want your son West, what do I do? I can't sacrifice Tuesday.

Mrs. Trevor would laugh and say, "No, really, what is going on?"

Meghan was a great fan of television real-life shows. She adored *America's Most Wanted*, and *Cops*, and *Rescue 911*, and all shows of rescue and law and order. She imagined herself calling the police. Hi, my boyfriend is driving around town with this girl who . . .

Right.

When they stopped laughing (and her call would be taped! Her voice would be forever captured on tape — so jealous of her boyfriend she called the police when somebody else sat in his car!) they'd say, "Okay, honey, get a grip on yourself."

"Do you think Lannie is capable of love?" asked Tuesday.

"No," said Mrs. Trevor. She didn't add to that.

Meghan couldn't stand it. She liked long answers. "Why not?" said Meghan.

"She never had any. I've never seen a child so thoroughly abandoned. Why, even when her mother was alive, I never saw anybody pick Lannie up, or kiss her, or hug her. She put herself to bed, nobody ever tucked her in. She ate alone, nobody ever shared a meal with her."

The coffee was made. Mrs. Trevor poured herself

a big mug and added lots of sugar and milk. Meghan thought anything a Trevor did would always be sweet and warm like that.

"Poor Lannie," said Mrs. Trevor. "It's enough to freeze your heart."

Chapter 5

Tuesday and her mother discussed the slumber party. Mrs. Trevor agreed to everything.

Meghan was impressed. Her own mother would be thinking up blockades, barricades. Battening down the hatches of the house to protect the Moores against the cheerleader invasion. Her own mother would confine the girls to the yard and the basement playroom. On the night of the party, Meghan's mother would constantly roam the place, keeping an eye on things and maintaining standards.

Mrs. Trevor didn't have any to maintain, which streamlined the whole event.

Meghan wished she was a JV cheerleader and could come.

But she was not and, as the afternoon passed, she felt more and more left out of the celebration. When eventually Meghan slipped out and headed home, Tuesday and Mrs. Trevor scarcely noticed.

When Meghan was little, the front yards on Dark Fern Lane had seemed like vast stretches of green grass. When they played yard games, what great distances their little legs had had to pump! When Lannie was It, what terrifying expanses of empty space Meghan had been forced to flee over.

Now the beginner bushes were fat and sprawling. Meghan's father liked to prune and trim his bushes, and in the Moores' yard, the bushes were neat and round, like plums. But the Trevors never trimmed, and the long thin tentacles of forsythia bushes arced through the darkness. Icy fronds touched Meghan's face and twisted cords grabbed her waist.

Lannie's fingers in winter.

Meghan sobbed dry tears, tottering among the obstacles.

A raised ranch house has three doors: front door atop many steps, back kitchen door opening onto a high deck, and a door into the garage. If you go in by the garage, you must ease your body between the silent cars and the debris stacked along garage walls. There is an oily waiting stink in a garage. The darkness that has collected over the years lies in pools, sucking your feet.

In winter, the garage door was always dark.

Meghan hated the garage door. But if she went in the front, she would be exposed to Lannie's view. If Lannie was home. If Lannie was looking away from West.

And she could not go in the kitchen door, because it was latched as well as locked.

The door in the garage opened with a raspy scream.

It wasn't the door, thought Meghan. It was me.

Would Lannie have frozen Tuesday? Had Lannie frozen her own mother? It had seemed silly when she was surrounded by the warmth of Mrs. Trevor. Now, in the oily dark, it seemed so very real.

Meghan did not feel frozen this time, but suffocated. The oil that had leaked out of the cars and soaked into the cement floor came through the soles of her shoes and crawled up her veins and lay like a sheet of rubber over her lungs.

West and Lannie. Hours now. Alone together.

She got out of the garage, up the stairs, into the safer more open dark of the living parts of the house. She turned on no lights. She did not want Lannie Anveill, across the street, to see that she was home.

Although of course Lannie always knew.

And Lannie, who could materialize anywhere, anytime, Lannie might suddenly be leaning against the wallpaper right here in this room, with her little chuckle of ice and snow.

It was a matter of will not to turn on the lights and make sure that the corners were empty. Lannie isn't here, Meghan told herself. I'm not going to be a baby and panic.

She sat in the dining room, which the Moores never used; it was just wasted space with a table and chairs. But it had a window view of West's driveway. She wanted to see him come home.

He didn't get home till supper.

He parked that car of his mother's and sat quietly for several moments behind the wheel before he opened the door and got out. What was he thinking about?

233

He had been alone with Lannie Anveill for three hours.

What had they done in that three hours? West . . . with his Trevor need to be courteous. Just how courteous had West been? What on earth had they talked about?

That hand on the pants leg of West's jeans. Lannie's hand. Thin and white like a peeled stick. What had that touch been like?

Had West shivered and felt sick?

Or could Lannie's hands, which froze bodies and hearts, make other changes, too?

West did not look over at Meghan's house. He did not look at his own, either. He got out of the car so slowly he looked damaged. He had to pull himself along, as if his limbs were a separate weight. He had trouble opening his front door, and trouble closing it when he was inside.

But then the door closed, and he was as lost to her as he had been driving around with Lannie.

The dining room curtains had been put up years ago and their positions rarely changed. They hung stiffly at each side of the sills, as frozen into place as if Lannie had touched them. It was utterly silent in Meghan's house. She had not turned on the television or the radio for company. Her parents were not yet home.

Meghan was so lonely she wanted to run over to the Trevors. Not even waste time getting to the door. Leap straight through the window.

But Lannie would be watching. Lannie always

watched. It was what she had done her whole life: stand in the shadows and watch.

Standing in her own shadows, watching the passing of others, Meghan thought — Life? This is not life. This is a warehouse.

Lannie had just been stored, all these years. Born and then stuck on a shelf, while others lived.

It was time to turn on the lights and go back to living herself. Meghan left the dining room, and walked through the house flipping every light switch. Then she sat by the phone.

It did not ring.

Meghan couldn't believe it. What was the matter with West? He had to know that the most important thing on earth was to call her up and tell her what was going on.

He didn't.

Meghan's parents came home. The routine in the Moore household never varied. Her mother and her father smiled at the sight of her, lightly kissed her forehead or her cheek, and asked how her day had been. How Meghan yearned for the passion at the Trevors' house — the clutter and noise and chaos and exuberance.

"I had a great day," said Meghan. The morning's academic successes might have happened ten centuries ago. "I'm really improving in Spanish. And history was very interesting."

Her parents wanted to hear her improved Spanish accent. They wanted to find out what had been so interesting in history.

But it was West's interest she wanted.

West did not call after supper.

He did not call at all.

At nine-thirty, Meghan gave up the wait and telephoned him herself.

West answered. "Hi, Meghan," he said. There was nothing in his voice.

"Are you alone?"

"No."

"Who's listening?"

"Everybody."

"What happened?"

"Tell you later."

"I have to know now. I can't sleep without knowing!"

West sighed and said nothing.

Meghan said, "I'll meet you at the truck."

They had done this a few times: crept out of their houses, walked silently over the dark backyards down the hedge lines, down the sloping grass, slick with evening frost. Then they'd sit in the front seat of the Chevy to talk. You couldn't slam the doors because it would make a noise the families might hear. Plus now that the handles didn't work from the inside, you didn't dare shut the doors anyway.

The truck interior was not romantic.

In summer, because it was in a low place where vines and tangles grew thickly, there were mosquitoes. In winter, a chill rose off the ground and could not be shaken. Meghan's feet got so cold she couldn't stand it. And this was January. Cold as Lannie's heart.

"Okay," said West finally.

"What time?"

"Same time."

"Eleven?"

"Okay."

"West, I can't tell a thing from your voice. What is going on? Is it okay? What did Lannie do?"

"It's okay," said West.

"I love you," she said to West.

There was a long silence. "Okay," he said at last.

But it was not okay.

Meghan's parents liked to be in bed by a few minutes before eleven, and at eleven, sitting up against the big padded headboard, they would watch the evening news together. In that half hour of broadcasting, Meghan could do anything and her parents would not know.

As soon as their door shut, she slipped downstairs to rummage in the closet, seeking out her heaviest coat.

On the back step, the wind bit her face and cut her skin.

She felt like an explorer on a glacier.

The backyard was long and deep.

There were no stars and no moon.

The wind yanked silently at the young trees and the hovering hedges.

The world swayed and leaned down to scrape her face.

She could not see a thing. But a flashlight would be a diamond point for Lannie to see out *her* bedroom window. Lannie must never know about the tangles, the privacy and the pleasure of the truck deep in the shadows.

How deep the yard was!

I must be taking tiny steps, thought Meghan. I feel as if I've gone so far I've crossed the town line.

The ground became mucky, and her feet quaked in the mire.

Where am I?

A hand grabbed her hair.

She tried to scream, but was too afraid. Her whole chest closed in as if a giant's hand had crushed her like newspaper for a fire.

"You walked right by," whispered West. "Come on. Truck's way back there."

Meghan's knees nearly buckled. "You scared me!" she whispered.

West led her back to the truck, where the driver's door hung open. She was amazed she had not walked smack into it and broken a bone. She climbed in first, and West got in after her, and on the wide single seat they crushed against each other.

"Tell me," said Meghan.

"About what?"

"About Lannie!"

West said nothing.

Meghan was used to the dark now, and could see his eyes. They were large and shiny. "Did you make it clear to her that you and I are going out with each other?"

West was silent for a long time. At last he said, "No."

"West! Why not?"

"Because."

Meghan hated him. Just as much as she loved him, she hated him.

West closed his shiny eyes and Meghan felt buried.

"She was serious," said West. He did not touch Meghan. He ran his hands over the torn dashboard, as gently as if he were stroking velvet. "When we talked, she slid over next to me, Meghan. She never took her eyes off me and she never blinked. I couldn't see down into her eyes. It was like riding around with a store mannequin. People shouldn't have eyes as pale as that. But she's like that all the way through. Too pale. What's human in her got washed out. Bleached away." West linked his hands together and studied them. Perhaps he had had to hold hands with Lannie. Perhaps he had scrubbed them to get the Lannie off. "She'll freeze Tuesday," said West.

"Why Tuesday?" said Meghan. "Why not me?"

West played with the broken door handles. The wind raked through the open cab door and chewed on Meghan's cheeks like rats.

Meghan thought: because West would risk me. He would call her bluff on his neighbor Meghan. But he would never call her bluff on his sister Tuesday. Tuesday matters.

West went in stages with his family. There were times he could hardly bear having a younger sister and brother. There were times he hated their dumb names and wished somebody would adopt them, or send them to boarding school. There were times when he and Tuesday and Brown bickered steadily, hitting each other, throwing things, being obnoxious.

But he loved them.

"Lannie is jealous of us," said West slowly. "We Trevors — our family works. We get along. We talk, we hug, we fight, we have supper, we share, we bicker. It works. We're a close family."

I'm jealous, too, thought Meghan. How weird that I can understand Lannie in that. Meghan thought of Lannie's cold cold eyes growing hot as tropical fever.

"Lannie is alone," said West. "She's always been alone. And she's tired of it. She's chosen me."

There was a strange timbre in West's voice, like an instrument being tuned. *She's chosen me.* Could he be proud? Could he feel singled out for an honor? That Lannie had chosen him?

"She wants an excuse, Meggie-Megs," said West softly. "She's ready to freeze somebody. I can't give her an excuse."

"Just stop her!"

"How?"

The little word sat in the cold night air and waited for an answer.

But there was none.

No parent, no police officer, no principal could prevent Lannie from touching somebody she wanted to touch. No bribe, no gift, no promise could ease Lannie's requirement. She wanted West.

"What about Friday night?" said Meghan at last.

Friday night they were going to a dance. West had never taken a girl to a dance. He'd attended plenty of them, of course. It was something to do. He didn't object to dances as an event. He'd go, and hang out with the boys, and do something dumb like hang off the basketball hoop, and bend it, and get in trouble, and have to pay for repairs.

But he wouldn't dance.

West knew all the top songs. He knew all the good groups. He owned all the best cassettes and CDs.

But he wouldn't dance.

He was a senior, and as far as Meghan was concerned, you could not have a senior year without dances.

There were to be raffles and games and prizes. There was a DJ (nobody wanted a band; they never played the songs right) and the chaperones were somebody else's parents. That was key. A good dance never had your own parents there. There was even a dress code this time: dresses for girls and a shirt tucked in with a tie for boys. Meghan could hardly wait.

"You have to understand," said West Trevor.

He meant he was not taking Meghan to the dance. Meghan could have overturned the truck on top of him. "Lannie won't freeze Tuesday!" shouted Meghan. "She knows you won't go out with her if she freezes your own sister!"

West swallowed. Meghan could hear the swallow. Thick and difficult. "She said she would."

If Meghan cried, West would not comfort her.

He was frozen in his own worries: he had to protect his little sister. That was first with him.

I want to be first! thought Meghan.

She slid away from him, and jerked open the handle on the passenger door. The handle being broken, of course it didn't work. She tried to roll down the window so she could open the door from the outside. That handle didn't work either. She fumbled and muttered instead of storming away. There was nothing worse than a slamming exit — and no door to go out of. Eventually she had to look back at West.

He was laughing.

"You bum," said Meghan. She absolutely hated being laughed at.

West's grief and confusion evaporated. His long crosswise grin split his face. His head tipped back with the laugh he was choking on. He had never been more handsome. "Don't be mad," he said. His hands unzipped her heavy jacket. "So I have to take Lannie to some old dance." His hands tugged at Meghan's thick sweater. "Big deal," said West. He leaned forward, hands and lips exploring. "I'll wear Lannie down somehow," he promised, "and get rid of her. It'll be us again, okay?"

The cold and the wind were forgotten. The torn seat and the broken handles meant nothing. The heat of their bodies left them breathless and desperate.

Yes, yes, it was okay! What was Lannie Anveill, against the strength of true love?

Meghan's adoration for West was so great it

seemed impossible they could survive the pressure; they would explode with loving each other. Her arms encircled his broad chest in the tightest, most satisfying embrace.

More, thought Meghan Moore, more, more, more, more, I will never have enough of you, West. More. More.

A thin white hand ran through West's hair and resettled it gently behind his ear.

The hand was not Meghan's.

A long narrow fingernail traced West's profile and stopped lightly on his lip.

The finger was not Meghan's.

A wrist as bony as a corpse inserted itself gracefully, slowly, between West's face and Meghan's. Fingers like falling snow brushed lightly on Meghan's cheeks.

"He's mine," whispered Lannie Anveill in Meghan's ear.

Meghan heard, but saw only mistily.

She felt, but through many layers.

Neither West nor Meghan moved away from each other. But there was no more heat between them. Their excitement had been iced over. They might have been anesthetized, waiting for some terrible surgery.

The only thing that moved was Lannie's hand, stroking here, touching there.

Lannie covered her victims like a snowdrift with her hatred for one, and her love for the other.

The game of Freeze Tag had gone on.

Lannie was still It.

Chapter 6

Winter wind prowled over Dark Fern Lane.

Snow crept behind shutters and blanketed steps.

Cars left in driveways were rounded white monuments, casting fat meaningless shadows where streetlights touched them.

In the yellow halos beneath the streetlights, snow seemed not to fall, but to hang, separate flakes caught in time. Listening.

Listening to what?

Dark Fern Lane was full of listeners.

Tuesday Trevor was so wide awake it felt like a disease.

Her eyes strained to climb out of their sockets.

Her lungs tried to turn themselves inside out.

Her blood circulated in marathons.

What is the matter with me? thought Tuesday. Her heart revved, and raced, and took corners on two wheels.

After a long time, Tuesday got out of bed. Silently she walked down the narrow hall to the boys' room. The door was cracked, in order that West could slip back in without making noise. Without making noise, Tuesday opened her brothers' door all the way.

West was not back.

Tuesday crossed the dark bedroom without bumping into anything. Since the windows looked out only onto yards and woods, her brothers never pulled the shades down. She looked out their window. Snow was falling. West's footprints in the old snow were covered now. She knew he was in the Chevy but nobody else would. If search parties went out, they would not think of the truck. How long had he been out there? Her heart revved again, fueled by worry.

"Do you think they're all right?" whispered Brown.

Tuesday jumped a foot. She'd been sure he was asleep. She shrugged.

She said, trying to sound knowledgeable, "I guess they're having fun."

"It's awfully cold out to have that much fun," said Brown.

Tuesday and Brown felt weird thinking about their own brother with their own best friend Meghan.

"Gag me with a spoon," said Brown, who hoped that when he was a high school senior he would not disgrace himself like that.

Tuesday had to deep breathe twice in order to say her next sentence out loud. "Lannie's there, too."

Brown sat up. "You saw her light go on?"

"I saw her cross the street."

Brown was full of admiration. Nobody ever saw Lannie cross the street. She just vanished and then reappeared.

"She loves West," said Tuesday.

"She always has. Talk about making me gag. I think we'd have to give West over to terrorists for a hostage if he ever loved Lannie back."

"Lannie's the terrorist," said Tuesday. I am terrorized, thought Tuesday. "Let's go down to the yard and check on them," she said.

"Yeah, but . . . what if . . . West and Meghan . . . you know . . . like . . . ick," said Brown.

What did Lannie have to do with it? Why was Lannie out there in the snow at one in the morning?

"Something happened in school," said Tuesday. How odd her voice sounded. Like somebody else's. She tried to catch her voice and bring it home. "This girl. In the cafeteria. At first everybody thought it was an unexplained paralysis. A girl named Jodie. But then somebody said it was Jennifer, and she had fallen down and broken her spine. And then somebody else was sure it was Jacqueline and she had a fever and some virus attacked her brain and turned her stiff as a board."

"Get to the point," said Brown.

"It was some girl, okay? And Lannie froze her. The way she did that time when we were little and Freeze Tag was real."

"It was never real," said Brown.

"Then why are you pulling the covers back up? It's because you remember that night, Brown."

"Do not."

"Do so." Tuesday looked back out onto the snow. The wind caught and threw it, as if the wind were having a snowball fight with its friends. The backyard tilted downhill, and vanished into the dark. A cliff to the unknown.

Tuesday stared at her little brother. He stared back.

"Okay," said Brown. "Let's go look. But it's going to be tough living with West if it turns out we're just interrupting the good parts."

The door of the truck cab was open.

Lannie was swinging on it, pushing herself back and forth with one small foot. She was smiling as she looked inside.

She knew Tuesday and Brown had joined her but she did not look at them. She was too pleased by the inside of the Chevy.

Brown took Tuesday's hand. She was glad to grip it. They did not let themselves touch Lannie. They peered into the truck.

Two statues. As cold and white as marble.

Carved in a half embrace; lips not quite touching; eyes not quite closed.

Lannie chuckled. "Hello, Tuesday," said Lannie. "Hello, Brown."

The snow ceased to fall. The wind ceased to blow. The world was smooth and pure and white. It lay soft and glittering and glowing on all sides.

"Are they dead?" whispered Brown.

"Just frozen." The chuckle was full of rage.

I have to reason with her, thought Tuesday. I remember that night in the grass. The last time we ever played Freeze Tag. West reasoned with her. He told her he was impressed. "I'm impressed, Lannie," said Tuesday. "They look very real."

Lannie favored Tuesday with a look of disgust. "They are real. They are your brother and your neighbor." She made "neighbor" sound like "roadkill."

"They'll die if they're left out here," said Tuesday.

"If they wanted to stay inside, they should have," said Lannie. "He promised to like me best." Her voice was slight, and yet filling, like a very sweet dessert. "He broke his promise."

Tuesday wet her lips. Mistake. The winter wind penetrated every wrinkle, chapping them. "Let's give West a second chance," said Tuesday. She had to look away from her frozen brother. "He'll keep his promise now." She wondered if West could hear her, deep inside his ice. Could he hear, would he listen, would he obey? It was his life.

"They didn't believe I could do it."

Tuesday suffocated in the sweetness of Lannie's tiny voice. "I believed you," said Tuesday quickly. She smiled, trying to look like an ally, a friend, a person whose brother was worth rescuing.

Brown was not willing to cater to Lannie. "You're a pain, Lannie," he said angrily. "You don't have any right to scare people."

"But people," said Lannie, smiling, "are right to be scared." Her hair was thin and did not lie down flat, but stuck out of her head in dry pale clumps.

"Undo them right this minute," said Brown. "Or I'll go and get my mother and father."

Lannie laughed out loud. "It won't be the first time in history two dumb teenagers froze to death while necking in a stupid place at a stupid time."

"Or call 911," said Brown. "They'll save them."

"No," said Lannie gently. "They can't."

Even Lannie's words could freeze. Tuesday's leaping lungs and throbbing heart went into slow motion, and her skipping mind fell down. No. Rescue teams cannot save them. Our mother and father cannot save them. That terrible little phrase "froze to death" hung in front of all Tuesday's thoughts like an icicle hanging off a porch.

At first Tuesday was going to say, *Brown and I will do anything you want, anything at all, if only you'll undo West and Meghan.* But she thought better of it. What promise would Lannie extract? What kind of terrible corner would Brown and Tuesday be in then?

So she said, "You love him, Lannie. He's better alive. Much more fun."

"He broke his promise."

"But he's learned his lesson now. He's in there now, listening. He's ready, Lannie."

Lannie appeared to consider it. Her eyes shifted from hot to cold like faucets in the shower. "I love doing this," she told Tuesday at last. Her voice was curiously rich.

Rich with what?

Desire, thought Tuesday. Not for West, and yet

it was desire. An unstoppable desire to cause hurt.

The texture of the snow changed.

It became very soft, like an old cozy blanket.

The moon shone through the thin moving clouds, and the snow sparkled in the darkness of night.

The temperature dropped like a falling stone.

She has to undo them! thought Tuesday. What can I offer her? What do I have? My brother! My best friend!

Tuesday scraped through her mind, hunting for anything, the barest scrap, to offer Lannie Anveill.

Lannie swung on the truck door again, making a wide smooth pocket in the snowdrifts. She might have been a six-year-old at a birthday party. Any minute she might lie down in the snow and make an angel.

Lannie. An angel.

Tuesday did not let herself fall into hysteria. She said brightly, "I know, Lannie! You can come to the JV cheerleader slumber party!" Her voice was stacked with false enthusiasm. "At our house! And we'll have a great time."

Lannie stopped swinging. She looked briefly at Tuesday, and briefly into the truck.

"But not Meghan," added Tuesday quickly. "She won't get to come. Only you."

Lannie tilted her head.

"All you have to do is unfreeze them," coaxed Tuesday. She made her voice rich, too. Desire for Lannie's company. Desire to be a friend to Lannie. "And you'll have a boyfriend, a dance, and a party, Lannie. All coming up soon. Won't it be fun?"

Brown was staring at his sister as if they had never met before.

"Well," said Lannie finally.

"Great!" cried Tuesday. "You're going to undo them! You're coming to my party!"

"I'll undo West," said Lannie. "Meghan stays."

Chapter 7

"Only," said West, "if you bring Meghan back, too."

His voice swirled in the dark. It did not seem like a voice at all, but like a wind, a separate wind. A dervish, perhaps.

Meghan lay frozen, stiff against the seats and the dashboard and the broken handles. Snow falling through the open door of the truck rested on her face. She could not feel its touch but she knew its weight. It was drifting around the hollows of her cheeks and eyes. Soon she would not be visible, she would be one with the rest of the blanketed world.

A statue forgotten until spring.

"No," said Lannie. Her voice was no longer rich with hurtful desire. It was a statement voice, a voice for making lists and issuing decrees.

No.

It was a forever "No." A "No" which would not change, which could not be bought, or compromised, or threatened. It was a real "No."

She was not going to undo Meghan Moore.

I am frozen, thought Meghan.

It was queer the way her thoughts could continue, and yet on some level they, too, were frozen. She did not feel great emotion: there was no terrible grief that her young life had stopped short. There was no terrifying worry about whatever was to come — a new life, a death, or simply the still snowy continuance of this condition. There was simply observation and attention.

It's like being a tree, Meghan thought. I'm here. I have my branches. I have my roots. But my sap no longer runs. I weep not. I laugh not. I simply wait. And if the seasons change, I live again, and if the seasons do not, I die.

She was surprised to feel no fear. She had been so fearful of Lannie before. Perhaps fear, too, froze. Or perhaps there had never been anything to be afraid of.

West shook his head. "Then it's off, Lannie."

What's off? thought Meghan. What did I miss, being a tree?

She could see very little now. The snow lay right on her open eyes. There was only a yellow hole in the black of the night. It was the nightlight shining out of Tuesday's bedroom window.

Nightlight, thought Meghan. What a pretty thought. The real night, this night, this night I am going to have forever — it has no lights.

She would be in the dark very soon.

The dark always. The dark completely. The dark forever.

"I don't want Meghan back," explained Lannie. "I like her frozen. She's fun to freeze. She knows it's coming, you see. It's much more fun when they see it coming, and they know what's going to happen." Lannie chuckled. "I like it when they get scared and you can see it in their eyes."

Yes, thought Meghan. I was scared enough for her. I screamed loud enough to bring armies, but armies didn't come. The snow soaked up my scream. The snow and West's embrace. I screamed into his chest. I don't know if he screamed or not. We stopped moving so fast.

"Now my mother," continued Lannie, "she didn't know." This was clearly a loss to Lannie. She had wanted her mother to know. Meghan found that she could be even colder, that her heart could still shiver, with the horror of Lannie Anveill.

"And that girl in the cafeteria," said Lannie sorrowfully, "of course she didn't know what was coming either."

The glaze on Meghan's eyes was greater. The snow lay on them and didn't melt. Meghan didn't blink. The yellow nightlight from Tuesday's room up on the slope grew dim and vanished completely.

"But Meghan," Lannie went on contentedly, "she knew. She watched my finger move closer."

Lannie's voice thickened with pleasure. Tuesday whimpered. Meghan wondered how long she would be able to hear. Were her ears going to freeze now, too?

"And closer!" breathed Lannie hotly. "My finger moved only an inch and it moved slowly. Like the blade of a guillotine coming down on her throat.

And Meghan knew what would happen and she was afraid."

Meghan could see nothing at all now, would never see anything again, but she knew that Lannie smiled. She knew the exact shape and texture of that smile. She knew it was the closest Lannie Anveill could come to happiness.

West's voice shook. Meghan loved him for that. She wished that West could know he was still loved. West said, "I will like you best, Lannie." His voice shook even harder. "But not if you leave Meghan out here in the snow."

Lannie sniffed. This noise did not fit the dark and the falling snow and the fear. For Lannie, fear and falling were perfectly normal, and so she sniffed, annoyed, calling West Trevor's bluff.

"And that's that," said West.

Lannie did not undo Meghan. It had been a forever "No." West had simply not understood. Meghan had. She lay quietly under her blanket of snow.

"Come on, Brown," said West. "Come on, Tuesday. School tomorrow. We have to get some sleep."

Meghan heard the snow crunch under their departing feet as West shepherded his younger brother and sister up the hill toward the house.

She heard no voices.

Neither Tuesday nor Brown argued with their brother.

They left her.

They walked on into the warmth and the safety and light.

Now the missing emotions came: they slid like a glacier falling off an alp. Meghan fell a great terrible distance into greater fear than she had ever believed existed. She was alone. Only Lannie Anveill stood beside her. She was cold. There was no warmth anywhere. She was lost. There was no rescue in this world.

Meghan's body lacked the capacity to reflect her agonies. She wept, but without tears. She shuddered, but without shaking. She screamed, but without sound.

Her only friends — the only ones who knew — who cared — Tuesday and Brown and West — *they had left her.*

Something besides her flesh froze.

She had fallen, truly fallen, heart and mind and soul and body, into Lannie's clutches.

Lannie had clutched her once, with only one finger, and would never have to clutch her again. Nature would do the rest.

Meghan's soul wept for the ending of her life, for the grief her parents would feel, for all those years she would never have, all those joys and hopes and frustrations she would never taste.

Lannie stomped her little foot in the snow. It made a pathetic little noise in the greatness of the night. "I thought he was bluffing," she said angrily. "I didn't think he'd actually leave you here in the snow, Meghan."

She knows I can hear her, thought Meghan. How does she know that?

She has frozen and tortured others before me.

She will freeze and torture more in the future.

Lannie kicked the snow around, like a little kid sulking in her room.

She doesn't really have much power, thought Meghan. Power is hers just one fingertip at a time, so to speak. West walked away, and he's gone, and she lost her game.

And I — I lost, too.

"Oh, all right," said Lannie. Disagreeably, as if she had been asked to share a small piece of cake. "All right!" she yelled up the hill at West. "Are you listening? I said, all right!"

All right, what? thought Meghan. She was very, very cold. She was not going to have many more thoughts. Or many more minutes. So it didn't really matter.

Lannie poked her in the side. It was a jab, actually, again like a little kid sulking — pinching the other kids because she wasn't getting enough attention.

Meghan's hand was moving. Brushing the snow off her eyes. She was shaking her hair. Struggling to get up. Bumping the narrow confines of the dumb, awful, cold, stupid truck.

Memory sifted away, leaving her with only bits and pieces of what had happened.

What am I doing here? she thought.

January? Meghan looked at her watch. She had to scrape off a crust of ice with her nail. One in the morning? And I'm out playing stupid games in a rusty truck in a snowstorm?

Meghan was so cold she really was frozen. She

was unable to gather herself up. She floundered, but did not manage to accomplish anything.

"Fine, stay there," said Lannie.

Oh, yes. Lannie. Lannie who liked to see them shiver before she froze them. Lannie who liked her victims to know.

Meghan remembered.

And then West's arms were around her. He was sliding her out the door, lifting her in his arms like a baby, warming her with his embrace.

Oh, West! West! You did come back for me! Her lips were very cold, but his were very warm, and when they met she melted a little, and smiled a little, and was safe a little.

You lose, Lannie, thought Meghan.

From the lovely protection of West's arms, from the sweet cradle of his holding her, she looked clearly at Lannie. It was the first time since she had been frozen that she could really see.

Perhaps it was not a good thing to see reality clearly. Reality was frightening. For Lannie Anveill stood very still. And very jealous.

And very close.

And her hand — that hand Meghan had watched descending so slowly — that hand was lifted like a weapon.

Not pointing at Meghan.

Not pointing at West.

But at Tuesday.

Tuesday stood very still, as if she'd met a deadly snake on a forest path. Been trapped by a mad dog. Threatened by a mad bomber.

Perhaps she was.

Perhaps Lannie was all three of those.

Lannie's eyes, bleached of humanity, focused dead and glassy on West. "Well?" she said.

West set Meghan down in the snow. He stepped away from her. "I'm sorry," he said to Lannie.

She did not accept the apology. Her hand remained extended, only half an inch now from Tuesday's bare cheek. And Tuesday knew what was coming. And Tuesday flinched. And Lannie chuckled.

"It was just habit," said West.

Lannie regarded him stonily. "You were going to carry her home."

What made me think that love could conquer evil? thought Meghan. What stupidity persuaded me that because West and I love each other, everything will be all right?

A cracked smile pasted itself on West's face. He was splintered and broken. But this was his baby sister. This was his family.

"You know what I'd like, Lannie?" he said. His smile was in a hundred pieces. But he flirted anyway.

"What?" said Lannie, testing him.

"I'd like to carry *you* home." His smile solidified and became real. He took a step toward Lannie. She lowered her hand. He took another step toward Lannie. She smiled at him. Meghan wanted to gag, but West smiled even more widely.

He picked Lannie up easily. She appeared to weigh nothing.

As if she were not a person at all, thought Meghan, but a husk of one. Stuffed with hay instead of flesh and bone. Perhaps that dry straw hair is her stuffing coming out.

West did not glance at his sister, his brother, or his girlfriend. He carried Lannie diagonally up the sloping backyard, heading toward her house. They both laughed now. What joke could they possibly be sharing?

West waded through a drift that reached his thighs. Lannie dragged her hand through it, leaving trails of long thin fingers.

"Are you okay, Meghan?" whispered Tuesday.

Oh, sure, thought Meghan. Fine. I go through this sort of thing all the time and it never leaves a mark.

And then she thought, If I can laugh at it, maybe I am okay. But will West be okay? What has he just promised? What have we just gotten ourselves into?

Brown, being younger, was on another subject entirely. "Nobody else woke up," marveled Brown, staring at the houses on Dark Fern Lane.

But the parents had never woken up to Lannie. They went on feeling sorry for her, because she had never been loved.

There was a reason for that, thought Meghan Moore. Lannie is not loveable. She is only hateable.

West was a silhouette in the dark, climbing and crunching the snow. Lannie in his arms was a pair of boots sticking out on one side, and wispy hair and dangling scarf on the other.

What is her power? thought Meghan. Did she

always have it? Who gave it to her? What evil force was her real parent?

It gave Meghan some peace to know that Mrs. Anveill, whatever she might have deserved, had at least not known what was coming. It was good that Lannie's mother had driven that Jaguar so fast she did not know she was to be frozen forever.

What was this game of Freeze Tag?

Was it truly *forever*?

Did Lannie have West *forever*?

Could Lannie hold the neighborhood hostage *forever*?

Chapter 8

In the days that followed, Meghan found out how cold it is to be without best friends.

How frozen you are when you are frozen out of love.

West never looked at her. Not once. Perhaps he did not dare. Perhaps Lannie had given an order and he knew the consequences were too terrible. But oh! how Meghan would have liked a phone call. A note. A single sad look across a room. Just so they could say: *yes, it happened; it hurts; we're afraid; we're apart.*

But West did not try to communicate with Meghan. Over and over she told herself: he's protecting me, he knows what Lannie will do if he so much as raises an eyebrow in my direction. But Meghan was not sure. Girls in love are never sure.

Bad as that was, not having a best girlfriend was even worse. For you could always count on your next-door-neighbor girlfriend. You could say anything and everything to each other, and you always did.

Tuesday never looked at Meghan either. She had that party after all: the JV cheerleader slumber party. And Meghan was not part of the preparation, and not part of the afterglow. Meghan was alone.

Tuesday's protecting me, too, Meghan told herself. It's my face Lannie's hand touched: the hand that holds freezing in its palm.

But Meghan Moore did not feel protected. She felt terribly, terribly alone. Abandoned and deserted. Without a friend in the world.

After school, when West had the use of his mother's car, it was Lannie who got in the front seat with him and drove away. It was Lannie who met him at his locker. Sat with him during his lunch. Telephoned him in the evening.

But it was Meghan who was supposed to make explanations to the world. Nobody wanted to walk up to West and say, "What are you doing, are you insane, have you lost your mind?" and nobody would have dreamed of walking up to Lannie.

West's best friend, Richard, who found girls a little unnerving at the best of times and preferred them to stay on their side of the room, actually sought Meghan out. "So what's going on? *Lannie? Is West crazy?*"

Meghan did not know what to say. What explanation was she supposed to give? The real one was too absurd. Nobody would believe it. They would say Meghan was the crazy one. So she said nothing and her eyes filled with tears because she did not know how to gather allies and mount an army against Lannie Anveill.

Richard said, "He was supposed to be restoring his Chevy this winter. I was going to work on it with him. It was bad enough that right after football he started *dating* all the time." This meant Meghan. Richard employed the word "dating" as if West had started selling military secrets to the enemy and should be shot. "But now — Lannie!" said Richard. "She has to be the creepiest person I've ever known in my life."

"I agree," said Meghan glumly.

"But after you?" said Richard, trying to get a grip on this girl thing.

Meghan said nothing.

Richard said, "Well. West and I were supposed to go to the big car graveyard down in Bridgeport, and find parts for his truck. We were going to look for handles so he can repair his, and open the doors from the inside. And Lannie said that didn't interest her, and West said he'd see her tomorrow then, and Lannie said, 'No, you'll see me today,' and West said, 'Fine.' Do you believe that? He didn't even argue with her? He's going to stay with her instead of going to the car graveyard with me?" Richard was scandalized. "At least when he dated you," said Richard, "he also would do normal things."

Meghan managed a real smile.

"What is there to smile about?" said Richard.

But it was impossible to explain.

Then there was Valerie. Valerie was a lovely girl, a junior, the year between Meghan and West. Valerie, too, had always had a crush on West. She was pretty relaxed about it, and teased herself, and asked Meghan for dating details so she could pretend it was herself dating West. Valerie took one look at Lannie on West's arm and said to Meghan, "What is going on here? I mean, I thought at least if he dumped you, he'd take me! But no — he's going out with that pale-faced shrimpette from the zoo."

"Don't let her hear you say that," said Meghan. She looked around fearfully. A girl who would send her mother to a frozen death in a Jaguar would certainly do the same to a Valerie about whom she did not care at all.

"Everybody says that!" cried Valerie. "She is *so* strange."

Meghan nodded.

"What does West see in her?" demanded Valerie. "He took her to Pizza Hut, Meghan! I mean, he was willing to be seen in public with that girl."

Eating off the same pizza wedge. It was enough to make you want to cram it in their faces, thought Meghan.

And then there was Su-Ann. Su-Ann, not Meghan's favorite classmate by any means, said with a snide smile, "Second half of West's senior year, Meghan, and it looks like you're out of the picture. No senior prom for you, huh, babe?"

Meghan said nothing.

"Back to riding the schoolbus like a peasant, huh, babe?" said Su-Ann. "No more rides from the cute boyfriend, huh, babe?"

"Don't call me babe," said Meghan. "Don't call me anything. Get away from me."

"Sure," said Su-Ann easily. "Like the rest of the crowd."

Su-Ann left Meghan alone.

Everybody, it seemed, was leaving Meghan alone. She was so lonely she could have wept all day every day. She wanted to talk to West, and ask what it felt like to be near Lannie like that, and what they were going to do about it. She wanted to talk to Tuesday, and ask what West was like to live with now, and what Mr. and Mrs. Trevor said, and what would happen next?

She wanted to be on a team.

She wanted to fight back.

But how did you fight a Lannie?

If West, who could wrestle and tackle, could not fight, how could Meghan? What was the weapon?

Was there a weapon?

"Hello, darling," said her mother. The kiss they always shared rested gently on Meghan's cheek. "How was your day?"

Meghan could not help it. Her eyes filled with tears.

"Sweetie!" said her mother. "Tell Mommy. What's wrong?"

Mommy. As if she had called her mother Mommy since second grade. "It's West," said Meghan.

"I know. Breaking up is so awful. Has he hurt you? Do you want me to kill him?"

Meghan managed a giggle. "I don't want him killed. I just — "

Just what? Meghan did not even know. Whenever she saw Lannie, she remembered, and she believed, and the frozen horror of the girl sapped Meghan's strength and turned her knees to jelly. But when she was not around Lannie, it was all impossible, and she was embarrassed, and felt stupid and hopeless.

They went down the hall together to the bedroom so her mother could take off her shoes. This was always first priority at the end of a workday. Mrs. Moore kicked off the high heels, wiggled her bare toes in the carpeting and said, "Aaaahhhhhhhhh."

"Why don't you get a job where you can wear sneakers, Mom?"

"I hate sneakers. I love high heels. I love shoes. I love being dressed up. I even love work. It just involves a certain sacrifice, that's all." Her mother kissed her again. "Now tell me everything." They flopped back on the king-sized bed, shoulders and heads hitting the fluffy rank of pillows at the same instant. Staring up at the ceiling, they snuggled their sides together.

Meghan suddenly remembered a thousand snuggles like this.

A thousand days after daycare in which she and her mother had bed-flopped to share heartaches and triumphs.

On cold days they pulled a comforter up over themselves and on hot days they turned the fan straight into their faces, so their hair blew up onto the headboard.

Meghan suddenly remembered the purse her mother used to have when Meghan was little. Oh, it was practically a suitcase. Mrs. Moore practically needed wheels to move it. How many days had her mother reached down into the capacious bottom of that handbag, and made all kinds of excited noises and raised her eyebrows and twitched her lips and said, "*What* do I have in *here*?" while the little Meghan waited, full of anticipation. And each day, a tiny treat: a single chocolate kiss, a package of bright colored paper clips, the monogrammed paper napkin from a restaurant or a giveaway vial of perfume from the department store.

How thrilled Meghan had always been.

When you were little, it only took a little.

But I never wanted to be here, thought Meghan. I always wanted to be over at the Trevors'. What was the matter with me? Home was wonderful. Why was I so sure theirs was more wonderful?

"Mom? Did it ever bother you that I spent so much time at the Trevors'?"

"Oh, yes. It bothered your father more, though. I knew you needed the company. You're very sociable. You like noise and people. There aren't enough of us here, and your father and I are too quiet for you. It used to hurt Daddy's feelings terribly that the instant we finished dinner you'd bolt out the door and go to the Trevors', where things were fun."

"Did it hurt your feelings?"

"In a way. I always wished the neighborhood kids would come here for a change. Sometimes I'd stock up on Popsicles or candy popcorn or jelly doughnuts and hope I'd be the one who got the kids, but I never was."

Meghan had always thought her mother disliked the mess of visitors. She turned on the bed to stare at her mother. They never did this. They seemed to talk most easily staring upward at the ceiling and not at each other. How pretty her own mother was. What a nice profile she had.

Why did I want Mrs. Trevor all this time? thought Meghan, and she was suffused with guilt. She buried herself against her mother's warm hug and they lay softly on the bed without speaking.

After a long time the lump in Meghan's throat went away.

She had told her mother nothing. She had said nothing about the horror of Lannie, and the taking of West, and the freezing of her own flesh. And yet, she was so comforted! Her mother was so solid. So there. So safe.

So *mine*, thought Meghan.

She knew with a stab of understanding that she had been able to spend such huge amounts of time at other people's houses because she had known absolutely that her parents would love her anyway. She had been safe doing anything at all. Safe in love.

And Lannie. . . .

What had Lannie been?

Unsafe.

Without love. Without even a molecule of love.

Unsafe.

If you are not brought up in the safety of love, thought Meghan Moore, you yourself become unsafe. It is unsafe to be near Lannie. She is as dangerous as a collapsing bridge or a caving-in cliff. All because of love.

"Ohmygosh!" said Meghan, remembering things out of nowhere, the way your mind does sometimes, all on its own. "Mom, don't you have a meeting tonight? We haven't even thought about supper! You're late! You haven't even changed yet! Ohmygosh!"

Her mother said. "It's only a meeting. You and I needed a hug. We haven't had a good long hug in ages."

Meghan's eyes filled with tears. Her mother had been there, waiting for this hug, and Meghan hadn't been home.

"It'll be okay in the end, darling," said her mother softly, lips moving against Meghan's hair as she squeezed her daughter. "I'm so sorry you're having trouble with West. I know you've always adored him. I know how it must hurt. But you'll tough it out. You're my strong girl. You'll do the right thing. You'll make it."

Chapter 9

Meghan *was* strong. But to be strong alone — it was hard.

She wanted to be strong together!

After two weeks of being discarded like something you can't even recycle in the garbage, Meghan went over to the Trevors' after school just the way she always had. She had the courage to do this only because she knew that West had his mother's car that day, and she had seen him drive away after school with Lannie, and the car was not back. So only Tuesday would be there, and possibly Brown, if he didn't have sports.

Meghan didn't knock. She had never knocked at the Trevors', just walked in. "Hi, Tues," she said nervously.

Tuesday leaped up from the television. She raced across the room and flung her arms around Meghan. "I'm so glad you're here!"

There. That was the welcome and those were the words. Some of the leftover frozenness in Meghan's lonely heart eased.

"It's been so weird," said Tuesday. "West doesn't talk to anybody. Not me, not Brown, not Mom, not Dad. I guess he uses up all his speech and energy with Lannie and he comes home this drained-out old thing. Sits over his homework without seeing the page, without lifting the pencil. Mom and Dad are beside themselves. You won't believe this, but they think he's lovesick."

"Over Lannie?"

Tuesday nodded. "Over Lannie. Brown and I tried to inch into an explanation that the sick one is Lannie, and the trapped one is West, and the one in danger is you. But you know parents. Even mine. They just got annoyed and stomped around when we reached the Freeze Tag part. West didn't like it either. He wouldn't even back us up. He just looked at his hands and said he didn't know what we were talking about."

Looked at his hands, thought Meghan. Why his own hands? Did Lannie pass it on? Can he do it, too, now? She swallowed, trying to gag down this horrible image. "I didn't even try with my parents," she said. She checked the window. There were no cars approaching. All they needed was for West and Lannie to drive up while she was on the premises.

"West had to take her to the library," said Tuesday.

"She studies?"

"She says so," Tuesday shrugged. "She's attached herself to him like a starfish to a rock."

"How can he stand it?" Meghan could not bear it

that West was managing. Was there something redeemable in Lannie that West had managed to find? If anybody was going to find good things in an evil person, it would be a Trevor. They were big on silver linings.

Mr. Trevor came in. He got out of work at about the same time the kids got out of school, so he was usually home in the afternoons. "Hey there, Meggie-Megs!" he said, much too heartily. "Say! We haven't seen much of you lately. How've you been, kid?"

"Fine," said Meghan, because what other answer could you give a grown-up?

"Sorry you and West sort of split up," muttered Mr. Trevor.

Meghan said nothing.

"They didn't sort of split up," said Tuesday. "Lannie forced herself on West."

Mr. Trevor did not look as if he believed that. Clearly, he believed it took two to tango; if West was dating Lannie, it was because West wanted to date Lannie.

"Lannie stinks," said Tuesday, laying it on the line.

"I'm sorry," said her father, addressing both girls, "that this turn of events has happened, but life is like that when you're young. You fall in love lots of times with lots of different people. So let's not say anything unpleasant about West's girlfriend."

Tuesday threw her arms in the air. "Let's," she

said. "Let's say lots and lots of unpleasant stuff about West's girlfriend. And then let's *do* something unpleasant to West's girlfriend."

Mr. Trevor frowned and left the room.

But Tuesday and Meghan grinned at each other. The grin of conspirators. Allies. Teams. They even winked.

"I'm staying at the Trevors' for supper, Mom," said Meghan into the telephone. "And I'll be studying with Tuesday. I'll be home around ten, okay?"

"That's pretty late for a school night," said her mother. "How about nine?"

Nine. Meghan wasn't sure it was going to be manageable before nine. "Fine," she said to her mother. "I'll be home by nine."

The thought of crossing the open space between the houses after dark was so scary Meghan almost quit right then. She would have Lannie's eyes following her, Lannie's knowledge, Lannie's plans.

"You can crawl across the grass the way they do in desert warfare," suggested Tuesday, giggling. "Belly flat, head down, bullets whizzing through your hair."

For Tuesday it had become fun. An adventure.

But then, Tues wasn't the one who had been frozen in the truck. Tuesday hadn't felt snow piling up on her open eyes. Tuesday hadn't felt the cold passing into her heart, taking her into another world.

Tuesday's pretty bed jutted out into the room, leaving a space between the hanging bedspread and

274

the wall. From the doorway you could not see down into that space. Meghan unrolled the sleeping bag in which she had spent so many nights and lay down, hidden. The afternoon grew dark. Tuesday and her brothers and parents had dinner. They made a lot of noise. None of it was West. Five people for dinner and four talked.

But he would talk tonight.

Mr. and Mrs. Trevor would watch their favorite TV programs and the children would be sent to their desks to do homework.

Well, they would do homework. But it wouldn't be a school assignment.

Meghan stayed beneath the level of the windowsill, just in case Lannie was lurking outside, peeking, staring, thought-policing.

It was eight-fifteen before Tuesday led West into her silent unlit bedroom.

"Sit on the floor," Tuesday said to him, and burst into a spatter of giggles.

"Tues, I'm tired," he said. "I can't play games anymore. Isn't it enough I have to play this endless game with Lannie?"

Meghan crept out from behind the bed.

West stared at her. She held a finger to her lips.

He sagged in a funny way, as if he were being rescued. "Oh, Meghan!" he said, and he said nothing more, but it was enough. He sat down next to her, and Tuesday sat with them, which Meghan regretted, but then, tonight's plan did not call for a kiss. It called for strategy.

"What's going on in here?" hissed Brown.

"Crawl in," whispered Tuesday.

Brown checked out the participants. "War council!" he said delightedly, and dropped down, and crawled. He would make an excellent desert warfare soldier, he had that belly technique down perfectly.

The four of them lay on their stomachs, propping their heads up with their cupped hands.

"What," said Tuesday, "are we going to do?"

"You're asking me?" said West. "You think I've come up with something?"

"Where does Lannie get this power?" said Tuesday. "Maybe we can cut off her source."

West shook his head. "I asked her how she calls it up. I was half thinking *I* could freeze *her*. If I knew how. She said she'd stage a demonstration for me. She said she'd freeze that gym coach I don't like."

"Wonderful," said Brown.

"Exactly. I start yelling 'No, no, no, no, no!' and Lannie says to me, 'Don't worry, West, it's easy, all I have to do is touch him, you won't be involved. I'd do that for you,' she says. Like I'd be happy afterward."

"But Lannie must touch you all the time," said Tuesday. "And you don't freeze."

"She does touch me all the time. But I don't touch her. It's not so bad if I just sit there and let her do what she wants."

It sounded pretty bad to Meghan. But still, Meghan began to enjoy herself. This was nice, this meeting of the best friends, plotting in the dark, hidden by the furniture, safe from the bleached eyes.

"I give Lannie hundreds of excuses for why I can't see her every waking minute," West said. "I use sports, chorus, homework, term papers, weather, baby-sitting, Tuesday, Brown, Mom, Dad, Grandma."

"Grandma?" said Tuesday.

"I said when you're eighty years old and you're stuck in a nursing home five hundred miles away, you want to hear from your oldest grandson. I've written a lot of letters."

Meghan giggled. West's face split into the old familiar grin. Oh, she loved him so much! Okay, they were going to whip this thing. Together they were going to knock Lannie out of commission.

"You should have been here at breakfast this morning," Tuesday told Meghan. "It was so funny. Mom says to West, 'You can have the car, dear.' And West says, 'No thanks Mom,' because the last thing he wants is to be alone with Lannie yet again. And Mom goes — 'There's no such thing as a seventeen-year-old boy who doesn't want the car. Are you sick? Are you taking drugs?' So after we make our way through the no-I'm-not-on-drugs conversation, Mom wants to know the truth about why West doesn't want the car. And the best my stupid old brother can come up with is — it's tough finding a parking space."

"Oh, yeah, Mom believed that," said Brown. Tuesday and Brown burst into gales of laughter. West flushed. Meghan rested her hand on his. It was their only touch. The only touch in so long! He lowered his gaze and seemed to draw comfort from her hand. No doubt it was very different from the one that had been touching him these last weeks.

Tuesday became very businesslike. She did not want this evening to deteriorate into some sort of icky romantic thing. "I think," said Tuesday, "that you've given it enough of a shot, West. Now in the morning, you march up to Lannie and you tell Lannie it's been fun, but it's time for you to move on."

West looked at his sister incredulously. "After what she did to Meghan?"

"It's worth a try," said Tuesday.

West shook his head. "She'll hurt somebody."

"We'll keep our distance."

"She'll run after you."

"Don't be a wimp," said Tuesday sharply. "You have to let Lannie know the score. Otherwise, this could go on forever."

Tuesday made it sound so simple. Meghan tried to believe her. That West could just say, *Hey, Lan, been fun, see ya around, back to normal now, don't hurt anybody, 'kay?*

"Okay," said West, nodding, trying to give himself courage. "You're right. It can't go on forever."

Meghan ate a huge breakfast, having skipped dinner the night before. Her mother was delighted. Mothers always loved seeing you eat breakfast. Even though Meghan had fixed it herself, her mother seemed to feel she could take credit for it.

But she was not so eager to go outside.

For this was the morning. West was to tell Lannie to skip off and leave him alone. Leave them all alone.

To whom was Lannie the most dangerous?

Would she turn on West, for breaking his promise? Would she turn on Meghan, for being the one West still wanted? Would she turn on Tuesday, for being the sister who started things?

This won't work! thought Meghan. He mustn't do it! Lannie isn't going to say, oh, well, it was worth a try, have a nice life without me, West! Lannie's going to attack!

Meghan rushed to the telephone and stabbed at the familiar buttons, to call West, tell him no, no, no, no, no!

She didn't get past the second number.

West, Tuesday, and Brown were already outside. West had his mother's car keys in his hand; was unlocking the doors. Tuesday was getting in front — Lannie's place. Brown was playing Indian and hollering and whooping and generally attracting attention.

Meghan set the phone down gently. She got into her coat. She pulled on her mittens. She tightened her scarf. Perhaps Lannie's touch could not go through clothing. Perhaps wool or goosedown could save Meghan.

Right, she thought. There is no getting away from Lannie.

Meghan came out her front door.

Lannie came out hers.

The Trevor children looked up Dark Fern Lane, and saw them both.

West, Tuesday, Brown, Lannie, and Meghan all knew. This was a test. The game had reached another level. They looked at each other and, even from her front door, Meghan could feel the heat and the cold, the hatred and the love, the fear and the need.

No one else did.

Two houses up, the rest of the Dark Fern Lane children waited for the buses. There were two kindergartners at that stop, two first-graders, no second-graders, one third-grader. Then there was quite an age skip up to Brown. Lannie intended for Brown to be on that bus, not riding in the car with West and herself.

The little children played in the snow.

They pushed each other down and then got up and admired the dents their bottoms had put in the snow. They swung their lunches and bookbags in circles and let go, so the bright colored containers spun out like trajectiles and hit the others lightly. They laughed six-year-old laughs and made six-year-old jokes.

The third-grader showed off, doing a cartwheel.

The littler ones had no idea how to accomplish such a marvelous move, but they tried. They flung their legs up an inch or two and giggled proudly.

Lannie Anveill walked through them. Stringing her fingers along as if she were hanging laundry on a line.

Perhaps she was.

They froze.

The two kindergartners, the two first-graders, the one third-grader. They hung in their positions like statues.

"No," whispered Tuesday, who had started this. "No, please."

Lannie stopped midway between her statues and the Trevors. Directly in front of Meghan's. Meghan might as well have been frozen. She could not move. Could not think.

"Hi, West," said Lannie across the frozen yards.

He did not speak. Perhaps he was as terrified as Meghan.

"Your heart is not in this, West," said Lannie.

He did not move either. Had she frozen him without even touching?

"I want your heart, West," said Lannie.

There was a thick dense silence.

Lannie's smile was tiny and yet tall: her mouth opened up and down, instead of sideways, in a terrifying leer.

The five little children remained frozen in the snow. Perhaps their mothers were not looking out the window. Perhaps their mothers thought it was part of a game.

It was.

But not a game anybody should ever play.

Freeze Tag.

No, please, thought Meghan. Not the little children. Not just because I want to be the one at Pizza Hut with West. Set them free. Let them go.

"Lannie," said West. His head sank down, so that he was looking at his own chest, the front of his own winter jacket. He seemed to lose some of the vertebrae in his backbone, and grow shorter and less strong. His voice scratched. He walked toward Lannie like an old man weighted with stones.

"You have my heart," said West.

Chapter 10

"You know," said Meghan's father, "I haven't seen Jason lately."

Meghan and her mother were going through the movie listings. Once a month the Moore family had Movie Saturday. Driving to the huge, twelve movie theater that had opened a few years ago, they saw one movie at four o'clock, came out dizzy and pleased, went to have hamburgers, french fries, and shakes, and came back for a movie at seven. During the first movie they had candy and during the second movie they had popcorn.

Meghan loved Movie Day. When she watched a movie, she fell into it. It was completely real and completely absorbing. Even a bad movie was good when you saw it on a big screen. Whereas bad movies when you rented them to watch at home were just plain bad movies.

This month was a toughie: They wanted to see everything. "It's better than the months when we don't want to see anything," her mother pointed out.

"I mean, I usually at least see Jason coming and going," said Meghan's father.

Meghan had not been thinking about Lannie for several weeks now. Ever since West had had to go on his knees to beg her to unfreeze the little children at the bus stop, she had decided just not to think about it again. There was nothing she could do. Nothing anybody could do. And as long as Lannie had West, the world was safe.

You have my heart, Lannie, West had said.

Meghan didn't think about that either. It had sounded so true. You could almost see his heart, that day, red and bleeding and beating. As if he carried it over to her and set it down so she could have it.

Lannie had danced back among the children, as light as an elf on top of the snow. Flying past the little ones, she seemed hardly even to touch them. She skimmed along like a swallow in the sky.

But the children fell over in the snow, real again. There was a moment when they were all close to tears. All close to calling, *Mommy! Mommy come and get me! Mommy, something's wrong!*

But the yellow schoolbus had turned the corner, and the children lined up to get on, bickering over who deserved to get on first. Shouting about who would sit with whom. And if they crowded closer to each other for warmth, and if a short, cold memory lay like ice on the backs of their necks, they did not say so out loud.

Nobody had ever said so out loud.

If I'm not thinking about Lannie, thought Meghan, I'm certainly not thinking about Jason.

Meghan tapped on the newspaper column with her bright blue soft-tipped pen. Meghan liked to write in many colors. She liked to underline in vivid yellow. She liked to make lists in black. She liked to address envelopes in red. She liked to take notes in blue. She had written very few letters in her life, but when she considered writing one, she considered writing it in blue, too.

Mrs. Moore said, "This movie is supposed to be a really truly weepy huggy romance. I am in the mood. I want love and loss. I want finders keepers. I want rings and music."

Meghan's vow to herself never to think about it again evaporated, as it did, in fact, nearly every day. Sometimes hundreds of times a day.

I want West, thought Meghan. He is all of those. I am going to a movie with my mother and father to watch an actress pretend to be in love with an actor. A month ago, I was the lover. I was loved. And now . . .

What was happening now?

"It kind of bothers me," said Meghan's father. He circled the kitchen, wanting his women to listen. Say something. Finish up his thoughts and his sentences for him.

Not me, thought Meghan.

At last Meghan's mother responded to him. "You could go over and check," she pointed out.

But Mr. Moore and Lannie's stepfather were not actually friends. They waved over the pavement. They occasionally met in the driveway when each was polishing his car. Once or twice they had each had a beer in hand on a hot summer day and had stood talking.

Jason never seemed to have a part in the life of Dark Fern Lane.

He drove out or he drove in, but he did not drive among.

In fact, now that Meghan thought about it, what did Jason do?

Mr. Moore left the kitchen, and the long white counter over which his wife and daughter had spread the newspaper. He crossed into the living room, spread back the curtains that lay gauzily over the picture window, tucked the fern fronds out of the way, and looked diagonally across the street at Jason's house.

"There's Lannie," said Mr. Moore. "Meggie-Megs, go find out from Lannie."

Leave the safety of her house?

Walk right up to Lannie Anveill? Who froze children like used clothes for a garage sale?

Get close to Lannie? Who when she was done freezing or unfreezing would set her hand back down? As if it were not attached, but was a purse or a book she was carrying around.

Say to her: *Lannie . . . we haven't seen Jason lately.*

"What do you think could have happened to him?" said her mother lightly.

Meghan could think of one thing, anyway. But her mother was not talking to Meghan. Meghan's fingers tightened. The blue dot beneath her pen spread an amoeba of ink over the movie listings.

"He's probably just out of town," said Mr. Moore.

But Jason's job had never seemed to involve overnight travel. Besides there was Lannie. Would he leave a fourteen-year-old?

Of course, it was Lannie.

It was not as if they were talking about a normal fourteen-year-old.

And yet . . .

"Go ask Lannie, Meghan," said her mother.

Meghan did not move.

"I know you're still upset about West going out with her," said her father, as if this were pretty small of Meghan; an event so minor her father could hardly believe his daughter even *noticed* when her boyfriend dropped her. "But I want you to ask."

Meghan was against part of growing up.

There suddenly were times when she was supposed to do the hard parts, when up till now they had always fallen into her parents' laps. "You ask her," she said.

Her father sighed a little, shrugged slightly, went to his office, and shut the door.

"It certainly isn't very much for your father to ask of you," said her mother sharply. "I think it's rather unpleasant of you to refuse him such a simple request. He's worried about his neighbor and you can't even be bothered to set his mind at rest."

At rest? Since when did Lannie's answers set anybody's mind at rest?

Meghan trudged heavily down the half stairs that divided their raised ranch house in the middle. Most of the families on Dark Fern Lane had replaced the thick hairy carpet that originally covered their stairs. When she was little, Meghan had loved that old orangey-brown carpet, with its loops as thick as an old-fashioned mop. Every house had either orangey-brown or else avocado green. It made even the houses of strangers seem familiar, because you remembered the carpeting so well. The year Meghan was in sixth grade, suddenly no grown-up on Dark Fern Lane could stand the sight of shag. Carpet vans were parked on Dark Fern Lane all the time. Now everybody had sophisticated nubbly champagne wool.

The orange shag had been cozier. Shabby, but comforting.

There was something cold and businesslike about the knots of pale wool.

Plus you had to remember to wipe your feet on the doormat before you came inside, a step everybody had omitted back when they had shag carpeting.

Meghan could not waste much more time worrying over carpet. She went out the front door.

Her father was correct. Lannie was there.

Standing thin and small in her driveway.

Perhaps she was waiting for West to pick her up.

Perhaps West had just dropped her off and she was still thinking about it, staring down at his house, watching him go inside.

Meghan walked slowly across the yard. The last

snow had melted and the temperature had dropped even lower. The ground was hard as pavement, and the frozen grass crunched like breakfast cereal under her shoes.

It was difficult to imagine herself and the Trevor children young enough and carefree enough to play yard games here. It seemed decades ago, a topic for history class.

It was me, thought Meghan. There was a time when I did not know what Lannie could do.

She had put on her jacket but not mittens or hat, and the wind chewed on her exposed skin, mocking her for thinking she could come outside and live.

Meghan gathered her courage and looked straight across the street. Straight at Lannie. Firmly, without flinching, because this was not a personal thing, this was a parental order. In the game of Freeze Tag, it didn't count.

Lannie had no eyes.

Only sockets.

Meghan stopped dead, gagging, unable to walk closer.

Lannie smiled. The smile rested húmanlike under the empty sockets. The smile was full of those baby teeth, small as birdseed. Meghan had a horrible feeling that birds had already been there: feeding on the face, taking the eyes, preparing to peck at the teeth.

Then Lannie was right up next to her, so wispy and unsubstantial that Meghan felt as heavy as a truck. Who had moved? How did Lannie do this —

empty herself from one spot and fill another, without Meghan ever seeing her accomplish it?

The sockets were not empty after all.

The same old eyes, bleached out and cruel, stared up at Meghan.

Lannie smirked.

It was the smirk that brought Meghan back. Such a middle-high kind of look. An *I've got what you want* taunt. Meghan's chin lifted. She would not be intimidated. "Hello, Lannie," said Meghan.

Lannie of course said nothing. Just waited.

"My father is worried," said Meghan.

Lannie of course said nothing. Just waited.

"About Jason," said Meghan.

Lannie smiled.

"He hasn't seen Jason lately," said Meghan. Talking to Lannie was like being in a track meet. She was winded from four short sentences.

"Well," said Lannie, linking her arm in Meghan's as if they were friends. "You haven't seen Jason lately either, have you?"

Lannie's arm turned to metal. It might have been a shackle on Meghan's wrist.

"It's time you saw Jason," said Lannie softly. "Come on over to my house, Meggie-Megs." Lannie had never used the nickname. It sounded somehow evil, as if Lannie had got a hold of some essential depth in Meghan and could control it.

"I just have to tell my father where he is," said Meghan, trying to resist. But Lannie did not let go. Meghan was going with Lannie Anveill whether she wanted to or not. They walked in lockstep.

I do not want to go into that house, thought Meghan Moore. I do not want to be alone with Lannie!

Lannie, who always knew what you were thinking, knew what she was thinking. "You won't be alone with me," said Lannie. Her voice dripped ugliness. Her tiny body shuddered with taunting. "Jason is there."

Lannie escorted Meghan in her front door.

It was identical to every other front door on Dark Fern Lane. It opened onto a rectangle of fake slate tiles. Four steps led down to the family room and the garage. Nine steps led up to where the kitchen opened straight onto the stairs. The living room was at the left, with only a metal railing to keep you from falling off the couch and into the stairwell. Jason had not replaced his shag carpeting. Layers of avocado green fluff, flattened in the center from years of footsteps, climbed both ways.

Lannie did not take Meghan up to the living room or kitchen.

They went down the four stairs to the fake cork floor that covered all family rooms.

Or had. Meghan's mother and father had continued the new nubbly champagne wool all the way down and across. They had replaced the plain metal railing at the living room rim with a delicate white wooden bookcase, half solid and half see through, so books were firmly placed and special possessions were beautifully displayed.

I'm thinking so hard about my own house, thought Meghan. I'm so afraid to think about Lannie's.

They did not go into Lannie's family room either.

It occurred to Meghan that she had never been in Lannie's family room. The same rather dark half-basement room with the high windows that let in so little light — the room where most people watched TV and sorted laundry and kept the video games and the board games and the outgrown Fisher-Price toys and the piles of paperbacks and magazines.

Did Lannie have any of those?

Had any family ever gathered in that family room?

When Lannie's relatives wanted to be happy, they drove away. They got in their cars.

Perhaps it was a room for solitary confinement, instead of family.

Meghan shivered.

Lannie smiled.

They turned right, into the tiny claustrophobic hall with a laundry closet on one side, a half bath on the other, and the garage door at the end. The garage door was flimsy; hollow wood that clunked lightly when closed. Most of these doors had broken and been replaced over the years. Lannie's had not.

Lannie opened it.

The two-car garage under the bedrooms was completely dark.

Lannie flipped the electric switch and the room

was flooded with light from two overhanging fluorescent tubes.

Jason sat in his Corvette.

He had a smile on his face.

One hand on the wheel.

One hand on the gearshift.

The motor was not running. But Jason was driving. The garage had been completely dark. But Jason was driving. The garage was very very cold. But Jason was driving.

Lannie's arm dropped from Meghan's.

Meghan walked slowly toward the Corvette. Jason did not look up at her. Jason did not stop smiling. Jason did not stop driving the silent motionless car.

Between the Corvette and the leaf rakes hanging against the side of the garage, Meghan stood trapped. Lannie's bright glittering eyes pierced her like stabbing icicles. Meghan backed up, pressing herself against the cold wooden studs of the garage. "You froze him."

Lannie nodded.

"But — but he's — your only family." ˙

"No. He was just Jason."

"He didn't deserve to — umm — I mean . . ." Meghan's voice trailed off. She was having difficulty thinking. "When did you do it?" she said. "Can you undo it?"

Lannie shook her head. "It's been quite a while. I'm surprised nobody missed him before this, actually."

Meghan had been in there, in that frozen state,

where Jason was now. She well remembered the feeling. She knew every sensation Jason had had — or not had — as the cold took him over.

But she, Meghan, had returned.

How long had Jason sat behind that wheel? How long had he sat there, knowing that the glaze over his eyes was to be permanent? That the cold in his bones would be forever?

"Does West know?" whispered Meghan.

"Oh, yes." Laughter etched new lines on Lannie's parchment skin. "I made him sit next to Jason for a while," she said, smiling. "West behaves very well now."

Meghan, clutching her stomach, retreated around the Corvette.

"Don't throw up," said Lannie. "I'd only make you clean it yourself, Meghan. Jason is fine this way. It's not that much of a change from his usual personality, you know."

Lannie came closer and closer. Meghan had nowhere to go. The lawnmower blocked her exit. She had no strength in her bones anyway.

Once again Lannie's hand closed on Meghan's arm. But nothing happened. Meghan did not freeze. She did not become an ice statue. Blood still ran in her veins and thoughts still poked through her mind like electric shocks.

Oddly practical thoughts. Groceries and electric bills. How was Lannie going to keep going all winter? All year? All future years?

"I'll be fine," said Lannie. "If anybody gives me a hard time, you know what will happen to them."

Meghan knew.

"I'd prefer you didn't tell your father," said Lannie.

Meghan felt thick and hopeless.

"Because," said Lannie Anveill softly, "you know what I will do if anybody gives me a hard time, Meghan Moore."

Chapter 11

The front seat of the old truck was warm and toasty. All the short February day, sun had gleamed on yesterday's snow. The truck cab was momentarily a greenhouse in which orchids could thrive.

Meghan sat far over on her side, and West sat far over on his.

The distance between them could be measured in inches or in hearts. They did not want to touch each other. They had not discussed this. Perhaps they thought that Lannie would know. That she could read the history of this afternoon in West's eyes.

Or perhaps whatever had once been between Meghan Moore and West Trevor had grown too cold for the sun to soften.

Meghan tugged each finger of her glove forward and bent the tips down, and then tugged each finger back till it fit again. She thought deeply about the pattern knit into the gray wool. She studied the long crack in the windshield.

"There must be something!" said West. His voice was low. Lannie was a hundred miles away and yet West thought she could overhear.

I must think so, too, Meghan realized. I am afraid of what will happen tonight when she comes over here. Some afterglow of me will be lingering on West, and for Lannie it will be as vivid a message as searchlights in the dark, and she will lust to hurt one of us. That terrible desire will be back in her speech and her heart. If she has a heart.

"Some reversal!" said West urgently. "Something we can turn against her."

Oh, how I want this to end! thought Meghan. But what can be turned against a girl who possesses Lannie's power?

Yet even Lannie had to follow certain rules. Her history class had gone to the state capitol for the day and would not be back until late. Meghan constantly checked her watch and the lowering sky. What was late? How did the school define that? What if Lannie were to return when Meghan and West were sitting together?

What would she do?

Meghan was irked with herself. Meghan knew perfectly well what Lannie would do.

"Some technique," said West. And then, with a sort of ferocity in his voice, like a pit bull fastening its jaws, he spat out, "Something to *destroy* her."

Meghan swerved in the little cozy space to look at him. He was not handsome, spitting his words. He was ugly and mean. He did not see Meghan. He did not see the truck or the snow or the sky. He saw only his neighbor. Lannie Anveill. Being destroyed.

A terrible word. Armies destroy cities. People who don't want them any longer destroy dogs.

I don't want to destroy a person, thought Meghan. Even Lannie. Even with her history. I do not wish to destroy. "Can't we just cure her?" said Meghan.

"Is there a cure for evil?" demanded West.

Meghan did not know. She was new to evil.

"You're the one Lannie was going to leave frozen! She laughed when she was going to let you die in the snow! You're the one she hates most, because you have everything!" said West.

To Meghan's horrified ears, West sounded as full of hate as Lannie. As though West, too, hated Meghan, and hated the world, and all good families. His mouth looked awful. Twisted and biting down. West, her sweet good West. Meghan looked away.

"You should be first in line to wipe her out!" cried West.

But I'm not, thought Meghan. I never want to be in that line at all. I want to be in line to save people. Not the line to destroy them.

She tried to explain this to West, but he could not listen. He huffed out an angry hot lungful of air, full of swearing and cursing. In the small space between the cracked windshield and the torn seats, his words expanded. She was breathing pain and ugliness instead of oxygen.

"You think you can teach Lannie to be sweet and

forgiving?" demanded West. His anger was as frightening as Lannie's.

Meghan flinched.

"We've set an example all our lives. Both our families are kind and generous. Lannie hasn't picked up any of it, believe me. A girl who would freeze her own mother? Freeze the dog? Freeze my sister? Freeze you? Freeze Jason and keep him there like a trophy?"

I never quite believed it, thought Meghan. I was there for all of that. I was one victim, and I saw the rest. Yet even now, in the afternoon sun, I cannot quite believe it.

West changed characters as swiftly and completely as if he'd been changing clothes. He set down anger and put on contemplation. Drumming his fingers on the dashboard, West frowned in an intellectual sort of way. As if he were a professor deciding how to explain a new concept.

He was handsome again, and yet Meghan was suddenly afraid of him, too. *Too?* she thought. Am I bracketing West with Lannie? What am I afraid of?

Now she was afraid of the truck, too. The handle that did not work. The doors she could not open. The bulk of West's body that blocked the only exit. Meghan laced her ten fingers together and ordered herself to be rational.

"No," said West meditatively. "I think Lannie has to be ended."

How little emotion lay in his voice. *Lannie must be ended.*

Meghan fixed her eyes on the swirling sunlight outside the truck. The sun spoke of truth and beauty and goodness. Perhaps it was locked out. Perhaps all she needed to do was open a door.

That day Lannie froze the children.

Girls have perfect conversational recall. Boys can hardly even remember the topic. If she were to quote West to himself, West would draw a blank. I said that? he would say. No, I didn't, Meghan.

Your heart is not in this, West, Lannie had said. *I want your heart.* And West had said, *You have my heart.*

She does have his heart, thought Meghan. Horror like some grotesque virus exploded her innocence.

Lannie has his heart. That's why I don't want to touch him. She has a grip on his heart. We're alone in this truck, and yet her fingers are curled around his heart.

Even West's voice was like Lannie's. The same flatness to it, because love and heart had been ironed out of it.

No doubt Lannie had whispered that to herself when she decided she had had enough of Mrs. Anveill. *My mother must be ended.*

"West," whispered Meghan. "Did you hear yourself? Have you thought about what you're saying? *Lannie must be ended.* That's evil. It means killing Lannie."

West hardly looked at her. Now a sort of hot thick eagerness poured out of him, like a poisoned drink. "Exactly," he said.

He shared her desires, too. Her aching, throbbing desire to inflict pain.

Oh, Lannie, Lannie! thought Meghan. Give me back his heart! His fine good heart! You've taken it!

She wanted to cleanse West of Lannie. They did that in olden days. They purged people of evil. Ancient priests and ancient rituals reached down into the heart and soul and tore out the evil and left the person exhausted but clean.

West is unclean, thought Meghan. His heart is Lannie's.

"Last night," West announced casually, "I considered driving into the bridge abutment."

The bridge had been rebuilt. Huge concrete pylons and immense concrete walls.

"Lannie won't use a seatbelt," West told her. He looked happy. "I seriously thought of simply driving into the cement at seventy-five miles an hour."

"West! You'd be killed."

He nodded without regret. "Yes. We'd both be killed."

She could not bear it that West had come to this. "No, West. We will not do that. We will not think of doing that. We are not going to *end* anybody. We are not going to end Lannie and we are not going to end you."

"Then where will *this* end, Meghan?" said West. He spoke reasonably, as if discussing homework or radio stations. "Where will Lannie take us? Are we going to grow up and reach our twenties and thirties and middle age and old age, with Lannie still there threatening us? Lannie still freezing people who annoy her? Lannie still ruining all our lives?"

Meghan could not sit in the ruined truck any longer. It was too symbolic. West was the rusted-out body. "Let's go up to the house," she said. Now it was her own voice that had become toneless. All the music had passed out of her. There would be no melodies and no harmonies now. Only the flat, ironed, heartlessness of Lannie . . . and West.

West got out of the truck. Meghan slid over the seat and hit the ground with both feet. She felt better standing on the ground. A little more connected to whatever goodness was left in the world. She headed up the hill while West fussed with the truck, checking the windows and slamming the door. As if the truck mattered. As if anything mattered when a fine young man could discuss without the slightest worry the "ending" of another human being.

"I just don't see what problem you have with this, Meggie-Megs," said West, genuinely puzzled. "I mean, think of Jason in that garage! How can you possibly mind Lannie being ended when you know what she does for fun?"

"That's Lannie!" cried Meghan. "Lannie's sick and twisted. But we're not! We can't do it just because she does!"

"Now, Meggie-Megs," said West.

She could not bear it that he was abusing her baby nickname like this. Meggie-Megs had been a curly-haired toddler to whom afterschool snacks and bear hugs were the whole world. Meggie-Megs had been a name for innocence and laughter, not the "ending" of another human being.

West was still discussing Lannie's "end" as they went into the house.

His brother and sister were watching a video. Tuesday was partial to James Bond and, as Meghan entered the family room, James Bond was also facing down Evil. He would win, of course. In the movies, Good triumphed over Evil. And so cleverly. Driving the best cars and using the finest of electronic devices.

Meghan did not feel clever. She felt utterly and completed depressed, and utterly and completely unable to stop the expansion of Lannie.

"See," said West, flopping down on the big raggedy armchair, "I was also thinking that I would teach Lannie to drive. And what I could do is, send her off by herself after I've rigged whatever car I use to teach her. There'd be a nice symmetry to that besides. She killed her mother in a car. It's only fitting that she should die in a car. Don't you think so?"

Tuesday and Brown looked up from the video.

Meghan could not bear it. "West, *murder* can *not* be next on our list."

"It isn't murder," said West, slightly surprised. "It's ending Lannie."

The family room divided into two temperature zones. There was the warm and friendly side on which Tuesday and Brown sat. There was the cold and vicious side where West sat.

Meghan stood in the middle of the room, the sleet of West's plans hitting her on one side; the stunned sweetness of Tuesday and Brown warming her on the other side.

"West?" said Brown.

West did not even look at his little brother. He was caught up in a daydream, a dream in which he would do all the things to Lannie which creatures do to each other in Saturday morning cartoons: They flatten each other, they push each other off cliffs, they drop dynamite down on each other's chimneys.

Meghan knew then that she really was an ex-girlfriend.

There was no going back.

This was not West: the Trevor she loved best. This was a stranger who would slice off another life as easily as slicing a wedge off a melon.

"And then . . ." said West eagerly.

Tuesday began to cry but West did not see her. A smile was curving on West's face. Meghan could see Lannie in it, as if Lannie had taken up residence inside West.

"Or another way . . ." said West excitedly.

Brown stared at his fingernails, the way boys did, making fists and turning them up. Girls spread their fingers like fans and held them away.

Meghan went home.
She could not bear another burden.

She lay awake for a long long time. Once or twice she got out of bed and went to a window from which she could stare at Lannie's house, and think of the people who lived there: the one who breathed and the one who did not. Once or twice she got out of bed and went to a window from which she could stare at the Trevors' house, and think of the people who lived there: the friends she still understood and the friend she had lost.

And once more she got out of bed, and very, very quietly opened a door at the other end of the hall, and looked in on two sleeping parents. Truly, thought Meghan Moore, I am loved. I have seen now what it is to be unloved and I know why Lannie is jealous.

I do have everything.

In school the next day, Meghan asked Lannie to sit with her.

"What is it you want from me?" said Lannie, when they were alone together.

"I just want to talk."

Lannie shook her head. "Nobody feels that way with me. You want something from me. Say what it is." Her eyes, like faucets, ran both hot and cold. Meghan could neither look at Lannie nor look away. She could not go on being courteous and full of fibs. "I want to talk about West," she whispered. Her lips did not move easily. How did Lannie do her freezing? She had even frozen Meghan's courage, and Meghan had had so much of it when she left home this morning!

"Oh?" said Lannie.

"I'm worried about him," said Meghan.

"Oh?"

"You've made him so cold!" Meghan burst out.

Lannie smiled. "His heart is colder," she agreed.

Meghan felt herself bowing forward, the weight of her worries folding her up. Her shoulders sagged, her muscles went limp, her arms drooped.

Coldhearted.

One of those phrases people toss about easily, without consideration, without knowing what it truly means. Meghan knew. She had two cold-hearted people to go by.

And what is a cold heart?

A heart without love. Without compassion.

A heart that does not worry about others. A heart that does not care if somebody else pays a price just for being near it.

Heart and soul. They are so close! So intertwined. What kind of soul could a coldhearted person have?

Perhaps, thought Meghan Moore, *no soul at all.*

Perhaps the cold heart has frozen the soul out.

"Did you touch him to do it?" she whispered.

"I didn't have to touch him. I just had to be there. Showing him my way." Lannie smiled her smile of ice and snow. "He's a good follower, West."

Meghan was crying now. Her tears were hail on her own cheeks: blisteringly cold tears that peppered her skin instead of running down her cheeks.

What would melt the heart of Lannie Anveill? What could possibly release the heart of West Trevor? "You froze him," said Meghan through the hail of her tears.

"Yes," said Lannie, chuckling. "He's mine."

Chapter 12

Sunshine is a blessing.

Morning is a blessing.

Agony is less and fear is diminished in the sparkle and the gold of an early sun.

Meghan was slightly restored. She dressed in a corner of her bedroom where a shaft of sunlight made a warm square on the floor. If only I could pick that up, she thought, and carry it with me. Stand in it all day long.

But she did not raise the shade to let more sun in, for Lannie's house also lay to the east.

There is a way out of this, she told herself. Then she said it out loud for additional strength. "There is a way out of this!" she called. If a cold heart has frozen West's soul, I will just have to warm him up.

She smiled to herself. "Perhaps West could be defrosted," she said to the sunshine square. It was a word for refrigerators or plastic bags of vegetables. "I am probably the only girl in America," she said ruefully, "who has to defrost her boyfriend."

Well, it made Meghan laugh, anyway. Now how

to get West to laugh so warmly? How to defrost his heart, and locate his soul, and peel him away from Lannie's influence, and save the world from Lannie?

In the sunshine, she believed that it could be done.

In the sunshine, she believed that she was the one who could do it.

And luckily, the sun stayed out all day. No clouds passed in front of it, no snowstorms blew in from Canada. Her classes in the morning were on the east side of the building and in the afternoon on the west. She never did lose that square of sunlight. And so after school, she went for help. She chose her history teacher, whom she adored and who seemed to have so many answers! The woman knew dates and wars and prime ministers and ancient enmities. She knew rivers and treaties and battles and kings.

Meghan launched right into it. "Suppose," said Meghan Moore, "that a person's soul froze. How would you teach him to love again?"

Her teacher smiled. "My dear, mankind has been trying to teach love to the frozen for thousands of years. That's half of every religion and every philosophy."

Meghan did not want to waste time reading every religion and every philosophy. "Who's right?" she said briskly.

"My dear, mankind has gone to war trying to decide who's right. They've lynched their neighbors, disowned their children, and built a million sacred edifices."

Meghan did not really want details at a time like this. "I understand, but in your opinion, who is right?"

"Everybody."

Meghan looked at her teacher with some irritation. "You wouldn't accept that answer on a quiz," she pointed out. "You'd say, 'Be more specific.' "

"Life is not a quiz," said the history teacher.

"Are you taking me seriously?" demanded Meghan. "I really need to know the answer to this question. *Who is right?*"

"And I said everybody. Love is right. In any language, in any history, in any religion, if you love your neighbor, if your heart is generous, if you show mercy and act justly, then you are right."

Love my neighbor.

Well, I have two neighbors here, thought Meghan Moore. Lannie and West.

Does this mean I have to love Lannie? That means I have to love Evil. Because Lannie is evil. She's a poison seeping from an abandoned tank into the water supply, and no one notices until all the children on the street have cancer. How can I love that?

I've always loved West. I've loved him all my life, and especially this year, and what do I have to show for it?

A cold heart in somebody else's hands.

Show mercy and act justly.

Show mercy to whom? Lannie's future victims? Lannie? Myself?

310

And what is justice? To do what West wants? End Lannie Anveill?

She had come for answers, and the history teacher seemed to think that they had been given to her. The history teacher smiled happily as she packed her briefcase with papers to correct that night.

To Meghan it did not feel like an answer. It felt like more questions.

She left the school. The sun still shone. The square of gold was still at her feet. But she knew nothing.

Least of all what to do next.

Chapter 13

The sun set and the snow began. Clouds as thick as continents rolled in, bleak and bruised. From out of those dark pain-ridden whirls came snow so white it stretched credulity. Nothing could be that white. That pure. That perfect.

Winter deepened in one brief afternoon.

Dark Fern Lane had never seen so much snow. It drifted thigh deep. Tires on the road surface made a whole new sound: scrunching and crunching in treads.

It was a Friday. The rules of school nights were suspended.

But not one child frolicked in the snow. Not one family had turned on a porch light or a garage light, and come out to roll a snowman in the dark. Not one snowball had been formed, not one snowfort built, not one angel made. No one had plucked the icicles from the porch overhang and pretended to be a unicorn. No one had gathered a plateful of the best and whitest snow, and poured hot maple syrup on it to make instant candy.

For another generation, yard games were over.

Those children who had been frozen like laundry — they remembered.

They had been aware, inside their motionless bodies and their unblinking eyes. They had known. They had felt Lannie's fingertips.

They were staying inside.

They would always stay inside.

Only Meghan went out into the snow, and only then because she had seen West in his mother's car stop for Lannie and drive away with her. Drive carefully, she had thought after the vanishing car. Don't do anything bad. Come home safe!

She waded through wonderful drifts, snow as deep as company on Thanksgiving.

"Meggie-Megs!" said Tuesday delightedly. "Come on in! It's freezing out there! You are so brave! Brown and I are hibernating till spring."

Meghan joined Brown and Tuesday in the family room. "Are your parents home?"

"Nope. They've taken up square dancing. Isn't that hysterical? You should see them. Dad's wearing cowboy shirts and a bowler and Mom's wearing a red calico skirt with ruffles."

Meghan wished she had seen them. It sounded so cute. She smiled, thinking of Mr. and Mrs. Trevor.

"It's good that they're gone," said Tuesday briskly. "We have things to decide."

Brown nodded. He sat up on the edge of the couch. Whatever they were going to decide could not be done slouching. "First," said Brown, "how much does West actually like her?"

Here we go again, thought Meghan. There's no getting away from Lannie Anveill.

"When West kisses Lannie, it looks real," said Brown. "Is he an actor? Or does he love her?"

"He started as an actor," said Tuesday, "but I think it became real. That's a danger with playing games so hard and so well. You forget it's a game. It gets into your bloodstream." Tuesday stood up. "Microwave popcorn anybody? Cheese or plain buttered?"

"Plain buttered," said Brown. "It's not only a game, but Lannie has beaten him at it. He's getting to be as sick and twisted as she is."

Tuesday brought out the popcorn. Their six hands went into the bowl together. They sat close to share. Food helps a person think.

"I have to believe," said Meghan, munching, "that good is stronger than evil. That somehow this will work out all right."

"It won't," said Tuesday.

"I saw Jason," said Brown. He crammed more popcorn into his mouth.

"Well, there's no helping him now," said Tuesday. "And probably no helping West either. We have to look out for ourselves."

The popcorn stuck in Meghan's throat.

"So the question here is," said Brown, rubbing a popcorn against the side of the bowl to slick up extra butter and salt, "how do we end Lannie?"

The cold seeped into Meghan's heart again. Yet another sweet Trevor suggesting that Lannie should be "ended."

"Could she freeze herself?" asked Tuesday. "Could we play Freeze Tag and somehow she freezes herself?"

Brown shook his head. "If that could happen, she'd have frozen herself when she brushed her hair or put on lipstick."

"I'm thirsty," said Tuesday. "Meggie-Megs, you want Coke, Dr. Pepper, cider, hot chocolate, raspberry ginger ale, or milk?"

This was too big a decision to be executed from the family room. The three of them went into the kitchen to inspect the actual containers. Once she had seen the bottles, Meghan knew she needed water first, to wash down the salt and butter, and then she could concentrate on the hot chocolate. "Do you have marshmallows?" she said.

"It comes with them. See?"

Meghan saw. She would ask her mother to get that kind. "I could offer myself," said Meghan. "I could say: Here. Freeze me. I am yours. Do not hurt other people who are not involved."

"Lannie'd just freeze you and leave you," said Brown, "and go on to her next victim. You wouldn't accomplish anything by that except to join Jennifer or Jacqueline or whoever she is on the hospital ward."

"I thought Lannie unfroze her."

"That was a while ago. There's been another one."

"What did Jennifer or Jacqueline do to Lannie?"

"Wasn't friendly, I guess."

"I know," said Tuesday. "We could lock her away."

"You own a jail, maybe?" said Brown. He shrugged and gave up. He found the remote and turned on the television. This was Brown's only answer to all difficulties.

Homework too hard? Watch TV.

Family too annoying? Watch TV.

Lannie too scary? Watch TV.

It had very little to do with the history teacher's answer to all difficulties. Mercy and justice.

Tuesday and Meghan watched helplessly. It's difficult to have a television on and not get sucked in. How remote, how impossible the family on the TV screen seemed. How could they laugh so hard and so often?

We used to laugh like that, thought Meghan. Back before we knew all about Lannie Anveill.

Beneath her feet she felt the rising and slamming of the automatic garage door, rarely used. She heard the growl of a car engine and its abrupt cessation. She heard a door slam. West is here, she thought.

She heard a second door slam.

"Lannie's with him," said Tuesday.

Brown turned up the television volume. It might have been a weapon or camoflauge. He was wrapped in a canned laugh track, safe even from Lannie Anveill.

Feet hit the stairs, and up through the raised ranch came West and Lannie.

Meghan's grandmother had had an awful saying of which she was very fond: Speak of the devil, and he appears.

They had spoken of Lannie, and she had appeared.

No one said hello.

Brown did not look up from the television. Tuesday did not look up from the popcorn. West did not look up from his shoes. Meghan practiced locking her fingers together.

Lannie chuckled.

It was such an inappropriate sound that Meghan did look up. She caught Lannie unaware. Lannie was nervous.

Because we don't like her! thought Meghan, astonished to see this flicker of humanness. Lannie wants to be popular like anybody else. We're afraid of her and we don't want her around and it makes her nervous!

Lannie and West dropped onto the couch opposite Meghan and Tuesday. It's good they have two sofas, thought Meghan. It would be tricky to have to sit next to each other.

"Turn that down," said Lannie.

Brown did not pretend he couldn't hear her. He notched the volume down, and he didn't play around, taking it slowly and being infuriating. He didn't want to see that finger of hers moving toward him.

The people on television giggled and sparred and chatted but you could not quite hear them; they might suddenly have become ghosts whose presence was only fractional.

Lannie smiled.

West looked away.

"Popcorn?" said Tuesday brightly.

"We ate," said West.

So they sat, waiting for Lannie to leave, waiting for the torture to be over. But this was Lannie, of course, who enjoyed torture, and so she was not going to leave.

"Oh!" said Brown suddenly.

They all looked at him.

He sparkled, the way you do when you've just had a brilliant idea. "Lannie!" said Brown.

She raised her eyebrows.

"I know what! Why don't you and I go out?" he said. "I'd be a great date. And that way, Meghan could still be with West."

Meghan was so touched she wanted to weep. Brown was offering himself in exchange.

Lannie hooted with laughter. "You?" she said. "You're a little boy! You're eleven years old! Get a life! You're so pathetic, Brown."

"You're the one who's pathetic! You know perfectly well, nobody would ever date you because he wanted to!" shouted Brown. "You have to threaten them with freezing to get them to sit in the same room with you. You have to keep Jason in the car to scare everybody to death just in order to get a ride to school!"

"West promised to like me best," said Lannie defensively, "and he does. So there."

"He does not!" screamed Tuesday. "He hates you! He loves Meghan!"

I cannot bear it, thought Meghan. I cannot go on like this. I will have to give up. I will have to have another life, with other friends.

Meghan looked at the three Trevors as if for the last time. She thought of school and all the people she knew there — thought of scrounging among them like a bag lady, hoping to find a discarded friend for herself. She thought: I'm a sophomore and I have nobody. I have to start all over.

"Do you really love Meghan?" Lannie asked West in a deathly cold voice. She held her hands away from her sides, like a police officer whose holster and stick make him walk funny. But Lannie didn't need a holster nor a stick. Just a fingertip.

"Of course not," said West. He put his arms around Lannie. She vanished in his embrace, as small as a kindergartner. Then he kissed her hair.

"How romantic," said Brown. "Must be like kissing a bale of hay."

West did not respond to this. Nor did he even glance at Meghan, whose hair he had once loved to touch. Is he protecting me? wondered Meghan. Or has he forgotten me? I can't tell. I don't know.

"Go home and get warmer clothes, Lannie," said West. "We'll go ice skating. It's Friday. The rink's open till midnight."

Lannie said shyly, flirtatiously, "I'm not very good."

West smiled. "I'll hold you up."

Meghan's heart broke.

Did anybody ever want to hear anything else? *I'll hold you up.* It's what we all want, thought Meghan. Somebody to catch us when we're afraid of falling.

Oh how I want him back! I want West Trevor! We held *each other* up. We were a pair. A perfect pair.

Meghan was weary. I'm going home, she thought. There's no point in coming back here. I have to stay away and start over. By myself.

Silently and seemingly without motion, Lannie eased herself out of the Trevor house. Lannie's vanishing always gave Meghan the shivers.

From across the room West said, "Never touch me again, Meghan."

She thought she would fall over. He didn't have to say that! He could leave it alone, without stabbing her with those words!

"Lannie knows we're meeting," West said tonelessly. "She gave me her power. If I touch anybody other than Lannie, they'll freeze."

West left to get the car out again, get Lannie again, go hopelessly on with his half-life again.

Brown watched his brother leave.

Tuesday watched her brother leave.

But Meghan could not bear to look at the West she would never again have, and so she watched Tuesday.

A strange flicker crossed her best friend's face.

An expression both calculating and cruel.

Meghan had to look away, and when she looked back, the expression was gone, and Meghan convinced herself she had never seen it. Tuesday — sweet Tuesday of summer nights and pink lemonade — would not look like that.

It was the face of a cold heart.

A frozen soul.

Chapter 14

Snow fell for days.

They had never experienced such weather. The sky would not change, would not back off, would not turn clear and blue. Endlessly, the sky dumped snow down upon them. School was canceled because the snowplows could not keep up with the amazing amounts of snow. After a while there was no place for the plows to push the snow, and the roads became narrower, flanked by mountain ranges of previously shoveled snow.

Brown didn't mind. He was the kind of person who could watch a million hours of television and then watch a million more. He just sat there with the TV on, staring. Tuesday had a "kitchen attack" and suddenly made real sugar cookies which she cut out in hearts and decorated with red glaze or chocolate chips.

Tuesday called Meghan to see if she had any other cookie cutters because Tuesday had a lot more cookie dough and no more shapes.

Meghan's mother had once been given a collection

of cookie cutters. They were still in the original box, lying on the original white tissue.

So much for finding new friends, thought Meghan. She put on her layers of protection against the winter and stormed her way to the Trevors' with her collection. She and Tuesday rolled out dough on the kitchen counter and argued whether — in February — they could properly use the Christmas tree or the Santa.

There was a knock at the front door.

Tuesday went to get it. Meghan took the opportunity to snitch a long thin slice of raw dough. Meghan loved raw cookie dough.

"Hi," said Lannie at the door. Like a normal person. A regular greeting and everything.

Meghan pressed herself into the corner of the kitchen, where she would be invisible if Lannie came up the stairs.

"Hi, Lannie," said Tuesday.

"Is West here?"

"Not yet. He went out to get a part for his truck. He's going to work on it today."

West hasn't looked at his truck in ages, thought Meghan. Strange how a person's only sister sees so little. You would think Tuesday would know that West is so caught between Lannie and real life that rusted trucks and stalled engines have slipped his mind. But no, she thinks he's still down there every day, working on the Chevy.

"Why don't you wait for West in the truck?" said Tuesday.

It's awfully cold out, thought Meghan. I'm not

sure that Lannie should be . . . what am I doing?

Meghan shook off her thoughts.

I'm trying to protect Lannie's health? I don't mind if Lannie catches cold. I hope Lannie gets such a bad cold she's home for a year!

"West will be back in a while and you know the first thing he'll do is run down there to look at his truck," said Tuesday.

From her corner Meghan looked out the kitchen window. There was only one, and it was a small dark square above the sink. Mrs. Trevor was trying to grow little plants on that window, but they didn't get enough sun, and all she had were thin bottles of water and sad little cuttings of fading greens. There had been no sunset because the sun had never been visible. The dark sky had simply grown darker, and now, in the hour before supper, the darkness had a fullness to it, as if it had finally consumed everything in its path and was ready for a nap.

Tuesday went on and on about the truck.

After a while, Brown woke from his television coma and joined Tuesday in the little entry between the stairs. "Here," he said, "I'll put on the backyard light for you." He hit the switch that turned on the light at the bottom of the deck stairs which led up to the kitchen door. Now the snow sparkled.

Barely, way down the sloping yard, Meghan could see the mounded tops of a row of cedars that had grown up near the truck. You could not quite see down as low as the truck. The white spires of the cedars marked the spot.

324

How peacefully the snow lay. Snow covers all ugliness, thought Meghan.

Tuesday coaxed Lannie around the house. Tuesday even went with her partway, although Tuesday had neither coat nor boots on. "He'll be there soon," Tuesday said twice.

Lannie waded down the sloping yard, past the snow covered vines and hedges and underbrush. Meghan turned off the kitchen lights so that Lannie would not see her, illuminated next to the cookie dough. She could hardly see Lannie. In fact, Lannie's shadow was clearer than the real Lannie.

Lannie's little body, forcing itself against the high drifts and packed snow, dipped down and disappeared from sight.

Meghan pulled the shade over the kitchen window before she turned the light back on.

"Now let's set the table," said Tuesday briskly. "Mom's exhausted from her new job. I've promised to do dinner twice a week. She cut a seafood recipe out of *Family Circle*. Doesn't this look yummy? You chop the onions and sauté them, and I'll start the biscuits."

"What does sauté mean?" said Meghan uneasily. She was not familiar with kitchens. Her own family had take-out, or fixed meals that involved heating rather than recipes, like steak and baked potatoes.

In the end, Tuesday even had to demonstrate the purpose of the chopping board. Had to show Meghan how to dice the onion without also dicing her fingertips. How to scrape the onions into the skillet without dumping half of them in the crack between the stove and the counter. "This is work," said Meghan. "I'm exhausted from a single onion."

She and Tuesday giggled.

"Now you've got to prepare the scallops," said Tuesday. She took a wrapped package out of the meat compartment of the refrigerator and ripped it open.

"Those horrible mushy white things? We're going to eat those?" Meghan was horrified.

"Yes. We're going to love them. Now here's what you do."

And then she had to do things with garlic as well, and parsley had to be torn, and then she was given a tiny little broom, or paintbrush, with which to slather melted butter on the tops of the almost-baked biscuits. When they came out of the oven again, minutes later, they were crusty and golden and smelled of heaven.

There was quite a rush as everybody else got home, and the table had to be set, and her parents had to be telephoned for permission for Meghan to eat at the Trevors' again, and Meghan had to work through her guilt for once again not being home with her own family.

The real treat was sitting next to West again.

His smile was normal, his laugh was genuine.

Mr. Trevor had had a great day at work and regaled them with stories. "This is the best dinner I've had in years!" he kept saying. "Meghan, you did the garlic and onion?"

"I taught her how, Dad," said Tuesday.

He shook his head proudly. "What a pair!"

"I'll have seconds," said West.

Meghan was beaming.

"Excellent dinner," pronounced Mrs. Trevor. Then she giggled in that special Trevor way. "Of course, I'd like any meal that somebody else fixed, so my standards are pretty low."

"You guys would not believe," said Tuesday, "what I had to teach old Meggie-Megs here. Good grief. She doesn't know an onion from a potato."

"What's for dessert?" said Mr. Trevor, holding a fork in one hand and a spoon in the other, ready for any eating style.

"Drop that silver," said Meghan.

"Cookies," said Tuesday, bringing out a tray lined with a Christmas napkin she'd dug up from somewhere.

"Santa Clauses!" shouted Mr. Trevor. He bit off a Santa head and declared it the tastiest cookie he'd had in his life.

Meghan had never dreamed that the mere cooking of food could bring so many compliments. She would have to tell her parents. Perhaps the Moores would try cooking, too, one day.

West cleared the table, scraped the dishes, loaded the dishwasher, ran hot soapy water for the pots. Dishes had always been his job. And he had never complained. His mother put on the coffee. Mr. and Mrs. Trevor always liked to sit around the table sipping that awful stuff after a big meal.

"So," said Mrs. Trevor, smiling broadly at her

son, and then equally broadly at Meghan, "you two are back together again? Lannie's out of the picture?"

I forgot Lannie! She's still waiting for him down in the truck! Meghan swerved to look at Tuesday, so Tuesday would give West the message. Certainly Meghan didn't want to deliver it. She was as full of happiness as the night was full of dark. She didn't even want to utter the name, because it would break her happy spell like an icicle hitting the pavement.

Both Tuesday's eyelids went down slowly, in a sort of double wink. How like Lannie she suddenly looked. Hooded, evil eyes. Eyes that had seen terrible things. Eyes that had seen through to the other side.

"Lannie's out of the picture," agreed Tuesday. She, too, smiled broadly. She met West's eyes and now his smile came out. Meghan could not move. Out of the corner of her eyes she checked Brown. No smile had ever been wider.

Meghan did not need to be out in the snow to be cold. Her hands, her heart, her thoughts: They chilled as if her friends had refrigerated her.

"All we need now," said Mr. Trevor, "is ice cream. A really good dinner isn't done till you've had your ice cream. Meghan, dish it out!"

Meghan got up from the table. She circled the big flat dining room table, and crossed the kitchen to the refrigerator.

The inside of the freezer was rimmed with frost crystals. Ice cubes tumbled out of the ice maker and fell into a clear plastic box. They looked like stones for a pyramid. Her fingers grazed the metal edge of the freezer and for a scary moment they stuck to the cold. She peeled herself away and got the ice cream container out.

So cold in there. How chilly the boxes of vegetables and desserts must be. Meghan shut the door, leaving the cold boxes to their dark frozen lives. They had to lie there until somebody wanted them. They had no exit without human hands. There were no handles on the insides of refrigerator doors.

Handles.

There are no handles on the inside of the truck doors, either, thought Meghan Moore. Lannie cannot get out of the truck.

Nobody knows she's there.

The snow is coming down. The truck is getting colder and colder. Lannie can scream and kick and bite. But she will never get out. There are no handles on the inside.

By morning . . .

By morning, Lannie Anveill will be frozen.

Like Jason, she will sit behind the wheel. She may sit all winter. Because Mr. and Mrs. Trevor never go down there.

And nobody else knows she's there.

"I boiled water," said Mrs. Trevor cheerily. "People who don't want coffee with their ice cream may have tea, herb tea, spiced cider, or instant hot chocolate."

West smiled. He would have coffee, please. Cream and sugar.

Tuesday smiled. She would have herb tea, please. With honey.

Brown smiled. He would have hot chocolate, please.

They were not smiling for coffee, tea, or chocolate.

They were smiling because they knew where Lannie was.

Those were not even smiles across their faces.

They were gashes.

Tuesday knew.

West knew.

And Brown, grinning down into his ice cream — Brown knew.

"Meghan?" said Mrs. Trevor.

"Spiced cider," said Meghan. It's not my responsibility, she thought. Tuesday sent her down there. Tuesday's the one letting it happen.

Only three people would know where Lannie Anveill was. How she got there. What happened to her.

No.

Actually, four people.

Three Trevors . . . *and one Moore.*

Meghan Moore.

Meghan's cider spilled on the table.

She set the mug down. Then set her trembling hand on her lap.

No. West. We will not do that. We will not even think of doing that.

Then where will this end, Meghan? Where will Lannie take us? Are we going to grow up and reach our twenties and thirties and middle age and old page, with Lannie still there threatening us, ruining our lives?

You won, Lannie. You froze him.

Yes. He's mine.

Evil can infect. Evil can spread. Evil has such great and terrible power that it infiltrates even the best of human beings.

I, thought Meghan Moore, am the one who became evil.

I am the one sitting here with a mug of spiced cider, waiting for the cold and terrible hours of night to pass, so that Lannie Anveill turns to ice and snow.

My heart.

My heart is frozen.

Meghan Moore got up from the table. She walked to the back door. It was difficult. Her feet dragged and she bumped into the jamb. The doorknob did not fit her hand and the wind when she opened the door assaulted her.

She heard voices behind her, but they were Trevor voices. The voices of people to whom things came easily. The voices of people who expected things to work out their way. Meghan did not know if she still loved the Trevors.

The one I have to love most, she thought, is me. If I don't love myself, I cannot go on.

The cold was no longer an enemy. Instead it woke her and embraced her with its demands.

This is what it means, thought Meghan Moore, to choose the lesser of two evils. Lannie is evil, but it would be more evil to stand aside and silently let her die.

Meghan had never gone through snow so deep, through darkness so thick. She found the truck by feel. She opened the door of the cab and Lannie fell into her arms.

Meghan helped Lannie walk.

"Come in my house where it's warm," said Meghan.

Lannie said nothing.

Perhaps she was too cold to speak.

Or perhaps . . . she had waited all her life to come in where it was warm.

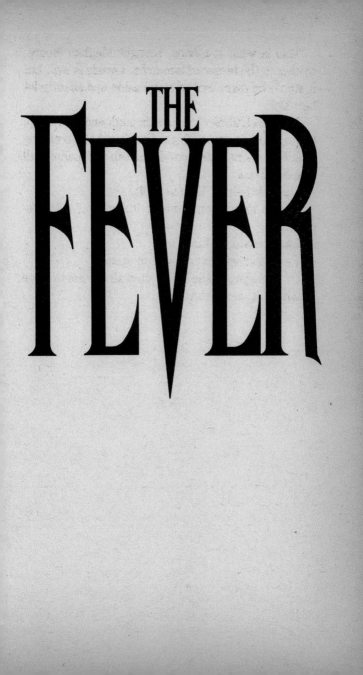

Prologue

Duffy Quinn tosses and turns in a restless, fevered sleep. Hot . . . hot . . . so hot . . . flames burning . . . tormenting her parched, dry skin, setting it on fire . . .

What . . . what is it? Sounds . . . noises . . . ripped into her tortured sleep. No . . . no . . . she doesn't want to wake up . . . no . . . leave me alone, she thinks . . .

Clanging . . . clanging . . . metal on metal . . .

Now a cry, muffled, frightened, "What? What are you — ?"

Now a soft, whispered flapping sound, flap-flap, flap-flap, like gentle waves hitting the shore of a lake . . .

Suddenly another cry, this time filled with terror, "No! Please, don't!"

Hot, hot, burning, blazing . . .

There's a soft thud . . . then silence . . . .

Silence floats about the room and then is broken again . . . flap-flapping underneath, rattle-

clatter-kadunk on top . . . clatter-kadunk, clatter-kadunk . . .

Duffy stirs, moans, tries to sit up.

The clatter-kadunk stops abruptly. Silence.

Duffy whispers, "What? What is it?"

But sitting up is too painful. Duffy sinks back down against the pillow on her hospital bed, murmuring her question. "What . . . what is it?"

The clatter-kadunk begins again. A faint shaft of light briefly crosses the room as the door creaks open. The door swings closed again and the light disappears.

Silence.

Chapter 1

The hospital stood alone in the center of town. A tall, grim structure of worn gray stone, sparsely covered with wilting ivy, it towered menacingly over the street. The bottom row of stone blocks were mildewed a grimy greenish-black around the base, shielded from the sun's drying heat by a ragged row of hedges. Visitors entering by the wide stone steps puzzled over the thick odor of mold and mildew. They did not realize that the building itself was gradually decaying from the dampness that began at its base and slowly but steadily made its way up the stone.

The upper-floor windows, tall and narrow, stared unblinkingly down upon the street below, as if a sightless gray giant were planting his feet in the uneven grass and boldly inviting strangers to approach . . . if they dared.

Residents of the town of Twelvetrees, Maine, had often remarked sourly that it was not the sort of look a hospital established to welcome the sick and ailing should have.

But they had no money for a newer, more modern building. The old one, unwelcoming as it was, would have to do.

On the fourth floor of Twelvetrees Community Hospital, Duffy Quinn awakened.

The fever had engulfed her, burning her body from the inside out, had transported her to a dizzying world of brilliant reds, hot purples, and blazing yellows. During the long hours since her admission due to a sudden, unexplained fever, the pungent, antiseptic smell of the fourth floor had become her only connection with the real world, as she drifted in and out of a surrealistic carnival of colors.

The smell, which wrinkled her nose even before she was fully awake, dragged her back into an unpleasant reality, a hospital world full of grim whiteness, of chilly, uneasy quiet, of medication, illness, even . . . death.

As depressing as the odor was, it guaranteed that she was still alive, still a part of the real world, no matter how isolated she felt.

As the grogginess of sleep left her, Duffy's head swung instinctively toward the companion bed. It stood silently opposite her own bed, empty and waiting.

Empty . . .

She couldn't have heard anything during the night. There was no one *in* that bed. There hadn't been, not since she was admitted on Thursday night, when her parents had raced to the hospital in the station wagon with Duffy prone on the backseat, raving weird, nonsensical things, in the throes of a raging, delirium-inducing fever. She remembered nothing about being admitted two nights earlier, but she was certain no one had shared the room even then. The other bed had been empty, and had stayed empty.

What had she heard, then? What had it sounded like . . . the noises? Metal on metal, she remembered . . . like the sound her gold charm bracelet made when it clanked against the metal edge on her desk at school.

Had it been someone out in the hall doing something useful with the old metal bedpans? Newer hospitals had plastic bedpans . . . not so freezing cold. Metal ones *could* make the noise she'd heard.

She was so hot . . . so hot . . . the room was so stuffy, not like at night when they turned off the furnace even though the early spring nights were still chilly. Then the room felt like a refrigerator. Her mouth was so dry, it felt like the cotton balls they swabbed her arm with before they stuck nasty needles into her flesh.

Somewhere within the thick stone walls, water ran. The exhausted plumbing shrieked in agony. The sound of running water made Duffy thirsty. But her hands, the left one impaled by the IV needle steadily feeding her antibiotics, had been robbed of strength by her illness. They floundered around like dead fish on the hills and valleys of her rough, off-white bedding.

What about the other sounds she'd heard? The

slapping sound . . . the rattly, *kadunk*ing sound?

And something else . . . a desperate, terrified cry for help?

No, that couldn't be right. She must have been dreaming.

Hot . . . she was so hot . . . burning . . . burning, as if she were lying on the beach in the middle of July with a cruel sun mercilessly beating down upon her flesh.

She needed water. "Nurse," she murmured, "nurse . . ." Where were all the nurses?

A figure appeared in the doorway. Her doctor. Jonas Morgan. Young, bearded, a gold ring in one ear, sneakers on big feet. Tall, bony, skinny. Not like a doctor at all. Doctors were supposed to be balding or gray. They gave you pills and sent you home. All Dr. Morgan had given her was a battery of tests, thousands of questions . . . and he hadn't sent her home.

He didn't seem to know the first thing about smiling. He frowned a lot, sending thick, shaggy, dark eyebrows on a collision course, and he seemed to take her illness very seriously. She supposed she should be grateful for that, but what she really wanted to do was say, "Lighten up, Doc!"

He took her pulse, listened to her chest, and ordered the nurse who had followed him into the room to take more blood. Duffy groaned. "*Again?* I don't think I have any left. I'm down at least a quart."

He didn't smile. She hadn't expected him to. "We

340

haven't learned anything yet," he said solemnly, "about what brought you here. It's probably the flu. But we have to make sure."

Minutes later, he was gone, bony shoulders slumped, probably weighted down with the worry of what on earth was wrong with Duffy Quinn.

"Were you in here last night?" she asked the tall, broad-shouldered nurse in white, who took her temperature and then her blood.

"Me? No, hon, I came on this morning at seven. Why?"

"I just wondered. Someone was."

"Another nurse, probably. Your temp has to be monitored."

But no one had taken her temperature. Not when she'd heard the sounds, anyway.

Or *had* they? Maybe she'd just forgotten. Everything was so fuzzy now, with her brain on fire. How could she be sure of anything? Yesterday her mother had told her some of the things she had cried out in her delirium on the way to the hospital. Silly, bizarre things, like warning her mother to get her umbrella out and shouting at her father to change the light bulbs in the kitchen. Crazy stuff.

Maybe last night had just been more of the same.

The nurse took her blood and left, and was immediately replaced by a second nurse, young and pretty, who gave Duffy an expert sponge bath, a clean hospital gown, white with tiny blue flowers, and a delicious back rub.

But she hadn't been on duty the night before,

either, and couldn't tell Duffy anything about who might have been in her room. She, too, said it was probably one of the nurses.

Wouldn't a nurse have answered when Duffy called out?

Amy Severn, a classmate of Duffy's and a Junior Volunteer at the hospital, brought her breakfast tray.

Duffy liked Amy . . . now. At school, Duffy had hardly noticed the quiet, dutiful student, who wore neat, "preppy" clothes like plaid skirts and sweaters, and always had every single blonde hair perfectly in place, sprayed so stiffly each strand looked like plastic. But here, in the hospital where Duffy felt so incredibly helpless, the qualities Duffy would have found uninteresting in Amy in the "outside world" proved comforting. She was kind and helpful, the two things Duffy needed most . . . besides a complete cure, which Amy couldn't provide.

"Are you just getting up, sleepyhead?" Amy asked with a sweet smile as Duffy stirred and moaned. Making a place for the tray on Duffy's cluttered bedside table, she helped the patient struggle to a half-sitting position, which was all Duffy could manage.

"Did you have a bad night?" Amy asked sympathetically as she expertly swung the top of the portable table across the bed and put the breakfast tray on top of it. "Poor Duffy. You've never really been sick before, have you? I can tell. You're not used to lying around with people fussing over you."

Duffy shook her head. It was always so hard

returning to awful reality, waking up and hearing the sounds of the hospital's daytime routine: the rattle of the food carts as they arrived on the fourth floor, the muted thuds of countless rubber-soled shoes, nurses calling back and forth to one another, the squeaking of wheelchairs and, occasionally, someone in pain crying out for relief. And there was, always, the pungent, antiseptic smell of the hospital.

"No," she murmured in response to Amy's comment. "I've never been sick before. Not like this. And I *hate* it!"

Amy's blue uniform whispered crisply as she nodded a head full of stiff curls, neatly held back from her pink, round face by a pale blue ribbon. She took a packet of silverware from the pocket of her uniform and removed the plastic wrapping. Then she slid a bowl of clear soup closer to the edge of the tray. "I know it's awful being sick. Have they taken your temperature yet this morning? Maybe it's gone down." That was Amy . . . forever optimistic.

Duffy made a face of disgust. "I wouldn't know. The nurse who took it wasn't in a sharing mood. I *asked* her what it was. I mean, it is *my* temperature, not hers. But she just shook her head, as if telling me would get her sent to prison or something. It was the nurse with the linebacker shoulders, the one with gray hair."

"Margaret. She's a good nurse, Duffy." Amy's voice was stern.

"Why can't she tell me how I'm doing? Nobody tells me anything around here." Duffy looked up at

Amy. "Amy, couldn't you sneak a peek at my chart? See if my fever's gone down?"

Horror washed across Amy's face. "Duffy! Volunteers are absolutely, positively not allowed to handle the patients' charts. If I got caught even *touching* one, I'd be thrown out of here, and I *love* being a volunteer. Forget it." She unfolded a cheap paper napkin and tucked it under Duffy's chin. "Your doctor will probably tell you about your temp when he comes back in this afternoon."

"No, he won't," Duffy complained. "He never tells me anything, either." But she gave up, knowing she wasn't going to get any information from Amy, who obviously thought that rule-breaking ranked right up there with murder and manslaughter.

Her hands were shaky. The spoon clanked against the bowl. But . . . not the same sound, she told herself. Not the same sound as last night at all. That sound was . . . sharper.

She was so tired. She glared at the bowl of thin, pale liquid staring up at her. "This is my breakfast? It looks like something you'd spray on flowers to kill insects." She gave the bowl a rude shove, sending its contents slopping out across the tray. "If I eat this, I'll barf!"

Amy swiped frantically at the mess with an extra napkin she carried in her pocket.

Of *course* she carries extra napkins, Duffy thought nastily. But she was grateful that Amy didn't scream at her, or even scold her. All she said was, "Duffy, you have to eat. You have to keep up your strength. You want to get out of here, don't you?"

Duffy's fevered eyes swept around the high-ceilinged, rectangular room. The walls, road-mapped here and there with small cracks, were a dingy white, the windows tall and narrow, shielded by old-fashioned wide-bladed Venetian blinds. The floor had worn black and white tile squares, and she had already memorized every spidery vein in the yellowed ceiling tile overhead. At night, when the hospital was deathly quiet, the grim little room was illuminated only by a tiny nightlight perched beside the heavy wooden door leading to the hall outside and beyond that, the nurses' station.

It was a lonely, isolated place, and Duffy wanted more than she'd ever wanted anything in her life to be free of it.

"Yes," she said softly, "I want to get out of here."

"Well, then, you have to eat. Here, I'll help." Amy sat on the edge of the bed and began to carefully spoon broth between Duffy's fever-cracked lips.

Duffy opened her mouth reluctantly.

Every time the spoon clanked against the bowl, she was reminded of the night sounds she'd heard.

Chapter 2

She had sipped only a few spoonfuls when a husky voice said, "Hey, she's eating! Medical progress is being made in this room today," and a tall boy dressed all in white entered the room, a broad grin on his sharply angled face. "Congrats, Amy! Yesterday, the sight of food made the patient, excuse the expression, puke. You must have magical powers."

Smith Lewis was an orderly at the hospital, but Duffy had seen him around town more than once before she became a patient. His arrival in town several months earlier had sent pulses racing among the female populace at Twelvetrees High School. They didn't get many new arrivals in town. It was the kind of town young people left before the ink was dry on the diploma. So the new arrival, older than they and already out of high school, had been unexpected. And, to most of Duffy's friends, a delightful surprise.

Smith's hair was thick and straight, slightly darker than his eyes, which were the color of root beer. His body moved carelessly, as if he were proud of being tall . . . or proud of being Smith Lewis. Most girls found the proud walk sexy. Duffy found it arrogant.

"Why don't you like him?" Duffy's best friend, Jane Sabatini had asked once when Smith, the top down on his black sports car, passed them in the mall parking lot.

"I didn't say I don't like him. I said I couldn't possibly like him as much as *he* likes him."

She had heard that he was given to practical jokes, which should have endeared him to her, since she had pulled a few pranks herself. But he talked too loudly, drove too fast, and grinned too easily, as if he were saying, "You think I'm adorable, right? Me, too." Every time she saw him, he was with a different girl. It was hard to imagine that someone like Smith Lewis could ever settle down to a medical education and career, which was what someone had told her he planned.

And whether she ate or not wasn't any of his business.

Duffy scowled at him. "I don't need an orderly. Amy's helping me."

Smith shook his head. "Eating hasn't improved your disposition, I see. Too bad. Didn't any of the nurses tell you that being nice to people isn't a bad idea when you look like something washed up on the beach?"

Duffy felt herself flushing and knew it had nothing to do with body temperature. Obnoxious though he was, she knew Smith was right. Her hair felt like an oil slick and she had no makeup on. And although the sponge baths given daily by the nurses were better than nothing, she yearned fiercely for a long, hot shower.

"Leave her alone," Amy told Smith, but she smiled sweetly as she said it. "She's sick. Quit picking on her."

"I just came to get the extra bed," Smith said, ambling over to stand behind the item in question. "You're not using it, and they need it in Pediatrics."

Duffy glanced over at the bed, remembering the night sounds she'd heard. The bed stared back at her. *You were hearing things,* it seemed to accuse. *Can't you see that I'm empty? There was no one here last night but you.*

"Amy," she asked slowly, "that bed's been empty ever since I came in, right?"

Amy nodded. "Sure. You'd remember if you had a roommate, Duffy. The hospital *is* filling up, though. A lot of flu in town. That's probably what you've got." She grimaced, her round, pink cheeks sliding up under her blue eyes. "There's an awful lot to do. And not enough nurses. They've put some of the volunteers on extra hours to help out. I've got band practice, so I can't do it, but Cynthia and a few of the others are helping out." Cynthia Boon was Amy's best friend.

Smith pushed the wheeled bed to the door. "Try to swallow something with sugar in it," he teased Duffy. "A sour female is a sad sight to behold. Take it easy, Duffy Quinn." And he left the room, laughing.

"Pig!" Duffy said heatedly. "A sour female? I should have thrown a pillow at him."

Amy laughed. "Oh, Smith's okay, Duffy. He told me once that his mother named him Smith because it was her last name. She'd always hated having such a boring last name, but thought it would be interesting as a first name. Smith has that same twisted sense of humor. He stole a skeleton from the lab a couple of weeks ago and stashed it in one of the empty beds. That little nurse from the third floor, the one with braids, found it. I guess she almost had a stroke."

Duffy swallowed a laugh. The stunt appealed to her. It was the kind of thing she'd love doing herself. But Smith had said she looked like beach debris. "What a stupid, childish thing to do," she announced primly.

Amy grinned. "Who are you kidding, Duffy? Everyone at school still talks about how you and Kit Rappaport and Jane stole the bust of Walt Whitman from Mrs. Toggle's English room and hung it from the flagpole."

Ignoring that, Duffy asked, "Why didn't Smith get fired? I know the head of the hospital, Dr. Crowder. He doesn't look like he'd have a sense of humor."

Amy shrugged. "Smith did get a lecture. But he told Dr. Crowder it was an experiment. Said he wanted to study the physiological effects of shock." Amy laughed. "Can you believe it? I don't think Dr. Crowder fell for it, but he didn't fire Smith."

Duffy was annoyed with Amy for laughing. She

knew it was only because Amy, usually too stiff-necked to find any humor in rule-breaking, thought Smith was cute. Smith was probably the sort of person who got away with murder, just because of his looks. She hated that. It was so unfair.

"I'd think the nurses would all hate him, he's so obnoxious," she said hopefully.

Amy slid off the bed and picked up Duffy's tray. "Nope. Just the opposite. He's a real hard worker. Sometimes he stays late when he doesn't have to, to help out. He's always hanging around the hospital. The nurses appreciate that, especially right now."

"Amy . . ." Duffy hesitated, not sure how to phrase her question. "Are you absolutely sure there wasn't anybody in that other bed last night? I mean, I was so out of it yesterday. . . . Maybe they brought someone in while I was sleeping, but she got better during the night and went home this morning before I woke up and you came on duty."

Amy frowned. "Duffy, this isn't a hotel. People don't just check in for a few hours. The patient in that bed was discharged last week and it's been empty ever since." Tray in hand, Amy fixed round blue eyes on Duffy. "This is the second time you've asked me about that bed. What's up?"

Duffy shook her head. "Nothing. Only . . . never mind. Forget it." How could she explain what she'd heard when she didn't *know* what she'd heard? She wasn't even sure, in broad daylight, that she'd heard anything. Amy would think brain-rot was setting in.

Maybe it was.

"Look, I've got to go," Amy said. "I'll bring you some magazines later, okay? Is Jane coming this afternoon? Kit?" After Jane, Christopher "Kit" Rappaport was Duffy's closest friend.

"I hope so." What Duffy hated most about being in the hospital, even more than the ugliness, the grimness, and the smell, was the horrible sense of isolation. She missed her friends, her family, her normal routine. This was Saturday. If it weren't for this stupid fever, she'd be home planning a trip to the mall, maybe a movie after dinner. . . . Real life was going on outside these moldy stone walls, and she was no longer a part of it. She *hated* that.

Nodding, Amy turned and hurried out of the room, the skirt of her crisp blue uniform swaying stiffly after her. "Get some rest," she called over her shoulder as she reached the door. "Dr. Morgan says that's the best cure."

Then Duffy was alone in the stuffy silence of her small, dreary prison. She knew Amy was right. Dr. Morgan *had* said, "Rest and quiet, that's the ticket. Sleep restores the body like nothing else can, so get plenty of it and you'll be out of here in no time."

Duffy settled down among the scratchy, yellowed bedding. Of course, Dr. Morgan hadn't added that getting plenty of sleep in a hospital wasn't easy, when nurses and volunteers and orderlies were forever taking your temperature or your blood and giving you baths and emptying your wastebasket or cleaning off your messy bedside table. Sleeping in a hospital was a luxury.

Especially when your room was full of frightening, unexplained sounds that came at night when everyone else had finally left you alone.

She closed her eyes, but she was suddenly afraid to sleep. She didn't want to have the clanking, clattering, flap-flapping dream again. The dream with the cry of terror.

If it *was* a dream. . . .

Chapter 3

Duffy lay in her hospital bed, her pretty, oval face flushed with fever, her eyes on the yellowed ceiling. She couldn't sleep. She flopped over on her side, unmindful of the IV needle embedded in her left hand.

I wish Jane and Kit would hurry up, she thought. If I tell them about my dream last night, Kit will react logically and rationally, the way he always does. Maybe he can help me figure it out.

Kit Rappaport, graduated the year before from Twelvetrees High School, was a math wizard who had been offered several scholarships and turned down all of them to continue working in his uncle's shoe store. The worst fight Duffy and Kit had ever had was about that shoe store.

"You're nuts!" she had shouted, and he had answered, "You just don't get it, do you? I *owe* the man!"

Kit Rappaport had been Duffy's good friend since she was nine. He had come into her fourth-grade class, his reddish hair very like hers except that his was carroty while hers was more cinnamon-colored. His plaid shirt was too small and flapped loosely outside of his jeans, his shoelaces untied. He had taken the seat opposite hers. Halfway through arithmetic, the frog he'd hidden in a pocket escaped and jumped to the floor. Without thinking, Duffy had reached down and scooped it up, hiding it in the folds of her gray sweatshirt before eagle-eyed old Mrs. Lauder could spy it and confiscate it. After class, she had returned the frog to Kit.

They'd been friends ever since, even after Kit skipped ninth grade and moved straight on to tenth, leaving her behind.

They'd never been anything more than friends, although Kit was cute enough, even if he was unaware of it. But he was so wrapped up in the misery of his home life that he had no thought for romance. Orphaned at nine by an automobile accident, he had been taken in by his aunt and uncle. "It's our duty," they told everyone sanctimoniously. Grim, humorless people, without affection or warmth, they believed that children should be useful. So Kit was put to work immediately in his uncle's shoe store, stocking shelves, sorting sizes, and pricing boxes. He hated every second of it.

A day or so after Duffy's argument with Kit about rejecting the scholarships, she had learned the truth from Jane. Upon Kit's graduation, his uncle had demanded that Kit "pay back every cent we've spent on you over the years" by working in the shoe store until the "debt" was paid off.

"Why didn't he tell me?" Duffy shrieked at poor Jane.

"He thought you'd call him a wimp."

Duffy had been ashamed then, because that was accurate. She would have.

Kit told her later he would have ignored his uncle's demands and left town, but his aunt had suffered a heart attack a week after graduation and was unable to help out in the store. He felt then that he had no choice. He would have to stay.

Their friendship had continued. Duffy knew that a lot of her friends didn't understand. Kit was cute and smart and nice. Why wasn't she in love with him? Well, she *did* love Kit, but not the way most girls loved a boy. She loved him because he understood her, her restlessness, her odd sense of humor, even her temper — and he liked her anyway. And she knew he would always be there for her. Even when he finally did go away to college, they'd still be friends. Forever. That was just the way it was.

And if he could get away from the shoe store, he would come with Jane to visit her that afternoon.

She missed him as much as she missed her parents and Jane. He would calm her down, help her to accept the hospital's routine. Kit could do that when no one else could.

"Hi," came suddenly from behind her, and Duffy turned, hope in her gray eyes.

But it wasn't Kit. Or Jane. Instead, Dylan Rourke was standing beside her bed.

A classmate and an employee of the hospital,

Dylan was wearing the obligatory pea-green slacks and tunic. The tunic pulled impatiently at shoulders that spent an hour every day lifting weights and had been used repeatedly as a battering ram on the football field. Dylan's nose had been broken twice in the same spot and now leaned slightly to the right. It gave his square, honest, open face a look of devilishness, which was quickly cancelled out by the trail of freckles leap-frogging across that same nose. Unlike Kit, Dylan had to struggle for good grades, a battle Duffy thought he was losing. That might keep him out of medical school.

Still, while Dylan might not be as smart as Kit, he was shrewd. Working at the hospital part-time put him in touch with doctors who, if he impressed them favorably, could put in a good word for him in pre-med programs at colleges across the country.

One way or another Dylan was determined, like Cynthia and Smith, to become a doctor. Maybe his methods were different, but Duffy had known him since ninth grade and when Dylan wanted something that much, he usually got it. He might look like an ad for a physical fitness magazine, but there was a lot more to Dylan than brawn.

"Your friendly maintenance engineer is here, at your service," he said, grinning, making the freckles dance across the bridge of his nose. His deep blue eyes focused sympathetically on her flushed face. "Anything I can do for you?"

"You mean my friendly *janitor*," Duffy said crankily.

Dylan shrugged good-naturedly. "Whatever.

Duff, you look really sick. You okay?"

Duffy glared at him. "Dylan, would I be in this horrible place if I were okay?" She waved her needle-pinioned hand at him. "This stuff isn't doing a bit of good. I'd get better faster at home, where I belong."

Concern filled his square, open face. "I know you hate it here, Duffy. It's not the greatest place in the world to spend your weekend. But when someone's as sick as you are, this is the safest place to be."

When he turned away to pick up her wastebasket, his broom clanked against the side of the metal container.

That sound last night — was this the same sound?

No. It wasn't quite right . . . it didn't . . . *clank* enough.

"Dylan," she asked, "did you work last night?"

"Uh-uh." He lifted the nearly full basket. "I was wiped out from a chem exam yesterday in Deaton's class. Man, that guy can really dream up some wicked questions! Think I passed, though. No, I wasn't on last night. Why?"

Disappointed that Dylan couldn't help her with last night's puzzle, Duffy sank back against the pillow. "I had this dream . . ." she began. Maybe Dylan *could* help her figure it out. "At least, I think it was a dream. There were these noises . . . it was really bizarre, like there was someone in the room. It was too dark to see, and I was kind of asleep. I was sure someone was doing something in here. But when I called out . . . if I really *did* call out, no one answered me."

Dylan looked interested. "Maybe someone *was* in here. The other bed is gone. Maybe someone was taking it out while you were sleeping and that's what you heard."

Duffy shook her head. "No. Smith just came and got the bed a little while ago. Took it to Pediatrics. And Amy said at breakfast that no one's been in that bed the whole time I've been here, so. . . ."

Dylan thought for a minute. "One of the nurses told me your temperature was headed for the record books when they brought you in. No wonder you've been hearing things. I'm surprised you're not seeing things, too." He stopped and gave her a quizzical look. "You're not, are you? I mean, did you *see* anything last night?"

"No. It was too dark. That little night-light over by the door isn't worth two cents. A jar of fireflies would make a better light."

He laughed. Then he took the wastebasket out into the hall and emptied it into a giant wheeled container.

As he left the room, Duffy sat up straight in bed. There was something . . .

When Dylan returned to put the small basket in its proper place, Duffy commanded, "Do that again."

"What? Do what again?"

"Go out and come back in. Go *on*! Quit looking at me like I just sprouted a second head. I have a good reason. Just do it, please."

Frowning, Dylan obeyed. When he came back in, he said, "What was that all about?"

"It's your *shoes!*" Duffy leaned forward to peer over the edge of her bed. "That's one of the sounds I heard last night . . . that funny slap-slap on the tile. Rubber-soled shoes!"

Dylan was visibly unimpressed. "Duffy," he said kindly, "this is a hospital. Practically everyone wears rubber-soled shoes, so we won't disturb the patients."

Duffy struggled to figure out if she'd just learned anything important. "Yes, but if a member of the staff was in my room last night, why didn't they answer when I called out? There was just this weird, creepy silence."

"You said you weren't quite awake. Are you sure it wasn't a dream?"

Disappointed that Dylan had no better answer than that, Duffy flopped back down on the pillow.

"Hey, don't be mad," he said softly, reaching down to take one of her hands in his. Hers felt parched and dry, his strong and comforting. "Maybe it's your fever. High temperatures can do crazy things to people."

Crazy? *That* wasn't what she wanted to hear.

Seeing the look on her face, Dylan said hastily, "Look, you had to be dreaming, Duffy. If no one was in the other bed, the only reason a nurse would be in this room would be to take care of you. Since you *say* no one was doing that, it's pretty clear that there wasn't anyone here, right?"

"I don't *say* that no one was taking care of me,

Dylan . . . no one *was*. I'm not making this up."

But she didn't want to be mad at Dylan. Especially not over something she herself didn't understand. It wasn't fair to expect Dylan to understand it. They'd been friends a long time. She probably would have dated him once upon a time, but he, like everyone else, had thought she and Kit were a couple, and he'd begun dating Amy Severn. They had broken up only a couple of weeks ago. And he'd been so nice to Duffy since she was admitted to the hospital, she was beginning to wonder if he might be interested in more than friendship now.

She was too sick to think about romance. Besides, how could anybody possibly be interested in someone who looked like roadkill? Dylan was only in her room because he had work to do.

But when she was well again . . . maybe . . .

"I guess you're right," she said after a moment or two of silence. "When my temp spikes, I can't tell the difference between what's real and what isn't. It's like being in another world. A very *hot* one."

Satisfied that she wasn't going to stay mad at him, Dylan began sweeping the room, using his considerable bulk to heave the broom sideways in strong, straight strokes.

"Have you seen Jane or Kit?" Duffy asked.

Dylan glanced at his watch. "Too early for visiting hours. You'll have to wait until after lunch. Isn't he working today?"

Dylan said "he" with a noticeable note of resentment in his voice. He and Kit weren't friends.

Dylan, strong and determined, had been Football. Kit, light and fast, had been Track. Maybe the difference between the two of them was just that simple. Or maybe it went deeper, had something to do with the fact that Dylan was the center of a huge, happy family but had trouble in school, while Kit, who had no family to speak of and lived a lonely, depressing life, had been valedictorian of his graduating class and won scholarships that Dylan would have killed for.

When Dylan talked about Kit, his face suddenly didn't look quite so warm and friendly.

But that only lasted a second. His face cleared quickly as Duffy answered his question.

"I don't know if he's working. I haven't seen him or Jane since I got here. They wouldn't let me have visitors the first day. But it's Saturday. I can't imagine The Grinch Who Stole Kit's Future letting him have a weekend day off. So yeah, he's probably working."

"Kit owed the man," Dylan argued mildly, "he said so himself. He'll go to college next year."

"They brainwashed him. Dumped guilt on him. He should have gone, anyway." But Kit wasn't like that, and both Duffy and Dylan knew it.

When he had finished his task, Dylan came over to the bed to hold her hand in his briefly. Then he said, "Keep your chin up and do what the doctor says, even when you don't want to, okay? I'll be back later to see how you're doing."

The hushed *slap-slap* of his rubber-soled shoes echoed in Duffy's ears for a long time after the sound had faded away. It reminded her . . .

She was being stupid. Of course she'd heard that sound before. As Dylan said, practically everyone in the hospital wore the same kind of shoes.

But if a member of the hospital staff had been in her room last night, why hadn't he or she answered when she called out? Wasn't that what they were there for, to help when help was needed?

What kind of nurse or doctor or orderly or volunteer would ignore a night cry from a patient?

No kind. They wouldn't *do* that. So Dylan had to be right. She'd been dreaming.

But it had certainly *seemed* real.

In an effort to clear her mind of the maddening puzzle, Duffy rolled over on her side and tried to doze until lunchtime and then, she hoped, the arrival of Jane and Kit.

Except for an interruption by the nurse Duffy called "Vampira" because she came in only to collect blood from Duffy's already-sore arm, she remained alone, and finally fell asleep.

Chapter 4

When Junior Volunteer Cynthia Boon entered Duffy's room shortly after the dismal lunch tray had blessedly been taken away, the patient was struggling to force a comb through her tangled, cinnamon-hued waves.

"Oh, I give up!" she cried in despair, heaving the comb across the room. It made a sharp, insulted click when it hit the floor tile. Bouncing twice, it landed in a corner.

"Easy, easy," Cynthia cautioned softly. She walked over swiftly and picked up the comb, returning it to Duffy. "You're not supposed to get upset. Your temperature will spike again."

"Oh, what's the difference?" Duffy grumbled. "I'm never going to get out of this awful place, anyway. I'm imprisoned here for life."

Cynthia, her long, straight, sand-colored hair pulled back in a neat but too-severe bun at the back of her neck, smiled. "Oh, Duffy, you've only been here two days. You should be grateful you don't have a chronic illness, like some of the kids in Pediatrics. They're in and out of the hospital all the time and *they* don't complain."

"Don't lecture me, Cynthia." Duffy hated the way Cynthia looked: her hair so smooth and neat, her pale blue uniform so clean and crisp, her skin shiny and healthy-looking. The only consolation was those tiny lines of tension around Cynthia's pale eyes and full mouth. They made her look older than seventeen years.

Cynthia was the most ambitious person Duffy had ever known and the most energetic. She had probably walked home from the hospital immediately after she was born, unwilling to wait for someone to carry her. Right now, Cynthia was taking her junior and senior years simultaneously because she was so anxious to finish high school and go on to college and medical school . . . which she would probably finish in six weeks or less, Duffy figured.

Duffy glared resentfully at Cynthia. She had almost certainly had a long, beautiful shower and shampoo that very morning. Reason enough to hate her. If she wasn't so nice . . .

"Why can't I have a shower?" Duffy begged. "Cynthia, you could fix it . . . you could sneak me out of here and into the showers down the hall, couldn't you? Please? Smith told me I look like beach garbage, and he's right. He's disgusting, but he's right."

Cynthia shook her neat, narrow head. "Duffy, I know how you feel, but you have to be patient. When Dr. Morgan thinks it's okay for you to have a shower, you'll have one. I'll take you down there myself. But not yet."

"The newer hospitals have showers right in the rooms," Duffy muttered. "But I have to be stuck in this ancient, medieval torture palace where the plumbing screams all day and the elevators creak and — "

"Duffy," Cynthia said gently but firmly as she fluffed Duffy's pillow, "lighten up."

Duffy groaned. "You're right. I'm being a creep. I'm sorry, Cyn. I know I'm a crummy patient. It's just . . ."

"I know. You're not the type to be stuck in a bed, Duffy. It must be making you crazy." Cynthia put on what Duffy called "that hospital face," with the fake smile that failed to reach the eyes, and the voice so falsely cheerful. "But you'll be out of here in no time, I promise." All of the nurses said things like that when a patient was giving them a hard time. It was probably something they learned in the first week of nursing school.

Duffy glowered. "Right."

"Hey, what happened to your other bed? It was here yesterday."

"Smith took it to Pediatrics."

Cynthia marched over to the faded flowered curtain hanging limply on a circular metal rod bolted to the ceiling above the second bed's now-empty space. "Well, then, let's open the window blinds and pull this curtain all the way back. It's blocking the light. No wonder you're depressed." She went first to the window to raise the blinds and then returned to the flowered curtain and yanked it backward on its metal rings.

And Duffy's eyes widened as the curtain sliding along the metal rod made a jingle-jangle sound identical to the one she had heard during the night.

She *had* heard it. She hadn't been dreaming.

She groaned silently. She didn't *want* to be back on this again. Everyone would think she was crazy.

But if someone *had* been in her room. . . .

What were they doing there?

"There *was* someone in here last night," she said aloud.

"Hmm?" Satisfied with the early spring sunshine now flooding the room, Cynthia turned back to Duffy. "What did you say?"

Duffy leaned back against her pillow. "I thought I heard someone in here last night. Dylan told me I'd probably imagined it, because of the fever. I'd just about decided he was right, until you pulled that curtain. Now I *know* I heard something. That curtain was pulled back . . . or forward . . . last night."

Cynthia returned to Duffy's bedside and looked down at her. "I don't get it," she said. "Of course someone was in here. Taking care of you. Your temperature has to be watched carefully. It was *your* curtain you heard, not the other one." She smiled. "We don't have time to waste on empty beds."

Duffy shook her head. "No. Whoever was in here didn't answer when I called out. They didn't want me to *know* they were here. *That's* what's weird, Cynthia."

Before the Junior Volunteer could answer, they were interrupted by the arrival of a short, chunky girl in too-tight Bermuda shorts and an oversized hot-pink sweatshirt, her dark, curly hair carelessly fastened with a huge hot-pink bow. Her face was breathtakingly beautiful, heart-shaped around almost-violet eyes with thick, dark lashes and perfectly arched brows. Her skin was ivory and flawless, as smooth and unblemished as a retouched photograph. She was carrying a pile of magazines and was seriously out of breath.

"Elevator . . . broken . . . again . . ." Duffy's best friend, Jane Sabatini, gasped. "Other . . . one . . . crowded. Had to . . . walk . . . stairs . . ." Her lovely cheeks were flushed with exertion and sweat beaded her upper lip.

"Sit!" Cynthia commanded, shoving a chair at Jane. Jane sat. Cynthia hurried to Duffy's bedside table and poured a glass of water from the heavy metal carafe. "Here, drink this," she ordered, thrusting the glass under Jane's nose. "And next time, wait for a working elevator," she added sharply. "Four flights of stairs carrying a load of magazines is not a smart idea for someone . . ." She stopped, obviously not wanting to be unkind.

"Go ahead, say it," Jane gasped. "For someone overweight. You don't seriously think I'm not aware of it, do you?" An impish grin crossed her lovely face. "You don't approve of exercise, Cynthia? I thought all you medical people preached exercise."

"Nobody recommends that you do it all in one day." Cynthia turned to Duffy. "Look, since you've got company now, I'd better get back to work. I'll report that elevator, Jane. We might actually get lucky enough to have someone fix it. Wouldn't that be a kick?"

Smiling with satisfaction at her own little joke, Cynthia marched from the room.

Jane sighed. "So thin, so efficient, so smart . . . couldn't you just smack her?"

Duffy smiled weakly. "It's even worse when you're stuck in this bed with greasy hair, sweaty skin, and no chance of a shower." Then she added more seriously, "She's been a big help, though. I don't know how she finds the time, but she comes in to see me a lot." She shifted uncomfortably in the bed and then asked, "Where's Kit? Didn't he come with you?"

Jane shook her head and slipped her tired feet out of worn black flats. "Uh-uh. Couldn't get off work. That uncle of his, the one who makes Scrooge look like Santa Claus, has been really riding him lately. Maybe Kit'll be over tonight, if the massah lets the slave out of his chains."

"Poor Kit," Duffy murmured. She was bitterly disappointed. She was glad to see Jane, but she had wanted to talk to Kit about the "dream." She needed his calm, rational input.

Jane nodded. "Anyone else been in to see you?" she asked too casually.

Duffy knew she meant Dylan. Jane had had her

violet eyes on Dylan ever since she'd heard that he and Amy were history.

Duffy knew how lonely Jane was. Her mother had died when Jane was twelve, when Jane's older brother, Dean, had already graduated and gone away to college. Three years later, her father had remarried, but Jane didn't get along with her stepmother.

Popular enough with girls because she was friendly and fun, she had less success with boys, in spite of her beauty. At first, when they'd both started dating, Duffy couldn't understand it. Jane was so gorgeous.

But after watching Jane several times on double dates, Duffy had decided that Jane's problem with boys had to do with her obvious neediness. Jane wanted so desperately to have someone in her life . . . someone who loved her, who thought she was special. The way she latched onto a boy on the very first date, as if they'd known each other forever, as if they were destined to march through life together, was very scary to Duffy.

And obviously very scary to the boys as well.

Duffy had tried talking to Jane about it. "You don't need to go so fast," she had said gently. "You're so gorgeous, Jane, if you'd just relax and take it easy, some neat guy would come along and fall head over heels for you."

But Jane couldn't help it. She was so lonely.

"Yes," Duffy answered, "Dylan was here." And then cringed as disappointment shadowed Jane's face. Because it didn't seem to her that Dylan

Rourke was interested in Jane Sabatini. It seemed to her that Dylan Rourke was interested in Duffy Quinn. That could be a serious problem between two best friends.

But Duffy couldn't think about that now. She had more important things to think about. "Dylan thinks I'm losing it," she told Jane. Then she repeated for Jane her story about the night sounds. "Dylan thinks I was hearing things, because of my fever. Think that's possible?"

Jane shook her head. Several clumps of dark, curly hair escaped the big bow. "It was probably one of those hunks out there in white sneaking in here with a date. I mean, you were probably zonked out, dead to the world, right? All they'd have to do is pull the curtain and they'd have instant privacy. Possible?"

The thought hadn't occurred to Duffy. Since she'd fallen ill, she felt so isolated from the real world. Things like romance and dating and having fun seemed foreign, unreal, as if they existed only on another planet.

But Jane's idea made sense. Two people grabbing a couple of minutes of privacy. She was sure it was against the rules, using a patient's room that way. That would explain why there'd been no answer when she called out. Whoever it was, they wouldn't want to admit they were there.

"I miss you, Duffy," Jane said sadly. "I hate it that you're sick. I know I shouldn't be thinking of myself, but I can't help it. My dad and Susan are busy, my brother's all wrapped up in his wife and kids and his job at the lab, and Kit is being held prisoner by his horrible uncle." Hope edged into her voice. "You do look a *tiny* bit better. Think you might be coming home soon?"

Duffy could do nothing but shrug.

Disappointment again filled Jane's face.

She stayed a long time, most of the afternoon. It was nice to have company, but Duffy, her fever up as it had been the two previous afternoons, tired quickly. When the nurse came in at three-thirty to take her temperature, she sent Jane home. "This girl needs her rest," she said briskly. "Off with you, now!"

It wasn't until Jane, reluctant to leave, had gone that Duffy remembered something that didn't fit Jane's theory about what she'd heard the night before. The whispered protest — had that been the voice of someone nervous about breaking the rules, afraid of being caught?

It hadn't sounded like that. It had sounded much more fearful . . . terrified. There had been so much urgency in that whispered, "No, no, don't!"

What would put such fear into a voice?

Only something very scary. Something terrifying.

Dylan had said she was "safer" here than at home. But the person last night — if there had been someone there — hadn't felt safe.

So maybe Dylan was wrong.

Maybe she wasn't safe here at all.

Chapter 5

The nurse who came in to take Duffy's temperature shortly after another dinner of thin soup frowned as she pulled the thermometer from her patient's mouth and peered down at it. "Doctor isn't going to like this. You're up a whole degree. You haven't been resting like Doctor told you," she accused.

She must think she's in Pediatrics, Duffy thought resentfully, talking to me as if I had a pacifier in my mouth. "I have, too," she replied defiantly, sounding exactly like a two-year-old. That angered her further and she added, "I need to get some exercise, that's all. Anyone would be feverish lying in this stupid bed all day! Why can't I get up?"

"Because you have a fever," the nurse answered patiently. "If you would just do what Doctor says . . ." Then, Duffy's chart under her arm, she turned and left the room.

I've *been* doing what "Doctor" said, Duffy thought, and where has it got me? Nowhere, that's where! What I really need is to get out of this stupid bed, move around, so that my body knows it's still alive. Then it will start acting like it's alive.

Having made up her mind, Duffy decided to wait until after visiting hours for an excursion. The gift shop would be uncrowded then. She'd take the elevator down to the first floor and go buy a magazine and some shampoo. That wouldn't be too much exercise. It would be just enough to get her juices flowing again. Maybe it would even lower her temperature. Then she could go home.

Visiting hours came and went. Apparently sensing that Duffy would rather spend valuable visiting time with her friends, her parents didn't stay long.

But while they were there, she tried once again to talk them into taking her home. "I'm not getting better here," she begged, "and there are all these weird noises when I'm trying to sleep. . . ."

"Sweetheart," her mother said patiently, "Dr. Morgan will tell us when you can go home. It won't be until he's positive that you're well enough. He knows what's best."

And her father added, "You know, Duffy, you scared us half to death . . . our healthy, busy girl lying on the sofa like that, not moving a muscle, your face all flushed with fever. We're not taking any chances by letting you come home too soon."

Gently warning her not to "give the staff a hard time" (they knew her so well), her parents left.

Shortly after they left, Jane arrived, alone. Without Kit. Duffy was filled with disappointment. But before she had a chance to ask Jane where he was,

Cynthia and Amy, now off duty, joined Duffy and Jane. Cynthia looked tired, but Amy seemed as perky as she had earlier in the day.

"I can't stay long," Cynthia confessed, sinking into a wooden chair near the foot of Duffy's bed. "I've got a chem test tomorrow. I'll probably be up all night."

"You work too hard," Amy said gently, settling down beside Duffy on the bed. "Why do you volunteer here when you've got a double load of schoolwork? I *know* why Dylan does it. He needs the contacts here. But you'll slide right into medical school, Cynthia, so why do you spend so much time here?"

Cynthia smiled wearily. "To learn more. Besides, they need the help. They're so understaffed. Especially now, with this awful flu."

Just as Cynthia finished speaking, Smith poked his head in the doorway. "Hey, what's going on? A party? And you didn't invite me?" Without waiting for an answer, he ambled into the room, saying, "Rourke's on his way, too," nodding toward the hall. "He's hot on my heels. All we need now to make this a real party is a couple more guys to even things out."

Ignoring him, Duffy turned to Jane. "Speaking of guys, I thought you'd bring Kit with you."

"I stopped in the shoe store on my way home from here this afternoon, but he wasn't there. His uncle was spitting nails, so I guess they had another fight and Kit didn't show up for work. I don't blame him."

"You talking about Rappaport?" Dylan asked as he arrived, still in his green garb. "He split."

Duffy frowned. "Split?"

"Yeah. Took a hike. Left town. Piled up his car with all his junk and headed for sunny California."

Duffy stared at him. No. No! Dylan was wrong. He had to be. Kit wouldn't take off, just like that. Not without saying good-bye, without explaining. "When? When did he leave?" she cried.

Hearing the distress in her voice, Dylan looked guilty. "Gee, maybe I shouldn't have said anything. I guess I just figured you knew already. I don't know exactly when he left. I ran into him last night. He said he was taking off, leaving. Said he couldn't take his uncle anymore."

"He wouldn't go without telling me good-bye," Duffy said in a soft, bewildered voice. "Not Kit." Then, hope replacing shock, she added, "Maybe he hasn't left yet."

"He's gone, all right," Dylan told her. "His uncle called my dad this morning." Dylan's father was a lawyer. "Said he wanted to cut Kit out of his will. He's not leaving him a penny. He said he didn't see why he should after Kit 'abandoned' him. What an old grouch! Why are you so surprised?" he asked Duffy, his voice kind. "We all knew he couldn't stick it out in that shoe store forever. Who could? Old Man Rappaport's a royal pain. You said so yourself, more than once."

Yes, she had said that. And she'd meant it. She knew the past six months had been rough on Kit. He and his uncle disagreed constantly. And his recuperating aunt was an expert at dishing out guilt. Duffy admired Kit for sticking it out as long as he had, because she knew she never could have done it. In the same circumstances, she would have been throwing dishes, smashing furniture, and screaming her lungs out. And although Kit had seemed to be biding his time with incredible patience, she'd always known that he might bolt at any time.

And now he had.

She didn't blame him. Not the tiniest bit.

But she was sick with disappointment. Not to get a chance to tell him good-bye . . . to wish him luck. . . .

Reading her mind, Cynthia said gently, "Duffy, I'm sure Kit came to tell you good-bye. But you were so out of it, he wouldn't have been allowed to see you. It wasn't his fault. He'll call you when he gets settled, you know he will."

A wave of sadness hit Duffy. Kit . . . gone? She had spent Sunday afternoon with him, in a boat out on the lake. It had been warm when they started out, but then the clouds hid the sun and it became cold and drizzly very quickly. Her mother was convinced it was that outing that had brought on her illness.

Duffy could only hope that if Kit had called the house to see how she was, her mother hadn't accused him of making her sick. He would have felt so guilty.

An uncomfortable silence fell over the room. Realizing it was because she was being so obvious about her feelings, Duffy made an effort to put the bad news aside for the moment. "He'll call me when he's settled in California," she said, blinking back tears. "Cynthia's right. Meanwhile," taking a deep breath, "I've got to get out of this bed. I'm going for a walk the minute the halls are empty tonight. I'm sick of being sick." Then she added in a low voice, "If I hadn't been sick, Kit would have told me good-bye and I could have wished him luck."

As Duffy had expected, both Cynthia and Amy argued with her. She wasn't well enough to leave her room, they said. She'd send her fever soaring, Cynthia pointed out, and Amy said quietly that it wasn't smart to disobey the doctor's orders.

Duffy ignored them. She was getting out of her horrible little room and nothing anyone said would change her mind.

Cynthia and Amy eventually gave up and left. But Jane, anxious to have her friend back at her side, said, "I think it's a great idea. Just don't overdo it."

Although she could tell that Dylan and Smith both disapproved of her plan, they knew better than to argue with her, and shaking their heads, they left with Jane.

When Duffy first sat up and swung her legs over the edge of her bed, the room turned bright pink and swayed around her. That passed. When her vision had cleared, she slipped her feet into white terrycloth slippers and wrapped herself in a matching robe. Then she stood up.

Red waves of heat slapped at her, blurring her vision again. One step . . . if she could just take one step without falling . . . tentatively, she put a foot forward, gripping her IV pole for support.

She was still standing. Another step, then another, and soon she was at the door.

Peering out, she found with satisfaction that the hallway was deserted. Silent and empty. No nurses, no visitors, no orderlies, no patients. She had the hall all to herself.

It was great being out of bed, although she felt like a toddler taking its first steps. Her legs threatened to cave in at any moment. But she was too eager to be free of her prison, and moved slowly and carefully out into the long, narrow hall.

"You don't like being cooped up, do you?" Smith Lewis asked her softly as he appeared out of nowhere.

She jumped, startled, and slammed into the wall. Her plastic IV bag slapped against the metal pole. "Don't *do* that!" she hissed, furious.

"I don't blame you," he said, ignoring her anger. "Being cooped up would make me crazy, too."

Crazy? Sensitive to the word because of her confusion about last night's strange sounds, she snapped, "I'm not crazy! Being cooped up isn't making me crazy, and neither is my fever."

Smith raised his hands in front of him in mock defense. "Whoa! Easy, girl. Chill out." And shaking his head, he moved forward to take her elbow. "I just wanted to make sure you could handle this little hike. You look pretty shaky to me. Your legs going to hold up?"

Duffy was ashamed of herself for biting his head

off. Being so unsure about what had really happened the night before *was* making her crazy. But she didn't want Smith to know that.

"I've changed my mind," she said suddenly. "The nurse was right. I'm not up to this. Would you help me back to my room, please?" If she was going to take her little "hike," she was going to take it alone. She didn't want Smith Lewis hanging on her, as if she were some feeble old lady. She'd get rid of him first, then she'd get her exercise.

But before she left her room a second time, she'd make absolutely sure no one was around. Especially Smith.

"This Kit person," he said as he accompanied her back to her room, "someone special to you?"

She didn't think she could talk about Kit without crying, and she had no intention of crying in front of Smith Lewis. "A friend," she said, her voice strained.

"Just a friend?"

"Just" a friend? No, much more than a friend . . . but she didn't want to talk about Kit with Smith. "A good friend," was all she would say.

"Oh. Great."

He left her at the door to her room and disappeared down the hallway.

After checking her pocket to make sure she had money for a magazine and shampoo, Duffy peered into the hall again. A nurse came out of the shower room with a patient. Duffy ducked back behind her door. A shower — how wonderful! Maybe, if the exercise regulated her temperature the way she hoped it would, she could talk someone into letting her take a shower the next day so she could wash her oil-slicked hair and look like a human being.

When the hall was finally deserted again, the overhead fluorescent lights dimmed for the night. The nurses' station was empty. Murmuring voices from other rooms told her the staff was busy readying patients for the night. Now was the time to make her dash for freedom.

She scuttled down the hall quickly and quietly, sliding the IV pole along behind her like a puppy on a leash.

One of the elevators wore an OUT OF ORDER sign. Duffy remembered Jane's heavy breathing that afternoon. Poor Jane.

Duffy pushed the button for the working elevator and waited impatiently for the silver arrow over the door to point to the number four. As the arrow began to move upward, Duffy stepped closer to the wide metal doors, prepared to enter as soon as they slid open.

The arrow moved, turtle-slow, around its half circle.

Gripping her IV stand, Duffy took another step forward.

The elevator finally reached her floor, and the doors, groaning with the effort, began to slide open.

"Duffy!" a voice off to her right shouted. *"Stop!"*

As her right foot lifted to step onto the elevator floor, Duffy turned her head to see who had shouted at her. She had no intention of letting anyone stop her little journey, and continued to aim her foot into the elevator.

But before it could land, a blur of white flew through the air and collided with her, knocking her off-balance and sending her flying backward. Too startled to cry out, she landed on her back on the tile floor, half-smothered by the white projectile now sprawled across her. Trying to catch her breath, Duffy realized in stunned shock that the bulk pinning her down had hair . . . arms . . . legs . . .

Smith Lewis.

Smith Lewis had just tackled her bodily in the hospital hallway and sent her flying across the tile.

"You're insane!" she gasped, struggling to sit upright. "You maniac! What are you *doing*?"

He pushed himself up into a sitting position. "Look!" he breathed, pointing a shaky finger toward the elevator. "Look!"

Duffy's eyes followed the pointing finger.

The elevator's doors were open all the way.

But there was no elevator cage inside.

There was only a black, yawning void.

Chapter 6

Duffy slumped against the wall, her shoulders shaking as Smith stood up and bent to retrieve her overturned IV pole.

"There . . . isn't anything *there*," she said dully, her eyes on the wide black mouth waiting to swallow her up. "I . . . I would have stepped into . . . air. Nothing but *air*!"

"And fallen five floors to the basement," Smith agreed grimly. His voice was full of anger and contempt as he added, "This is Rourke's fault. I *told* him it was the *second* elevator that wasn't working, *not* the first. He put the sign on the wrong one!" Shaking the thick thatch of dark, curly hair, he said, "Someone could have been killed." He moved his gaze from the black gaping hole to Duffy. "*You* could have been killed," he said emphatically.

As he moved to set her IV pole upright and then help her to her feet, he muttered, "Wait'll I get my hands on that Dylan! I'll have his head on a platter. His supervisor's going to hear about this, too."

Duffy couldn't tear her eyes away from the empty

elevator shaft. Empty. No cage there to carry her safely down to the first floor. Nothing there but a deep, hungry emptiness. For one horrible second, she could actually feel herself falling . . . falling . . . into the shadowy nothingness. A sickening, terrifying sense of helpless horror overwhelmed her.

Duffy stood up. If it hadn't been for Smith's firm grip on her elbow, her knees would have buckled and sent her to the floor in a slow, buttery slide.

A nasty little voice in her mind chimed repeatedly, *You almost died . . . you almost died . . . you almost died. . . .*

"What on earth is going on here?" a voice demanded. The night nurse bustled down the hall toward them, indignation written all over her middle-aged face. "What are you two doing out here? Lewis, you're not on the schedule tonight. And Quinn, what are you doing out of bed?"

Shock and fear had stolen Duffy's voice from her. She was unable to speak.

Smith quickly explained what had happened as briefly as possible. "I came back to get my paycheck," he added. "It wasn't ready when I left earlier. And I saw Duffy about to step into the elevator, the one I knew was out of commission."

"Oh, for heaven's sake," the nurse said in an exasperated voice, "that elevator was supposed to be fixed by now." She took Duffy's arm. "You take care of that sign," she ordered Smith briskly. "I'll see that Quinn gets back to her room."

Duffy found her voice. "Smith," she said quietly as he moved away, "thanks. Thanks for — "

"Forget it," he interrupted. "No big deal. Go back to bed. And," he added harshly, "maybe you'd be better off staying there. Safer that way."

Nodding, Duffy allowed herself to be led back to her room.

"You've got no business being out of bed," the nurse scolded as Duffy crawled into bed. "You look flushed. I'm going to take your temperature right now. Then you'll have your sleeping pill so you can forget all about this nasty business."

Duffy didn't see how that was possible. How could she forget that she had almost plunged five floors to her death?

I came to this horrible place to get well, she thought as the thermometer was thrust under her tongue, and instead, I almost died.

How could Dylan have made such a terrible mistake?

She lay curled up in bed, trembling violently, until the sleeping pill began to take effect. Her body relaxed, involuntarily. Her arms and legs turned to warm water. But her mind continued to shudder with fear, until that, too, fell under the spell of the drug.

She was drifting off into a pleasant cotton-candy fuzziness when Smith came quietly into the darkened room and stood beside her bed.

Leaning down, he asked softly, "You okay?"

"If you get caught in here," she said drowsily, "Attila the Nurse will have you shot. She just left, but she could pop back in at any time, probably with a whip in her hand or a set of thumbscrews."

Smith didn't smile. "They gave you a shot? Or a pill? Must have. I expected to find you in hysterics. Medication is a wonderful thing." He awkwardly patted her head, said, "Sleep well," and turned to leave.

But there was something Duffy needed to ask him, if she could only grab the thought dancing around crazily in her mind and turn it into coherent words. The question she needed to ask Smith was . . . was . . .

No, the sleeping pill was getting in her way, making it impossible to form the question into words and send it on its way to Smith.

It would have to wait until tomorrow. She hoped it wasn't important.

But she had a strong, uneasy feeling that it was.

In spite of the uneasiness, she was asleep before Smith reached the door.

When she awoke Sunday morning, having slept soundly through the night, the question had crystallized in her mind. It was so clear and so urgent, she asked the nurse who brought her breakfast tray if Smith was on duty.

The nurse, a young, pretty student, grinned. "You, too? All the other female patients are ga-ga over Lewis. I don't see him as your type, but — "

"It's not like that," Duffy protested, annoyed. "I just need to ask him something."

"Right. Like what he's doing next Saturday night, just in case you're sprung by then?"

Duffy glared daggers at the girl. "Will you just

call him for me, please? Tell him I need to see him, right away."

Although the student nurse was grinning when she left the room, she must have passed on the message, because five minutes later, Smith hurried into the room.

"Well, you look better. Your eyes are still sort of glazed with terror, though. What's up?"

"Smith," Duffy said earnestly, "when exactly did you tell Dylan to put the out-of-order sign on the elevator?"

Smith thought for a minute. "About four o'clock. Right after that friend of yours, Jane, had to struggle up four flights of stairs. I was afraid someone would have a heart attack before maintenance got the cage fixed. Why?"

"Well, think about it," Duffy said impatiently. "This place was full of visitors all afternoon and all evening. People were going up and down like yoyos. If Dylan's sign was hanging on the wrong elevator all that time, how come no one but me came so close to taking a dive into an empty elevator shaft?" She shuddered just thinking about it.

Smith moved closer and sat on the edge of her bed. "You're right," he said slowly. "It doesn't make any sense."

"Unless . . ." Duffy began, "unless Dylan *did* put the sign on the right elevator and somebody moved it just before I got there."

Smith looked skeptical. "Why would someone move it?"

"How should I know? But they must have."

He thought for a minute and then said, "I just thought of something. Day before yesterday, the *other* elevator was screwed up. It was fixed right away. I guess it's possible that someone who came in late today wouldn't have expected the repairs to be made so fast. And they wouldn't have known the second one had broken down. So, when they came in today and saw that sign, they would have thought it was a mistake. And they would have moved the sign . . . back to the elevator they *thought* was still broken."

"Someone who had the day off wouldn't have known the broken-down elevator had been repaired?" Duffy echoed. "Don't you people *tell* each other things?"

"I'm talking about when the guy came in, first thing, before he'd talked to anyone. Some of the crew comes on at nine P.M. I know Elmer Dougherty came in at eight last night, just before you left your room. He could have switched the sign, thinking someone had put it on the wrong cage."

"I guess that makes sense. Can you find out for sure?"

Smith nodded. "I can find out who, besides Elmer, had Thursday off. I'll ask around, see who else came in late yesterday, find out if they switched the sign." He grimaced. "I'm glad I didn't read the riot act to Rourke. I don't think I want him mad at me. He works out regularly. My idea of exercise is draping myself over the wheel of a sportscar." He stood up. "Take it easy today, okay? You still look a little shaky to me."

Glad that the mystery had been solved, Duffy watched him go. He *was* thinner than Dylan. But he was taller, and she liked the way he moved, so easy and careless, as if he wasn't afraid of anything.

But then, he hadn't almost fallen into a deep, black hole last night, she thought with some resentment. He could afford to walk as if he didn't have a care in the world.

Kit had walked the same way. He wasn't afraid of anything.

She, on the other hand, would probably start shaking violently from now on every time she went near an elevator.

Shuddering, Duffy closed her eyes.

Chapter 7

Dr. Morgan had already heard about Duffy's brush with death by elevator but seemed concerned only with how the near-accident had affected her illness. "I didn't give you permission to get out of bed," he reprimanded her sternly. "If you're not going to follow my orders, how do you expect me to help you?"

By fixing the elevators when they break, Duffy wanted to say, but she didn't. She was feeling totally crummy, hot, and sick. The IV needle pinched her hand unmercifully.

Noticing the stiff way she held the limb, Dr. Morgan said in a softer voice. "Maybe we can get rid of that for you soon. Would that help?"

It would definitely help.

But the IV was still in when the doctor and the nurse who had accompanied him into the room and taken Duffy's temperature left.

Amy and Cynthia were horrified when they heard what had happened to Duffy, and came rushing to her room the minute they had a break in their duties. Jane, taking advantage of Sunday morning's visiting hours, arrived at almost the same time. She paled visibly when she heard what had happened.

"Oh, Duffy," she said, her flawless skin as white as Duffy's sheet, "you could have . . . you could have been . . . killed." Her violet eyes filled with tears at the thought of losing her best friend. "What if someone hadn't been there to save you? What if Smith hadn't been around?" Weakened by the thought, she sank into the wooden, straight-backed bedside chair.

"She's right, Duffy," Amy agreed. "You owe Smith. If it hadn't been for him . . ."

Duffy didn't like the idea of "owing" Smith Lewis, but she knew Amy was right. She shuddered. "I keep seeing that black hole . . ." Taking a deep breath, she changed the subject. "I am," she announced in a relatively steady voice, "going to take a shower this afternoon if it's the last thing I do. It's the only thing that will make me feel better. I deserve it, after what happened, right?"

"Didn't you learn anything last night about disobeying doctor's orders?" Cynthia asked brusquely. "Honestly, Duffy, you are the worst patient in the world!"

And Amy added hesitantly, "Duffy, you can't take a shower with that IV in your arm."

"They're going to take it out. Dr. Morgan said so."

Cynthia shrugged. "Well, do as you please, Duffy. You will, anyway. But don't blame me if someone catches you in the act and yells at you."

"You'd better not rat on me," Duffy warned. "Any of you. If you do, and I miss my shower, I'll jump off the top of this stupid building. And then I'll haunt you guys for the rest of your natural lives."

Jane laughed. "Oh, Duffy, you're the least likely person in the world to jump off a building . . . unless it's because you've rigged up some fancy parachute and you want to try it out."

When the three had gone, promising to return that afternoon, Dylan arrived, bearing a healthy green plant in a white ceramic swan, purchased in the downstairs gift shop.

After thanking him for it, she asked him about the out-of-order sign. "Did you put it on the elevator at four o'clock, when Smith told you to?" she asked.

"Of course I did!" Dylan's words oozed injured pride. "Why? Did Lewis say I was goofing off?"

"No, and don't be so touchy. Did you put the sign on the first elevator or the second?"

"The second. That's the one Lewis said wasn't working. Why are you asking so many questions? What's going on?"

"No one told you I almost fell into the empty shaft of the broken elevator last night?" Duffy knew the story had circulated through the hospital rumor mill. That was how Cynthia and Amy had heard it.

"I just got here," Dylan answered. "I haven't talked to anyone. I went to the gift shop and then came straight here."

She told him about her narrow escape. And then,

while he sat, shocked and silent on her bed, she added Smith's theory about how the sign had been innocently switched.

"Elmer Dougherty was off on Thursday," Dylan mused. "I think Pete Ramsey was, too. And Smith could be right. Neither of them would have expected the first elevator to be fixed so fast, especially when they weren't here to do it. They don't think much of the other two maintenance guys. They're always complaining about them. So yeah, Elmer or Pete could have moved my sign." Dylan looked at Duffy, concern in his blue eyes. "You sure you're okay?"

"I'm fine." That wasn't true. She wasn't fine. Every time she thought about how close she had come to diving into that deep black hole her heart pounded and she felt dizzy and breathless. She didn't think that feeling would ever go away completely.

"Thanks for the plant," she told Dylan. "You'd better get to work. I don't want to get blamed if you're late."

He surprised her by kissing her before he left, bending to touch her cheek lightly with his lips. "You do feel a little bit cooler," he said as he straightened up. "Maybe they'll let you go home soon."

"The sooner the better. I've already made up my mind that I'm *taking* a shower whether anyone says I can or not. Tonight. Even if I have to sneak down the halls like a criminal."

"Good idea. It'll help you keep cool. Take it easy."

When Dylan had gone, Duffy lay with her eyes wide open, wondering why Smith hadn't come back to tell her who had moved the sign.

When the nurse came in to take her temperature, she beamed down at Duffy and said, "I've got good news."

"My temperature's normal and I can get dressed and go home," Duffy offered, a false note of hope in her voice. She didn't feel *that* cool.

"No, afraid not. But I have orders to remove your IV. That should cheer you up. Your doctor wants to try you on antibiotic capsules in place of the intravenous. So I can take this nasty thing out of your arm. That should be a relief."

It was. Free of the painful pinching sensation, Duffy gently rubbed the football-shaped black-and-blue mark left by the needle.

"Here," the nurse said, shaking a tiny fluted paper cup, "these should do the trick. Take two now, and I'll give you more when it's time."

"So when do I get sprung?" Duffy asked when she'd obediently swallowed the capsules.

"That's up to your doctor. I think he's waiting to see if you develop additional flu symptoms, just to be sure that's what you've got. So far, your blood tests have been negative." She glanced out the window. "The doctor even said you could go outside if you wanted, get some fresh air. Get one of the orderlies to take you. In a wheelchair, of course. And *don't* get out of the chair. Not yet. It's too soon."

When the nurse had gone, Duffy aimed her own gaze out the tall, skinny window. It was a sunny, blue-skied early spring day. She was sick to death of her grim prison. If she could get someone to wheel her outside . . .

Her legs were newborn-weak when she slid from her bed. But since she would be in a wheelchair, it didn't matter that her legs, like everything else in this hospital, weren't functioning properly.

The only orderly out in the hall was Smith. He was advancing toward her, pushing a wheelchair.

"You're supposed to take me outside," Duffy commanded as he reached her doorway. She was annoyed with him for not getting back to her with the information she wanted. She still didn't know for certain that he was right about how the sign on the elevator had been switched.

Smith laughed. "No kidding? And here I was planning on pushing this empty chair up and down the halls all day, because it's so much fun. Now you've gone and spoiled my plans."

"Why didn't you come and tell me who switched that sign?" Duffy hissed, climbing into the chair. "I've been waiting for hours!"

"Because I didn't find out anything," he answered amiably, coming around behind her to begin pushing her down the hall. "No one could remember moving the sign. Or maybe they were afraid to say, considering what almost happened. Probably thought they'd be in hot water if they admitted moving it. Sorry."

Duffy sulked in disappointment. She had hoped to prove that Dylan hadn't made a mistake. She didn't like thinking that he'd put the sign on the wrong elevator. "Maybe you didn't ask the right questions," she accused.

But before he could answer, she realized that they were headed toward the elevator.

Her body began trembling violently, rocking the wheelchair.

"Whoa!" Smith said, leaning down to look into her face. "You okay?"

"No," Duffy whispered. "No. I can't go in there. I can't ride in that elevator. Take me back to my room."

"Look," he said patiently, "you want to go outside, right? You have to go downstairs to do that, right? The only way I can get you downstairs is on the elevator. C'mon, relax! I'll park your chair back against the wall and make absolutely sure the cage is there before I push you over to the door, okay?"

Duffy couldn't control her shaking or the trembling of her lower lip or the nausea that rose in her stomach. The thought of those big metal double doors opening again terrified her.

But she wanted so much to go outside, to get out of this building, out of her room.

"Don't move it one inch away from the wall until you're sure that cage is there," she ordered from between teeth chattering with anxiety. "Promise?"

"I promise. Try to relax, okay? You shouldn't be getting upset like this. Could send your temperature up again and you'll never get out of here."

When he parked her chair against the wall, several feet from the elevator doors, she closed her eyes. When she opened them the cage was there, just as it should be. Smith wheeled her in, and kept one hand on her shoulder the whole way down. That helped.

"I can't stay out here with you," Smith said as he wheeled her around a corner of the building. "I've got things to do. But I'll be back in half an hour or so. I'm supposed to remind you *not* to move from that chair. Doctor's orders. So, no jogging, okay?"

Her bad mood broken by the bright sunshine and blue, cloudless sky and the faint April breeze, Duffy nodded. "I won't move, I promise. Park me anywhere here." Then, feeling guilty for her earlier rudeness, she added gratefully, "And thanks. The fresh air feels great."

"It'll probably do more good than those capsules you're taking," Smith agreed. Then he set the brake on her wheelchair and, whistling, left her alone.

Duffy relaxed in the old wooden wheelchair. She was seated at the top of the steep slope carpeted in bright-green new grass. Other patients sat in similar chairs, reading or talking to one another. Far below her, where the slope ended, she could see silvery-blue water glistening in the sunshine. The lake — the only pretty part of the hospital grounds. Several children were sailing boats in the water and a pair of workmen in jeans and white T-shirts were planting new shrubbery around the lake's shoreline.

It felt wonderful to be part of the real world again. I almost feel human, Duffy thought, a half smile on her face. My IV is gone, and I'm actually outside, away from that horrible room and those grungy halls. I wish I could wheel this chair all the way home and never come back here again.

She couldn't do that. But she could relax and enjoy the time she had outside.

She slid down in the chair, trying to find a comfortable sitting position so that she could tilt her face up toward the sun in hopes of getting an early start on her tan.

A noise that startled her came from somewhere behind her. Just as she turned her head to locate its source, the wheelchair jerked abruptly, lurched forward, and began slowly moving down the slope.

Duffy bolted upright in the chair. It wasn't supposed to be moving. It was supposed to be *parked*. Sitting safely in a stationary position. Safe. Safe and unmoving.

Instead, the wheels continued to revolve. As they turned, they picked up speed.

"Hey!" a student nurse studying in the sun cried out in surprise as she glanced up and saw the wheelchair bearing down upon her. "Hey, stop that thing!"

Duffy, her mouth open in shock, had no idea how to stop it.

The student nurse managed to throw herself out of the way just in time. A second later, the heavy chair careened across the blanket she'd been sitting on. "Hey!" she shouted after it, "what's the big idea?"

Other shouts joined hers as the wheelchair, with Duffy in it, rolled faster and faster down the hill. When it reached the steepest part of the slope and tilted precariously forward, Duffy had to cling to the wooden arms with every ounce of her strength to keep from being thrown out across the hill. Slamming out onto the ground now would break every single bone in her body.

With a sinking heart, Duffy realized her mistake. She should have jumped from the chair the second it began to move. At the top of the slope where the ground was level, she would have sustained only a few minor bumps and bruises. But she had been so startled by the sudden, unexpected movement, that she hadn't been thinking clearly.

Now, it was too late. Her hands fumbled frantically near the wheels, searching for the brake, but she couldn't find it. And the fear of crushing her fingers in the speeding wheels brought her hands back up to clutch the chair arms again.

She tried to scream. But the wind ripped viciously at her mouth, stealing her voice.

"Help me, help me, help me," she mouthed desperately as the chair tore down the slope. Her terrified heart pounded in her chest, her knuckles turned white on the wooden arms, her lips moved soundlessly, frantically, as she tried in vain to scream for help.

The lake, glistening in the sun, beckoned below. Duffy was headed straight for it. The water, this early in spring, would be freezing cold. If the chair dove into the lake, it would sink like a stone, and she with it. Even if someone saved her from drowning, exposure to that freezing water would set her illness back weeks. It might even kill her.

Suppose she got tangled in the wheels, underwater?

Here and there across the hillside, people raced to her rescue, waving their arms and shouting.

None was close enough to reach her in time.

Why couldn't she scream? Why was the wind stealing her voice? "Help, help, help," she mouthed over and over again as the chair sped down the slope, closer and closer to the icy waters of the lake.

The two workmen glanced up in astonishment and, without dropping their shovels, dove out of the way of the heavy wooden chair barreling down upon them like a missile.

In utter despair, Duffy moaned helplessly and closed her eyes.

Chapter 8

As the runaway chair, holding Duffy prisoner, continued its suicidal dive toward the chilly waters of the lake, she gave up hope. She was going into that lake . . . no way to stop it . . . no way . . . so cold . . . it would be so cold. . . .

Eyes closed against the terrible reality of it, lips mouthing frantic prayers, she shrank into a little ball curled up against the back of the chair and clenched her teeth. She would have to swim for it.

Duffy opened her eyes and was instantly blinded by the glare of the water just inches away from the speeding chair. She sprang upright, leaning forward, preparing to dive the instant the chair left land.

And she nearly catapulted out over the water as the wheelchair jolted to an abrupt, grinding halt at the very edge of the lake. Her head snapped to one side. She gasped as the chair jerked backward, tilted slightly, its wheels spinning frantically, and then settled shakily onto the sand.

When the chair finally sat sullenly and completely

still, Duffy sagged against its back. Her chest heaved in an effort to restore normal breathing.

"You okay?" Dylan's voice whispered in her ear. "You okay, Duff? All in one piece?" And then he was there, kneeling beside her, taking her shaking hands in his, gazing up into her face with worried eyes.

She couldn't speak. Her breath came in ragged gasps. Her eyes remained fastened in bewildered horror on the cold, silvery water. Then tears of hysteria began pouring down her cheeks, spilling over her lips and chin. "Oh," she whispered numbly, "oh, oh . . ."

"Man, that chair weighs a ton!" Dylan exclaimed as staff members and patients alike began to gather around Duffy, expressing concern for her safety. "No wonder you couldn't stop it on your own. For a minute there, I didn't think I was going to be able to, either."

Dylan had saved her life. He'd risked being pulled into the water right along with her and the runaway chair. He had saved her. If only she could stop shaking and crying long enough to thank him.

"Thanks," she whispered, her tear-streaked face crumpling as the realization that she was safe began to sink in. "Thanks, Dylan." Then she hid her face in her hands, her body trembling from head to toe.

The group of onlookers, uneasy with their inability to comfort her, murmured among themselves. One said in a low voice, "She needs a doctor," and turned to run up the hill.

Smith Lewis, followed closely by Amy Severn,

came running down the hill. "What's going on?" Smith asked angrily as they arrived at the foot of the hill. "I thought I told you to stay where I put you," he began to accuse Duffy, and then realized the state she was in. "What happened?" he asked Dylan. "What's wrong with her? How did she get down here?"

"Take it easy, Lewis," Dylan warned, putting his hands protectively on the back of the wheelchair. "Duffy's had a really bad time. Did you check the brake on this chair before you left her?"

Smith flushed angrily. "Of course I did, Rourke. I checked it twice." His voice rose. "What *happened*?"

Then everyone began talking at once, a jumble of excited voices. None of it made any sense. Smith looked more confused than ever.

Duffy, her eyes glazed with shock, said numbly, "The chair ran away. It just . . . took off. If it hadn't been for Dylan, I'd . . ." Fresh tears began to flow. "If it hadn't been for Dylan, I'd be in the lake right now." Her voice broke, "Oh, God, I came so close . . ."

Smith looked stupified. "Ran away?"

"Yeah," Dylan said. "Took off. Escaped. Straight down the hill. With Duffy still in it."

"Dylan saved my life," Duffy said softly. "Can I go back to my room now, please?"

Smith's flush changed to pallor as he lifted his head to survey the steep distance the chair had covered so quickly. "You . . . you came down *that* hill in a wheelchair?"

"Yes, she did," Dylan answered emphatically, "and I think she should have her doctor check her out. Everyone move out of the way, please, so I can take her back inside."

"Yes," Duffy said, trying in vain to tear her gaze away from the sun-glistening lake. "Yes. I want to go back inside."

"Duffy," Smith said quietly, looking down at her with guilt-filled eyes, "I was sure I checked that brake. I'm sorry."

A fellow orderly standing by offered loyally, "Wasn't your fault, Lewis. Those brakes aren't much good. The chairs are ancient. Old Man Latham donated them years ago when he first came on the hospital board."

But Smith looked unconsoled.

Duffy wanted to tell him to forget it. But how could she, when she knew *she* never would. Never . . . never. That race down the hill . . . feeling so helpless, so terrified . . . she knew she would feel the harsh wind slapping against her face in nightmares for a long time to come.

I'm not dead, she thought with a sense of morbid wonder. I'm not dead . . . but I almost was. Again. For the second time in two days, I almost died.

How was that possible in a place where she had come to get well?

Duffy's doctor found no sign of physical damage, but the look on the nurse's face when she removed the thermometer from Duffy's mouth signified bad news.

"Your temperature's shot back up," she said briskly, shaking the glass tube back down to normal before replacing it in its antiseptic holder. "Small wonder, after what you've been through. The whole hospital's abuzz. Here," extending one of the tiny paper cups with pills in it, "take these and try to get some rest. I'll look in on you in a little bit."

Amy and Cynthia stayed with Duffy until her parents and Jane arrived.

Amy's eyes were wide with shock. "Oh, Duffy," she whispered in awe when the nurse had gone, "you must have been terrified! I can't believe how lucky you were!"

Cynthia, sitting at the foot of the bed, nodded in agreement.

Duffy settled more deeply beneath the covers, hoping to still her trembling limbs. She stared at Amy. "Lucky?" she whispered. "Lucky?" She closed her eyes, trying to blot out the sight of that lake rushing closer and closer to her.

Amy turned a deep pink. "Well, I know it was terrible, what happened to you," she stammered. "What I meant was, you didn't go into the lake. Dylan stopped you, just like Smith stopped you from stepping into the empty elevator shaft. That's what I meant by lucky."

"Amy," Duffy said, her voice quivering, "this place isn't safe for me. I have to go home, right now, before something else terrible happens to me. Ask my doctor, okay? Tell him . . . tell him it's absolutely crucial that I not spend another night in this horrible place." Tears of fear and despair filled her eyes. "Please, Amy?"

Matching drops of saltwater trembled on Amy's own pale lashes. She couldn't speak.

"Duffy," Cynthia said, folding and refolding an edge of Duffy's yellowed blanket. "I know you've been through some really awful stuff. But it isn't the *hospital's* fault. The hospital isn't out to get you. You've just had a couple of accidents, that's all. You were in the wrong place at the wrong time. It could have happened to anyone."

"But it *didn't*." A sudden wave of nausea washed over Duffy, and her head began to ache. "It happened to *me*. And . . . and I just remembered . . . there was this weird noise . . . right behind me . . . just before the chair took off down the hill. I'd forgotten . . . but I remember now. This sound . . ."

Amy leaned forward. "Noise? What kind of noise?"

Duffy needed to sleep. She could barely keep her eyes open. She struggled to remember what kind of noise it had been. "I'm not sure . . . like someone was tiptoeing up behind me . . . you know, the way people walk when they don't want to be heard? And then . . . a little creaking noise . . . the sound those old chairs make when the brake is put on . . . or . . . *off*." Duffy's eyes flew open. "Amy! That *is* the sound I heard . . . the brake being released on my chair!"

Amy and Cynthia exchanged glances.

"Duffy," Cynthia said patiently, "that's silly. I know you're upset, but you're really beginning to sound paranoid. Anyone fooling around with your chair would have been seen by the other people outside."

Duffy fought rising nausea. "Maybe not. I was at the top of the hill. Alone. Everyone else was on the slope. Why would they be watching me? Someone could have run up behind me, released the brake, and then run away."

"Duffy!" Amy exclaimed in horror. "That's crazy! Why would anyone do such a horrible thing?"

"That's ridiculous," Cynthia agreed. "It's just your fever talking. The nurse said it was up again. You have to stop this, Duffy: hating the hospital, not letting yourself feel safe here. It's keeping you from getting well. You have to relax."

Duffy made a rude sound. "Relax? Are you crazy? How can I relax?"

"Maybe what happened," Cynthia proposed calmly, "is, a student nurse came along and intended to take you inside. She released the brake, and then something caught her attention . . . another patient needing something . . . and she forgot she'd released the brake. I'll ask around, okay? Will that make you feel better?"

Duffy felt tears of frustration threatening again. And she realized then what felt so wrong about the way people were reacting: They were all so sure the chair's race down the hill had been an accident. How could they be so sure? How *could* they?

She wasn't.

Frustrated and feeling extremely ill, she muttered, "You won't get any answers from anyone, Cynthia. Smith didn't when he asked about the sign on the elevator door. No one will admit to releasing that brake. Forget it."

Her parents arrived then. She could tell by the look on her mother's face that they had already heard about the runaway chair. Maybe now they'd take her home.

Amy gestured to Cynthia that they should leave. "We'll come back later," she told Duffy. "You'll be feeling better then."

That was Amy. Always looking on the bright side.

Was there a bright side?

The only bright side, it seemed to her, was that her parents might take her home now, agreeing that she wasn't safe here.

That idea was quickly squelched. While her parents were upset about the downhill race, they were not only convinced that it had been an "unfortunate accident," but their total faith in Twelvetrees Community Hospital and Dr. Jonas Morgan remained unshaken. If they had a concern, it seemed to be that their very imaginative daughter might be overreacting.

"Honey, you have to calm down," her mother said. "Although," she added, "I do think someone could have stayed with you out on that slope. It's so steep."

And her father said, "Duffy, of *course* it was an accident. What else could it be? You wouldn't be reacting this way if you weren't so sick."

When they had gone and Duffy was waiting for Jane to arrive, she tried to tell herself her parents were right. It had simply been an accident.

Because she couldn't think of a single thing she had ever done to anyone that would make them deliberately send her flying down a steep hill, trapped in a wheelchair. So if there was no reason, there was no plot to kill her. It had been an accident, period.

But . . . she felt the wind again ripping at her face, felt the horror of being trapped in the speeding chair, saw the icy waters of the lake approaching . . . and heard again, as clearly as if she were once again out on the top of that hill, the sound of stealthy footsteps approaching behind her, the creak of the brake being released.

Accident?

How could she be sure?

She wasn't sure of anything anymore.

Chapter 9

Duffy missed Kit fiercely. Images of the two of them exploring the woods, Kit with his ever-present camera, she with a stick in hand, played across the dingy white walls of her room. Being with Kit had always been so easy. He never demanded brilliant conversation or her complete attention, didn't get his feelings hurt if she sat down on a log and became engrossed in a book while he wandered around taking pictures, and he always seemed to understand when she was in what her mother called "one of your moods, Duffy."

Where was he now? He couldn't have reached the coast yet. She tried to picture a map of the United States in her mind. Where would Kit be by now? Didn't you have to go across the desert to reach California? What if that old rattletrap of his broke down?

A flash of anger at Kit darted through her consciousness. He should be *here* now. She needed him. He'd always been there before. Couldn't he have put up with that awful uncle of his for just one more week?

Ashamed of her selfishness, a wave of nausea flooded over her.

But even when the shame eased, the nausea didn't. And her head had begun to ache, a new symptom. Was the flu finally attacking her full force?

As she struggled to pull herself to a sitting position, she noticed something odd about the ceiling light. It seemed surrounded by a frothy halo, something she had never noticed before. Were all fluorescent lights like that, or had the flu suddenly attacked her eyesight as well as her stomach and her head?

She felt much worse than she had when she had first arrived at Twelvetrees Community Hospital.

"This is not the place to come when you want to get well," she told the aide who brought her dinner. "I didn't feel this rotten when I first came in here."

"You're just having a bad day," the aide said matter-of-factly. "If I were you, I'd consider myself lucky to be alive. Smith Lewis said he couldn't believe you survived that race down the hill. And you without a scratch! It's a miracle."

That sentiment was echoed a while later by the nurse who came in to take Duffy's temperature again and dispense more pills. "You should count your blessings," she said. "Surviving such an escapade — it's incredible. You're a very lucky girl, Dorothy."

"Yeah, right," Duffy said harshly. Then she added slyly, "Since you admit I'm having a bad day, how about making it better by letting me take a shower before visiting hours? Please? Just one tiny little shower?" A shower would definitely calm her down and ease the queasiness in her stomach.

"Absolutely not!"

Duffy groaned.

"Someone would have to go with you and no one has time. And didn't you just say your stomach was upset? Why on earth would you want to get out of bed and walk all the way down the hall when you're feeling so crummy?"

"Because maybe if I had a shower, I wouldn't *feel* so crummy," Duffy retorted. "God, I hate this place!"

Amy and Cynthia stopped in briefly when they were collecting the dinner trays.

Duffy thought Cynthia looked beat, and said so.

"Yeah, I guess I am," Cynthia admitted. "I keep falling asleep at night when I should be studying. But no school tomorrow . . . teachers' conference, so I figured I could afford to work today. They're awfully busy here."

"I know," Duffy said grimly. "They won't let me take a shower because they think I need a keeper and everyone's too busy to go with me. I think maybe I'll just take one, anyway."

Amy gave her a warning glance. "Duffy, honestly, why can't you just obey the rules for a change?" Sighing, she turned her attention to Cynthia. "You work too hard," she said softly. "What you need is a man in your life. Someone to take you to a funny movie or out dancing, help you unwind a little."

"I don't have time to date," Cynthia said.

"Well, *I* do," Amy said, her mouth curving downward. "For all the good it does me." For a brief moment, her round face filled with sadness. "I thought that Dylan and I . . ." Then, just as quickly, her face cleared and her usual cheerful expression returned. "Oh, well, that's life, right, Duff?"

"Right." But Duffy was surprised by the momentary bleakness in Amy's face. Dylan had told everyone that his split with Amy was "mutual," meaning, Duffy thought, that they'd both decided it was time to split up. But it certainly didn't seem as if Amy was happy about the decision.

After Amy and Cynthia had taken her tray and left, Duffy began to wonder. Had Dylan been lying about his breakup with Amy? Maybe to protect her from embarrassment? That was the kind of thing Dylan would do. He didn't like hurting people. But Amy seemed hurt, anyway.

Duffy felt briefly ashamed, because she had often wondered what outgoing, popular Dylan saw in a girl who got upset if her library books were one day overdue. Knowing now what a nice, thoughtful person Amy was didn't ease Duffy's discomfort. And remembering how attentive Dylan had been since she'd become a patient didn't help. She wondered nervously if she had, innocently enough, had anything to do with Dylan and Amy's breakup. She hoped not. She would hate that.

It was silly to think about stuff like that now, Duffy reminded herself. Right now, all she wanted was to feel better. And despite what everyone said, Duffy knew that a soothing, hot shower would help.

After all, it hadn't actually been the shower the nurse had objected to. Only the need for someone to accompany Duffy.

Well, I don't *need* any help, she thought, preparing to slide out of bed. I can take a shower all by myself. I've been doing it for years.

The room spun wildly. She saw double, and her knees melted. Her stomach heaved. "Oboy," she murmured, clutching her stomach. This was not going to be easy.

Kit always said nothing worth doing was easy. And he should know. Nothing had ever been easy for him.

Duffy managed to slide her feet into her slippers, although looking down she saw four feet instead of two. The room spun crazily as she slipped into her robe and stood up straight. But although she teetered dangerously, she remained upright.

"Great!" she whispered, and collected her shampoo, razor, soap, washcloth, and towel from the cabinet in her bedside table, Then, walking very carefully, she made her way to the door and peered out.

It was still very early evening, that quiet time after dinner when patients often nap before visiting hours. The halls were empty, the nurses away from the station, eating their own dinner or busy dispensing medication in other rooms.

Duffy decided to risk it. Maybe she'd get lucky.

She did. Clutching the wall for support, she made it to the twin shower rooms at the end of the hall without being stopped. The first door was locked, but the second doorknob turned easily in her hand. Heaving a deep sigh of relief, Duffy slipped inside and flipped on the ceiling light, locking the door of the small, beige cubicle behind her.

She noticed with mild curiosity that this light, too, had a strange halo. Her head pounded anew, and her stomach did a dizzying dance. But there was the shower stall, so inviting in spite of the ugliness of the grim little room. A shower would make her feel better. Probably do more good than a thousand little pills.

The shower felt unbelievably good, like a drink of water after a long desert trek. The tension in her muscles melted away under the flow of the wonderfully hot water. Her skin responded with joy, and Duffy felt momentarily well enough to hum a tune as she lathered and rinsed. Still dizzy, she was careful to lean against the cold, clammy tile as she scrubbed.

She had just finished wrapping her blissfully clean hair in the towel and was in the process of awkwardly shaving her legs in the narrow tiled cubicle when she felt a sudden blast of cold air against her shoulders. She paused, lifting her head to listen.

Had the door opened? No, that couldn't be. She clearly remembered locking it.

As she straightened up, there was the click of a light switch and the room disappeared into a thick cloak of darkness.

Duffy was standing, soaking wet, in total, silent blackness.

Chapter 10

Duffy's first clear thought as she stood, wet and disbelieving in the shower stall, was that there had been a power failure. Cynthia had warned her that such failures were frequent occurrences in the old building.

But . . . that wouldn't explain why the door had opened, admitting that wave of cool air over the top of the glass shower door . . . or the sound of the light switch being flicked off.

How could the door have opened? She hadn't heard the sound of a key turning in the lock.

But the water had been running the whole time. The sound of someone turning a key would have been muffled.

Was there someone in the room with her now?

Beginning to tremble, Duffy listened, not breathing. She heard nothing. Not a sound.

With her only towel wrapped, turban-style around her wet hair, she grabbed her robe from the top of the shower door and threw it on over her water-slicked skin. Then, anxious to leave the musty, pitch-black room, she turned to retrieve her shower supplies from the tiled ledge.

Suddenly, the shower door latch clicked open behind her. With only enough time to gasp in shock, Duffy was seized from behind and thrown bodily, facedown, onto the floor of the stall, where several inches of water had puddled due to the slow drain.

Warm, soapy water filled her mouth and nose. She choked, gagged, spat, and struggled to pull herself upright, out of the foamy water. But a knee in her back pinned her down, rendering her immobile.

What . . . what was happening?

She was too tall for the tiny space. Her legs, cruelly bent at the knee, were crumpled up against the cold, wet tile. A fist pressed down painfully on the back of her neck. She was completely helpless, her mouth and nose submerged in warm water, unable to move . . . to scream . . . to make a sound . . . unable to cry out for the help she needed.

Her mind, stunned and shaken, reeled in an effort to think clearly. All it could manage was a shocked, terrified, *What is happening?*

But as she struggled desperately to free herself of the deadening weight on her back, to lift her head out of the soapy water, her mind cleared, and began to race frantically.

I can't breathe. I will drown in this tiny little bit of water if I don't do something . . . something. But what? What can I do?

Then she realized that her razor was still clutched in her right hand. A small pink plastic grooming tool, she was afraid it could do no harm to her attacker. It was designed specifically *not* to do harm.

But it was all she had.

Desperate, she slashed backward, hard.

A harsh, guttural scream of pain echoed in the stall . . . a whispered curse . . . the fist left the back of her neck.

Duffy threw her head up out of the water, gasping for air.

The whispered, angry cursing above her continued as bright red droplets of blood began plopping into the soapy puddle surrounding her.

The little pink razor had come through for her.

Duffy lay in fear, her head stiffly held up out of the water at an awkward, painful angle. Had her desperate slash made her attacker angrier with her? Would the next attack, when it came, be even more vicious? She had no strength left to fight . . . how could she hold her head up out of the water if another attack came?

She waited . . . not breathing . . . her heart beating wildly against her chest, tears of terror stinging her eyelids.

With one final, whispered curse, the weight left her back. Another whiff of cool air entered the stall as the shower door was flung open.

And then came the blessed, beautiful sound of the wooden door to the room opening and ferociously slamming shut.

She was alone again.

But someone was very, very angry with her.

Duffy lay on the floor of the stall, sobbing tears

of fear and relief for what seemed like a long, long time, cradling her head on her arm to keep it up out of the water.

When she felt her legs going numb, she used the palms of her hands pressed against the clammy tile to pull herself to her feet. Unsteady, her head screaming in pain, her stomach lurching, she swayed and had to lean against the wall for support.

Her white robe was soaking wet. The towel wrapped around her head had been dislodged in the struggle; cold strands of sodden hair chilled the back of her neck.

She began trembling violently and although she tried to still her shaking limbs, nearly biting through her lower lip with the effort, her body refused to obey her.

It was so dark . . . so dark and damp. . . .

Taking a deep breath, she slowly pushed open the glass shower door, peering into the velvety darkness for any sign of a threat.

What if her attacker hadn't really left? Suppose it was a trick — slamming the door shut to make it seem as if Duffy were safely alone? Suppose he was hiding, there in the darkness, waiting for her to emerge from the shower stall?

Her bones paralyzed with fear, Duffy listened anxiously.

But the tiny room was utterly still. No sound of angry breathing broke the silence.

Finally sure that she really was alone, Duffy emerged from the stall, still shaking and unsteady, and moved toward the door.

If she could make it to the door, pull it open, step out into the hall, away from the horrid musty smell, the chilly dampness, the unbroken darkness, she would be all right. She *would*. The shaking would stop and someone would come to help her. She would be safe again.

Wouldn't she?

But the minute she stepped out into the dimly lighted corridor, she was blinded by the strange halos around the overhead lights. Shielding her eyes with her hands, she sagged against the wall. The full horror of what had happened to her flooded over her in an enormous wave, nearly knocking her off her feet.

This time there was no question of an *accident*. Someone had tried to kill her. She didn't know who, or why she only knew that they had.

And they had almost succeeded.

Chapter 11

There was no one in Duffy's end of the corridor, but she could see white uniforms scurrying about in the distance.

"Help," she whispered, shaking violently. "Somebody please help me."

No one heard or noticed her.

She raised her voice. "*Help* me!" It stunned her that people in the hospital could continue to go about their business as usual, after what had happened to her. Couldn't they see? Couldn't they tell? Why didn't someone rush to her aid?

And then hysteria took over. Completely losing control, Duffy opened her mouth and a scream came out. "Help, help!" she cried and lurched away from the wall, breaking into a staggering run. Still screaming, she moved down the hall, hands against the walls for support.

And the white figures in the distance stopped what they were doing to stare at her.

Her sodden robe hung open, her damp hair hung limply against her face, her bare feet slipped and slid on the cold tile as she staggered on. "Help me!" she sobbed, her voice hoarse with fear, "somebody help me!"

At the other end of the hall, Smith Lewis broke into a run.

When he reached her, she fell against him, gasping, still shaking violently.

"Help," she whispered, "please." And then, giving in, she slumped against him and her eyes closed.

When Duffy awoke, she was lying in her bed, covered with a sheet. She was surrounded by two nurses, Smith Lewis, Dr. Morgan, and Amy Severn. Smith and Amy looked worried. The older nurse was removing a blood pressure cuff, the younger one holding out a tiny paper cup, and the doctor was frowning down at his patient.

It took Duffy a few moments to remember exactly why they were all staring down at her. When the shower scene returned, in full graphic detail, she gasped and began moaning softly, "Nono-nono. . . ."

Smith was the first to speak. "What, Duffy? What happened?"

Duffy closed her eyes. "Someone . . . someone tried to kill me," she whispered. "In the shower . . ."

When she opened her eyes, what she saw shocked her. There was total disbelief in every face peering down at her.

The two nurses exchanged a glance that clearly

said, "delirium." Smith and Amy looked doubtful, and the doctor regarded his patient as he might a lab specimen, gazing down at her with detached curiosity.

"I've checked you over thoroughly," he told her, "and aside from some nasty bumps that are probably going to turn black-and-blue on your back and neck, you're okay. Took a bad fall, did you?"

"I . . . no, I didn't fall," she managed. "I didn't. Someone . . . I was attacked. In the shower . . ."

"Attacked? In the shower?" the older nurse repeated, in the same way that she might have said, "You say you have a fairy godmother at home?"

Duffy clenched her teeth. She had never expected that she wouldn't be believed. Not this time. Would she look the way she did if she hadn't been attacked? Couldn't they see?

"I know it sounds crazy," she cried. "But I'm telling you the truth! I was taking a shower and someone came in and knocked me down on the floor and sat on my back and wouldn't let me go, and there was water in the bottom of the shower and I almost drowned . . ." She stopped. She had never faced such disbelief in her life.

And that terrified her. If she couldn't convince anyone she was telling the truth, who would help her? What if the attacker wasn't finished with her? She needed someone on her side.

"You've got to believe me!" Duffy struggled to sit up in bed, but she was too weak, too nauseated. Sinking back against the pillow, she tried again.

"Please, it *did* happen. I wouldn't make up something so crazy." Her eyes appealed to Amy. "Amy? You believe me, don't you?"

Amy flushed and took a step backward.

"Of course you wouldn't make up such a story," the older nurse said soothingly. "It's the fever, dear. This kind of thing happens all the time, doesn't it, doctor?" As she turned away, Duffy heard her mutter under her breath, "Shouldn't have taken her off the IV. Too soon."

"I didn't *imagine* it!" Duffy shouted, her eyes flying from face to face in a search for understanding. "I was in the shower, and the door opened, and the light went off . . ." Tears of frustration spilled from her eyes.

"Didn't you lock the door?" the ponytailed nurse asked gently. "My goodness, Duffy, you should always lock the door."

"Of *course* I locked the door," Duffy protested. "I did! I locked it! I *remember* locking it."

"Well, there you are," the older nurse said cheerfully. "If you locked the door, how could anyone possibly have gotten in?" She smiled. "I don't think anyone around here can walk through walls, Dorothy."

Duffy wanted to scream. "Don't talk to me as if I'm two years old," she sobbed angrily. "I *did* lock the stupid door and someone got in anyway. They must have had a key."

"Wait one sec," the young nurse said, and disappeared. As promised, she was back immediately, a round metal ring of keys in her hand. "See, Duffy?"

she said, holding up the ring. "This is the only extra key we have to that shower room. And it's right here, on the ring where it belongs. And the ring was hanging behind the nurses' station, right where it's supposed to be. So . . ."

"So, nothing!" Duffy snapped, swiping at her tears with the back of her hand. "Someone must have taken it, used it, and then put it back. Let me see it."

"I would have seen someone taking it," the nurse said defensively. But she handed Duffy the ring.

"Which key is it?"

The nurse pointed.

"Dr. Morgan, Dr. Morgan, to ICU, stat!" a voice barked over the PA system.

The doctor patted Duffy's hair awkwardly, handed the older nurse Duffy's chart, told the patient to "Relax and take it easy," gave the nurse medication orders for Duffy, and left.

Ignoring his departure because it was clear he wouldn't have believed her, Duffy continued to study the key. It hung on a leather thong. "Look," she said, pointing, "there's a smear on the strap. It's probably blood. I slashed at the person who attacked me and I know I hurt him because there was blood in the water. See?" Pointing, she held up the key ring.

Smith and the younger nurse examined it, while Amy hung back, an expression of revulsion on her face.

"Oh, Duffy, I don't think that stain is new," the nurse exclaimed. "I'm sure I remember seeing it before. I thinks it's paint, from when they painted behind the nurses' station."

Duffy could see then that it was hopeless. The nurses, scolding her for taking a shower alone against orders, clearly thought that she had been hallucinating. Amy was looking at her with cow-eyed sympathy, and Smith was chewing thoughtfully on his lower lip.

Not a single one of them believed the attack had actually taken place.

If no one believed her . . . who would *help* her? She knew now that someone, for some crazy reason, was angry with her, wanted to hurt her, kill her. As insane as that sounded, she knew it was true.

Duffy was startled by a sudden pinprick in her upper left arm.

"Doctor ordered a sedative for you," the older nurse said. "It'll calm you down. My, you really let your imagination get the best of you, didn't you? That's not wise, Dorothy. Not in your condition."

Duffy flopped angrily over on her side and burrowed beneath the blanket, before anyone could see her helpless, frightened tears.

Chapter 12

Duffy was floating somewhere in that blissful haven between sleep and reality when she heard her father's voice.

"Look, if my daughter says she was attacked in the shower, then that's what happened." He sounded angry and very, very far away. But he had to be out in the hall. "She doesn't tell lies."

Sure, I do, Daddy, Duffy thought woozily. I lied that time I didn't get home until three in the morning and you were waiting up. My date didn't have a flat tire. I just didn't want to leave the party. Sorry, Daddy.

"Nobody said anything about lying, Mr. Quinn," Dr. Morgan's voice replied, also from a distance. Both voices sounded as if they were coming from behind a giant wall of cotton. "Your daughter had a bad fall, that's our theory, and the bump on the head, combined with her illness, caused her to hallucinate. It's not all that unusual."

A third voice joined them . . . the gray-haired nurse. "We did have Security check the shower room, of course. There was no sign of forced entry."

She tried to sit up in bed and call her father, but she toppled sideways immediately. She was floating in a sea of clouds. It was not an unpleasant sensation.

"We want to see her," her mother's voice said.

"I'm sorry," Dr. Morgan answered from his faraway place, "but I'd rather you didn't. I gave her a sedative. Let her sleep. She's had a rough time of it. Since tomorrow is a holiday, we've added morning visiting hours. You can see Duffy then."

What? No visiting hours tonight? Well, that certainly wasn't fair. Not the least bit. It wasn't *her* fault she'd had a rough time of it. Why were they punishing her by stealing her visiting hours?

And then her head fell back on the pillow, her eyes shut, and she disappeared into a thick, drugged sleep.

When she awoke sometime later, her room was still shrouded in darkness broken only by the faint glow of the small night-light by her door. She hated the darkness. She would never feel safe in the dark again.

Her head pounded, her stomach rode a carousel. But she was no longer lost in that drug-induced twilight zone.

The entire fourth floor was shrouded in silence. There were no quiet, rubber-soled footsteps out in the hall, no clattering of gurney wheels, no hushed conversation between nurses and orderlies, no clanking of metal rings on curtain slides. The hospital was as still and silent as . . . death.

Death . . . she had come so close, so close, in that shower stall. Duffy pulled the sheet up around her neck, clutching its hem with her fists. No one believed her. They all thought she was crazy or delirious. But it *had* happened. She remembered every single horrible second of it and as the memories returned, her heart began pounding.

Why would someone want to kill her?

Why had she been sent racing down that steep hill toward the lake? Why had she been attacked in the shower stall? And the elevator . . . had the out-of-order sign really been switched accidentally? Or had it been done on purpose, by someone who knew she was planning to go downstairs to the gift shop?

She couldn't remember who knew she had planned to leave her room to go downstairs. How many people had she told? Hadn't she announced it, loud and clear? And anyone she'd told could have told half a dozen other people. There were no secrets in this place. The whole hospital probably knew she planned to go for a walk, knew she was headed for the showers.

Duffy's head pounded, and her skin, dry and parched, burned with fever.

I really *am* sick, she silently told the cracked ceiling.

But am I sick enough to imagine a vicious attack?

Was the nurse right? Could being this sick make a person imagine all kinds of horrible things?

No . . . she was positive someone was trying to kill her. She couldn't have imagined the terrible scene in the shower.

Or . . . could she?

And no one had believed her. They were all so sure her life hadn't really been in danger. How could they *all* be wrong? How could she be the only person who was right?

Smith's dark head appeared in her doorway. "Just checking," he said as he moved toward her bed. "I see you're awake. Feeling better?"

Smith planned to be a doctor. Someone had said he read a lot of medical books. Maybe he could answer the question that was racing around in her mind. She would rather ask Dylan, but Dylan wasn't around.

"Smith," she began as he stood over her, looking down, "could a really high fever make a person imagine the kind of thing that happened to me today? I mean, it seemed so *real*. The light going out, the door to the shower stall opening, being pushed to the floor, the knee in my back . . . I know I have bruises to prove it. I can feel them."

Without waiting for an invitation, Smith sat, carefully, on the edge of her bed. "Let's look at it logically," he said. "Made anyone mad enough to want to wipe you off the planet?"

"No, of course not! I mean, I know I'm not the world's best patient . . ."

Smith laughed. "Boy, is that an understatement! But I've seen worse patients and as far as I know, no one ever attacked any of them in the shower. So . . . unless you can come up with a logical reason why someone would want to get rid of you, I guess the answer to your question is yes, a high fever *can* make you think all kinds of things."

That wasn't the answer Duffy wanted. "But my bruises . . ." she protested.

Smith shrugged. "Doc Morgan's probably right. You must have fallen. Knocking up against ceramic tile could turn anyone's skin black and blue."

He didn't believe the attack had really happened.

Kit would have. Kit would have believed her. And then he would have helped her figure out *why* it had happened.

But Kit wasn't there.

"Look," Smith offered, "if it'll make you feel better, I'll camp outside your door tonight. I'm off tomorrow so I can sleep late. I'll park a chair there and read, okay?"

No, not okay. Because he didn't *believe* her. He was just humoring her, as if she were a psychiatric patient up on the fifth floor. "Don't do me any favors," she said haughtily, turning her back on him. "Since you're so sure it's just my fevered little mind attacking me, I don't see why you'd think I need protection. Just go away, please. Leave me and my feeble brain in peace, okay?"

"C'mon, Duffy," he said in exasperation, "you *asked*! I just told you what I thought."

"Go away," she repeated stubbornly.

With a heavy sigh of resignation, he turned and left the room.

Duffy was overcome with nausea, attacking her

in huge waves. She fought it successfully and when it had passed, she thought about what Smith and the others had said. She wished she could believe their theory, and accept it. Wouldn't that make her feel better, if the whole horrible thing had been unreal?

Well, if they were right, there was no reason why she couldn't try to relax and get some sleep. That would make morning come faster and another miserable night in this awful place would be behind her.

She was just drifting off when she heard voices again, outside in the hall directly beyond her door, which stood slightly ajar.

"I don't know, doctor. I haven't seen it."

Duffy recognized the voice. The young ponytailed nurse.

"I was just going off duty, doctor, but if you want me to look for it, of course I'll be happy to."

Then a deeper voice, unfamiliar. "You do that. I don't care if it takes all night, I want that bottle found. In the meantime, if any of the patients start complaining about nausea or dizziness or happen to mention visual problems, for instance that the lights look funny, pay attention. It could mean we've found our missing digoxin." The voice deepened, became harsher. "You'd better hope and pray that medication wasn't given to the wrong patient, because I'm holding you accountable."

Duffy, listening intently, heard the threat of tears in the young nurse's voice as she replied shakily, "Yes, doctor, I'll start looking right this minute. I'll let you know when I find it."

There was no answer, only the sound of muffled, angry footsteps striding away.

Duffy lay unmoving in her bed, staring up at the ceiling. Nausea? Dizziness? Lights looking funny?

Those were *her* symptoms.

Chapter 13

Duffy huddled under the blankets, a paralyzed lump. Digoxin? That wasn't the name of her antibiotic. She had asked. Hers was "something-myocin." But the unseen doctor had just described, perfectly, the way she was feeling. He had said a medication was missing . . . that it wasn't where it was supposed to be.

That was scary.

Duffy chewed on her lower lip. Even if that medicine *was* missing, how could that have anything to do with her? Nobody had given her anything new or strange. Just the capsules.

The capsules . . . could someone have mixed them up with the missing medication? Given her the wrong kind of pills? Did the missing digoxin come in the same kind of pill as her something-myocin?

Anyone could make a mistake. Even in a hospital. After all, she already knew they'd lost the medication in the first place.

But . . . what if . . . what if it wasn't a mistake? If given to the wrong patient, could those missing pills *kill* someone? Cynthia had said the reason they had to be so careful with the charts was that any mix-up could lead to the wrong medication being dispensed. And she had said that the wrong medication could sometimes result in . . . *death*.

If someone really were trying to kill her, wouldn't that be the perfect way? Would anyone even question her death?

No, they probably wouldn't. They'd blame it on her fever.

Her mouth set grimly, Duffy grabbed the call button and pressed on it, not releasing her hold until she heard soft footsteps approaching her door.

Amy Severn, looking anxious, came into the room. "What's wrong, Duffy?"

"What are you still doing here?" Duffy asked with surprise as the Junior Volunteer hurried to her bedside. "It must be after midnight."

"It is. Two of the nurses have the flu and none of the volunteers wanted to help out tonight. So I said I would." Amy sighed heavily. "Cynthia and Smith and Dylan all work nights sometimes. I don't know how they do it. I'm beat! We've had two emergencies already, and old Mrs. Creole is giving us fits. That woman is the *worst* patient on this earth. She makes you look like a saint!" Another sigh. "At least I can sleep in tomorrow."

Ignoring that, Duffy asked, "Amy, have you heard anything about any missing medication? I overheard one of the doctors talking . . ."

"Oh, Duffy, the patients aren't supposed to know anything about that. As if we didn't have enough problems tonight, Dr. Brooks has everyone scrambling, hunting for a missing bottle of digoxin. He's really upset that we can't find it."

"What's it for? The digoxin."

"Heart."

"What does it look like? Not the bottle, the medicine."

"Capsules. I think the bottle they're looking for was part of the inventory in Mr. Latham's room, and now they can't find it."

"Who's Mr. Latham?"

"A patient. He died. Duffy, is this why you called me in here? We're awfully busy."

Amy turned to leave, but Duffy stopped her. "Wait, Amy! I'm not just asking out of nosiness. I heard the doctor talking about the side effects of that medication. And I have *all* of them."

Skepticism showed on Amy's face.

"I do," Duffy insisted. "Really. They started right after the nurse gave me the first capsules, when they took my IV out. My stomach's upset, I'm dizzy . . . and I heard him say something about the lights looking strange. Well, when I look at the lights, I see weird little halos. They were never there before."

"Duffy . . ." Amy's voice was weary. "There's no way your medication could have been mixed up with that digoxin."

"But you're not *sure* that it didn't get mixed up, are you?" Duffy pressed relentlessly. "And if it did, you don't know what it would do, do you?"

Amy shook her head. "No . . . I haven't read as

much about medications as Cynthia and Dylan and Smith. You should ask one of them."

"I want you to have my medicine checked out. Make sure they're not giving me that missing heart stuff by mistake, okay? You can do that, can't you?" Duffy knew how neurotic she sounded, how paranoid. She couldn't help it. Amy had to realize how important this was.

The weariness in Amy's voice was replaced by annoyance. That surprised Duffy. She didn't know Amy ever got annoyed. "Duffy, really, I wish you'd quit worrying. The nurses are very careful with medications. They don't screw up on something that important."

Duffy pounced. "They lost a whole bottle of medication, didn't they?"

Amy shrugged. "People lose things all the time. The bottle will turn up. It's not as if some nurse made a mistake and gave the digoxin to the wrong patient. It's just misplaced, that's all."

Duffy's voice rose as she fought panic. Amy *had* to listen to her. "You don't *know* the wrong patient isn't getting that missing medicine. I'm telling you I have all the symptoms the doctor was describing, and I want you to check my medication to make sure I'm not being given that digoxin stuff by mistake." Out of desperation, her voice hardened. "You wouldn't want my parents suing this hospital because you didn't do your duty, would you? The hospital board wouldn't like that at all. They'd blame *you*."

Amy's face crumpled in dismay and then, for the

first time since Duffy had known her, she lost her temper. "You're being hateful, Duffy Quinn!" she whispered in a hushed, angry voice. "People are just so sick and tired of you making such a fuss all the time. Why can't you be like other patients and sleep? You'd get better faster. Then you could go home and we'd *all* be happy!"

Amy's voice rose as Duffy, her mouth open, stared in astonishment. "I am sick and tired of being nice to you when you don't care a thing about how *I'm* feeling! I don't know what Dylan sees in you, why he would dump me for you — " Her voice broke and, near tears, she turned on her heel and rushed out of the room.

Duffy's nausea returned, turning her stomach into a seesaw. Feeling sick and abandoned, she buried her head in her pillow, moaning.

If Amy — quiet, gentle Amy, who always listened and who always seemed interested — didn't believe her, no one would. No one.

She was alone.

Did Amy really think Dylan had "dumped" her for Duffy?

Oh, God, I am so sick, she cried silently, self-pity overcoming her and wiping out thoughts of Dylan and Amy. She was nauseated and headachey and dizzy. Terror suddenly struck Duffy like a sledgehammer . . . could she be dying? Was this what dying felt like? Was she right about someone deliberately giving her the digoxin, and now it was killing her?

If the digoxin had been in the capsules all along,

ever since Duffy started taking them, she'd had more than a dose or two.

How much of that stuff would it take to kill someone?

She wasn't taking any more of them. If no one would listen to her and have the medicine checked out, she wasn't going to let another capsule pass her lips. She didn't care *how* mad the nurses got. Let them kick her out of the hospital if they wanted to. It would probably be the best thing that could happen to her.

Duffy lay awake all night, fighting nausea and fever, huddled deep in her covers.

Several times, panic overtook her and her hands flew to the call button. Then, remembering with bitter disappointment Amy's disbelief, she let the call button drop into the sheet folds. What was the use?

They all thought she was hysterical . . . or crazy . . . or delirious . . . or all three.

It was hopeless.

She had to find a way to prove the digoxin was in her capsules. First thing in the morning . . .

But morning seemed very far away.

Chapter 14

Frightened by how sick she was feeling, Duffy appealed to her doctor the following morning.

She knew there was no point in sharing her suspicions with him. He wouldn't believe that someone had switched her antibiotic with the missing digoxin any more than Amy had. She would have to try a different tack.

"I think the new pills are making me sick," she said as he glanced at her chart. "I feel sicker than I did when I came in here. Maybe I'm allergic to them. You'd better give me something else."

Dr. Morgan tugged at his earring and frowned. "That's just the drug fighting your infection," he said brusquely. "There's a war being fought in your system and I guarantee the medication is winning. We're pretty sure you've got the flu. The blood tests rule out anything more serious. You'll feel like new in a day or two. Just hang in there, okay?"

And without waiting for an answer from Duffy as to whether or not she was willing to "hang in there," he left.

"Those pills are making me sick!" she cried after him, but it was hopeless. He wasn't listening.

No one was listening. Where Duffy Quinn's fears were concerned, the whole world had gone stone-deaf.

The ceiling light blinked down at her coldly, its strange little halo reminding her that there was something very wrong with her "system" and it wasn't a war being waged by an antibiotic. There *was* no antibiotic in her system. She was convinced there was only digoxin.

A clattering sound out in the hallway preceded Smith's curly head appearing in the doorway.

Something about the sound made Duffy tilt her head and listen carefully. It was probably just one of hundreds of ordinary hospital noises, but . . .

"How's it going?" Smith inquired, leaning against the doorframe. "You recovered from the heebie-jeebies?"

"Go away," she said rudely. "I don't want to talk to people who think I'm crazy."

"Hey," he said, moving into the room, "I never said that. You're sick, that's all. You'd be surprised by some of the stories we hear from patients on heavy doses of medication. I know you *think* what happened was real, but — "

"It *was* real," Duffy said, but her voice lacked conviction. She had tried during the night, throughout the long, sleepless hours, to think of a reason why someone would want to harm her, and she'd failed.

That was the biggest stumbling block to believing

and accepting that someone was deliberately trying to hurt, even kill her. Didn't the police always look for a motive? Wasn't that the most important thing? The "why" of a crime? And there *wasn't* any "why" here.

So, unless there was a crazed psychotic killer in the hospital, one of those weirdos who didn't need a reason to commit murder, there shouldn't be anyone after her.

Maybe Smith and all the others were right. Maybe it *was* the fever.

She would try not to think about it. No point in making herself even crazier when no one was willing to listen. They'd whisk her off to a padded room if she wasn't careful.

But she was still going to find a way to check what was really in her capsules. She didn't know how yet, but —

"What was that noise out in the hall?" she asked Smith. "That rattling sound. What was it?"

"Oh, that. A gurney. One of its wheels is loose. Dylan was supposed to fix it, but . . ."

"A gurney? One of those rolling tables?"

Smith nodded. "Yeah. Taking it downstairs. To the morgue. Why?" He said "morgue" as easily as he might have said "mall."

Duffy shuddered. The morgue. Where they kept the patients who had . . . died. Had someone planned to send her there yesterday?

"Why?" Smith repeated. "Why do you want to know what the noise was?"

She shook her head. "Oh, it's just . . ." Her voice drifted off. She was positive that the sound was identical to the last noise she'd heard that night.

Why would someone be moving a gurney out of her room? Why had it been there in the first place?

"It's just that I heard that sound the other night," she said thoughtfully. "In my room, I think . . ."

His reaction was the same as Dylan's had been when Duffy recognized the soft *slap-slap* of rubber-soled shoes. "Yeah? Well, the hospital is full of them, Duffy. It would be weird if you *hadn't* heard that noise before."

"Yes, but . . ." Oh, what was the use? Trying to explain was a waste of time. "Forget it."

Had she learned anything new? Anything helpful?

The gurneys were used sometimes to take patients who had died down to the basement morgue.

Did that mean anything?

"What are you thinking about?" Smith asked, his eyes on her face.

"Nothing." Why had that gurney been in her room? If two people had been fooling around, as Jane suggested, they wouldn't have needed a gurney. They had the bed.

Could the rickety old gurney have been outside in the hall and not in her room at all?

Maybe. Sound carried better late at night when the hospital was quiet. Maybe the gurney had been out in the hall, passing by her room.

But it sounded closer than that . . .

If she'd heard it at all. How could she be sure? She couldn't.

"You've got that look on your face," Smith said, snapping her back to attention. "You're thinking weird things again, I can tell."

"Did . . . did anybody die a couple of nights ago? The night everyone tells me was just a bad dream?"

Smith sighed and shook his head. "No, Duffy, no one died. We had a couple of emergencies, just like we always do at night, but everyone pulled through just fine. If you did hear a gurney, it was probably bringing a post-op patient back up from surgery. Or maybe someone was just being moved to another floor."

No one had died that night.

Then she remembered something Amy had said, about someone dying recently. The man with the missing digoxin . . .

"What about Mr. Latham? Amy said he'd died. When was that?"

Smith tilted his head, thinking. "Old Man Latham? Pillar of the community, member of the hospital board . . . I'm not sure exactly when he died. Couple of days ago, I guess. Just before you got here. I wasn't on duty that night. Everyone was freaked out the next day, though. The old guy had donated mega-bucks to the hospital. Had a bad ticker, I heard."

Latham had died before Duffy was admitted. So his death couldn't possibly have anything to do with what was happening to her. Not that she had really thought it did. She hadn't even *known* the man.

444

After admonishing her to "get some sleep, you look awful, Duffy," Smith left.

When he had disappeared through the open door, a depressed Duffy rolled over on her side and stared out the window. As she turned, the sheets coiled around her legs, imprisoning her. Panicking momentarily, she began kicking out, desperate to be free of the scratchy cocoon.

"What on earth . . ." Cynthia cried as she entered the room and found Duffy wrestling with her bedding. "Duffy, what are you *doing*?" Then she added more quietly to Jane, who was directly behind her, "Oh, Lord, she's lost it! I knew this was coming!" and ran over to grab Duffy's wrists.

"Leave me alone!" Duffy shouted, her face scarlet. "I'm just tangled, that's all." She yanked the last bit of sheet away from her bare legs. Glaring up at the blue-uniformed Cynthia, she asked caustically, "Did you really think I was losing it? Did my doctor warn you to watch out for weird behavior in room 417?"

When Cynthia's cheeks reddened, Duffy knew she'd hit a nerve. The doctor *had* warned them all to keep an eye on her.

"I brought you some magazines," Jane said cheerfully, in an effort to ease the awkwardness of the moment. "I hope you haven't read them." She was wearing lime-green pedal pushers and a hot-pink short-sleeved T-shirt with the slogan, GO AHEAD MAKE MY DAY GIVE ME A CHOCOLATE CHIP COOKIE slapped across it in blazing scarlet.

"Don't tell me, let me guess," Duffy said bitterly.

"You brought me the *American Journal of Psychiatric Medicine* and the latest copy of *Guide to Mental Health Facilities*, right?"

A bewildered expression crossed Jane's face. "What? What are you talking about?" She plopped herself down at the foot of Duffy's bed.

"They all think I'm crazy here," Duffy said heatedly. Then she filled Jane in on the shower incident, leaving nothing out, ending with, "It *happened*, Jane. But no one believes me. They all think I was hallucinating."

She didn't add that there were moments when she agreed with them. Right now, talking about it, reliving it, she was convinced that every second of it had been real.

"Oh, Duffy, that's the worst thing I've ever heard!" Jane declared, her eyes wide with horror. "Didn't anyone call the police?" She swallowed a sob. "You could have been *killed!*"

"No one called anyone. I told you, they all think I made it up."

"You wouldn't do that." Staunch loyalty filled Jane's voice. "Why would you lie about something so horrible?"

"No one claims she's lying," Cynthia said. "It's just that everyone on the hospital staff knows what fevers can do, that's all. People see and hear all kinds of weird things when their temperature is sky-high."

Jane looked doubtful. Duffy could see that she didn't know what to believe. How could she blame

Jane for that? She didn't know what to believe herself.

"The shower room door was locked," Cynthia pointed out. "Duffy said so herself. And the extra key was at the nurses' station. So how could anyone have gotten into the room?"

Duffy thought about explaining her key theory and decided against it. Jane looked very upset and confused. What good would it do to keep harping on the same old thing when she couldn't *prove* anything?

"Never mind," she said despondently, "forget I said anything."

Discouraged, depressed, and exhausted from lack of sleep, Duffy was such poor company that Jane and Cynthia stayed only a few minutes. Jane, worry clouding her features, promised to come back later, which gave Duffy an idea, and Cynthia said she would stop in later before she left the hospital.

As they reached the hall, Duffy heard Jane say, "Cyn, Duffy doesn't *invent* things. I can't believe no one is taking her seriously." Then their voices faded and Duffy couldn't hear Cynthia's answer. She was sure it was a calm, sensible one.

But that didn't matter right now. Duffy had thought of a way she could learn something about what was in her capsules.

If Jane was willing to help.

Chapter 15

When Dylan stopped in to see how she was, Duffy fought off her nausea long enough to ask a question that had been tugging at her mind.

"Wouldn't the maintenance crew," she asked as he sat down on her bed, "have a key to the shower room? Besides the ones hanging at the nurses' station, I mean. If a pipe burst or the drain backed up and flooded the place, they'd have to get into that room in a hurry, wouldn't they?"

"Well, if no one was in there, the door wouldn't be locked. They wouldn't need a key to get in."

"Yes, but what if someone was in there when something broke?" she persisted. "And couldn't get to the door to open it. Like . . . like a heart patient who had an attack if . . . if the lights went out. They'd need a key then, wouldn't they?"

"Not really. They'd use the key at the nurses' station. It's hanging in plain sight."

Disappointed with the clear logic of that, Duffy

sighed. "I still think the maintenance crew should have their own key," she grumbled.

Dylan thought for a minute. "They probably did. But stuff gets lost around here every day. I know there's no shower room key hanging in the basement with the other keys."

But maybe there once *had* been. And maybe someone has swiped it. And maybe that someone still *had* that key. . . .

"I'm not so sure you imagined that attack," Dylan said slowly, thoughtfully, surprising her. "I know everyone thinks you were hallucinating, but . . ."

Duffy's eyes filled with tears. It was so wonderful to be believed. She reached out a hand. "You mean it?"

Dylan nodded. "Doesn't seem like you, that's all. I know fevers can do weird things, but it would have to be *some* fever to make Duffy Quinn see things that weren't happening. And I keep thinking, you were able to get up and walk all the way to the shower room, so how bad could your fever have been then? Doesn't seem like it could have been bad enough to make you think someone was trying to kill you."

"Oh, thanks, Dylan," Duffy murmured gratefully. "Thanks! It's so nice to have someone here who doesn't think I've gone off the deep end."

She felt hot again, burning up, ablaze. "Could you hand me a glass of water, please? I'm dying of thirst."

Dylan reached over and lifted the heavy metal carafe, pouring carefully. As he handed her the squat little glass, the sleeve on his green tunic slipped back half an inch, revealing a nasty, jagged scratch on his left wrist.

Duffy's heart stopped. She knew she had made a scratch on her attacker that day in the shower. But Dylan? *Dylan?*

Then she almost laughed aloud. She really *was* losing her mind. Dylan Rourke wouldn't hurt a fly.

Still, after taking a long sip of cool water, she couldn't resist commenting lightly, "That's a wicked cut. What happened?"

Looking annoyed, Dylan shook the sleeve back into its proper place. "Nothing. It's just a scratch."

Unable to stop herself, Duffy pressed on. "From what?" Jokingly, she added, "You weren't trying to end it all, were you, Dylan? I thought I was the loony around here."

His expression of annoyance deepened. "If you must know, it happened when I grabbed your wheelchair. Remember? Just as you were about to go into the lake? Slammed my arm against a rock when the chair dragged me."

Guilt flooded Duffy. He'd hurt himself saving her and here she'd been thinking . . .

Awash in shame, she cried, "Why didn't you *tell* me? No one said you'd been hurt! Honestly," she added in exasperation, "no one tells me anything around here. Did you have a doctor look at that?"

"No. I told you, it's just a scratch. And this is

exactly why I didn't tell you. I knew you'd make a big deal out of it." Then he grinned and took one of her hands in his. "It's nice to know you care about me, though. I wasn't sure. You're not the easiest person to read."

Funny . . . no one else thought that. Everyone else in the hospital seemed to think they knew exactly what was going on in her head and why.

"Of course I care, Dylan," she said and was about to add, "we're friends," when Amy appeared in the doorway.

The expression on her round, pink face told Duffy that Amy had heard her comment about caring for Dylan. She looked stricken. Her eyes were wide and bright with unshed tears, her lower lip quivered, her fists were clenched at her waist.

Duffy thought unhappily, That is not the picture of a girl who cheerfully agreed to end her relationship with Dylan Rourke.

She yanked her hand out of Dylan's grip.

Without a word, Amy turned on her heel and left.

Duffy felt as if she'd just ripped the wings off a butterfly. Amy was clearly still in love with Dylan.

And Dylan was just as clearly interested in Duffy.

"I need to sleep," she told him, her voice curt because of her embarrassment for Amy. "Could you leave?"

It was Dylan's turn to look surprised. "Shouldn't we try to figure out who might have gone after you

in the shower? Maybe someone upstairs got loose."
He gestured to the fifth floor where the psychiatric
ward was. "And if he got loose once, he could again."

"I'm too tired to think about that now, Dylan.
Besides," turning over on her side, "what's the use?
No one will listen, anyway."

He stood up then, laying one hand on the top of
her head. "I think your temperature's up. And
you're right, you need your rest. But I'm going to
think about this, Duffy. If the people in this hospital
aren't safe, someone needs to know that. So stay
right here in this bed, where you'll be safe, okay?
And take your medicine."

She didn't tell him she'd decided not to swallow
one more capsule. He'd argue with her, maybe even
tell one of the doctors or nurses. He might not believe her digoxin theory.

When Dylan had gone, she waited for Jane, who
had promised to return. Hadn't that been hours
ago?

But it was Amy who appeared in the doorway,
carrying Duffy's lunch tray.

They were awkward with each other. Each knew
the other was embarrassed because of the earlier
painful moment, and so both avoided mentioning it.
Their speech was stiff and stilted.

"Here," Amy said, "I brought you a newspaper.
There's an article on the track meet in there. I know
you and Kit always went to all the meets. I thought
you might be interested."

Kit had been a runner in high school, so Duffy

had become interested. And then, after attending several meets, she'd found that she really enjoyed it. After Kit graduated, they sometimes went to meets together.

Kit . . . how she missed him!

"Thanks. Thanks a lot, Amy. I . . ." She would *not* mention Dylan. That would be like twisting a knife in Amy's back. "I think I'll sleep now. I'm really tired."

Unsmiling, Amy moved forward to place the palm of one hand on Duffy's forehead. "You're really hot. Are you taking your pills?"

Duffy knew why everyone was asking her that. The hospital rumor mill had picked up on her suspicions about the capsules. They all figured she'd made up her own mind about the pills and wasn't taking them.

But they couldn't prove it.

"Yes," she said, "I am *taking* my pills." Which wasn't a lie . . . yet.

"See you later," Amy said curtly, obviously not forgiving Duffy for letting Dylan sit on her bed and hold her hand. "Take it easy." She turned on her heel and left, her back as stiff as a board.

And something caught Duffy's eye.

Amy usually wore white stockings to work. She said they made her feel "more professional," more "like a real nurse." But today, she was wearing sheer beige on her legs. And underneath the pale, nearly transparent fabric, Duffy could see, on the back of Amy's leg, an ugly dark red mark, etched across the flesh like a streak of lightning.

"Amy," Duffy called impulsively, "what happened to the back of your leg?"

Amy turned slightly. "What? Oh, that . . . cut myself shaving. Gross, right? Bled all over the place. See you." And she disappeared out the door and into the hall.

I've cut my legs shaving thousands of times, Duffy told herself, but I don't remember ever bleeding "all over the place." And I certainly never made a nasty cut like that. What was Amy shaving with, a power saw?

Or . . . had someone *else* made that cut? Someone desperate, armed with a small pink razor, in the darkness of a puddled shower stall?

What was the matter with her? She really *was* paranoid. If, she thought with disgust, it was my little pink razor that carved that gash in Amy's leg, she wouldn't have been so casual when I asked her about it. And she wouldn't have worn see-through stockings to work today. Or she would have covered the cut with a bandage so I couldn't see it.

Unless . . . unless Amy was so sure of herself, so sure no one believed Duffy's theory about someone being after her, that she felt she had absolutely nothing to hide.

Maybe she even *wanted* Duffy to know it was her. Maybe she was doing a little knife-twisting herself, knowing that a weak, sick person whose sanity was in question would be helpless to stop her.

And Duffy realized with a terrible feeling of

dread that of all the people she knew Amy Severn was the only one with a motive to hurt her. Amy was still in love with Dylan. And Dylan was clearly interested in Duffy.

The police always looked for a motive.

Duffy had just found one.

Chapter 16

Questions about Amy had to be put on hold as Duffy's parents arrived for a quick visit.

"I wish we could come more often," her mother said apologetically. "I worry about you every minute. But it's tax time, honey, and you know what that's like." Duffy's parents were accountants, and she did know what tax time was like. She had picked a lousy time to get sick.

"Can't I please go home?" she begged. "I'll get better faster there, I promise." They hadn't mentioned the shower attack, so she knew the staff had convinced them that it hadn't really taken place. They'd never bring it up, thinking it would upset her further.

"Oh, Duffy, please don't start that again," her mother pleaded. "You're much better off here. I just told you how busy we are. At least here, there's someone watching you every minute."

Well, not really. Where had all the nurses and doctors been the night she'd heard those sounds in her room?

"But I don't feel safe," she protested. "This isn't a safe place to be . . ."

Her parents exchanged worried glances.

She read the gaze. They, too, were concerned that the fever was affecting her mental health.

It was hopeless. She spent the rest of their brief visit in sullen silence and tried not to feel guilty when they left looking uneasy and unhappy. They should have listened to her. . . .

When they had gone, her thoughts returned to Amy. She had thought of Amy as a nice, sweet person, and she *was*, most of the time. But Amy had a temper, Duffy knew that now.

How angry could Amy get?

And had she really cut herself shaving her legs?

Or was she so angry about Dylan's interest in Duffy that she was determined to obliterate the competition?

To escape the questions that had no answers, Duffy picked up the newspaper and began skimming through the track meet article on the sports page. The words had no meaning for her. The fact that Twelvetrees High School's varsity track team would be advancing to the state finals failed to touch her. It seemed unimportant. If Kit were still on the relay team, maybe she'd feel something, in spite of her nerves being strung as tightly as violin strings. But he wasn't.

Where *was* he?

Would he be in California by now? Why hadn't he called to tell her he'd arrived safely and to give her his new address and telephone number? She was glad he'd finally dumped his cranky uncle and whining aunt and that terrible, deadly shoe store. But had he put his best friend, Duffy Quinn, behind along with the rest of Twelvetrees, Maine? Off with the old, on with the new?

No. Kit wouldn't do that.

What would he say to her now, if she told him everything that had happened, and the things she suspected? Would he laugh it off? Tell her, as everyone else had, that she had an overactive imagination or was suffering from fever delirium?

No. He wouldn't do that, either. One of the reasons Kit hadn't been the most popular boy in school was the way he took everything so seriously. Always reading, always learning, taking in new information. He believed that life was not a laughing matter. No wonder, considering the household he lived in.

He would have taken her story seriously. And then he would have tried to help her figure out what to do.

If only she could talk to him now. . . .

Duffy began leafing listlessly through the rest of the newspaper. A name jumped out at her from one of the middle pages, startling her.

Latham. Victor Latham, she read.

Latham? Where had she heard that name before?

The man who had died before she arrived, "Old Man Latham," someone had called him. Her interest piqued, Duffy read the brief article.

*A scholarship fund in the name of Victor La-
tham, a longtime resident of Twelvetrees and a
member of the Community Hospital's Board of
Trustees, has been established at the hospital for
future medical students. Latham, 64, died recently
after a brief illness. According to his daughter and
sole survivor, Claire Bristol, Mr. Latham's pri-
mary interest in life was medicine. He felt it was
important to keep young people interested in ca-
reers in the health field. And he was fond of the
young people who worked at the hospital while he
was ill. The scholarship is being established to return their kindness to him.*

Duffy couldn't help wondering which of the
"young people" at the hospital had been kind to
Victor Latham. Amy? Cynthia? Smith? Maybe even
Dylan. Had Latham given any of them money in
return for their kindnesses *before* he died? Was that
where Smith, an orderly, had found the money to
buy that fancy sports car he drove?

Anyway, that night . . . the night she'd heard
the clanging of the curtain rings, the *slap-slap* of
rubber soles, the clatter of the gurney wheels . . .
that hadn't been the night Victor Latham died. So
none of the sounds she'd heard had had anything to
do with him.

And his death had nothing to do with *her*.

She let the newspaper fall into her blanketed lap.

Victor Latham must have felt very safe here, in
the hospital he'd given so much to.

459

But he *had* died here.

The nurse came in then, armed with the little fluted cup, and briskly handed Duffy the two capsules.

Duffy took them without a word, obediently dipped them into her mouth, tucked them into the flesh of her cheek and prayed silently that the capsules wouldn't dissolve too quickly. She sipped the water handed her by the nurse and slid down beneath the covers, feeling a pressing need for an afternoon nap.

It worked. The nurse turned quietly and left . . . *slap-slap, slap-slap.* The heavy wooden door closed after her.

Duffy sat up and spat the soggy but still intact capsules into the palm of her hand. She wrapped them in a paper napkin and hid the folded napkin under her pillow. She'd have to make sure no one came near it to fluff it or change the pillowcase.

Without the pills, maybe she'd start feeling better.

She was disappointed to find that although dumping the pills gave her some slight feeling of control, she was still unable to relax. Where was Jane, anyway? What was keeping her?

Amy, as bright and cheerful as if the scene between Duffy and Dylan of the day before had never taken place, arrived before Jane. She came breezing into the room, every hair in place, a blue ribbon imprisoning her curls. She was smiling.

Duffy couldn't tell if the smile was real or phony.

"Have you heard?" Amy asked. "Did anyone tell you?"

"Tell me what?"

"Kit called last night. I just heard."

"What? What did you say?"

Amy poured a glass of water for Duffy. "Kit called. To talk to you."

Duffy took the water gratefully. She forgot her suspicions about the cut on Amy's leg. She forgot her hatred for the ugly hospital room and her fear for her own safety. Kit had called?

But before she drank, she said slowly, "But I never talked to Kit last night. The phone didn't ring once. I was awake . . . I would have heard it."

Amy leaned against the nightstand. "They wouldn't put the call through. He forgot the time change between here and California. It was only eight o'clock there, but it was eleven here. The switchboard doesn't put calls through to patients that late at night."

Duffy leaned back against the pillows, weak with disappointment. "Darn! I really wanted to talk to him. He must have read my mind." She smiled slightly. "He could do that, you know. Sometimes. He used to finish my sentences for me. Drove me crazy." She sipped the water slowly, struggling with the bitter news that Kit had actually called, had wanted to talk with her, and hadn't been able to.

"Who took the call?" she asked Amy. Maybe Kit had left a message for her.

Amy shrugged and began straightening the litter

of tissues, hair supplies, get-well cards, and candy boxes that cluttered the nightstand. "Switchboard operator, I guess. One of the nurses told me about it. I thought it would cheer you up, but you don't look very cheerful. Maybe I shouldn't have told you."

"Yes," Duffy said quickly, "yes, you should have. I'm glad you told me." If Kit called again, she didn't want people afraid to tell her. At least now she knew he was okay and had made it to California in one piece. But she was so disappointed at missing his call.

"Thanks, Amy. I hope the operator reminded him of the time change so he won't make the same mistake again."

"I'm sure she did. Maybe he'll call back today." Amy paused and then added, "Dylan knows, Duffy."

Duffy lifted her head. "Knows what?"

"He knows that Kit called here. Everyone knows that some guy from California called you at eleven o'clock last night. I saw Dylan in the hall a few minutes ago and he didn't look happy. He's jealous of Kit, you know. Always has been, even when he was dating . . . me. We argued about it a couple of times."

Before yesterday afternoon, when Amy got so angry with her, Duffy would have had trouble imagining Amy arguing with anyone. But not now.

"I'm sorry," Duffy murmured. "Really, Amy, I am."

"I know." Amy's voice was as soft and sweet as it had always been. "It's okay, Duffy. Not your

462

fault. Look, can I get you anything before I get to work? I might not have time to stop in later. We're pretty busy. More flu cases."

There was something. "Amy, do you remember Victor Latham?"

Amy began fussing with Duffy's blankets. "We're not supposed to talk about him, Duffy. Everyone feels bad that he died. We all liked him. And he was getting better. And then . . ." She shrugged.

"What happened?"

"I don't know. But he was old, and he had a bad heart. So . . ."

Old? The paper had said he was sixty-four. Was sixty-four that old? Duffy's grandmother was seventy-six and still healthy and active.

But then, she didn't have a bad heart.

"Gotta go," Amy said. "Jane'll probably be here in a minute to keep you company. See you later."

She was right. She had barely left the room when Jane hurried in, looking guilty.

"Where have you been?" Duffy cried. "I've been waiting all day for you."

"Sorry." Jane flopped into the bedside chair and put her feet up on the edge of the bed. "Had to run some errands for my father's wife." Jane always used that particular phrase to describe her stepmother, and she rolled her eyes toward heaven as she said the words.

"Well, I'm glad you're in a mood to run errands, because I have one for you," Duffy said. "And it has to be done right this minute."

Jane groaned.

Chapter 17

"Before you tell me what the errand is," Jane said, her lips sliding into a big grin, "I hear you got a telephone call last night. Didn't talking to Kit make you feel better?" Her dark hair was in braids tied with orange ribbon that matched her jumpsuit.

"I never talked to Kit," Duffy explained. "They wouldn't put the call through. Too late. How did you know he called?"

"Dylan told me." A bleak expression flitted across Jane's round, plain face. "He didn't seem too happy about it." She paused and then added, "He likes you, doesn't he?"

Duffy didn't know what to say to that. Yes, he probably *did* like her, but right now, that seemed so unimportant — except to Jane and Amy. Duffy Quinn had far more pressing matters on her mind.

During Jane's absence, Duffy's idea had taken shape. But she needed Jane's help. "Never mind Dylan," she said tersely. "About that errand . . ."

Jane heaved a sigh. "I just got *through* running errands! Is it really, really important?"

"Do you want me to get better?" Duffy asked sternly.

Jane flushed. "Of course I do, Duffy. Okay, what is it? Where do I have to go?"

"To the lab."

Jane frowned. "You mean Dean's lab?"

"Of course. I need a lab, and your brother works in one, so why would I send you to someone else's lab?"

"What do you need a lab for?"

"You're stalling, Jane. Quit asking questions just so you won't have to leave this room. I need my pills analyzed, and Dean's just the person to do it." She handed Jane the capsules she hadn't taken, still wrapped in their paper napkin. "Take these over there, right away, and ask Dean what they are. Then come straight back here and tell me."

Jane's frown deepened. "Why don't you ask your doctor what they are?"

Duffy glared. "Because my doctor doesn't *know* what they are. I mean, he *thinks* he does, but I think he's wrong. I think someone screwed up and gave me the wrong stuff, and Dean can tell me if I'm right. So hurry up, okay? This is important."

Something in her voice sent Jane to her feet. She took the napkin, then hesitated. "Duffy, I can't believe someone would make a mistake like that."

"That's because you aren't a patient in this hospital." Conscious of the minutes passing rapidly, Duffy urged, "Jane, just *do* it, okay? Trust me. I know what I'm doing. I promise, I won't ask you for another single favor as long as I live."

"Yes, you will. And I'll probably give it to you." Jane grinned weakly. "I want you to know I'm only humoring this bizarre request because you're my best friend and I miss you and I want you out of this place so life will be back to normal again. But I'll bet you anything you're wrong about the medication being screwed up, Duffy." She shuddered. "I can't believe someone could make such a mistake."

Duffy shuddered, too. Because she wasn't at all sure it was just a "mistake." She wasn't sure of that at all.

"I'll hurry," Jane said quickly, noticing Duffy's shudder. "I'll tell Dean it's for you. He's always liked you, Duffy." She bent to give Duffy a quick hug. "I'll be right back, I promise."

When Jane had rushed out of the room, Duffy wondered just who she would tell if it turned out that the pills contained the missing digoxin. It would have to be someone she trusted completely. Names flitted through her mind and were rapidly discarded.

The list of people she trusted completely was getting shorter all the time.

A nurse coming in to give Duffy a back rub nearly collided with Jane.

"Where's your friend going in such a big hurry?" she asked amiably as she uncapped the bottle of lotion.

"Gee, I don't know," Duffy fibbed. She wasn't telling a single soul in this place where Jane was going, or why. Not until she was sure of who she could trust.

"You feel hot again," the nurse said as she rubbed Duffy's muscles, so tense with fear and uncertainty, they were cramping between her shoulders. "Your temperature must be up."

Duffy knew it was because she wasn't getting the antibiotics she needed. But until Jane returned with the lab report, she wasn't about to tell anyone she'd quit taking the capsules.

The nurse was leaving when Dylan arrived, mop in hand.

And when he bent to kiss her cheek, Duffy was shocked to find herself recoiling. She didn't do it on purpose. It was strictly an involuntary movement. But she knew it was stimulated by fear.

Fear of *Dylan*?

That really *was* crazy. Dylan hated hurting people. In grade school, he hadn't done well in football because he was so afraid of hurting someone when he tackled them. He'd got over that in high school and was on the varsity team now, but the coach was always yelling at him for "holding back," not "giving his all." Duffy knew it was because he was still a little afraid of breaking bones. Someone *else's* bones, not his own.

It would take something really powerful to overcome Dylan's reluctance to hurt people.

And she couldn't think of a single thing powerful enough to do that.

But neither could she bring herself to return his

kiss, or even smile as if she meant it, not until she felt completely safe — if she ever did again.

How long would Jane's "errand" take?

Frowning, Dylan asked gently, "You okay? Taking your pills?"

Wearing a frown of her own, Duffy remembered that this wasn't the first time Dylan had asked that question. Why was he so preoccupied with her medication?

Maybe, she thought, her stomach twisting in revulsion, maybe he knew something about those pills. . . .

"Yes," she snapped, "I'm taking them."

Could Dylan, who seemed to like her so much, be the one who wanted to hurt her? What reason would he have?

If Kit were still around, maybe jealousy would make Dylan act weird, do strange things.

But Kit was in California. He wasn't a threat to Dylan. Not that he ever had been, but Dylan didn't know that. Maybe he was the sort of person who didn't believe girls could have male *friends*. Like Jane, who had always had a hard time believing that Duffy and Kit weren't in love.

"If you don't want him for a boyfriend," she had said more than once, "you shouldn't monopolize his time when there are so many girls out there without boyfriends."

Meaning Jane, of course.

But Kit had never been attracted to Jane. Duffy had suggested once, casually, that Kit ask her out, and he had said, "I don't think so. She's not my type."

Meaning he liked "thinkers" and Jane wasn't a thinker. She was a "feeler," running mostly on emotion. Kit, who lived in a household devoid of emotion, couldn't understand that.

Dylan wasn't happy when he left her room, but Duffy couldn't dwell on that.

Where was Jane? I need to know the truth, Duffy thought, and I need to know it *now*.

A very long hour and a half later, she did. Because Jane, red-cheeked and breathless, came into the room carrying a brown paper bag.

"Well, here it is," she said wearily. She handed the bag to Duffy. "The pills are in there, and so is the report. Dean was glad to do it . . . for you." She hesitated, and then added in a voice that hinted of hurt feelings, "Duffy, why didn't you tell me you had a heart condition?"

Duffy looked down at the slip of paper in her hand, already knowing what it said.

D I G O X I N

Chapter 18

Duffy tried to still her racing heart. She told herself it wasn't as if she hadn't suspected . . . the word DIGOXIN shouldn't have been that great a shock.

But it was.

Seeing it there on the small slip of paper, seeing the proof that her suspicions, which had once seemed so wild, had been accurate after all, punched her in the stomach. Someone had actually done this to her? On purpose? Sent this awful, sickening drug flowing through her body?

Who could hate her that much?

She had been right. Someone had switched the digoxin with her antibiotics. Someone had actually stolen her pills, split the capsules in two, emptied out the "something-myocin," and replaced the antibiotic with the missing digoxin.

And no one knew that but her.

Except for the person who had *done* it.

Who *was* that person?

As she stared, frozen, at the slip of paper in her hand, Jane repeated her question. "Duffy? Why didn't you tell me you had a heart condition?"

"I don't," Duffy replied. "There's nothing wrong with my heart." Except that it was pounding wildly in her chest.

"Dean made a mistake? But . . . but he seemed so sure," Jane said. "I mean, I told him digoxin didn't sound like an antibiotic, and he said it wasn't. He said it was heart medication. I said you didn't have anything wrong with your heart, and he said, 'Then she shouldn't be taking this stuff. It won't make her well. It'll make her *sicker*.'"

Duffy said nothing. She was debating whether or not to take Jane into her confidence. What if, in spite of Dean's analysis, Jane didn't believe her. What if she wrote it off as a simple mistake and accused Duffy of "paranoia"? Worse, what if she *told* someone that Duffy had had the pills tested? Word would spread quickly through the hospital that Duffy knew the truth . . . once whoever had done this knew Duffy was on to them, something really terrible might happen. Maybe to *Jane*, because she had taken the pills to the lab.

No. She couldn't tell Jane. It was too risky.

"Never mind," Duffy said, "let's forget it. Let's talk about something else. Seen Dylan today?"

"Duffy!" Jane squealed. "Are you kidding? Dean tells me you're taking heart medication, and you say you don't have a heart condition, and you expect me to forget it, just like that? What's going on?"

When Duffy, her mind racing to come up with a plausible explanation that would keep Jane safe, failed to respond, Jane pressed. "Duffy, we don't keep secrets from each other, right? Are you in some kind of trouble? You sounded so scared earlier. What are you doing with those pills? Where did you get them?"

Duffy wanted desperately to confide in Jane. She was so tired of worrying alone. And what was the point of having a best friend if you couldn't tell her the truth?

But what kind of friend were you if you deliberately put your best friend in danger?

A rotten kind of friend.

She couldn't stand the thought of anything terrible happening to Jane. Bad enough that Kit had left. What would she do without Jane?

Forcing a grin onto her face, she said, "Gotcha!" and added slyly, "Does the phrase 'wild-goose chase' have any meaning for you?"

It took Jane a few minutes. When the words finally sank in, her cry of outrage echoed throughout the room. "Dorothy Leigh Quinn! I don't *believe* this! You didn't! You didn't send me all the way across town for no reason, did you?"

Duffy's grin splashed wider.

Jane flopped back in her chair, throwing her hands up in the air. "This is not happening. Sick people are not supposed to play stupid practical jokes. I do *not* believe this."

But Duffy could see that she did. And her relief was mixed with a terrible sense of loneliness. She had kept Jane out of it. Jane was safe. But now she was alone again, with no one on her side.

"Honestly, Duffy," Jane babbled, "this is just like

the time you told me Michael J. Fox was making a personal appearance here and if I hurried, I could get tickets." The corners of her lips began to turn up in the birthing of a laugh. Glaring at Duffy in mock anger, she said, "You laughed *so* hard. I thought you'd crack a rib."

Then she added with a grin, "So, I guess this means you're getting better, right? And you'll be sprung soon?" Her voice softened, "I miss you something fierce, Duff. I hate it when you pull this kind of stunt, but nothing's the same when you're not around."

Thinking of the digoxin in her system, Duffy fell silent. *Would* she be going home soon? Would she be going home at *all*? In one piece?

She needed to think about what the lab report meant, and what to do about it. "I'm really all worn out," she told Jane. "I think I need to sleep for a while. Maybe you could come back tonight?"

Immediately, Jane jumped to her feet. "Oh, sure. I'm sorry. I shouldn't have stayed so long. I keep forgetting you're sick. I'll come back later." Her smile then was sweet to see. "I'm mad at you for sending me across town for nothing, but I'm glad that you felt well enough to do it. 'Bye."

Duffy watched her go, her thick dark hair swinging on her shoulders, and was glad she'd made up that silly story about a wild-goose chase. Being in this alone wasn't easy, but at least she didn't have to worry about something horrible happening to Jane.

Alone again, she asked herself if the digoxin in

her pills could possibly have been a mistake.

There had been a lot of "mistakes" — the elevator sign being switched, the wheelchair being pushed down the hill, the attack in the shower, the digoxin. There was no way all of those things could be simple mistakes. Someone had engineered them.

If only she had some clue as to who it was, and why.

Duffy settled back against the pillow, her head throbbing, and closed her eyes.

As hard as it was to believe, Duffy realized with horror, it had to be someone she knew, someone who'd been around the hospital and knew where she was and what she was doing.

Amy was still in love with Dylan, that was obvious. But Dylan was interested in the ailing Duffy Quinn. That must either hurt Amy terribly . . . or make her very angry. And she had a temper, Duffy knew that now. She also had a very nasty scratch on the back of her leg.

How far would Amy Severn go to get Dylan Rourke back?

Dylan had a cut, too. On his wrist. He had said he'd hurt himself when he saved her from hurtling into the chilly waters of the lake.

But Dylan had no reason to hurt her, did he? What had she ever done to Dylan?

Amy had said Dylan was jealous of her friendship with Kit, had been for a long time. *How* jealous? And why would that make Dylan want to hurt *her*?

Could Dylan and Kit have had an argument before Kit left? Was Dylan hiding a hatred of Kit so deep that he would attack anyone who was close to Kit? Duffy Quinn, for instance?

But . . . wouldn't that mean Dylan was severely unhinged? If he was, he hid it well.

If she only had Kit's phone number, she could call him and find out if Dylan and he had fought.

What about Cynthia? She seemed to be interested only in Duffy's health. But was that just a clever disguise? Duffy tried to recall something she might have done to anger Cynthia. But she came up with nothing.

There was Smith Lewis, too. He had been there at the empty elevator shaft, and again behind her wheelchair on the hill. As far as she knew, Smith had no reason to want her out of the way. And he had seemed so helpful. . . .

What am I *doing*? Duffy covered her face with her hands. Everyone is right about me, she thought in disgust. I *am* losing it. Suspecting my friends, people who have helped me since I got sick. No wonder everyone is treating me as if I've gone off the deep end. Ever since that night I heard those weird noises in my room.

Those noises . . . that night . . . the sounds . . . what if everyone was wrong and those sounds hadn't been figments of her fevered mind's imagination? What if there really *was* someone in her room? Someone who didn't want to be seen? Someone who was afraid Duffy *had* seen him? Or her?

But . . . what could that someone have been doing in her room that was so awful, killing the only witness had become absolutely necessary?

"Fooling around" with a date, as Jane had suggested, couldn't be it. That was ridiculous. Whatever had happened in her room, if anything had, it had been a lot deadlier than a few stolen kisses.

What *was* it?

Had she really seen something? And forgotten it because it was too awful to remember?

And who, exactly, had she shared the experience with? Who knew she'd heard something that night?

Everyone.

Everyone knew.

Duffy felt tears of exasperation stinging her eyelids. What difference did it make? Why waste time racking her brain to figure out who wanted her sick or dead, when it was so clear that the only way to be safe was to escape from the hospital.

Now that she knew the digoxin in her body had been put there deliberately, she couldn't spend one more night in this place.

She had to get away.

I am not, she thought with resolve, spending another night lying awake, waiting. If only I could call Kit, tell him to come and get me. He would. And he wouldn't ask any questions until we were safely out of here.

But Kit wasn't here.

She would have to figure out, all by herself, how to carry out her resolution to leave this place.

Chapter 19

Duffy decided on the midnight hour to attempt her escape. The patients would be asleep by then, the nurses occupied with night care and writing reports. She would have to be careful to steer clear of the maintenance crew. On her sleepless nights, she'd heard them out in the halls at all hours, mopping the floors or changing light fixtures. Any one of them would be suspicious of a patient lurking in the corridor at such a late hour. They might report her, clip her wings before she took flight.

That couldn't happen. She *had* to get out of here.

Her skin, hot and dry to the touch, felt too tight. It squeezed against her, a bodysuit one size too small. The hands on her watch crawled slowly, slowly, as if struggling through glue. Seven o'clock, eight . . .

When her parents came, she asked once more if they would take her home. She knew they wouldn't. They trusted the hospital completely, or they wouldn't have brought her here in the first place.

"If you would just relax, Duffy," her mother scolded lightly, "you'd get better so much faster. Dr. Morgan says it's nothing serious, but that you're impeding your own recovery."

Impeding her own recovery? *She* wasn't the one doing the impeding!

Knowing she would just upset her parents if she kept insisting that she wasn't safe in the hospital, Duffy gave up. She'd get out of this place on her own if it was the last thing she ever did.

Jane never arrived. When Cynthia came in later that evening to bring Duffy fresh water, she said Jane had called the nurses' station to say she wasn't feeling well.

"Didn't you get her message?" Cynthia asked when Duffy's face registered distress. Jane, ill? Duffy thought. She'd been perfectly fine that afternoon.

"People around here don't seem to be very good about delivering messages," Duffy said dourly. "I almost never found out that Kit had called, either. Did Jane say what's wrong with her? I hope I didn't give her my bug."

Cynthia shook her head. "Maybe she was just tired. All that running around she did for you today. I saw her come in and go back out and then come in again. Did she bring you goodies?"

Hardly, Duffy thought. She brought me the news that someone is out to get me. Aloud, she said, "No. Just shampoo."

Cynthia nodded, said she was going home soon

and she'd see Duffy in the morning, and then she left.

You won't see *me* in the morning, Duffy thought to herself, because I'll be long gone. I *hope*.

When the last visitor had left, the eerie silence she was waiting for crept, foglike, across the fourth floor until the last soft murmur had been swallowed up. Duffy tiptoed to her closet and slipped inside, dressing in the dark, narrow space: jeans, a sweater, socks, sneakers. Leaving her gown on the floor of the closet, she hurried back to the bed and slid under the covers to wait for the perfect moment.

She had no plan. There was no way to plan without knowing exactly where everyone might be at every second. She would wait and be very careful and do a lot of praying and hoping. If she could make it to the elevator without being seen. . . .

"You still awake?" a voice said from the doorway.

Duffy jumped, startled, and quickly yanked the blanket up to hide the telltale sweater. "Smith? What are you doing here?"

He came into the room, moving toward the bed. In the weak glow of the night-light beside the door, she could see his grin. "Checking up on you," he answered. Noticing the blanket tucked up underneath her chin, he frowned. "You cold? Doesn't seem that bad in here to me."

"*You* don't have a fever," she pointed out. "One minute I'm burning up, the next I'm freezing. Right now, I'm freezing." She could hear the tension in her voice. Would Smith pick up on it? What if he got suspicious?

She had left the closet door open. Jerk! If he glanced in and noticed that her clothes weren't hanging on the hangers . . .

He wasn't looking at the closet. He was looking down at her.

What if he decided to check her pulse? He did that sometimes — showing off, playing "doctor." If he did that now, he'd be surprised to find her wrist encased in a sweater cuff.

She'd just have to say she'd been so cold, she'd thrown a sweater on over her hospital gown.

"How come you're not asleep?" he asked.

"It's hard to sleep when someone's standing over your bed talking to you," Duffy said sarcastically. And was surprised to see Smith recoil, as if she'd struck him. Had she hurt his feelings? Did it matter?

Maybe some other time it would. But not now, not when her life was on the line. The only thing that mattered was getting away from here, and she couldn't do that with Smith Lewis standing over her bed. If it took hurting his feelings to get rid of him, so be it.

"Sorry," he said stiffly. "Didn't mean to bother you. Thought you might need something." He hesitated and then added, "I . . . I wanted to make sure you knew I did check the brake on your wheelchair. I've thought about it, and I'm sure of it."

The horror of that terrifying ride swept back over Duffy, and she shuddered violently.

"Sorry," Smith said for a second time. "Shouldn't have brought it up. Probably still gives you nightmares. No wonder you can't sleep."

Even in the darkened room, she could see the guilt in his face. But how could she be sure he was sincere? Of course he would say he'd checked the brake. He certainly wouldn't admit it if he'd deliberately sent that chair racing down the hill.

"I *could* sleep," she said caustically, "if you'd go away and leave me alone."

"Your tough act doesn't fool me," Smith said quietly. "I think you're scared to death, and I don't blame you. You've had a rough time. Fevers can be nasty things."

Fever? Duffy thought nastily. It wasn't my fever that switched the signs on the elevator or sent me down that hill or came after me in the shower. Who is he kidding?

"Say you believe I checked that brake and I'll get out of here," he said, bending low over the bed. "I need to know you believe it."

"Sure. I believe you." Anything to get rid of him. "In fact, I'm pretty sure I *saw* you check the brake." Actually, she thought now that she *had* seen him check it. But maybe what she'd really seen was Smith sabotaging the brake so that it would release and send her flying down the hill toward the lake shortly after he was safely away from the scene.

But she must have sounded convincing because Smith heaved a sigh of relief. "Great! Okay, then. You sleep now and I'll check on you when I come on duty tomorrow." Then he caught her by surprise by bending quickly and kissing her cheek.

Before she could protest, he was gone. She could hear the soft *slap-slap* of his rubber-soled shoes as he disappeared down the dim hallway.

Duffy found herself wishing fervently that she could somehow be sure that Smith was on her side. Then she could ask him to help her make her mad dash for freedom and she wouldn't be so terrified.

But . . .

Smith had been the only person near the elevator, and he'd been the only person close to her wheelchair. How could she possibly trust him?

No, better to do it alone. She'd be safer that way.

But she didn't *feel* safe when, some twenty minutes later, she listened and listened again and then slid out of bed, put on her ski jacket, and tiptoed to the doorway to listen once more.

Nothing. Silence. Not a total silence . . . she could faintly hear the sound of murmuring voices. Nurses, probably. But they sounded too far away to be at the nurses' station, where they could see her as she passed. Maybe they were in some patient's room, and if the door was nearly closed, as hers always was at night, she should be able to slip by unnoticed.

If she could just make it to the elevator. . . .

Duffy's skin pinched at her again. What if someone were in the elevator? Maybe she should try for the stairs. They were hidden behind a steel door in the middle of the corridor, closer to her room than the elevator at the end of the hall.

But they'd be dark. Wouldn't they? And she had no flashlight.

The elevator was faster.

Faster seemed better.

Her heart went on a rampage in her chest, thudding so violently she wouldn't have been surprised to see it leap out and land on the floor at her feet. Her hands, icy cold in spite of the fever that raged in her body, shook as she pressed her back so close to the wall she seemed almost a part of it, and began moving slowly, slowly, down the hall.

Her teeth began to chatter, and she bit her tongue. She felt warm blood on her lower lip. Another step, another . . .

"You take this side, I'll take the other," a voice Duffy recognized said. The ponytailed nurse. The remark came from inside one of the rooms.

Duffy inched her way right up to the door of the room from which the voices came. The door was half open. If they saw her passing . . .

Slowly, carefully, she peered around the corner of the door frame. Two nurses . . . their backs turned to the door . . .

Holding her breath, Duffy skittered past the door and stopped on the opposite side, paralyzed.

She waited for one of them to call out, "Hey, there, you! Duffy Quinn! What are you doing skulking around in the halls? Get back to your room this minute."

But no one called out.

They hadn't seen her.

Breathing again, the violent trembling slightly eased, she continued her turtle-pace down the hallway. After what seemed like agonizing hours, she was within two steps of the elevator.

Just two more steps . . .

"Going somewhere?" a voice said in her ear.

Chapter 20

Duffy froze in place. Nononono! Not when she was this *close* . . . one more step and she'd have reached the elevator button.

But now . . .

Reluctantly, awash in bitter disappointment, she turned to face the person who had interrupted her flight.

Dylan.

Dylan frowned at her, his square, open face full of concern. "Duffy, I can tell by your eyes that your fever isn't down. What are you doing out of bed?" He had changed from the green smock into street clothes, a sweater and jeans. Going off duty, like Smith. Could she talk Dylan into taking her with him?

Duffy, her energy sapped by the fever and her disappointment, sagged against the wall.

Dylan reached out and held her around the waist. "Whoa, easy there! How come you're dressed? Why aren't you asleep?" Then, "Boy, you're burning up!

Geez, Duffy, are you nuts or what? You should be in bed."

She had to trust him. She had no choice. If she didn't tell him what was happening, if she couldn't convince him that someone was after her, he'd lead her back to her room and she'd belong to the hospital again. And she wouldn't be safe.

Dylan wouldn't hurt her. They'd been friends for a long time. How could she have suspected him? He had the nicest face in the world, and he had covered up the truth about his breakup with Amy to protect her feelings. That had been a kind thing to do. Someone like that would certainly help her, wouldn't he?

So she poured it all out. "Dylan, listen," she began, clinging desperately to his arm, "I can't stay here. I have to go home. Please, you have to help me. You can take me there. Then I can tell them about the lab report . . ."

"What lab report?"

"Jane took my pills to a lab today, and I was right . . . they had digoxin in them . . . the missing heart medication. You heard about it, didn't you? That it was missing?"

Dylan nodded.

"Well, someone took it and put it in my capsules. I said I was getting sicker, but no one believed me. So I asked Jane to get them tested, and she did. And the lab report said just what I knew it would . . . that there wasn't any antibiotic in the capsules I was taking. Just digoxin. That's what was making me sicker."

"Duffy . . ." Dylan's voice registered doubt, but

486

he kept his arm around her waist. She couldn't have remained standing without it.

"No, listen, *please!* Someone here, I don't know why, is trying to kill me. I didn't imagine the attack in the shower, Dylan, the way everyone thinks I did. It really happened." Tears of frustration gathered in Duffy's eyes and spilled down her fever-pinked cheeks. "*All* of it really happened. Someone switched the out-of-order sign on purpose and someone pushed my chair down the hill on purpose — "

"Duffy, take it easy." Dylan's voice was gentle and quiet as he gathered her closer against his chest.

"You have to believe me, Dylan. You're the only one I can trust."

Dylan flushed with pleasure. "How about if you show me that lab report? It's not that I don't believe you, Duffy, but seeing that would help. I mean, it's hard to believe that someone would give you the wrong medication."

"Of course, you're right. Here . . ." Duffy gasped as she slid a hand into her jeans pocket. It was empty. "The report . . . I must have left it on the bed. Dylan, I have to have it. It's the proof that my capsules were switched."

A nurse came out of a patient's room and hurried to the nurses' station. But Duffy and Dylan were standing in shadow and weren't seen.

"We'll just go get the report," Dylan whispered. "Then you'll have it to show your folks. I'll take you home, if you're sure that's what you want to do."

"I'm sure, Dylan, oh, I'm sure! But . . . I don't

think I can make it back down the hallway again. I'm too tired. Could you just go get the report . . . it's on my bed, probably hiding in the covers? I'll wait here. I'll hide over there in that corner until you get back. Hurry, okay? I feel like I'm going to pass out any minute."

The last bit of doubt faded from Dylan's blue eyes. "Okay. Stay right here, don't move. I'll be right back."

And he hurried off down the hallway as Duffy moved to take refuge behind a tall white column disguising a heating duct.

It was almost over. Dylan would come back with the report, take her home, and her parents would take it from there.

Relief washed over her, and her hands finally stopped shaking. It was going to be all right. It was. Whoever was doing this to her would be caught, and put away somewhere where they couldn't do bad things anymore.

And she'd find out why all of this had happened. But best of all, she'd be safe, the way she used to be. Duffy closed her eyes.

Suddenly, Duffy heard voices approach.

"I'll take care of her," a crisp, efficient voice said.

And Duffy looked into the face of the middle-aged head nurse. In her right hand was a hypodermic needle. "You go on home, Rourke. You did the right thing. This poor child shouldn't even be out of bed. She'll be fine now, thanks to you."

Duffy drew in her breath and took a step backward. "No, no," she murmured, her horrified eyes flying to stare accusingly at Dylan, who lingered behind the nurse. "You — you promised!"

"There wasn't any report," he said, his eyes pleading for forgiveness. "Honest, Duffy, I looked and looked. There wasn't anything! You must have thought there was, but there wasn't."

Duffy continued to back away until she ran into the wall. The nurse continued to advance, needle in hand.

"Call Jane!" Duffy begged, her eyes wildly searching for a way out. There was none. "Call Jane, she'll tell you! She'll tell you she had the pills analyzed and that Dean said they had heart medication in them." Her voice rose to a piercing scream. "Dylan, *call* her!"

"He's not calling anyone at this hour, Dorothy," the nurse said briskly, "and you just calm down now. This isn't doing you any good at all. You quiet down and let us take care of you. You should thank your friend here instead of shouting at him like that. He probably saved your life. Going out on a cold night like this with that fever of yours . . . why, heavens, child, that's just crazy!"

And in the next instant, with Duffy safely trapped between the wall and the nurse's bulk, her sleeve was pushed up and in went the needle. Duffy, devastated by Dylan's treachery, felt the sharp, piercing sensation and began sobbing, "No, no, oh no. . . ."

The nurse, saying, "There, there, now, there's no need for this, no need at all," took one arm, and Dylan, worry in his eyes, took the other, and they began leading Duffy down the hall toward her room.

"Duffy," Dylan said, "don't be mad, okay? When I couldn't find the report, I figured you'd been, well, thinking things had happened again that really hadn't. I mean, like you did before, remember? Remember, there really wasn't anyone in your room that night, but you thought there was?"

"I hate you, Dylan!" Duffy spat. "I hate you for this! I trusted you . . ."

But then the medication from the needle began to kick in, and the lights in the hallway began to spin, and the walls began weaving, and Duffy's legs gave way. By the time they reached her room, her captors were half carrying, half dragging her.

"Dylan," she murmured as they carefully deposited her boneless, drugged body on the bed, "I won't ever . . ." What was it she wanted to say? It was so hard to think, with her brain all fuzzy and sticky. "Dylan, I won't ever forgive you. Never, never . . ."

And, as her voice faded out and a thick, gluey sleep took over, she knew that she meant it.

Even if he hadn't done the other bad things, even if he had meant to do the right thing, even if he told her a million times how sorry he was . . .

She would never forgive Dylan.

More asleep than awake, Duffy floated on a thick, dark gray cloud. Fighting to resist the drug, unwilling to give up hope, she lay on her back in the darkened room, her head filled with fog, her arms and legs heavy as cement.

Slap-slap, slap-slap . . . footsteps whispered toward her bed.

"What . . . ?" Duffy murmured woozily, "what?" Was it Dylan, returning to apologize?

There was a slight rustling noise. The mattress sagged beneath Duffy as an added weight clambered aboard and settled itself across Duffy's stomach.

"What? What's happening . . ."

There was no time to scream, no chance to fight. Without warning, her pillow was yanked out from underneath her head. Duffy grunted in surprise as her head fell backward, flat upon the mattress.

Then something soft and thick and suffocating was pressed down upon her nose and mouth and held there with great force, completely cutting off her air supply.

Duffy Quinn couldn't breathe.

Chapter 21

As the pillow pressed down cruelly over Duffy's nose and mouth, she began flailing about wildly with her arms, the only limbs not pinioned by the weight on her legs and stomach. But her hands, searching the air desperately for help, grasped only empty, useless space.

Frantic, she sent her hands to the pillow covering her face. She clawed at the worn fabric . . . pulled . . . tugged . . . while her entire body bucked and heaved in an effort to dislodge the weight pinning her down.

But it was no use. Weakened from her illness, her reflexes slowed by the sedative, Duffy had no more strength than a small child.

Guttural sounds of panic stuck in her throat, held prisoner there by the pillow viciously shoving her lips back against her teeth. Her upper lip felt as if it were being cut to ribbons.

Air . . . air . . . there was no air . . .

No no no no . . . this couldn't happen . . . she

couldn't die now . . . not now . . . not yet . . .

Her hands abandoned their futile tug-of-war with the pillow and again searched the air for aid.

Her right hand slammed into the bedside table. The table . . . the hand rose tentatively to the table surface, the fingers scrambled across the Formica, feeling, searching . . .

Something cold and hard . . . the carafe, the heavy metal jug that held her water.

Red and purple spots danced before her eyes, the lids pressed harshly into the sockets. The pain in her chest was unbearable. Her lungs were going to explode . . .

Her fingers closed around the handle of the metal carafe, gripped it tightly.

But her arm . . . her arm had no strength. Weak and drugged, her muscles refused what her brain in desperation, willed them to do.

The spots increased, a cloud of red and purple and now yellow, bright yellow . . . she was going to pass out.

Move, she screamed to the arm holding the carafe, move, dammit!

Her arm moved. It moved across the space from the table to the bed, it moved up, up, up and, as Duffy felt herself beginning to fade away into the cloud of red and purple and yellow, the arm slammed the carafe blindly downward.

There was a sickening thud as the carafe smacked into a skull. A surprised grunt of pain echoed in the room, and the weight on Duffy's legs and stomach shifted slightly as her captor swayed, stunned, above her. The suffocating grip on the pillow eased.

Duffy gulped for air. She knew she had only seconds — her attacker hadn't been knocked unconscious. In another second or two, the smothering attack would be renewed with angry vigor. The time to move was *now*.

Duffy shoved upward on the pillow, knocking it away from her. She could see nothing but the dim shadow of a figure sitting, tilted sideways, above her.

Still gasping, her chest heaving in pain, Duffy brought her drug-heavy legs upward, her knees lifting her attacker further off balance. The precariously tilted figure uttered an oath and went flying up and sideways, off the bed in an arc. It landed on the tile floor with a muttered "Oosh!" There was a sharp crack, and the room fell silent.

Free at last, Duffy threw herself out of the bed, landing on the floor in a heap. Lurching, she scrambled upward, clutching the bed for support. Then she staggered to the doorway.

A moan from behind her sent her reeling outward, into the dimly lit hall. Clutching the wall for support, her drug-dulled eyes searched the corridor for signs of life.

Nothing. Quiet as a . . . tomb. . . .

Dizzy and dazed, Duffy stumbled down the hall, the wall her only source of support. She tried to hurry. That moan had meant her attacker was regaining consciousness. Any second now, someone would be pursuing her, and she was moving so slowly . . . so slowly . . .

If she could just make it to the stairs, open the heavy door, close it behind her before anyone saw her . . .

There would be no support as she crossed from the wall to the door. What if she fell? A fall now would destroy any chance of escape.

I *won't* fall, she told herself, biting her already sore lower lip.

She didn't fall. But for one awful, terrible minute when she reached the door, she thought she wasn't going to be able to open it. It was so heavy. And she was so very, very tired. Her arms and legs seemed to weigh a ton.

Somehow, she managed to pull the door open and stumble into the landing, watching in terror as the door took forever to close, so slowly, after her. When it had, she clung to the iron railing and allowed herself a tiny sigh of relief. She was hidden from view now. If her attacker had revived enough to venture out into the hallway, there would be no sign of Duffy.

Now . . . to get down the stairs and find a door leading to the outside . . . and freedom.

She was on the fourth floor . . . one, two, three flights of gray stone steps to the first floor.

No . . . she shouldn't leave the stairway at the first floor. That was the lobby. There would be a security guard at the door, another person who wouldn't believe her and would send her back to her room — and into the hands of her attacker.

Better to continue down one more flight and sneak out through the basement. There had to be a door down there somewhere. She would find one.

If she could get that far without falling on her face . . .

Hurry! She'd forgotten, for a moment, the need to hurry.

Down the steps . . . not enough light . . . only a small yellow light at the top of the landing . . . maybe on each of the landings . . . she needed more light, but at least it wasn't pitch-black.

Hard to see each step . . . dizzy, so dizzy, so headachey, chest hurts, but . . . hurry, hurry . . .

She was stumbling around the corner of the second landing when she heard the unmistakable sound of the heavy steel door above her opening.

Duffy froze.

Light from the hallway on the fourth floor bathed the staircase in a pale yellow glow as the door was held open.

Duffy shrank back against the wall in an effort to hide.

The pale glow disappeared slowly as the door swung shut.

And the sound of soft footsteps moving quickly downward echoed in the silence of the stairway.

Her pursuer had arrived.

Duffy, her heart pounding dangerously, swallowed a sob of terror and lurched away from the wall and down the stairs, her legs heavy and unsteady. She slammed against the steel railing more than once, banging an elbow or a wrist, but she kept going, her breath coming unevenly in harsh gasps.

And behind her the soft, threatening steps continued.

Chapter 22

Duffy stepped too hard as she reached the last step leading to the basement, jarring her body and nearly falling to her knees. Regaining her balance, she spied a door at the end of a long, narrow corridor of smooth cement walls. One small fluorescent ceiling fixture did a poor job of illuminating the entire length, and the space was unheated. It was very cold.

The door beckoned to her. Although Duffy shivered from the chill as she moved in a jerky run, the damp, cold air helped pull her further from her drugged fog. She was going to make it. She *was*.

The *slap-slap* on the stairs behind her moved closer. And there was a new sound now . . . a cheerful humming . . . her pursuer was humming!

What kind of person hummed on his way to kill someone?

Was he that sure that he would catch her?

That made her angry and fired her movements, speeding them up slightly.

The door had to be open. It *had* to!

It was. She reached it just as the padded footsteps behind her left the stairs and hit the cement floor. The difference in the sound was unmistakable. That put him at one end of the corridor, which he could cross far more quickly than she had, and her at the opposite end.

But the door was hers now. In one more second, she'd be outside.

Would her pursuer follow her outside?

Would he feel, as she did, that if she made it to the outside, she'd won? Would he then give up?

Or would he find some way to kill her out there, too?

The humming behind her increased in volume, the footsteps *slap-slapped* closer. "Dorothy," a voice whispered, "give up. You can't get away from me. Give up now."

Give up? Never!

She closed her hand around the doorknob and yanked, hard. It opened easily.

But . . . not to the outside.

Bitter disappointment washed over her as she yanked the door closed behind her and stared at a cold white room: white tiled floor, white walls, white ceiling. There was only one light, high on the far wall, casting yellowish shadows over all that white. The space in the center of the wide, square room was taken up with three tables on wheels. The wall nearest Duffy was filled, ceiling to floor, with small metal doors with latches.

And then Duffy, with a sharp gasp of horror, realized where she was.

She was in the morgue.

She was in the room where they brought the patients who had died. There, Dylan had told her, the patients were kept, until other arrangements could be made, on tables that slid in and out of the small steel cabinets.

"Oh, no," she sobbed softly, her hands covering her face, "oh, God, I don't want to be here!"

But when she turned to retreat, the doorknob was already turning. A second later, the door swung open.

Cynthia Boon stood on the threshold.

Still in her blue uniform, her hair neatly fastened behind her ears, her thin face pale and tired-looking, she stared at Duffy with concern in her eyes. Her arms embraced a thick pile of grayish-white towels.

"Duffy, what on earth are you doing down here?" she cried.

Weak with relief, Duffy sagged against the wall. "I have never been so glad to see anyone in my *life!*" she said. Then, glancing nervously around Cynthia toward the door, she whispered, "Didn't you run into anyone out there?"

Cynthia looked at the door. "Out where?"

"Out in the *hall*. Wasn't there anyone out there?"

"Duffy, it's almost one o'clock in the morning. No one in his right mind would be wandering the basement halls. What are you doing down here?"

She can take me home, Duffy thought, her brain working more quickly as the drug wore off. She can drive me to my house where I'll be safe.

"Take me home and I'll tell you. I know it will

sound crazy, but every word is the truth and you have to believe me." Duffy's words rushed together in her effort to convince Cynthia to drive her home. "Just take me home, please, Cynthia. . . ."

Cynthia raised her hands in a gesture of defeat. "Okay, I give up. The whole hospital gives up! We're all tired of trying to make you well when you have all these crazy notions in your head that someone is out to get you. You might just as well go home. I'm through here for the night, so I'll — " She stopped. "Duffy? What's the matter?"

Duffy, frozen in place against the square metal doors, was staring, white-faced, at Cynthia's left wrist.

Just above where the sleeve of her blue blouse ended, there was a two-inch ugly, jagged cut, fresh enough not to be healed.

"Cynthia?" Duffy asked through numbed lips. "Where did you get that cut?"

And Cynthia sighed and smiled, a smile that never went near her suddenly cold, empty eyes.

"I got it in the shower," she said lightly. Her smile widened. "I don't know why they call them safety razors, Duffy, do you? There certainly wasn't anything safe about *that* razor."

And she began moving slowly toward Duffy, a look of cold purpose on her pale, thin face.

Chapter 23

"You?" Duffy croaked, shrinking back against the wall of metal drawers. "You were the one who . . . in the shower . . . no . . ." She shook her head. Her cinnamon-colored hair seemed to stand on end. "No . . . we're friends, Cynthia. I've never done anything to you. Why . . . ?"

"Because of Kit, of course." Cynthia slipped one hand into a pocket of her blue uniform.

"Kit?" Duffy's fever-flushed face registered complete bewilderment. "What about Kit?"

Cynthia's hand moved within the pocket, as if she were fingering something. "You're the only one who knows what really happened to him." She shrugged. "You can't really figure it out right now, of course. But you will. Probably when your fever goes down for good, you'll figure out what you heard and saw in your room that night." Another shrug. "I can't take that chance."

Duffy licked her lips nervously. "Cynthia, I don't know what you're talking about. Nothing happened to Kit. He's fine. He called here, to talk to me."

Cynthia's mouth curved in a sly smile. "Don't be ridiculous. He didn't do any such thing. That was just a rumor. And guess who started it?" She beamed proudly. "All I had to do was *say* he'd called from California, and it was all over the hospital in no time. And you believed it, like everyone else."

Duffy's stomach heaved. The room was so white . . . so white . . . and so cold . . . nothing but cold whiteness everywhere. And Cynthia, her face a pale, icy mask, seemed to belong in this room.

"Kit never called?" Duffy whispered.

Cynthia shook her head. "Of course not. How could he?"

Duffy recoiled against the wall of metal. She didn't want to know why Kit couldn't have called. Didn't want to know . . . didn't want to hear . . .

"You switched the elevator signs? You sent my wheelchair down that hill and attacked me in the shower? It was you the whole time?"

"Took you long enough to figure it out," Cynthia said. "Maybe that fever has lowered your IQ, Duffy. What did you *think* all those weird sounds in your room that night meant? I tried to be quiet, but Kit was . . . uncooperative."

Her voice was completely cold, matter-of-fact, unfeeling. Cynthia . . . so kind, so helpful, so dedicated . . . Cynthia . . . not Dylan, not Smith, not Amy . . . it had been Cynthia who had tried to kill her.

But *why*?

Kit . . . something to do with Kit, who was in California now.

How could it have anything to do with Kit?

Duffy's eyes searched frantically for a way out of the white room. But the only means of escape was the door through which she had entered.

And Cynthia was barring the way.

"Duffy," Cynthia said softly, leaning closer to her prisoner as she withdrew her hand from her pocket, "don't you want me to refresh your memory about Kit?"

Duffy's eyes, wide with alarm, were on Cynthia's emerging hand. Teeth clenched tightly to keep them from biting her tongue in half, she shook her head vigorously . . . no. No!

"Shame on you, Duffy. Kit was one of your best friends. I would think you'd be more concerned about him than that."

The hand wasn't empty, as Duffy had known it wouldn't be. Her terrified eyes remained fastened on it as it slipped from the edge of the pocket.

Cynthia's fingers were wrapped around a long, nasty-looking hypodermic needle.

Holding the wicked-looking needle high in the air, Cynthia smiled and said, "Well, I'm going to tell you about Kit, anyway." She glanced around the room. "I think it's very appropriate that I tell you in this room." Her cold smile widened.

"Because this is where I brought him after I killed him."

Chapter 24

"I killed him, Duffy," Cynthia repeated when Duffy made no sound. "And I brought him here."

Duffy had made no sound because sound wasn't possible. Her voice had abandoned her, left her body the second that Cynthia's flat, emotionless statement registered.

Killed him? *Killed* Kit?

No. No, that wasn't true. It couldn't be.

But Duffy saw the look on Cynthia's face — cruel and sharp and mean.

Kit . . . Kit wasn't in California, registering for film school? He wasn't thinking about calling her, writing her a long letter telling her all about his coast-to-coast trip?

Kit was . . .

Kit was . . . *dead*?

Duffy's mouth opened wide and her piercing, anguished scream split the air.

"No," she cried, facing Cynthia, tears pooling in her eyes. "No, you couldn't have. You wouldn't. Why would you? *Why?*"

Cynthia had flinched at Duffy's scream and taken an involuntary step backward. Now, she pressed closer again. "Because he knew," she said calmly.

Duffy couldn't stop crying. Kit . . . Kit dead? "Knew what? What did he know?"

"He knew it was my fault Latham died."

Duffy shook her head, trying to clear it. "Latham? Victor Latham?" The newspaper article. "You killed *him*, too?"

Cynthia's voice lowered to a nasal whine. "I didn't *kill* him, Duffy. It was an accident. But that wouldn't have made any difference to the hospital board." Her thin lips twisted angrily. "They'd have seen to it that I never saw the inside of a medical school. Never mind that I've studied my head off, that I'm a good worker. All they would have focused on was that their precious benefactor was dead and it was all my fault. My whole life would have been ruined. Forever!"

"What did you do to Victor Latham, Cynthia?" Duffy forced the words out. Dizzy and sick, she couldn't bear to hear another word. But she had to know.

"Nothing. I swear, nothing!" The whine droned on: "I was just reading his chart one day. I know we're absolutely forbidden to touch them, but I knew how important Latham was to the hospital. I thought his chart might give me a clue about getting close to him, getting on his good side. I knew if I did that, he'd put in a good word for me at any medical school in the country." The voice became sullen. "And it would have worked, too, because a note on his chart said he wasn't allowed to smoke. I'd heard him complaining about how he missed his cigars, so I figured I'd buy some and sneak them into his room. That would have made me his friend for life."

The pale blue eyes filled with rage. "But just then Kit came along. He was delivering a pair of nurse's shoes to that twit with the ponytail. He made some comment about me being too nosey for my own good, and I tossed the chart back into place. But not before Kit saw the name on it."

" 'Latham?' " he said. " 'Isn't that the big shot who has that mansion out on River Road?' "

Cynthia stamped one foot, momentarily snapping Duffy out of her shocked daze. "He noticed the warning sticker, too."

"Warning sticker?"

"Latham was allergic to penicillin. The hospital uses a little round red sticker on a patient's chart for dangerous allergies. Kit saw it. I knew he'd put two and two together when Latham's death made the news."

She's right, Duffy thought in a daze, Kit would have. And he would have gone to Cynthia and asked her questions.

"What did you do to Mr. Latham?" she repeated in a whisper.

"I put his chart back in the wrong place. It was Kit's fault," Cynthia said sullenly. "He got me all rattled, sneaking up on me like that, and I just dropped the chart into the chart table."

"You put the chart back in the wrong spot?"

507

Duffy shook her head, uncomprehending. "But you told me yourself the nurses always check the names on the charts, so how could that hurt Latham?"

Cynthia's upper lip curled in a sneer. "They're *supposed* to," she said, her voice hard and unforgiving. "But sometimes when things get really busy, they don't. I accidentally put Latham's chart into Mrs. Creole's slot. She was on penicillin. For an infection. The order's right there on her chart. The night Latham died, we had a couple of nurses out with the flu so two nurses came up from the city. They weren't familiar with the patients. One of them gave Mrs. Creole's penicillin to Latham. It killed him. He was so much better that he wasn't on any monitoring equipment. By the time someone checked on him, he was already dead."

"And . . . and Kit said it was your fault," Duffy breathed.

"But it wasn't!" Cynthia cried. "The nurse who had Mrs. Creole's chart must have dropped it into the only empty slot when she brought it back, without checking the room number. That empty slot was Latham's. So later, she gave *him* Mrs. Creole's penicillin, and left the room. She never saw what the penicillin did to him. She got blamed for what happened."

Duffy, knowing it well, said, "Kit wanted you to tell someone about the chart mix-up, didn't he?"

"He said I had to go to Dr. Crowder, the head of the hospital, and tell the truth. Get that nurse off the hook, was the way he put it.

"But of course I couldn't do that," Cynthia continued matter-of-factly. Her eyes widened. "I mean, how could I? Telling the truth would have ruined everything. I would have been fired for handling the charts, and I never would have got into medical school, not ever." Her eyelids drooped sadly. "Without medical school, I wouldn't *have* a life. I tried to tell your precious Kit that, but he wouldn't listen. And the hospital's being sued by Mr. Latham's survivors. So I'd be blamed for that, too. Everyone here would hate me."

Duffy, watching in awe as Cynthia's expression changed from anger to injured innocence thought, *Oh, God, she's insane. She's as crazy as everyone in the hospital thinks I am.*

"Cynthia," Duffy whispered, "where is Kit?" Eyes wide with fear, she glanced around the room. "Is he here? Somewhere?"

"No. I couldn't leave him *here*, Duffy. Why, my goodness, somebody would have *found* him! I had to get him out of here." There was great pride in Cynthia's voice as she announced to a white-faced Duffy, "I put your friend and his car in the old quarry."

Chapter 25

"The quarry?" Duffy's voice was barely audible. Imagining her friend lying deep in the quarry's cold, muddy water, she shuddered.

"Um-hum." Cynthia's gaze centered on a spot somewhere above Duffy's head and took on a dreamy expression. "It was so easy. He really was leaving town, Duffy. Dylan wasn't lying about that. Kit's car was all loaded up and he was ready to take off for California. Only he stopped off here first, to tell you good-bye and," bitterness seeped into her words, "to warn me that if I didn't promise to go to Dr. Crowder with the truth, he'd go *for* me, as soon as he'd seen you." Her gaze returned to Duffy's face. "He was going to *rat* on me, Duffy," she said in a hurt voice. "I couldn't let that happen, could I?"

"What . . . what did you do?" Duffy, her heart bleeding for the loss of Kit, knew there was no way she was going to be allowed out of this room alive. She had to stall, keep Cynthia talking until she could think . . . think . . . how could she think when her whole mind was still wrestling with the horrible fact that Kit was dead?

"I told him I would go see Dr. Crowder, but first I would take him to your room. And that's what I did." Cynthia smiled. "But I grabbed an empty syringe when I left the nurses' station. I knew exactly what to do with it," she said proudly. "I read a lot of medical books, you know. There's this spot on the back of the neck — "

"I don't want to know!" Duffy screamed. "Don't tell me!" She began crying again. Kit . . . she would never see him or talk to him again. How could that be?

Her left hand involuntarily bumped up against the latch of one of the metal doors. The tables inside the cabinet were designed to slide out. Dylan had said so. Did they slide slowly? Or did they whiz out, like sleds on an icy slope? There was no way of knowing. Could she take a chance? It was so hard to think . . . so hard to plan. . . . But she wanted to *live*. And this wild-eyed, pale-faced maniac in front of her didn't want her to.

"Your friend Kit was in such a hurry to see you," Cynthia continued. "Followed me to your room like a puppy. Right straight to your room. You were dead to the world." Cynthia giggled. "Excuse the expression. You were sound asleep, and he didn't want to wake you. He said he wasn't in any big hurry and he'd just sit on the other bed and wait for you to wake up." Cynthia sniffed in disdain. "He said he couldn't leave town without telling you goodbye. Wasn't that *sweet*?" Contempt laced her words.

The thought of Kit sitting on a bed in her room, patiently waiting for her to wake up, Cynthia about to pierce the back of his neck with a needle full of air, made Duffy sick with anguish. If only she could have stopped it somehow, if she could have pushed the call button.

"But he saw the needle," Cynthia went on harshly. "It was dark in there, but he could still tell what I was about to do. He was sitting on the other bed, and I came up behind him. He saw me lift the needle in the air and he made these noises . . ."

Duffy gagged and closed her eyes.

"I missed the first time." There was regret in Cynthia's voice. "Clumsy me! For a minute there, I thought he was going to get away." Then she brightened visibly. "But he didn't. I tripped him," she said cheerfully, "and he went down on his knees. He sort of whimpered then." Cynthia mimicked Kit's deep voice: " 'Please, no, don't!' But I *got* him!" Her voice was triumphant, almost jubilant.

That joy stirred something in Duffy. Anger began to replace her fear, slowly at first, then more quickly, coursing through her body until it became a rage as red hot as her fever. Cynthia was *glad* she had killed Kit! And she was about to kill again.

Duffy screamed. "No! No, no, no!" echoed around the room, and her arms came up and pushed, with all of her might, shoving a surprised Cynthia backward, where she teetered off balance, her mouth open.

But she didn't fall. And she didn't drop the syringe.

Still, her surprise gave Duffy just enough freedom to dart away, running to the desk to search frantically for a weapon: a letter opener, a pair of scissors, anything . . .

There was nothing. A box of paper clips, a lamp, piles of notebooks and leaflets, and a scattered puzzle of pens and pencils . . . nothing the tiniest bit lethal. But there, in the corner, behind a tall, thick medical book standing on end . . . a can of bug spray. Maybe . . .

Duffy turned to face her captor. Behind her, her hands closed around the can.

"Relax, Duffy," Cynthia said calmly, her balance restored. She began to advance slowly, her eyes cold and determined. "You're going to have a little accident," she said, "and it won't be my fault. All *I'm* going to do is be kind enough to give you a ride home. Isn't that nice of me? Of course, *I* won't be hurt. But you . . ." She shook her head. "You'll end up in a ditch by the road in a fiery car crash. I'll tell everyone you grabbed the wheel out of my hands, that you missed Kit so much you committed suicide. They'll believe me. Everyone thinks you're nuts, Duffy. And I'll say that since I'm not crazy like you, I had the good sense to jump out before the car burst into flames." She raised the needle higher. "And no one will ever be able to tell that you were dead before the car ever went off the road."

Her eyes never leaving Cynthia's face, Duffy moved sideways, back to the wall of steel cabinets. She backed up against them, her hands behind her. This time, she found a latch and opened it. It made no sound.

"Wasn't it nice of Kit to decide to leave town?" Cynthia went on, as if they were two friends having a casual chat. "There was his car, all loaded up. . . . After I killed him, I wheeled him down here in the gurney and then later, when everyone was gone, I wheeled him out to his car and drove out to the quarry." She sighed happily. "They'll never find him *or* his car. The water's too deep." After a minute, she murmured, "Sank like a stone. Took me forty-five minutes to hike back to town. Boy, was I beat!"

Duffy, her hands hidden behind her jeaned hips, held the bug spray can in one hand. With the other, she lifted the latch on a metal door. The door opened easily. It made no sound. She tugged gently. The door moved forward an imperceptible fraction of an inch.

"You're crazy," she told Cynthia, her voice shaking. If she kept talking, she hoped Cynthia would continue to watch her face instead of wondering what her hands were doing behind her back. "You're sick. You need help. Why don't you let me go now?" she begged, fastening her eyes on Cynthia's. "We'll go up and talk to Dr. Crowder. He'll see that you get the help you need."

If she was going to get the door open all the way, she had to move forward several inches. But Cynthia was in the way.

Cynthia's cheeks reddened with rage. "I'm not going to *see* anyone!" she shouted. "I don't need *help*! You're the one who needs help!" And she raised the hypodermic needle high in the air, poised just above Duffy's head.

It was now or never. Duffy's hand holding the bug spray can whipped out from behind her, her index finger on the spray button. Her arm flew up, her finger pressed down.

Cynthia screamed as the foul-smelling mist hit her eyes. Her hands, one still gripping the needle, instinctively flew to her face.

The needle's wickedly sharp point missed her left eye by a fraction of an inch, penetrating with full force the top of the cheekbone. This time Cynthia's scream was one of agony. A thin stream of blood slid down her cheek as the needle protruded from her face like a dagger.

Duffy gagged again, but she knew there was no time to waste in sympathy for Cynthia. Cynthia, her anger fueled by new fury, wouldn't give up now. This moment, with Cynthia temporarily blinded, was the only moment Duffy had.

With her empty hand, she threw open the door of the cabinet and, jumping out of the way, grabbed the edge of the slab inside the cabinet and jerked.

The slab flew out, slamming into a moaning Cynthia, her hands still covering her eyes. It kicked her in the stomach at waist-level, lifting her off her feet with a startled "Uuh!" She flew up and then forward, landing with a scream, facedown, on the slab.

She screamed again and then went limp as she lost consciousness.

The weight of her body hitting the slab sent it whizzing back into the depths of the cabinet.

Her eyes glazed with shock, Duffy reached out automatically and gently closed the door. Then her legs gave and she sank to the cold white floor, covering her eyes with her hands.

Chapter 26

When Duffy awakened in her hospital bed the following morning, four pair of eyes regarded her with concern. Smith and Amy stood on one side of her bed, Dylan and Jane on the other. The sight of the little group jolted her out of sleep.

Then she remembered. She remembered all of it: the pillow over her face, the desperate struggle for air, the body thumping to the floor, the cold, dark journey to the basement, Cynthia's arrival at the morgue and . . . Kit . . . Kit! Kit was . . .

Uttering an agonized moan, Duffy buried her face in her hands.

Her friends moved closer. Amy hurriedly poured Duffy a glass of water, Smith took up a position as close to Duffy as he could get, while Dylan and Jane fixed worried eyes on the patient.

Smith was the first to speak. He looked tired, his dark eyes shadowed by bluish circles. "I'm sorry about your friend," he said.

Duffy lifted her head. "You know? You know about Kit? How did you find out?"

"You told us. It was hard for you to say it, but you did."

Duffy's gray eyes widened in fear. She reached out in sudden panic and clutched at Smith's sweater sleeve. "Cynthia?" she asked.

"It's okay, Duffy," Jane hastened to reassure her. "They took her away. She's gone. You don't have to worry about her."

Duffy exhaled in relief.

"Your doctor was in," Smith told her. "They're going to do some tests this afternoon to make sure the digoxin didn't do any permanent damage. He's pretty sure it didn't. He feels really awful about not believing you, Duffy. The whole staff does."

"It was your fever that fooled everyone," Amy added quietly. "Nobody could be sure that you weren't delirious." She waved her hands helplessly. "We're all really sorry we didn't believe you. And," in a hushed voice laden with shame, "I'm sorry I lost my temper. You must hate me."

"No." Duffy shook her head. "It was all Cynthia's fault." Her eyes filled with fresh tears. "She killed Kit . . ." she stopped, unable to continue.

"They found him early this morning," Smith told her, his voice gentle as he took her hands in his and held them tightly.

Duffy sobbed. A sad, sympathetic silence fell over the group.

She wiped her eyes with a corner of the sheet and asked, "Who found me?"

"We did," Jane and Dylan said in unison. "And Smith. It was his idea to try the morgue."

"Dylan called me," Jane explained. She smiled at him before returning her attention to Duffy. "He asked me about the lab test Dean had done on the pills."

Duffy fixed her eyes on Dylan. So he *had* taken her seriously, after all. But too late. He probably had meant well when he brought the nurse to her in the hall. But she would never feel the same about him again, and she could tell by the look in his eyes that he understood that.

Jane didn't need to know about that part of it. The way she was looking up at him, her eyes so full of admiration, she'd never blame Dylan, anyway.

"I *told* Dylan," Jane went on, "that it had all been a gag, but he wouldn't drop it. So finally I told him what Dean had found out and Dylan screamed, 'Duffy was right!' and hung up. That's when I knew it hadn't been a joke, after all. And I knew you were in trouble, Duffy." Her violet eyes reflected hurt. "Why didn't you tell me the truth? I could have helped."

"Then you would have been a target, too." Duffy forced a weak smile.

Jane's eyes glistened with unshed tears. "Oh, Duffy," she said, "I'm so glad you're okay."

And Smith smiled and said, "I wouldn't mind having you in *my* corner, Quinn."

Duffy turned to Jane. "You came to the hospital last night?"

Jane nodded. "I really was feeling crummy . . . bad headache. But when Dylan hung up like that, I knew something was wrong. So I threw on some clothes and raced over here. When I got to the fourth floor, I found Dylan and Smith and Amy hunting all over for you."

"We could tell you'd been in a battle with someone," Dylan said. "Your room was a mess. So we started searching. It was Smith's idea to try the basement."

"We found you on the floor, crying for your friend," Smith told Duffy. "You were really out of it, and at first, you couldn't tell us what happened."

"But you finally did," Amy said. "It was all very disjointed and it took us a while, but we finally figured out that Cynthia was behind one of the doors." Her face was very white. With gratitude in her voice, she added, "It was Smith who found her, and he wouldn't let Jane and me see."

"She tried to kill me," Duffy said. "Like she . . . like she killed Kit." Kit . . . she would never see him again, never talk to him, could never visit him in California.

"When I told you what Cynthia had done," she asked slowly, thoughtfully, "why did you believe me? You could have thought I was the one who did the attacking, that I finally flipped out totally and went after her with the hypodermic needle. Why didn't you?"

"Because we know you'd never do that," Jane said quickly. "And anyway, I knew about the digoxin. And we all knew Cynthia had access to your medication."

"We called the police," Dylan added, "and they sent divers out to the quarry." He hesitated, and his voice was low and reluctant as he added, "They found Kit right away. He was still in his car."

Duffy gasped in pain. She began crying again, quietly, unaware of the tears sliding down her cheeks.

"I can't believe he's dead," she whispered. "What am I going to do without him?"

There was a sad, awkward silence, and then Dylan and Jane said, in one voice, "We'll be here, Duffy." And Amy added in her soft, sweet voice, "Me, too."

And Smith gripped Duffy's hands more tightly in his own and fixed his dark eyes on hers and said solemnly, "I can't take your friend's place. I didn't even know him. I wish I had. But maybe, after a while, I can make a place of my own."

Duffy was too tired to answer. But maybe, after a while, he could . . .

Smith stood up. "This girl needs rest," he said sternly. "I want this room emptied *pronto*."

Nodding obediently, Dylan and Jane and Amy turned to leave. Smith leaned down close to Duffy and said, "It's okay now. You can sleep. You can start putting all of this nasty business behind you and close your eyes. It's over. It's really over."

Feeling safe, surrounded by people who cared about her and wanted her to get well, Duffy closed her eyes.

And slept peacefully.